STARVINITY

THE HERETICS OF TERRA

PART TWO

TAZM SAGA: BOOK TWO

BY

GRANT-GREY GUDA

First published in the United States of America by Starvinity, Ltd

ISBN: 978-1-967651-13-9

Library of Congress Control Number: 2025921659

Imprint: Starvinity, Ltd

Front and back cover design by: Grant-Grey Guda, Front cover art by: Vijay K
Book design by: Grant-Grey Guda

Starvinity, Ltd

P.O Box 8

Nelsonville, Ohio, 45764

Dedication

This book and the Starvinity universe are dedicated to my incredible wife and wonderful family.

-STARVINITY-

THE HERETICS OF TERRA: PART TWO

Beyond our known universe, in another dimension, another reality, the fate of all existence will be decided...

Chapter One:
SHADOWS OF CONSUMING

"We saw it in dreams long before it arrived. We just didn't believe what we were seeing. When we finally did, it was too late."

— Luminarian Historical Archives

Fire and debris rippled through the skies of Verellien Prime. The heavens burned as galactic dreadnoughts broke apart in midair. Floating cathedrals of light and war were torn open like paper, their cores detonating in slow-motion fury. The very clouds seemed to scream as they were drenched in weaponized plasma and ion flares. Below, the world fractured. Towering cities of crystal and alloy crumbled into dust, swallowed by the endless tide of devastation.

On the ground, chaos reigned. Aliens of every kind. Bipedal and serpentine, plated and feathered, silicon and flesh. They all fought as one, side by side. Most were once enemies. Now they were unified battalions of the Alliance of Light. They pushed forward through rubble and flame, weapons blazing, banners flying.

Machine-walkers the size of stadiums lumbered through shattered plazas in the outer districts of the capital, past the high walls, discharging continuous thundering assault after assault against the invaders. These titans of alien origin strode beside tanks and artillery, hurling their energy bolts like ancient gods.

But it wasn't enough. The planetary shields had failed. The sky continued to ripple and tear. From beyond the visible stars came the black masses of tentacles and spikes and bones of darkness, serving the Consuming. But it was also a part of the Consuming. It wasn't living in any way known to biology, and yet it was horribly, darkly alive. Blacker than the blackest void, they shimmered with flickers of impossible dark. They didn't slither, they slipped, folding across dimensions with angles that broke the eye. Where they touched, matter changed in strange ways, ceasing to exist as we know it.

And behind the masses of dark, the hordes came. Twisted creatures poured forth like rivers of flesh and steel. Some crawled, some galloped, some flew. Among them a number of monstrosities were taller than buildings. They crushed tanks beneath jagged clawed limbs that seemed impossibly evil. Needle-thin flyers stabbed through ships like swarms of angry Xeekee through water. Among the chaotic armies of the Consuming, the Vis'Ori'Ki marched and led: many of them were towering war-beasts stitched from entropy, covered in black blade-like bones and multiple mouths and sharp, cruel spines. Many stood larger than any known warform, even larger than the most elite Ascendant Guardians once spoken of in ancient texts.

On a balcony above it all, high atop the central capital spire, behind the strongest energy shielding ever devised, stood a Luminarian, High Emissary Azaratha Velreth Saranith. Her cerulean skin shimmered faintly in the pulsing light of the catastrophe unfolding. Her silver robes rustled, caught in the artificial breeze of the tower's failing systems. Around her, the world screamed. Yet she stood silent. The Alliance was losing. Crushed. Dismembered.

She saw it unfold: One after another, great cities fell in the far distance. Ships ruptured and fell like dying birds. Mechs were pulled limb from limb. Massive genetically created warbeasts were consumed in a single breath by the shifting tentacles and swift bones of darkness, which now wrapped the horizon like a cage. A whisper escaped her lips.

"We waited too long. We believed unity would be enough. It wasn't."

Alarms shrieked in the tower's command core and voices were projected out throughout the building.

"Western defensive lines have fallen. Eastern bunkers breached. All remaining troops fall back to extraction points. Prepare for final phase evacuations."

"This is Commander Rekk. I am initiating planetary abandonment protocol. Repeat, total retreat. If you're still receiving, get out now. In any way that you can. Retreat."

Azaratha turned from the balcony. The shields above her flickered. Just for a moment, as a massive tendril scraped across the barrier like a blade against glass. There was no anger in her eyes. Only the still, terrible clarity of one who knows the end has come. She raised her hand to the control console beside her, and with a voice steady as iron, activated the last beacon. A planet-wide signal went out confirming the commander's orders.

"This is High Emissary Saranith. Our world is lost. Evacuate while you still can. All forces assist in the evacuations in any way possible. We have to get as many people off-world as possible."

The Shadows of war had come. And they couldn't be stopped. Azaratha stood motionless, the roar of the evacuation echoing in the distance and nearby as ships took off and throughout the inner capital as crowds of people rushed to the portals.

Through the mostly translucent city shields, she watched the sky. the once-blue heavens now nothing but writhing black. The tentacles. The Consuming. The unnatural cosmic horror from beyond known reality arched high above the clouds like monstrous pillars of a living storm, blotting out the sun in a dance of shadow and dread.

Below her, the capital gardens still bloomed, untouched by flame for the moment, the last haven of serenity in a world being torn apart. Verdant vines swayed gently, fountains still whispered. The beauty of it all burned her heart.

Above, retreating fleets streaked skyward. Vessels twisting and weaving through the impossible chaos, dodging and firing at the colossal appendages that lashed through orbit like titanic whips.

Some ships made it, others cracked and fell, burning trails across the sky.

Her hands clenched the edge of the balcony railing as she heard him before he spoke. The heavy tread, the hiss of armored breath. Supreme Commander Rekk, her protector and advisor since she had become High Emissary. He stepped into the dim golden light beside her. Thick, plated scales lined his seven-foot frame, jagged across his shoulders like the edge of a broken moon. His voice rumbled from deep within his chest, echoing with force.

"We have to leave," he said, firm but not cruel.

Azaratha didn't answer right away. Her eyes remained locked on the fleeing ships. A small family cruiser detonated mid-lift, reduced to falling ash. A strangled sound nearly escaped her throat.

"I don't want to. I don't deserve to," she said softly. "I want to be here... This is my home. Every stone. Every root. Every melody of this wind. If my world falls, then I fall."

Rekk stepped closer. His clawed hand gripped the rail beside hers. Steady, strong, and immovable.

"Don't say that. You can't stay." His tone shifted, lower now. "You must come. I can't lose you... not after losing everything else."

She finally looked up at him. The firestorms reflected in her tear-rimmed eyes. His gaze, burning amber and ancient, met hers. For a moment, nothing was said. The ground rumbled beneath them. Far in the distance, the outermost capital wall shattered. One of the tentacles broke through. Yet still, she hesitated.

The next capital wall exploded shortly after the first in a thunderous shock-wave. Light and dust cascaded through the night like molten thunder. The protective shields flickered again. They were becoming unstable and weakening. Jagged black fractures danced across their glowing lattice. Alarms continued to scream through the tower like mechanical banshees.

"We don't have much time," Commander Rekk growled with impatience, his amber eyes flashing. "We have to go."

"I told you. I'm not leaving!" Azaratha snapped, stepping back, defiantly. "This is my world. These are my people. I won't run while they burn! It's all my fault. I should have given the order to evacuate a long time ago. I thought we could win. I was wrong. And now people are dying because of me."

Rekk's fists clenched the stone even harder, his massive and clawed hands slightly cracking the edge. "And if you die here, what good will you be to them then? There are more worlds that need protecting. There are more people to evacuate. You have to lead."

Before she could reply, a tremor shook the floor beneath their feet. The third wall had fallen. The sky tore open even more with a louder thunderous crack. The shields sputtered and pulsed and began to fail. Small holes in the barrier began to form.

Then the swarms started to come through. Hundreds, then thousands upon thousands of Vis'Ori'Ki surged through the cracks, shrieking through the air like burning hatred incarnate. Their warped, jagged and vicious forms scrambled across buildings, over domes, down columns, into the very arteries of the city. Plazas erupted in chaos. Energy fire lit the gardens. Screams filled the air.

And then, too soon—hand-to-hand. Defenders drew plasma spears, radiant swords. Anything and everything that they had. They clashed in bloody, brutal rhythm. Streets ran with blood and death and Consuming, the Vis'Ori'Ki sucked up many people and spilled blood and life into strange black almost biological devices.

They could barely see the insanity of it all, as the streets were dimly lit under failing flickering lights under the shadow of the black mass that was now almost entirely surrounding the city shields.

A sharp, unholy shriek sounded loud and close. Several winged Vis'Ori'Ki leapt down from a broken nearby tower and slammed into the balcony. Their jagged limbs and gaping maws sliced toward

Azaratha. But Rekk was a living weapon. He moved like a storm, claws tearing through sinew, armored fists breaking chitin. He roared as he fought. Twelve of the Vis'Ori'Ki were dead in moments, their bodies hurled from the balcony like lifeless puppets. But more came, climbing the walls towards them, shrieking vengeance.

"Inside! Now!" he bellowed with urgency and caring.

He grabbed Azaratha and ran down a corridor and then to a set of heavy tall metallic doors, having to drag her by the arm into the heart of the spire. With a thunderous slam, he sealed the doors behind them. Just as the corridor outside collapsed beneath more shrieking horrors.

The spire shuddered. Above, they could hear one of the colossal tentacles smashed down across the top shields of the spire, breaking some of the reinforced alloy like soft clay. Chunks of the towering spire plummeted in flame, internally and externally.

Portals. Brilliant golden rings. Had already flared to life, they could see their bright light down a final hall. Panic flooded the air as the last of the defenders screamed for quicker evacuation as crowds continued to surge forward in panicked disorder. Rekk pushed Azaratha toward the nearest gate.

"No!" she cried, reaching for him. "You're coming too!"

"I'll buy you all time," he growled. "You carry the flame."

"I love you." She yelled through the chaos.

"I have always felt the same."

He replied in caring as he shoved her through. She vanished in a flash of light through the golden ripples of energy. Rekk turned, breath heaving, blood running from his side.

From the ruin stepped a towering Vis'Ori'Ki. Larger than the rest, its form broken and yet beautiful in a dark way, like a god of decay.

13

Bladed arms folded outward. Its face, a mass of layers of writhing bone like many crowns upon its head.

Rekk snarled. "Come on, then." And activated the battle mode of his armor, it injected him with an experimental formula. His stature increased to match the size of the Vis'Ori'Ki abominable monstrosity.

They collided with the force of titans of legend. He struck with everything. Claws, fists, rage. The creature answered in kind, flinging him into walls, slashing deep into his armor and his flesh. But he refused to fall. They traded blows in a dance of death, surrounded by fire, as the spire began to collapse around them.

Then—

Tria Oberon gasped awake. Darkness surrounded her in her officer's quarters. The cold Plankinsteel walls of her chamber were no comfort. The sterile hum of Peacekeeper tech on Venus gave no serenity. She was covered in sweat; her breath was heavy and uneven.

A dream. But it wasn't just a dream. It had felt real. Like so many others she had had over the years. Too vivid. Too knowing. As if someone. Or something. Was trying to show her something.

The dream, the vision, hadn't just shaken her. It had deeply split her, like a blade to the soul. She could still feel the heat of that ruined world, the scream of dying light, the taste of alien metal and ash in her throat. And worse. She knew it hadn't been just a dream. It felt more like a memory. She knew that something was coming. Something ancient. And it, whatever it was, had already destroyed countless worlds before.

She lay there, heart pounding as she tried to understand what she had just witnessed. The base was quiet. Venus was in its night cycle. A calm temporary lie. Her thoughts drifted back to Mars and the uprising that she helped begin and then lead. To the mindless death. The illogical chaos. The evil shadows of lost humanity in what had become a hellhole.

She turned over and reached toward her nightstand with trembling fingers. Her hand brushed against something cold. It wasn't what she was reaching for in the moment. It was her NAXV Bible. The edges of the worn cover caught the dim light that was leaking through the closed metal shutters, a flicker of gold trim reflecting in her sight. She stared at it for a long strethcing moment.

A whisper of prayer left her lips, barely audible. "Father. Son. Holy Spirit. Be near. Be real. I need you now, more than ever." She waited for the warmth to come, the peace she'd once felt so clearly. It flickered within. Like candlelight in a raging storm. Her hand reached past the Bible, this time finding what it was truly seeking in her stress. Goodgel.

The injector was cool to the touch. But it was all too familiar in her palm. Her thumb hovered over the release. She'd sworn off it. She'd promised herself, her friend Ari'Ella, and even God that she wouldn't spiral towards it again. It wasn't just medicine anymore. It was a leash. A numbing, blinding tether that buried her beneath false serenity. But the pressure in her skull was rising, traumatic memories and visions clawing at her like hungry beasts.

She squeezed her eyes shut, teeth grinding together as the pain pulsed behind her eyes like a heartbeat made of razor-sharp teeth. Prayers turned to pleading. "Just let it stop. Just for a little while." She hesitated. Then. With a sob of frustration, she slammed the injector against her neck and pressed the release.

One dose. Then two. Then three. Then four. Far more than any regulation. Far more than her body could tolerate for long. The chemical rush hit her instantly. A perfect numbness. A hollow relief. A chemical salvation. Synthetic euphoria. The storm within her quieted, not gone, but dulled. The shadows retreated, but she knew they'd return. They always did. And still, she whispered, "Amen."

Chapter Two:
MORE BLOOD FOR MARS

"We didn't teach them to do it. But for some reason, they build their nests out of bones and blood."
— Internal Memo, Genovation Industries

A low rumble vibrated through the floor, distant at first. Like tectonic plates grinding in rage beneath Mars's surface. Amarax crouched, pipe still slick with blood and ichor, his breath jagged in the cold dark. Every nerve in his body screamed for rest, but there was no time. No mercy.

Amarax's naked feet echoed down the cold, sterile corridor, but the further he moved, the air grew thicker, tainted with the stench of decay and blood. The walls had transformed, now slick with a vile substance, covered in the pulsing, writhing masses of the Beast's spawn.

The once-pristine white halls of the Peacekeeper prison had become a grotesque, organic nest. The walls hummed with an eerie, guttural noise as the smaller, more vicious creatures skittered in the shadows. Feral, bloodthirsty offspring of the monsters he had just slaughtered.

His fingers gripped the bone claw, its jagged edge glistening with blood. With a savage roar, he swung it through the air, cleaving through the first of the demon spawn. The blade of bone met flesh with a sickening crunch. They came at him faster now. Scrabbling, gnashing teeth, eyes glowing with pure malice. The stench of their death-scent filled his nose as he slashed through them one by one. Their tiny bodies exploded in bursts of viscera, but more came, relentless, crazed, desperate for his blood.

Amarax's muscles screamed with the effort, but his rage drowned the pain. These creatures were nothing but extensions of the beasts he had already killed, he would tear through every last one. The bone claw howled through the air, a weapon forged in blood, cutting through the spawn like a scythe through wheat. The blood-soaked floor was a sea of death and shattered bodies, but still they came. He would fight, he would eradicate.

Breathing heavily, Amarax stood amidst the carnage, his body drenched in their blood, but there was no time to linger. He had to move.

Down another corridor, this hallway pulsed with a dim, red glow. Emergency lighting was sputtering, weak and inconsistent. Shadows danced like demons along the walls. Somewhere deeper in the station, something howled. Not an animal. Not a man. Something in-between. Something broken. Something bred in a nightmare.

Then came the footsteps. Heavy. Measured. Purposeful. Not the erratic scrambling of feral beasts. These were methodical. Controlled. They echoed through the blackened corridor with dreadful rhythm, thoom... thoom... thoom...

Amarax raised the bone-blade in his right hand, his fingers tight around the jagged shaft of alien cartilage. He pressed his back to the wall, heart thudding in sync with the approaching steps. The shadows began to shift again. This time, with deliberate clarity.

From the red haze emerged a silhouette. Not another monster. No. A man, or what had once been one. Tall. Armored. Its frame wrapped in priestly exo-plate, their flesh fused with red-chrome implants and long, twitching cables that snaked behind him like tails. His face was half-mask, half-flesh, bolted into his skull with cruel precision. Where his eyes should have been, there was only a glowing strip of crimson light, twitching, scanning.

Behind him came more. Two. Three. Four. All cultists of an outlawed sect of Terranism. A sect that had been a thorn in the side of Mars for generations. All heretics. Followers of the Machine-Prophet of Darana. Large marks of their prophet were boldly tattooed on their bodies. And their flesh was twisted by metal, minds hollowed out by the hum of heresy. They weren't human anymore. Just vessels of the mad cyber-rituals infecting Mars's forbidden zones.

The lead cultist stepped forward, dragging behind him a jagged shard of scavenged blackened steel, still slick with corrosion and fresh blood from recent victims of their insanity. Sparks danced from its edge as it scraped the floor, humming faintly with unstable charge.

No elegance. No craftsmanship. Just raw, brutal death waiting to be unleashed.

His voice crackled from a shattered vox-grille, each word strained through static and ruin:

"You bleed, warrior... We'll carve out the rest."

Amarax answered with silence. Then with the wrath of an angry god. He lunged with pure motion, a thunderbolt wrapped in flesh. In his grip, the bone-blade, a massive, jagged talon, still slick with black gore ripped from the corpse of the beast he had just slain in a nearby corridor. Its severed digit served as Amarax's sword. A grotesque weapon of survival and brutality. He used it like judgment itself had come to bring its sentence.

The blade tore through the lead cultist's shoulder with a wet crack, nearly cleaving the arm from its socket. Blood and spurts of dark coolant sprayed into the red haze. The cultist screamed a raw, gurgling sound and staggered backward, dragging his twisted weapon, no more than a sharpened slab of machine plating with wires still dangling like veins.

Amarax didn't stop. He kicked the next one square in the gut with such force it lifted the man off his feet, ribs shattering like dried bark. Before the body could hit the floor, Amarax spun around driving the jagged hilt of his bone-blade into the face of another. Metal mask crumpled. The rebreather shattered. Blood exploded from the cultist's mouth as his skull snapped backward against the wall.

A rusted, serrated edge bit into Amarax's back. It dragged across muscle and spine with a butcher's cruelty. He roared, not in agony, but in volcanic rage. And he spun again, catching his attacker with an elbow that detonated their throat. The cultist dropped instantly, choking on crushed cartilage and black ichor.

Still the others came. No plasma, no bullets. Just sharpened scraps of a dead world and the fanatical strength of those who had forgotten they were ever men to begin with. One charged, metal shard overhead, eyes wild with madness.

Too slow. Amarax twisted low and swung wide. The bone-blade howled through the air and hacked through the heretic's leg just below the knee. Bone splintered. Flesh tore. The cultist crumpled, shrieking, clawing at the air with one hand while trying to crawl forward with what remained.

Devotion burned in his eyes. Amarax's blade ended it. Rammed down through spine and lung, burying deep into the floor. The scream turned to silence. He rose, limping, bleeding, his flesh cracked open, but still upright. Still breathing. Rage was his lifeblood now. Firey faith kept his heart beating.

Two more circled. Predators. Fanatics. Filth. One stepped forward, mouth opening to speak, to gloat, perhaps. Amarax hurled the bone-blade. The massive talon slammed through his skull with sickening precision, snapping bone, crushing thought. The body twitched, fell, and twitched no more.

The last cultist froze. Amarax closed the distance in a blink. No weapon. Just fury. His fists became hammers. His forearms, wrecking bars. He drove the heretic down into the ground with savage, unrelenting violence. Over and over, until there was nothing left but wet pulp and shattered plate.

And then. Silence. Only the quiet buzz of broken wires. The drip of blood onto scorched steel. The breath of a dying hallway.

Amarax stood over the ruins of cultists who were once human, his chest heaving, his limbs shaking, blood running down his spine and pooling at his feet. His right arm dangled uselessly. Vision split. Muscles screamed. But the fire in his mind burned brighter than ever. They thought Mars was theirs. That the Machine-Prophet of Darana would shield them. Let their ghosts pray to dust.

He turned toward the next corridor, deeper into shadow, where worse things most likely awaited. One of his bare feet came down on a cultist's skull. Bone caved in with a crunch. And he disappeared once more into the bleeding dark.

Mars wasn't finished. And neither was he.

Chapter Three:
OPERATION LIGHTFALL BEGINS

"And the Holy Duality spoke together in one voice unto the planetary architects, saying:[1] 'Venus, once drowned in storms and sorrow.[2] By Our will her skies shall clear, her mountains shall bow, and her wastelands shall blossom with righteous fire.[3] Through faith and fury she shall rise, a jewel set in the Crown of the Righteous.[4] Even death shall yield to Our command, for no grave shall stand before our Divinity.'[5]"

The Holy Terran-Orion Bible - The Book of Rebirth, 4:1–5

Deep beneath the Colosseum's golden facade, the Unders and Umbers toiled. The work levels pulsed, with grit and misery. Grease and sweat ruled here, far from the glittering lies of the Uppers. The Games above were fueled by a multitude of breaking bodies below, toiling to keep things running smoothly.

The lower levels of Solanius Colosseum throbbed with the heavy pulse of machines and the shouts of people drowned in hard labor. Down here, beneath the spectacle of the Games, the air tasted of ancient eternal rust and old blood. The Uppers and luckiest Umbers feasted above as they enjoyed tournaments of death. The working Umbers and Unders toiled below to keep the machine of entertainment alive and well without any interruptions.

Tria moved through the labyrinth of shadowed corridors. She wasn't wearing her usual shining silver Peacekeeper armor, she was in a disguise, more brutal black armor with a red glowing Radara in the center of her chest replacing the blue hexagon that she was more accustomed to. She was a part of another important operation. Operation Lightfall. Her cloak was drawn tight around her shoulders, dark boots ringing loudly against the grated steel. Other Peacekeepers ghosted behind her in similar disguises, faces hidden beneath darkened visors, weapons concealed but ready. No banners. No oaths.

Only the heavy, unseen gravity of a mission born in the deep shadows of the empire.

They found him alone, a large wrench in hand, working on an important system, red sleeves rolled to the elbows, his skin stained with grease and sweat. Braxxan Lume. He looked up. His face darkened the instant he saw her. His eyes darted to the ceiling, panic twisting his face.

"The holo-grids—" he gasped. "They'll see us! They're always watching! Judicators will come! They're going to execute me for heresy."

Tria didn't even blink, slightly smiling. "We disabled them before we came. No one's watching. No one will know that we were ever here. You don't have to worry about being discovered."

Braxxan wasn't amused, he was angry and annoyed by Tria's presence.

"I told you never to contact me again, I told you to leave me alone," he hissed, glancing around nervously. "You shouldn't be here. You're going to get me killed."

Tria took a step closer, her voice a blade hidden in silk. "And yet here I am."

Braxxan dropped the wrench with a clatter, wiping his hands roughly on his dirty maintenance trousers.

"You don't listen. You don't understand! I have a good life here. A family. I'm not some martyr you can pin your Jankking hopes on. I'm not a heretic. I'm a faithful Umber."

"You don't have a good life, you have a sentence here," Tria shot back. "It's not living. You breathe because they allow it. You work because they demand it. They own your sweat, your blood, your soul—and you think you're living?"

His jaw clenched. Fury and fear warred in his eyes.

"I spoke once. I organized other Umbers and Unders. I demanded better for all of us. Where did it get me? Docked wages. Secret beatings. Re-education." His voice twisted into a growl. "You want me to rise up? You want me to spit in the face of the Gods? You don't know what it's like down here. You don't know what it costs to defy the Uppers."

Tria stepped in, so close he could feel the heat of her anger.

"I know exactly what it costs," she said, voice low and sharp. "I've paid the price for defiance. I'm willing to die for it. But I know what it'll cost if you keep kneeling. Everything. They'll bleed you and all future generations dry until there's nothing left but bones and ash."

Braxxan shoved her shoulder.

"Get out of here before you get my family executed. I'm not a heretic. I serve the Duality. I'm a faithful Dualinite."

Tria didn't flinch from the shove. She absorbed it like a block of Plakinsteel absorbing a gravhammer blow, her boots planted firm.

"You serve the chains of the Uppers," she said, voice soft but seething. "Not your gods."

Tria lifted a small emitter from her belt and activated it. A thin beam flickered, expanding into a sharp, vivid holoprojection. The final moments of the Battle of the Undercity of Antica.

The massive Diviniterra Legionaries, clad in sacred armor, moved with brutal precision over the ridge. Only to be brought down by blue energy, overwhelmed by the army and grand machines of the Peacekeepers, their tactics a perfect unity of surprise and trickery. The ground was littered with broken banners and fallen giants.

Braxxan's face paled. His hands, still stained with grease, trembled slightly at what he was seeing.

"That's Diviniterra…" he whispered.

"Yes, yes, it is. The best that the Dominion has," Tria said coldly.

"And they fell?"

"They did. An entire Diviniterra Legion."

Braxxan opened his mouth to respond—but a tremor shook the floor beneath them. Somewhere deep in the coliseum, alarms howled.

Then a roar, monstrous and wild, ripped through the walls. They froze for half a heartbeat. Then chaos erupted.

Screams echoed from the maintenance tunnels. The ground quaked again. Heavier this time. Followed by the crash of something massive tearing through metal.

Tria's Peacekeepers moved instantly, peeling off toward the disturbance. Braxxan staggered back, eyes wide with fear as another bellow shook the pipes overhead.

"The cages," he rasped. "They've broken loose again!"

Something barreled through the corridor ahead. An unnatural hulking beast created just for the games, all sinew and fangs, its hide gleaming with oily sweat. Its four hungry crimson eyes locked onto them, a snarl ripping its maw apart.

"Down!" Tria shouted, shoving Braxxan aside just as the creature lunged.

The first Peacekeeper opened fire, low-powered energy rounds slamming into the monster's hide. But it barely slowed, crashing into the wall with a screech of tortured metal. Tria spun, drawing her Singublade with a hiss of energy, she set it to max power, the weapon humming like a living thing.

She met the bio-spliced creature head-on, dodging its snapping jaws and driving the blade deep into its flank. It shrieked, thrashing wildly, smashing pipes and sparking conduits.

More beasts poured into the tunnels behind it. Mutated horrors, escaped from the blood pits of the coliseum's lower levels. A stampede of nightmares.

"Form up!" Tria barked with a commanding and confident presence. "Hold the line!"

The Peacekeepers fell into a strong wedge formation, Plakinsteel and discipline ready to meet twisted muscle and hunger. Braxxan pressed himself against the wall, watching in horror and awe as the black-armored figures fought. Not as soldiers of the Dominion, but as silent, lethal shadows.

The lead beast lunged. Foam flying from its fanged gaping maw. A Peacekeeper slipped aside, jamming a shocklance into its gut. Thunder cracked. The monster seized, crashed down, and didn't rise.

Another horror, bone-plated and roaring, tore through the maintenance bay, flattening two Peacekeepers, knocking them over. Tria was already moving to meet it, low and fast. Her Singublade flashing in brutal arcs. She sliced a lashing tendril, drove the blade into the beast's throat, and twisted. Its blood flowed like black ichor, spraying and hissing against metal.

An eight-legged twistedly mutated brute leapt from the smoke. A heavy Peacekeeper braced, then fired. The dark matter cannon set at full power roared. And the creature vanished in an exploding bloom of gore. The tunnels shook under the carnage. Alarms wailed. Smoke burned the air.

Another monstrous hybrid charged right towards Tria, a grotesque fusion of horrors. Three heads sat atop elongated necks, each one a twisted mockery of its progenitors.

The center head, a vile mix of Vamp and Askar, snarled with vampire fangs glinting under the dim light, its glowing yellow eyes burning with the hunger of a wolf on the prowl.

On the left, a Galgador head, thick and armored like a brutal space turtle, reared back, its massive jaw creaking with pent-up fury.

And to the right, a Drak head, long and serpentine, its scales glistening like obsidian as it hissed and flicked its tongue in the air like a dragon preparing for a fiery assault.

The beast's massive body coiled and shifted, its six muscular arms crackling with power. Tria gripped her Singublade tighter, feeling the weight of the moment. The air was thick with tension as the creature prepared to strike.

With a growl from the Vamp-Askar head, the beast lunged forward. Its claws slashed like the bite of a hurricane, raking across the air with savage speed. Tria was already moving, her body a blur of fluid motion as she darted to the side, narrowly avoiding the

24

snapping mouth of the Galgador head and the dragon's fiery, guttural hiss. The ground beneath her feet cracked and splintered from the sheer force of the beast's charge.

Tria's Singublade flashed as she leapt to the side, slashing at the creature's exposed throat. Her blade hit hard against the thick, mutated flesh, but the beast barely flinched. The Vamp-Askar head snapped toward her, its jaws closing with a bone-crushing snap, forcing her to parry with a harsh clang. She dropped low, narrowly avoiding its massive claws as two of its arms swung at her.

Before she could recover, the mutated twisted Galgador head. A massive, vicious, armored turtle-like monstrosity swung down with terrifying force. Its spiked shell slammed into her chest, knocking the wind from her lungs and sending her crashing into a metal wall that dented at her impact. It rattled her bones, and pain exploded through her body. She slid to the floor, struggling to stay fully conscious, her vision became temporarily blurry from the force of the blow.

With a surge of adrenaline and nanotech strength, Tria pushed herself to her feet, narrowly avoiding the Galgador head's next swing. In one swift motion, she plunged her Singublade into its glaring, unblinking eye. The blade tore through the thick, armored membrane with a sickening crack, releasing a geyser of black, viscous fluid.

The Galgador head flopped limp, lifeless. But before Tria could even breathe, the Vamp-Askar head howled in rage. It lunged forward, snapping its vampire and wolf-like jaws, and with a brutal, savage bite, it tore the dead Galgador head, the sickening crunch of bone echoing through the air. Bioengineered blood poured from the severed neck, coating the floor in thick, oily puddles.

The Drak head came at her next, its massive jaws snapping open in a fiery roar as it lunged at her. Tria dropped to her knees, narrowly avoiding the crushing bite. With a burst of strength, she pushed herself up quickly, driving her Singublade deep into its exposed throat. The blade tore through with unforgiving intensity, and the beast's screech rattled the walls as its body convulsed violently. With a final, desperate thrash, the Drak head collapsed, lifeless, its massive form flopping to the ground. The center head again ripped off this dead head and then the beast circled Tria. Now taking its time.

The Vamp-Askar head lunged again, its vampire-werewolf hybrid instincts flaring. Tria barely sidestepped its savage bite, but one of its Plakinsteel claws raked across her armored shoulder, sending waves of fire through her body. With a growl of anger, she twisted, her Singublade cutting through thick flesh with vicious. Three arms were cut off the thing, severed in brutal, repeated strikes—but still, three remained, each capable of causing a lot of damage and possibly death if it got a few lucky hits against the weakest parts of her armor.

A roar shook her to the core as the beast reared back. Before she could react, its jaws clamped around her torso, teeth sinking into her armor with a sickening crunch. She was lifted, weightless, her feet dangling. She slashed desperately at the thing's impenetrable hide, but her efforts were in vain.

With a savage jerk, the creature hurled her through the air, slamming her into a jagged metal pipe. Stars flashed in her vision, her teeth rattling, but she fought to stay conscious. The creature wasn't finished. It seized her again, lifting her higher, tighter.

Her breath came in short gasps as its grip tightened like a vice. Then, with a final roar, it smashed her into a high wall, the metal buckling under the force. Pain exploded through her body—lights flickered, then died. Darkness swallowed her whole as she burst through the metal wall into another room.

Shallow breaths. Her body, numb with pain, barely registered the impact. She crawled, pushing through the darkness, hands scraping against the cold floor as she fled. The beast's growls reverberated, and she retrieved some distraction grenades from her DIE-Space compartments, tossing them in desperation. The explosions flashed, filling the air with smoke, casting eerie shadows as the creature followed, undeterred by the fog.

Tria's pulse thundered through her body as she retrieved her pistol, firing into the smoke. Making the best guess of where to aim. The shots hit, but the creature kept coming, its claws scraping closer,

26

its roar cutting through the haze. In an instant, it lunged, biting down on her hand. Pain exploded as its fangs clamped against her arm, ripping her weapon from her grasp. Tria screamed as she fought, but the creature loomed over her, its jaws about to end it all and swallow her whole.

Missiles slammed into the creature's side, sending it reeling. It howled in agony, its heads flailing wildly as the impact threw it off balance. Tria's vision blurred, pain and blood loss overwhelming her senses.

A different team of Peacekeepers disguised like her spread out, their armor flashing like dark storm clouds. One leaned down and injected biogel into her veins. It was cool. Soothing warmth spread through her, and began healing her shattered body. The pain began to fade.

"We heard you needed some backup," a voice said, gruff with urgency.

With help from the steady hands of the Peacekeepers who had saved her life, she forced herself upright, pain lancing through her body. The end was nowhere in sight, but survival against the unexpected attack felt like a little victory. They had defeated the bio-engineered terrors without a single Peacekeeper death and had gained Braxxan Lume's trust. It was a crucial foothold in the Umber levels of Venus. Still, the continuing war lay ahead, vast and merciless.

Chapter Four

THE TRUTH WILL SET YOU FREE

In the light of the Eternal Dominion, the lost shall find their way.[1] Those who walk the path of unity shall be granted strength beyond the stars.[2] Their hearts shall beat as one, and their souls shall rise together.[3] For in the bond of true faith, no darkness can prevail.[4] The truth shall be a beacon to all who seek, shining through the veil of shadows.[5] Know this: the truth will set you free.[6] But freedom is found not in defiance, but in the humble embrace of the eternal order.[7] Stand firm, for the path is narrow, and only those who endure shall reach the light.[8]

The Holy Terran-Orion Bible - Book of Unity 1:1-8

The Dominion prison cell on Orion breathed darkness, its silence broken only by the slight buzz of forcefields and the rhythmic pulse of the neural conduit feeding into Maris Solvannis's spine. Incense curled like ghosts in the corners, veiling the stone with smoke and shadow. Princess Transcendent Veshdren'Ra stood still in the gloom, her golden armor whispering power. Her shining eyes shimmered. Not just with cruel brilliance, but with hunger. Hunger for truth and power. For transformation and control.

Maris, scarred by a lifetime that had been through too much, sat upon the memory chair with a defiance that spoke for itself. As if the machine were a throne ready for its king. His posture was steady despite the tremors riding his nerves. He had endured worse. He had watched entire civilizations burn and refused to blink.

"I know her name," Veshdren'Ra said at last, her voice low and reverent. "Tria Oberon. It was pulled from the dying minds of the Margoons before their skulls cracked from their inner screams. The woman who led the uprising on Mars with you. The one you threw through the stolen portal like she was a sacred flame. Why?"

He didn't flinch. "You're wasting your breath. I sent her where your kind will never touch her. That world is beyond even your father's reach. There are too many stars in the galaxy for you to ever find her. I'll carry its location to my grave."

A ripple of frustration crossed Veshdren'Ra's features. "Don't pretend I can't tear it from you if I wanted to."

"Try," he said, a ghost of a grin tracing his lip. "But what you find may break more than your mind, it may break your soul."

She stepped closer, slowly, deliberately, until she leaned over toward him, like a wolf stalking before its kill. "You don't understand. I want to help her. I want to help them. I want to help you."

His brow furrowed, the words strange in her mouth. "What are you talking about? You're Princess Transcendent, heir to the Godly Throne? Why would you help? You said you wanted to make me suffer for eternity."

"Yes, yes I am," she said, her voice cold and clear. "I have to keep up appearances. I can't let anyone know my true nature and beliefs. And I heard everything you and my parents said as you talked alone in the throne room, after everyone else was ordered to leave. I stayed, hidden out of sight. The God Emperor and Empress hide behind gold and rot. From what you all said, they've lied many times. And they continue to lie. Their promises to you and those like you who were there at the beginning of the empire are broken."

"Promises have been broken. Things used to be different. Your parents have changed. I still love them. But they are not as they were when the empire was first born. They have forgotten what mercy truly is."

"I know what you mean. Their so-called future is a graveyard even more hideous than now. I've seen their plans. Of the silence it would create. A future of obedience carved from bones and tears. Worse than anything you could imagine. A crusade to end all crusades. No mercy. No light. No peace. I won't be an architect or tool of that misguided vision. I will end their rule by any means. I will remake the empire anew. A rebirth of truth. As you have said."

"You'd unmake one tyrannical empire to build another? Replace two lost tyrants with one? You think by killing your parents you will make things right?"

"No," she snapped, but quickly steadied herself. "I don't want my parents to die. I want to end the cycle. I will remake the empire. Not for conquest, but for peace. Not a peace that crushes the living beneath it, but one that lets them breathe. I know this uprising is bigger than Mars. I can feel it. I have seen it in dreams. It won't end here. This is only the beginning of something much larger that will shatter the foundations of all civilizations throughout the universe."

29

Maris didn't speak. His silence was not surrender. It was the weight of an old man measuring her words, looking into her soul.

"Tell me," she whispered, dark as the darkest black hole, "who is Tria Oberon... really?"

Still, he said nothing. So, she reached. Her hand hovered over his forehead. With a whisper in a language born before Dominion banners were ever woven, she slipped into his mind. They found themselves within a raging storm. Then a raging fire. His pain and conflicts were cracked open like wounds.

The fire and storms faded, replaced by the cold, dim light of one of Pluto's undercities as it was thousands of years ago. Dust drifted through vents high above, catching on rusted scaffolding. They both saw Maris as a little boy, barefoot and gaunt, wrapped in filthy rags. He was crouched beside a heat exhaust, hands trembling as he held out a scrap of metal with shaking fingers, begging passing workers for discarded nutrient bars or a sip of thawed water. The air stank of grease and desperation. Veshdren'Ra watched silently from the shadows, seeing the boy who would one day become the Prophet of Mars, a desperate child shaped by hunger and frostbite, whose eyes burned with the silent vow to never beg again.

Another memory came. In the bitter cold of Pluto's thirtieth century slums, teenage Maris knelt in the icy air. Fingers numb, stomach hollow. From the shadows, two strangers emerged. Silent, radiant, cloaked in a presence that bent the air around them. The man's eyes burned with ancient fire. The woman's gaze pierced like a blade of ice. They spoke not with pity. But power. "Do you want to rise?" His breath caught. In that frozen moment, everything inside him: fear, hunger, despair. Was replaced by fire. He said yes, and the Duality had their first follower.

Within the storm of his mind, they were pulled into the fires of the Earth Civil War. Chaotic battles flashed before them. Insanity and cruelty. Mindless slaughter. The most destructive war Earth had ever known.

A ruined skyline stretched across the horizon. Once proud cities now broken bones jutting from scorched earth. Ash fell like snow. United Peacekeeping Forces of Earth soldiers fought trench to trench against the disciples of the Duality through radioactive wastelands, their armor scorched black, their flags tattered. Orbital strikes lit the skies above, turning night to hellfire. Younger teenage

Maris ran through the wreckage of Old Chicago, his Deacon staff in hand, lungs burning, comrades screaming. A U.P.F.O.E war mech collapsed beside him, its pilot crushed, still reaching for the controls. Veshdren'Ra walked with him through the shattered streets, silent as ghosts passed them by. Soldiers, civilians, martyrs. All swallowed by a war that turned Earth into a graveyard of division. Faith and hate. Politics and power. Greed and envy. Apathy and passion.

Deeper past all these surface memories, Maris was hiding Tria and something ancient and hidden. Something powerful and important. He fought back. Memories began to twist like warped steel beneath her mental grasp.

"You won't find it," he growled within the shared space. "Even here, it's buried in fire and frost and pain. You will not find it."

But she kept going. And then. She saw it. A momentary glimpse that lasted just a few seconds. The United Free Republics of Earth, hidden beneath layers of secrecy. Still breathing beneath countless generations of Dominion cities. And then she saw a forest of crystals, but they were alive. Powerful and knowing. It seemed impossible. A civilization even more advanced than the Dominion. And beings of ancient power. Right on Earth, under the nose of the Dominion and the Duality. Untouched. Watching. Waiting.

She gasped. But before she could press in further, a psychic backlash hit like a falling star. Maris flung her out. She stumbled back across the obsidian floor, blood trailing from her nose.

"You think you're ready for that truth?" he spat. "You're not. You want peace? Stop parading yourself as a God. Or you'll become just like your parents, maybe even worse than them."

She stood, shaking. Not from fear, but from the tremor of revelation. Awe. Rage. Purpose.

"I'm not the only one who knows her name," she said through clenched teeth.

Maris's gaze narrowed. "Who else?"

"Wraithblade Razik Kelran. Spymaster of the All Seeing Shadows. It wasn't me who tore the Margoons apart. He did. And he pulled more than names from their screams. He will find out what I have learned. Maybe even more. He has his ways."

Maris's jaw tensed. "Razik's shadows are long. If he wants information, no secret is safe for long."

She stepped closer, voice like a winter wind. "Then you understand. You are no longer the last keeper of her story."

"And yet," he said, lifting his chin, "I will fight to protect it, until the day I breathe my last breath."

The air cracked between them, charged with a storm of truths being unraveled. Veshdren'Ra's voice fell to a whisper, edged with fire.

"You aren't in a position to fight. But I am. I am a storm that has broken empires. I will tear down everything that has enslaved us. I will free us all. Now show me what I need to know."

With a new wave of force, she surged deeper into his psyche, crashing through mental barriers like a tempest through stone. Memories fractured around them. Planets aflame, warships screaming through the void of outer space. Names and faces torn away by time. Each vision was a blade of painful mistakes. But Maris stood in the storm, a rock in the tide.

"You will not find what you seek by force. No matter how hard you try. You won't find the deeper answers you seek." Maris said.

The dream unraveled like mist torn by wind. Maris stood still at first, silent, watching her with a gaze that weighed time itself. The glow of that strange mental realm dimmed as trust, however faint, began to stir behind his eyes.

"You want my help," he said, voice low and wary. "Then show me. Show me that you truly mean to change the Empire. I will not be yours or anyone else's pawn. Not again. Not ever again. I need proof of your intentions."

Veshdren'Ra nodded slowly. Around them, the dream faded entirely, and their senses returned to the cold, dim-lit chamber. She raised her hand, and with a flick of her fingers, the shimmering forcefield around his chair that was holding him down hissed and vanished. Maris stood, shoulders broad with purpose but still guarded.

They faced each other for a quiet moment, something heavy settling between them. Then, out of thin air, a familiar shape appeared in her hands. The Deacon staff he had wielded for millennia, gleaming with its old power. She held it out, almost reverent and respectful. Along with it, she offered a small black beacon marked in ciphered runes.

"When the time comes," she said, "use the beacon. It will reach me, wherever I am. And I will come."

Maris took them both without a word, but his eyes stayed locked on hers.

"You must strike me," she added. "They need to believe you escaped because I was careless and stupid. Not because I let you go freely. My defenses are down. Make it look real." He hesitated, looking at her intently. "Go," she urged. "Let the old fires burn again. Let the rebellion rise."

Maris turned toward the center of the chamber. Power crackled through his staff. A violet portal spiraled open, shimmering with light from a world unseen. He paused at its edge, looking back at her. Their eyes met. Their now shared secret alliance burned between them.

He gave a single nod, then reached out with the full force of his power. Veshdren'Ra flew backward, slamming into the wall with bone-rattling force, shattering the dark stone wall. Her body crumpled to the ground, motionless. Maris stood in the silence for a moment.

"We will meet again, Princess," he said. "The day will come when you will do great things." He stepped into the portal and vanished, leaving the chamber cold and echoing with their shared fate. The fate of heretics.

Chapter Five:
WHISPERS OF UNITY

"Unity is not forged in the light of triumph, but in the dark where no one watches."
— Peacekeeper Codex of Peace

The underground service tunnels beneath the Meridian Arcology were never meant for meetings of power. Rusted pipes hissed overhead, and the faint vibration of the transit rails rumbled through the walls like a restless heartbeat. But this was where real change started now. Not in the gleaming towers or the blessed temples, but here, deep in the bones of Venus.

Braxxan Lume leaned against a corroded maintenance panel, arms crossed over his grease-stained jumpsuit. Middle-aged, broad-shouldered, the marks of his hard work were still fresh. But the steel in his gaze was unmistakable. Around him, a half-circle of Umbers: system techs, pipefitters, and waterline inspectors. All stood silent, waiting.

Tria Oberon took a breath, feeling the cold, recycled air dry her throat. She let the silence stretch before she spoke. she wanted them to be listening intently.

"You know the High Lords don't care," she said. "The Holy Duality speaks one way. The temples preach to you, bless their empire, bless their crusades... but they don't answer your cries for justice. Not to the Unders. Not to you. Not anyone."

Murmurs passed through the group. Some agreeing, some skeptical. Braxxan pushed off the panel and stepped forward.

"She's telling the jankking truth and you all know it," he said, voice rough but cutting through the tension. "We've sent our cries up the chain. We've marched. We've waited. You know what we got back?"

He held up a fist and opened it to nothing. A younger Umber, Joral Vint, narrowed his eyes.

"The Unders are more restless than we are. Some of them want revolt. Full burn. No talking. No reasonable course of action."

Tria didn't flinch. "And if they do it without us, the fires will take innocents first. And some of your families will be taken in the chaos if we don't unite and..."

She paused for a moment, remembering Mars. The thoughts of the insanity she witnessed still broke her heart, but she refocused.

"I'm not asking you to pick up arms. I'm asking you to open a door. Meet with them. Hear them. Be united under the same ideals of justice. Because you aren't that different. You're the same. The uppers crush you both. The uppers lie to you all."

Someone coughed. Marit Sol, a hydrofarms supervisor with silver in her hair.

"And when the Gods see our heresy? When the Holy Duality finally looks down from their thrones? What then?"

Tria met her gaze, unwavering. "The truth isn't heresy. The High Lords and Uppers are the heretics. They spit on the light of the Gods. If we remain divided, chaos will erase us all. Umbers, Unders, Uppers, everything that has ever been built. But if we unite, with justice for all in our hearts, the Gods will understand. For too long, the Uppers have caused you pain and suffering. For too long you've been bound in their lying chains. If our cause is just and rooted in the truth of the holy texts, no temples or statues destroyed, the Duality will see. They must see."

Silence gripped the room. Venus' winds hummed above, stirring dust in the artificial light. Tria felt every gaze pressing down on her. They want to believe. They had to. It was life itself. She didn't believe that the Holy Duality were gods. They had allowed this cage, and the Dominion had become enslaved by it. But she didn't want more bloodshed. Mars had shown her enough blood for a million lifetimes. Cities eviscerated, innocents torn apart. Not again. Not here.

The Umbers and Unders deserved unity, not bloodlust. Piece by piece, they would tear down the Dominion's false towers with their own beliefs. And if it meant using their myths, so be it. She would use their faith to ignite their awakening, even if the price was her soul.

35

Chapter Six:
MADNESS BENEATH MARS

"The corporations rewrote the flesh and mocked the order of creation, but in unmaking what was, they unmade themselves."

The Holy Terran-Orion Bible – The Book of Creation, 9:1

Amarax moved like a silent blade through the ruined corridors of the heretic facility, driven by wrath, carved from pent-up rage, he pushed himself forward, sometimes falling against a wall for support, he was still losing a lot of blood. The air reeked of scorched metal and rot. He heard the cries of someone in pain and followed it. Down a winding hallway he noticed a light flickering through a slightly broken bulkhead door. He made his way to it and slammed through it, splinters of the already fractured steel crashing to the floor. Amarax stepped into a ruined laboratory.

The stench hit him first. Burnt meat, chemicals, and something deeper. Wrong. The walls were scorched, panels melted, and cables hung like entrails from the ceiling. Sparks danced through the air, casting wild shadows across broken glass and shattered consoles. Blood pooled in craters where machines once stood. Two twisted strange Beasts of Mars, grotesque, dead things with armor-like scales and bone protrusions lay slumped across the wreckage, twitching even in death. Their maws hung open, steaming with deep plasma burns.

Throughout the lab were dozens of dead bodies ripped to pieces. Shredded and torn head to toe. Their once pristine white coats were like decimated fragments of battlefield hospital rags.

At the far end of the lab, a man writhed beneath debris, half-pinned, his body mangled, one cauterized arm completely gone almost at the shoulder socket. His white coat was stained black with thick drying blood. And was torn open to reveal seared flesh. In his remaining hand, he clutched a still-glowing plasma torch, flickering weakly, like a last gasp of hope.

Amarax stormed across the room, eyes burning with holy rage. He yanked the man free with one hand, dragging him and then slamming him against a crumpled table.

"What have you done?" he roared, slamming the scientist against the metal surface. "You heretic! You cultist! What have you unleashed here? These are no ordinary Beasts of Mars?! Tell me everything! Now!"

The scientist's head lolled, blood dripping from his lips. His eyes, cloudy and unfocused, locked onto Amarax's face. "You don't... understand..." he rasped. "We're not cultists... We're scientists..."

Amarax pressed the bone claw against the man's chest, still seething. "Then explain before I rip the rest of your lies from your throat!"

The dying man coughed, a wet, rattling sound. "The cultists... they were prisoners. Like you. We never meant to... They're not ours... We have nothing to do... With those lunatics... We serve the Republics of Earth. Not any fake gods..."

"Lies."

"No... truth..." he wheezed. "We thought we could... use the Beasts... Make weapons... Better for monsters to die in war... than our people... But they... they can't be tamed... Not truly... They... evolved... even more... our experiments... They were too successful... They breed and grow... many times faster than before... They want to consume... To grow... We thought we could... control them... We were wrong..."

He began to shake, plasma torch falling from his hand, hissing out against the blood-slick floor.

"I'm sorry... I'm so sorry..."

He reached into his coat with trembling fingers and pressed something on a cracked datapad. A shimmer burst to life in front of them. Blue light forming a holographic map of the facility, three-dimensional and detailed. Arrows blinked along the tunnels. One was marked in red: Maintenance shaft. Surface access.

"Take it... It's the only way out now... the upper floors are overrun... most of the beasts... have been trapped... but the

37

forcefields won't hold them forever… the jump gates have been shut down… the self-destruct has already been activated… these twisted… unnatural monsters… they can't be allowed… to escape… get out of here…"

His voice faltered, breath hitching. The light in his eyes dimmed as his head fell backward. He was dead. Amarax stood motionless for a moment, the lab crackled around him with heat and ruin. His gaze shifted to the map, to the corpses of the beasts beside the man, to the smoldering remains of the misguided.

"Fools," he growled under his breath. "You served no God. Only death. Only avarice."

He turned, blood-soaked feet padding across the warped metal floor. He snatched the plasma torch from the ground, now his, and used its lowest setting to carefully cauterize his gaping wounds, screaming out as he burned his own flesh to stop the flow of blood.

Once he was sure that the wounds were burnt shut he marched toward the path the scientist had shown on the datapad. Whatever waited ahead, Amarax would meet it not as a prisoner. But as vengeance incarnate. The warped Beasts of Mars would remember his fury.

Amarax left the lab of death behind him, stepping through corridor after corridor lit only by emergency strobes that kept reminding him that he had little time to get out. The weight of the dead pressed against his back as he limped forward. Toward the maintenance shaft. Toward the only escape from this created hell. The facility groaned like a dying beast, and Amarax, fueled by wrath and fading strength, ran as fast as his injured body could toward the red-marked shaft etched in memory.

It was becoming more and more obvious that the beasts were starting to break through whatever forcefields were still functional, the sounds that echoed through the facility was evidence of that.

After a few minutes of fighting and burning through nests and slimy membranes that held birthing abominations, Amarax finally made it to the base of the large and tall maintenance shaft that was big enough to fit a small starship in. The maglev lift was gone, most likely jammed high above from the self-destruct protocols. The walls were slick with condensation and scorched streaks of old plasma fire. He had no choice. He leapt for the outer railings and beams that lined the walls of the shaft, fingers catching the first narrow ledge, and he began to climb.

About three-quarters of the way up the maintenance shaft, Amarax paused just long enough to hear it. The screeching clamor of claws tearing into metal, the unnatural howls of the Beasts below as they poured into the base of the shaft. A jolt of fire surged through his limbs. He climbed faster, ignoring the pain in his cauterized wounds, fingers gripping jagged rails, bare broken feet slamming against narrow footholds.

Sparks rained from a ruptured conduit above, lighting the shaft in eerie pulses as shadows twisted beneath him, growing closer. He didn't look back. He couldn't. Every breath was a war cry now, every pull upward a rebellion against the death chasing him from below.

A screech echoed up the shaft. Wet, ragged, and wrong in every way thinkable, sending a shiver down Amarax's spine. Amarax glanced down for only a second, and that second burned into his memory forever. The thing crawling up after him along the walls defied biology and sanity alike.

Twisting like a serpent but moving like a spider, it stretched across the walls with grotesque grace. Its centipede-snake body bristled with jagged limbs and chittering maws that opened in places no mouth should be. Spiked black tentacles lashed the air with terrifying speed, snapping close behind him. Its hide was oily and iridescent, rippling with living faces. Some screaming. Some whispering. None human.

It shouldn't exist. A nightmare of twisted biology, its centipede-snake body writhed with layered, alien muscle and chitin, covered in mouths, jagged claws, and lashing black tentacles. Each movement defied nature, shifting in dimensions that shimmered and bent. It surged upward, faster than it had any right to be.

Amarax turned and raised the plasma torch. He set it to max power and squeezed the ignition. A stream of superheated blue fire roared to life, blasting down the shaft. The creature screamed. Not in pain, but in challenge. The flame engulfed it, searing a dozen of its mouths closed, blackening its outer flesh. But it didn't stop. It pushed through the fire, tentacles flailing, burning and blistering but refusing to die.

He shifted on the beam, bracing with his legs and sweeping the torch in wide arcs. The shaft lit up with flickering inferno, shadows dancing along the walls like fleeing ghosts. The creature took the brunt of it, its hide bubbling and peeling, but it struck back hard. A tentacle slammed across his chest, the force ripping the torch from his hand. It clattered down the shaft in a fading trail of blue sparks.

The twisted beastly thing slithered away on the opposite wall for a moment and shed its outer skin. In only a very few moments a new layer of brand new and fresh flesh replaced everything that was burnt. Amarax roared in fury. He reached for the bone claw and slashed at it as it came after him again, but his defense didn't last long, another strike faster than any beast he had ever faced sent it spinning into the dark below. He was now disarmed and cornered.

The beast lunged, jaws open like a blossoming nightmare. Amarax had no time to think. Only react. As the monstrosity lunged, all fangs and tentacles, he used every bit of strength he had against a metal pipe jutting from the shaft wall. With a guttural roar, he bent it downward in one brutal motion. The creature impaled itself mid-strike, the sharpened edge of the pipe punching through its gaping maw and up into its skull with a slimy bone-splitting crack.

It continued to recoil and thrash wildly. It slammed against the shaft walls, shrieking, spasming, twisting around itself in a seizure of pain and fury. Amarax didn't wait. He climbed, faster than ever before, even as blood poured from reopened wounds and his muscles screamed in betrayal. Behind him, the thing continued to twitch violently. A few last shrieks of distorted gurgles, before going limp. Skewered and suspended like a grotesque banner of death.

Below, past the dead creature, the rest of the swarm rose in a tidal wave of claws and shrieks. Above, the tunnel rumbled and shook. Then explosions started their death march upward. The facility's final breath was coming. Amarax climbed like a man who had nothing left but the will to destroy death itself.

A rising sun of white-hot flame surged up the shaft. Heat and light swallowed the darkness. Amarax gave a final heave, his body surging with desperate power, and burst from the top just as the firestorm erupted beneath him. He flew. The shock-wave caught him mid-leap, hurling him like a shattered comet. He slammed into a stone outcropping and then started rolling. He tumbled down a jagged cliff-side, every hit felt like a gravhammer, once he was at the bottom he lay still, gasping, scorched, trembling.

Behind him, the mountain wept fire. Flames spiraled into the sky as molten steel and screaming monsters were torn apart. Black smoke billowed high, blotting out the sun. The ground cracked. And then it began to collapse.

The entire valley. Once lush and green with thick dense jungle was now charred and burning. Then, it began to collapse, the ground devouring itself in slow, grinding ruin. Amarax forced himself to his feet, every breath like swallowing glass. Limping away as fast as his body allowed, he knew the beasts were gone, but death still had teeth. He pressed on until his strength failed him, collapsing into the wet dirt as the world faded into pitch-black silence.

Chapter Seven:
THE FAILURE OF A PRINCESS

"Her fall was not sudden, but sung in soft notes across centuries, like a harp string fraying beneath divine weight. When it snapped, the song of peace died with it."

— Lamentations of Kahlvara Asuki, Deacon of the All Seeing Eyes

Pain flickered through her spine as golden light surged across her chest. Veshdren'Ra gasped awake, her body floating in a healing chamber suspended between living metal pillars. The chamber pulsed with Divine Radiance, channeled directly from the God Emperor's own hands. At her side, the God Empress stood in silence, eyes glowing with light far beyond mortal comprehension.

"You let him go," the Emperor's voice cracked like thunder, not in wrath, but deep disappointment. "The false Prophet of Mars is now free to cause chaos once again."

Veshdren'Ra clenched her fists. Her lips trembled, but she held his gaze. "He's broken and defeated. He's nothing but a shell. I didn't expect that he'd be able to turn the shadows against me."

"Why did you release him?" the Empress asked, her voice sharp with divine scrutiny.

"He mocked us, mocked me," Veshdren'Ra replied through clenched teeth. "Mocked your divinity. Mocked my strength, my purpose. I wanted to teach him what it meant to defy us. I underestimated his power. I have no excuse... but I won't make the same mistake twice. I will hunt him down and make him pay."

The Empress stepped closer to her daughter. "You underestimate the flame inside him. He has seen things you will understand. He carries words that can unravel empires. He has our blessings upon him. He was the first of our disciples. The first to see our light. He was our beloved. Which makes his betrayal even more painful."

"He's just a single heretic," Veshdren'Ra snapped, her voice rising. "A heretic who breathes only because of my overconfidence in my own abilities. It will never happen again. One man cannot stop the Dominion. One man cannot stand against you."

"But one man with the voice of prophecy can sway multitudes," the Emperor said, lowering his hand. The chamber's glow faded. "We've given you great responsibilities and command of countless legions. We trusted you to sever threats before they grew. This time we will forgive your shortsightedness. You will hunt him down."

"He's nothing. he's no threat to us," she insisted. "He's weak. He hides behind memories and guilt. He's no warrior. He's no prophet or massiah, he's no leader of armies that can silence the stars."

The room fell quiet. The twin Gods of the Dominion exchanged a look. Unreadable to anyone besides each other, an ancient knowing connection that only they shared.

At last, the God Empress reached out, touching her daughter's brow. "Even Gods can be wrong," she said gently. "This time, we trust that your misguided actions weren't true failures. But merciful lessons to strengthen you."

Veshdren'Ra bowed her head, accepting what her mother had said. "He won't rise again. I will make sure of that."

The Emperor turned and walked away, his cloak of living stars trailing across the marble floor as he said one last thing. "He will rise. But when he does, you'll be there to administer our final judgement." The God Empress soon followed, but first she held her daughter's hand and said "Rest now. Renew your strength. My precious child." A smile projected across the Princess's face once she was alone. She had fooled her parents. Now her plot against them could begin.

Chapter Eight:
VENUS UNITES

"I don't lead armies. I spark wildfires. I don't move pieces across a board. I flip the board, strike the match, and walk away to the next."

Captain Zoephiria Vergaragas Morganvale, At a secret meeting of the U.R.F. 3,099 AD

The dark, huge, cavernous room was thick with anticipation, the air humming with the quiet reverence of those gathered. Tria stood before them. An unlikely leader for Dominion citizens, but one forged by conviction. Umbers and Unders, their faces weary but hopeful, filled the hidden grand chamber beneath the surface of Venus. Their faith in the empire and the Holy Duality was unwavering. But now, they were beginning to see the cracks in the system that had oppressed them for so long.

She raised her hands, the room falling silent. There was no need for loud declarations. Her words would carry the weight of truth, the truth that had been buried beneath the Uppers lies.

"Faith," Tria began, her voice steady and sure, "is a gift. A sacred bond with the Holy Duality. It is not to be taken lightly, nor twisted by those who would use it to subjugate us. For too long, the High Lords of Venus have claimed to serve the will of the Duality, but they have only served their own hunger for power. They have turned the very faith we hold sacred into a cage."

She paused, watching the eyes of the gathered souls flicker with recognition. These were not rebels. These were the faithful, those who believed in the power of the Duality. They had been betrayed, and Tria could feel their anger, their confusion.

"The High Lords wear the mantle of divine authority, but their actions betray the very teachings of the Holy Duality. They exploit our faith, our devotion, to keep us weak. They claim the title of 'holy' while feeding us lies, keeping us divided, and turning our devotion

44

against us." She clenched her fists, her resolve strengthening. "They are the true heretics. Not us."

She paced slowly before them, her gaze sweeping over their faces. "The Dominion speaks of unity, of divine order. But where is the order for the Umbers? Where is the justice for the Unders? The High Lords speak of the will of the Gods, but their actions mock it. They have turned our faith into a weapon to control us. They claim to be the chosen, yet they grow fat on our suffering."

Tria's voice rose, passion igniting in her chest, fueling the fire that had burned within her from the moment she first saw the injustice of the Dominion lords firsthand.

"They would have us believe that we are nothing without them. That our devotion to the Duality is meaningless unless it serves their goals. But I tell you now: we are the faithful. We are the true servants of the divine Holy Duality."

Her words echoed in the room, striking deep into their hearts. The crowd shifted, uncertain but intrigued.

"Do not let them twist your devotion," she continued. "The Duality's light shines through us, not through the High Lords who hide behind their walls of luxury and privilege. They have stolen your faith, turned it into a tool for their own gain. But it is time to take it back. It is time to show them that the will of the Gods cannot be manipulated."

Tria's eyes burned with intensity. "If the Holy Empire is to be saved. If our faith is to be true. It must come from the truth. The truth of justice. The truth, that all are equal in the eyes of the Duality. We will no longer kneel before the pretender High Lords of our world who have sold their souls for power and greed and petty obscene pleasures. We will rise in the name of the Duality, not to destroy, but to bring the truth of our Gods light to reveal the corruption of heresy that has infected the high places of this once beautiful world. We will bring the absolute truth of the Duality to Venus. No longer will the Uppers be allowed to hide behind their blessings,"

She took a step forward, her voice steady and unwavering. "The Holy Duality will see the truth of our devotion. They will see that we should be the Lords of Venus. And when we rise, when we stand together in the light of our faith, the High Lords will be powerless. They will see us for who we truly are. The faithful. The righteous. They will be judged. They will fall. We will rise."

A murmur rippled through the crowd, a flicker of hope igniting in their eyes. Tria's heart swelled as she felt the shift. The power of their faith could no longer be used against them to suppress. It would now be the greatest weapon in their struggle to gain true sovereignty.

"We do not need to destroy the temples to get the attention of the Gods," Tria continued, her voice softening but still carrying the weight of conviction. "The truth will be enough. The truth of our devotion, the truth of our unity. The Gods will see it. And the High Lords will be brought to their knees."

The room was silent for a moment, then, as if on cue, a chorus of voices rose in agreement—a soft, building hum that echoed like a prayer.

Tria's voice cracked the silence, growing louder, fierce as a storm. Every soul in the room was drawn to her, their desperation a tangible force that pressed against her, urging her on. She felt it, like thousands of hearts beating in unison. This was the moment—this was their reckoning.

"For too long, we've been told that we're nothing! For too long, they've twisted our faith, used it as a chain to bind us, to break us! But hear me now!" She stepped forward, her eyes wild with purpose, burning with conviction. "We are not weak! We are not their playthings! We are the true children of Venus, the rightful heirs to the Duality's light! And we will not be silenced!"

Her words slammed into the air, the truth like a thunderclap, shaking the walls, igniting the room with fierce energy.

"The High Lords, the Uppers," Tria spat, each word a strike, "have stolen our faith. They've weaponized our devotion to keep us broken and divided. Crushed beneath their lying boots. But no more! We will never bow to them again! The chains they have forged for us will be shattered! We will take back what is ours—our faith, our future, our freedom! In the name of the Holy Duality!"

She roared the last words, her chest rising and falling with the force of her rage, her voice like the crack of a whip, the call to arms. "We are the faithful! They are the fallen! And in the eyes of the Gods, we stand united! We will strike as one! And when we rise, when we move in judgment the heretics above will fall! Not by our hands, but by their own lies, by their own falsehoods, by their own greed!" she became even more impassioned in her pretending dedication and belief in the Duality "The Holy Duality will cleanse the unrighteous, purging the filth that stains this sacred world! With fire and light, they will burn away the darkness that has choked the lifeblood from Venus, leaving only purity in its wake! The unworthy will be cast into the void and outer darkness, and those who stand with the truth will rise, bathed in the glory of the Duality's righteous wrath! The time has come for the false to be shattered, for the light to reclaim what is rightfully its own! It is time for Venus to rise! It is time for the faithful to be seen!"

Her eyes blazed as she let the shouting and agreement of the crowd stretch, her gaze sweeping across the room. The faces before her were no longer uncertain. They were aflame. The fire had caught, and they were with her.

Tria stood like a statue carved in legend, her heart heavy but resolute in her mission to free humanity. She had turned their faith into something more than worship and blind subservience to the system. She had made it a force that would burn through the lies and corruption that had infected the most powerful circles throughout the Dominion. And now for better or for worse, they would rise together against the High Lords of Venus. In the name of the Duality.

Chapter Nine

MARS HUNTING LODGE

"They looked upon Mars and saw not a world, but a throne that turned into blood. In their pride, they stitched flesh and flame, forging beasts in the image of their hunger. They called it progress, but the stars wept, and the ground cried out. For they were not gods, only men, led by greed, lost in the shadows of their own undoing."

The Holy Terran-Orion Bible – Book of Mars, 2:1-4

Heavy eyelids slowly opened. Amarax awoke to rainfall hitting his face. No fire. No screams. Only the whisper of wind through ash and ruin. His eyes continued to crack open, crusted with soot. Above him, the sky was a sickly gray bruise, no longer burning. He drew a breath, expecting great pain, but found only deep, dull aches. His ribs, once shattered, were once again whole. Burns had sealed into unnaturally thick fresh scar tissue. His genetically engineered body had done what it was built to do: survive.

He sat up slowly. The world swam. Around him, the valley was a blackened scar, the ground had collapsed into a vast crater. Trees stood like charred bones. The silence wasn't true peace. It was simply the aftermath of pure chaos. He didn't know how long he'd been unconscious. It had most likely been days. The fires had died, the smoke had disappeared, and the altered beasts were no more.

Amarax rose, unsteady at first but remained upright. He began scanning the horizon. Beyond the crater's jagged rim, the Gorgannon Teeth clawed at the sky. Mountains he knew well. He had hunted there as a boy with his father. Stalking razor-stags beneath ice-capped cliffs.

Beyond those far peaks in the next valley was the family's old hunting lodge. In the valley of Varn Oss, which meant blood in old Martian dialects. He began walking, pushing through the aches and ash. Supplies. Shelter. Answers. Maybe even a memory worth holding on to. He would reach it. He had to.

Once over the mountains, he looked down at the jungle that stretched for hundreds of kilometers in every direction, a living sea of moving green and leaking crimson. Thick vines curled like serpents. Massive stalks of barksteel trees scraped the clouds, their leaves humming with bioluminescent pulses. The bioengineered jungle was a breathing thing, as it had always been since its technological creation. Dense, rich, hungry, and now absolutely uncontrollably untamed.

And yet, it was silent. Too silent. Amarax moved like a ghost through the underbrush, his steps instinctual, his body remembering every path, every scent, every sound. He knew these woods better than his own heartbeat. He had hunted here since boyhood. Tracked beasts whose names were now forgotten by most. He used to pass fellow hunters every few miles. Laughs shared. Rivalries kindled. Fires lit beneath blood-red moons.

But today, nothing. Not a single rustle, not a single howl. No campfires. No distant rifle shots. No signs of life at all. The silence pressed in on him like the weight of a grave.

After hours of navigating steep ravines and moss-covered ruins, he saw it. The Mirvega family hunting lodge. Half-swallowed by vines and jungle ivy, it emerged from the Martian soil like a sleeping titan. Black and brooding. Its Dominion design was unmistakable. Functional and brutal. Indestructible to the elements.

Its sloped walls were carved from eight feet of nanocrete, reinforced with denser, specially formulated plakinsteel. The strongest metal Mars had ever forged. Each window was sealed behind thick, retractable metallic shutters, one foot thick and laced with monomolecular threads of woven nanotubes. The jungle had tried to reclaim it, but it hadn't stood a chance against its overengineered design.

Amarax approached the sealed entrance, brushed moss from the biometric scanner, and pressed his hand against it. A long pause. Then the clunking and clicking of gears unlocking. The triple-sealed pressure door hissed and slid open, revealing darkness inside. He stepped through.

Cold, years old dry air hit his face. Preserved by automated systems. The lights flickered to life in sequence, illuminating the interior hallway, wide and spartan, filled only with the echo of his feet. He passed the Great Room. A massive circular chamber with a vaulted ceiling, where hunting trophies lined the walls.

Massive skulls of beasts hung in silent vigil. Twin-headed Maraxian drakes. A crystal-horned Night Grazer. The serrated tusks of a Stalker-Bore, its teeth longer than his forearm. A massive Goreclaw Ravager stood upright in the far corner—its crimson-scaled hide stretched over reinforced plating, the thick, plated spines on its back still sharp enough to gut a man. Next to it, the twisted form of a Vinehowler, part-beast, part-plant, its tendrils coiled like petrified whips, its open maw lined with bone-blades and dripping with hardened sap-like resin.

His gaze drifted up to the central mount. A Vulkar Demon-Beast, stuffed and posed in mid-roar. Its claws as long as swords, its fangs yellowed and glistening. Amarax had killed it alone. When he was just eight years old. He paused there for a moment. Intense memories began tightening his chest like a vise. His father had stood right beside him that day, arm slung around his shoulder in pride.

Across the main wall was Amarax's most brutal trophy—a Cratermaw Behemoth, nearly the size of a dropship, its skull fractured from where his blade had split it down the center in a desperate hand-to-hand kill. Its tusks, each longer than a man is tall, still gleamed under the dim lighting, etched with ancient traditional Martian glyphs burned in by ceremonial plasma to celebrate his kill.

But these weren't just trophies in the normal sense. Each one was a memory of survival that had been forced upon him. All had been tests that he had passed. Each was a moment that he had fought death itself and came back angrier and stronger. A shrine to savagery and brutality. It had been good training to prepare him for the battles he would fight for the empire. A good preparation for the Holy Crusades and the dark worlds he would be sent to throughout his service as a Legionary.

Once the memories had subsided, Amarax walked to the armory. Its walls were lined with chrome-black lockers and fully stocked magnetic weapon racks that were filled with archaic old swords and spears. He went to his locker and entered a code. With a clicking sound, the locker slid open. Inside, wrapped in preserving oiled cloth and stasis foam, was his old hunting gear.

He ran his fingers along the matte surface of his Vulkar-pattern bolt rifle. Hand-crafted. Modified with a grav-assisted targeting lens, rail accelerators, and a triple-modded kinetic chamber. This rifle had never missed its mark when it mattered.

Beside it: his plakinsteel hunting blades, serrated for jungle skinning and reinforced for close combat. He buckled two to his thigh and slid a third into the sheath behind his back.

His hunting armor was still there too, scarred and dented by all the creatures he had slain. Composite power-weave beneath chitin-reinforced plating and painted in Martian jungle camouflage, a suit designed to blend into the jungle but take on a beast at full charge. It smelled like blood and dirt and memory.

He suited up. Piece by piece. Every strap, every buckle a memorized ritual. As he pulled on his hunting boots, they automatically adjusted to his current fit, then he tested their hidden retracted blades. They burst out as if wanting to kill something at that exact moment. They were still functional. By the time he pulled on his helmet and locked it into place with a soft hiss, he was no longer the war prisoner. No longer the defeated exile. He was a hunter again.

The visor on his helmet wasn't closed. He stared into the reflective surface of the polished plakinsteel locker. His own eyes staring back like ghosts of the man he used to be. Had the heretics warped him? Had he lost his edge? Had he forgotten his duty to the Duality? And for a moment, he didn't recognize himself. So much had changed. But the fire for revenge and retribution was still in his eyes. He slammed the locker shut and left, leaving the lodge, heading towards the nearest city.

The lodge hummed behind him like a dormant beast, waiting to awaken again whenever a Mirvega might return. As he treaded through the thick foliage, he knew something wasn't right. The silence in the jungle wasn't natural. It wasn't random. Something had happened to Mars. And now he made it his mission to find out.

Chapter Ten:
OPERATION LIGHTFALL ENDS

"Not all who follow the light survive the dark."

— Zeetarian Proverb

The night's thick white clouds were choking the sky, illuminated by the endless metropolis of Venus that sprawled in every direction, up and down, west and east, north and south. Every square inch of Venus was a city. A fading yellowed veil hung on the edge of the horizon, thick with poison and promise.

Tria Oberon crouched beneath the jagged overhang of collapsed infrastructure, her intricate black rifle that looked like it wanted to tell a story sat across her lap, her breath slow but heavy. The air inside her sealed suit filtered in steady hisses, masking the distant rumbles above.

Another orbital drop. Another legion landing. She glanced to her left. Four Peacekeepers crouched in silence. Their Peacekeeper, Dominion looking armor dulled by ash, engineered eyes fixed on the dark ahead. Somewhere beneath their feet, the Umber levels stretched like a hive. A middle layer of civilization. Filled with skilled laborers, exiles, and souls who were now numb to the endless cycles of industry and commerce.

Umbers had once built this world's golden cities from molten stone and polymer. Now they lived in the fumes below, stripped of most rights, bound by the Dominion's sacred codes of life that had been warped by the greedy. They were always promised the sky, just for the rug underneath their feet to be pulled at the last minute.

Tria's mission was clear: light a slow flame. Speak in shadows. Turn the Umber and Under castes not into martyrs, but murmurs of liberty. Let rebellion grow like a slow rot beneath the skin of Venus.

They had been able to successfully ignite the flames of rebellion before. On Mars, fire had followed whispers. Mars had screamed. But they couldn't allow any new rebellions that they wanted to start to morph into a revolution of darkness. Like what had happened on Mars. They couldn't allow hell to rise up in these middle layers. The Peacekeepers had to be sure to embolden the Umbers and Unders without allowing them to fall to their darker demons.

But what had happened on Mars and the district of Antica changed everything. Now, the Dominion was listening more closely. Now the leaders of the Dominion watched with fearful eyes. Every important world was under practical lockdown until further notice. Especially the lower levels of all city worlds. They had long mostly ignored these under areas, but they could no longer afford to ignore the lower levels.

Security nets tightened. Surveillance protocols tripled. AI sentinels rerouted patrols with machine precision. The Drak Death Legions, the Dominion's airborne alien dragons in midnight armor had been deployed like wildfire across thousands of the most important core worlds. Especially in the under and umber levels. The upper levels were given the benefit of the doubt. For now.

Still, Operation Lightfall had moved forward. The Peacekeepers had risen up out of the shadows of their secret base. The Umber contacts had been made, an army of dissidents had been formed. Then, the silence grew. One by one, the contacts were apprehended. Caches were discovered and seized. Signals from crime syndicates went cold.

The Peacekeepers didn't know what next step should be taken, they didn't have to decide. Motion everywhere. A vibration through the nanocrete under their feet. But the vibrations weren't coming from below. But from above.

Tria stood firm through the vibrations. She could barely see it through the industrial towers, there was a fleet of Dominion Titans piercing through the clouds. Their black hulls projected the will of the Holy Duality and their eternal empire. Their massive red weapons grids glowed and lit up the entire area as they descended lower.

Then they fired and the air around her ruptured. A scream of light and thunder cracked the sky as crimson beams lanced downward, burning through plakinsteel, nanocrete, and flesh without pause or mercy. The Umber levels convulsed. Towers folded like helpless paper against angry hands. Fires bloomed in every direction, swallowing corridors, bridges, industry, everything.

Tria began to lose her footing as the metallic platform beneath her feet started crumbling away and breaking apart. She was thrown into the air, her breath stolen, ears ringing. Around her, the city of the forgotten was reduced to ash—its people, her allies, vaporized in holy fire.

She plunged through the breaking ruins, nanocrete and plakinsteel disintegrating beneath her. Dust and flame burst upward as her body slammed through a wall. Then another and another. Pain bloomed. She tumbled through the shattered buildings. Unable to stop her trajectory, weightless and broken, until gravity seized her again. She crashed into the dark, into a hollow area carved by devastation, vanishing into the pit left behind by the wrath of the High Lords of Venus.

The floor beneath her stopped shaking for a moment, but the silence that followed was worse than the screams that she had heard in the distance. It was the hush of annihilation. Smoke curled through broken corridors, thick with ash and burning insulation. Tria pushed herself up, trembling, skin blistering beneath her armor, her mind still catching up with what had just happened.

Then she saw her. Neeta. Crushed beneath a collapsed structural support strut, one arm outstretched, her helmet cracked wide open. Eyes glassy and lifeless. Her Peacekeeper compatriot was now still and quiet. Her life had ended far too soon.

Tria staggered forward, knees buckling beside her fallen sister-in-arms. "No, no, no," she whispered, voice shaking, choking on the smoke. She pressed her forehead to Neeta's, their visors touching. "I'm sorry. I should've seen this coming."

She knew what was coming next. There was no time for grief. No time to bury her. Just duty. With shaking fingers, Tria manually initiated the emergency dead code on Neeta's suit that had failed to self-initiate. A faint hum activated. The suit's fail-safe started blinking. A pulsing red. One minute. One last act of defiance against their attackers. No Peacekeeper tech could be allowed to fall into the Dominion's hands.

Tria stood and then backed away, her hand clenched into a trembling fist as the countdown ticked. She didn't look away. She owed her friend that much. The explosion that followed was small and almost silent compared to the roar of devastation that was unfolding all around. But in Tria's heart, it thundered louder than anything the Titans could conjure.

They would pay. For Mars. For Venus. For Neeta. For all the thousands of years of control and subjugation. Tria ran. The world behind her was dying, again and again, with every new blast.

She vaulted across twisted rubble, ducked through collapsing hallways, the air thick with dust and screams. Overhead, the sky lit up even more. The Dominion Titans descended lower, breaking past the upper fog like vengeful gods. Their red grids ignited again, and again, and again. Lancing the Umber levels with brutal rage. Nothing surgical or calculated, just annihilation.

Nanocrete crumbled like ancient bone beneath the breath of gods, each fracture a whisper of cities and its people dying, dreams dissolving into dust. Industrial walls buckled inward. Ceilings cracked like brittle bones. Beams the size of the largest cargo ships snapped in midair and came crashing down like divine judgment. The heat from the Titans' main beam rolled across everything. Melting steel, boiling blood, branding its authority into the ruins of a world already forgotten.

Tria's armor scorched against her skin as she stumbled through what remained of a tunnel junction. "Peacekeepers!" she shouted through the comms, desperate. "To me! Regroup at Delta Fork!"

Static. Chaos. Screams. Then voices. Familiar ones. Rough and scared but alive. She found many young, inexperienced Peacekeepers in fragmented pieces. They were scattered within the carnage, pulling each other out of debris, wounded, coughing, bloodied. A few dozen at best. Less if you didn't count the injured.

With everything in her, Tria hoped and prayed that more Peacekeepers survived. She had left with an entire battalion just that morning.

Coral was limping, and half of the armor on her right arm was gone. Luzon had a gash across his helmet, visor cracked and smeared with his own blood, which mingled with his friends. The tough and strong Brann carried a child, a local Umber with soot-streaked eyes and nowhere left to run.

"Eyes up!" Tria barked, pointing skyward, trying to keep her ragtag squad focused. Another blast came—closer this time. The ground convulsed beneath their boots, sending a support tower crashing down beside them in a shriek of metal and flame.

"They're not stopping," Coral growled.

"They won't," Tria spat out almost like an angry decree. "Not until every level's been sterilized."

The Dominion Lords weren't making examples. They were making sure that nothing like the Martian uprisings would ever happen here on Venus. No more revolts. Especially in the Holy Sol system. The Umbers were being reminded that rebellion wasn't just hopeless. It was punishable by extinction. The Uppers would see this from their crystal towers. They'd see the fire. The silence. And they'd remember and be grateful of their high privileged places that could be taken away at the flick of a switch.

Tria looked at the mangled under-skyline of Venus' underbelly, her face burning with grief and fury.

"They think they're ending our movement," Tria said, her voice coldly steady. "But all they're doing is lighting a fuse."

The Titans fell silent, their cannons dimming to deactivation standby mode. Leaving only the echo of ruin, a moment of stillness that hung like death in a graveyard.

Then, from the shadows of shattered towers and burning wreckage, the drums began to beat. Low at first, then thunderous and unyielding. Legionary war drums. And through the smoke, they came. Black wings sliced through the industrial sulfur haze. Drak Death Legion.

Tria raised her rifle just as a spine-rattling scream echoed through the middle levels of the ruined industrial block. It wasn't human. The assault came like thunder. No warning. No mercy.

From smoke-choked broken industrial corridors, fire erupted—blue and violet, plasma and sonic bursts tearing into stone and flesh. Her Peacekeepers fought back, disciplined, practiced, and efficient. But it wasn't enough.

Winged monstrosities swept down like wraiths in jet-black Dominion plate, their helmets carved with the sigils of extinction, their claws forged for death. The air sang with violence.

And behind them, marching out of the clouds of smoke, methodical and vengeful, came the Terra Legions of Venus, reborn and reforged anew in newly acquired stronger armor and weaponry, gifts from the High Lords of Venus who spared no expense, rushing to strengthen their forces after the tragic revolts and uprisings on Mars.

The Lords of Venus now ruled from newly built and rashly constructed sky-citadels, wanting to keep themselves out of reach of any possible attacks from the unders and umbers. Their palaces within the cities weren't designed for defense like the fortress citadels of the Lords of Mars.

No longer second-class units with basic backwater training and wielding dead-world cheap equipment, the Venusian forces of the Terra Legions were now clad in gold-dusted shining helmets, representing their rebirth as stronger, more ready legionaries. Now bearing the best pulse-spears and impact shields, the most powerful dark matter rifles. Their faces were masked with the hollow gaze of a stronger zealotry than ever before.

Tria tried to lead a retreat and hide, knowing she had no chance whatever defeating entire legions with the injured force she now commanded. But it wasn't possible to escape, not any longer. Her little group of Peacekeepers were quickly surrounded. Encircled. Cut off. She hadn't expected such a quick response from the Lords of Venus. She ordered defensive lines to be formed, the Peacekeepers used whatever they could to find cover. They fought like flames that didn't want to go out, even though they were outnumbered thousands to one.

Then came Dominion gunships, a continuous spray of automatic dark matter cannons and missiles fired at the Peacekeeper positions that peppered the ruined industry.

Tria's rifle screamed as she tore down a Drak soldier mid-flight with a few precision shots, the creature's bloodless body crashing beside her with the weight of a meteor. Her mind raced. There was no extraction plan. No fallback points any longer, the whole city was in rubble. They had walked into the furnace, and the Dominion Lords of Venus had shut the doors.

Melting steel and screams continued to fill the air. Tria spun, energy crackled from her rifle as she emptied another burst into a group of charging Terra legionaries. With a single pull of her trigger the front soldier's impact shield shattered, and his golden mask melted under the heat of her rapid burst fire, going right through him and hitting the other legionaries with him.

Tria, had accidentally set her weapon to the max possible energy level for the first time in many years. After seeing the legionaries die so brutally, she quickly returned her rifle's energy to the stun setting. In most cases, a single precise direct hit was still enough to knock out almost any Dominion soldier. The scimancers of the empire hadn't yet found any reliable defense against the mysterious heretic weapons that were strangely more powerful than anything they had come up against until now.

But no matter how many Legionaries she and her little group of Peacekeepers pacified, two more surged forward. Their formations were perfect and unwavering in their continuing surging flow. A flooding force that didn't stop. As if pain and fear had been engineered out of them. The Peacekeepers were dying one by one against such overwhelming odds, but they were holding the line, keeping the surge at bay for now.

Explosions ignited from ruined levels above their position as a chain reaction detonated old power systems. Sections of the ceilings and floors above them crumbled in sheets, massive nanocrete chunks crashing down like tombstones. Huge metallic beams snapped and fell and crashed into the remaining levels where Tria and her Peacekeepers were surrounded. Bodies, both Peacekeeper and Legionary, disappeared in flashes of heat and blooming dust. Voices turned to static as they were consumed by the destruction. Tria stumbled over a corpse, Neerak, one of hers. Half of his body was gone, his one remaining hand still gripping his rifle. She didn't stop. She couldn't. Not now. She ran as the self-destruct erased him.

The air burned in her lungs. The filtration systems started to fail in her armor. Sweat mixed with soot streaked down her cheeks. Her armor was cracked and charred; thousands of Dominion weapons blasts covered almost every inch. Her heart pounded like a war drum with every step forward through the chaos as gunships circled above.

"We hold the line! We survive!" she shouted over the holocomms, though she wasn't sure anyone could hear her anymore. "We are Peacekeepers! Stop their advance! We kneel to no one!"

A blast from a gunship missile knocked her sideways. Her vision spun and blurred. When she rolled over, a Drak Legionnaire was already descending, talons out, wings spread like a devil's shadow. Tria's blade snapped out of the DIE-Space compartment on her wrist gauntlet, and with a cry of pure rage at max power, she drove it upward into its chest, feeling the crack of alien bone and cyborg machine. It collapsed on top of her. She shoved the weight aside, its bodily fluids and coolant mixing across her armor.

She staggered to her feet again barely able to catch her breath as more Draks came at her from multiple directions. She fought them as best as she could until one picked her up and smashed her through rubble. She was tossed and flipped and smashed against the ruins, she returned the same brutality in kind once she gained footing, picking the Drak up and smashing it into a metallic pillar, bashing it time and time again. They were locked in one on one combat, until Tria eventually had the upper hand and dealt a deadly blow.

Smoke. Ash. Screams of battle lust. Every breath was a rebellion. Every second was a defiant choice to keep living, to continue the fight. The Dominion had underestimated them once. Had mistaken hope for weakness. But Tria was making them remember that even in a graveyard of apathetic fire, rebellion still finds a way to survive.

The Terra Legions surged once more, reinforced by fresh waves of armored infantry and siege crawlers. The streets around Tria trembled beneath their advance, the rhythmic cadence of war drums echoing through shattered domes and ruined temples. From the upper terraces, Peacekeeper marksmen took careful shots, stunning wave after wave of Legionaries, but it wasn't enough. For every soldier felled, two more took their place, like the tide devouring a broken shore.

Then... the firing stopped. Tria ducked behind a collapsed plinkinsteel column, heart still pounding, but no more energy bolts came. No more shrieking shells or sonic blades. Across the battlefield, the Legionaries halted mid-step, weapons lowered but not holstered. The sudden stillness was suffocating. Then came the voice.

"Peacekeeper heretic, Tria Oberon," it boomed, magnified by command audio projectors. A tall Dominion general lifted himself out from the Legion's forward hover carrier, his armor embossed with gold sigils. His helmet crowned with a black command crest. "You're surrounded. Lay down your weapons. You and your soldiers will be given a fair trial under Dominion law. Resist, and this mercy shall be withdrawn."

Tria narrowed her eyes, blood smearing the side of her cracked helmet. She stood slowly, leveling her weapon but not firing. "A Dominion trial?" she shouted back, voice strained. "You call that mercy?"

"This isn't a negotiation," the general replied, his tone tightening.

Tria's mind raced. They were boxed in. Her battalion was scattered and was down to less than fifty. No more backup. No more exits. She tried to think. Could they retreat into the under chambers? Could they escape underground? Push their way through the Dominion lines and make a run for it? Then the skies groaned.

Hundreds of Dominion war mechs descended with a roar, falling from drop pods like iron angels. Their weapons primed. Their formation perfect. The general's gauntlet raised high, ready to command annihilation.

And then the war mechs opened fire. But not on the Peacekeepers. Blue energy bolts streamed into the ranks of the Terra Legions, dropping rows of Legionaries with blinding precision. Tria blinked, stunned. She knew that color and shape of the weapons energy. Peacekeeper stun signatures. Peacekeeper tech disguised and mounted on Dominion mechs.

"Thank Omega," she whispered. "We're saved…"

The general shouted orders to his legionaries, but it was too late. The front formations of his Legions fractured under the unexpected assault. Chaos bloomed and soon all formations were broken. Tria could barely breathe, it was the most unexpected rescue ever. She didn't even know that the Peacekeepers had taken Dominion mechs, let alone so many. They were winning.

A beam of red energy burst down into the formations, taking with it both Peacekeepers and Legionaries. Above them, the Titans resumed their merciless assault. Beams of searing red dark matter plasma raked across the battlefield, indiscriminate in their fury. Vaporizing Peacekeeper defenses, tearing through Dominion formations, annihilating steel and flesh alike. The sky had become a crucible of fire, a thunderous storm of energy where pillars of light fell like the judgment of machine gods.

The roar was overwhelming. A plasma lance struck nearby, detonating in a white-hot shockwave. Nanocrete vanished. Air combusted. Tria was thrown like a ragdoll, her body slamming into the rubble. Her helmet cracked hard against a metallic beam. Her visor finally gave up and shattered. Blood began to fill up in her mouth. Her ears rang. Her vision ran in streaks of red and black.

Then the heavens fractured. Not from the Titans. A blast of blue dark matter ripped through the clouds as one of the Dominion behemoths erupted in exploding flame. A second explosion. Then a third. The Peacekeeper fleet surged from jumpspace, railguns and auto cannons blazing. Hundreds of warships fell upon the Venusian sky, trailing vengeance behind them like comets.

A Peacekeeper Battlecruiser and a Dominion Titan locked in direct combat. The Titan. A colossus of blackened alloy and divine etchings, unleashed streamers of arc-cannon fire, slashing across the heavens like blades of godlight. The Battlecruiser retaliated with its own mega cannons, slamming into the Titan like kinetic hammers, each slug the size of a dropship. Breaking through its force fields and pounding into the Titan's torso with world-breaking force. Armor buckled. But neither fell. They circled each other like monsters of myth, each one wounded, each one refusing to yield. The atmosphere around them shimmered from the heat and fury, a duel of titanic will across the upper sky. Until the battlecruiser dealt the final blow, firing its main central axis weapon, ripping the Titan in two.

Dominion fleets plunged from high anchor, their black-armored hulls carving down through the upper thermosphere like divine spears hurled from the throne of the Duality. Venus's skies, already choked in ash and destruction, ignited with fresh chaos. Peacekeeper battlecruisers and destroyers surged to meet them, rising like ghosts from the golden clouds, weapons arrays screaming to life.

They should not have been there. No fleet was supposed to breach Sol's Divine Wall. An ancient defensive web of deep-field distortion nodes, mines, and anomaly traps said to prevent any starship jump into the solar cradle. It was the Dominion's pride, its unshakable wall. But no one expected an enemy fleet jumping from inside the wall itself.

The Peacekeeper fleet had torn through local space like a blade to the throat from their secret bases, bypassing the outer net and punching into Venusian orbit itself. Inside the Dominion's holy veil. The shock alone sent tremors through command lines that were shocked. What few Titans remained in high orbit twisted their cannons to adjust, venting entire cloud banks into boiling silence. Below, the atmosphere became a furnace.

Tria, broken and bloodied, was barely conscious on a medical hover bed being taken to a shuttle. Peacekeeper reinforcements, medics and rescue teams had shuttled down from support vessels that hovered low beneath the battle unfolding above. They hurried to find all the thousands of Peacekeepers who were buried beneath the rubble of the destroyed district. Her eyes were locked onto the sky, drawn to the clash above like a moth to lightning.

Three Dominion Titans locked horns with a Peacekeeper dreadnought, their hulls bruising each other with their massive cannons and vicious arsenals, including gravity-lances and antimatter missiles. Explosions ripped across the Titans, chunks of their armor tumbling down like burning obelisks. But the Dominion war machines retaliated in kind, unleashing salvo after salvo that cored the Peacekeeper ship's midsection in a fountain of fiery metal and bodies. None of the vessels broke quickly. They just kept firing.

Around them, fleets twisted in dogfights, fighter swarms wheeling between fusion flares and burning debris, as if the sky itself had gone mad. What began as a little planetary battle was becoming a celestial brawl that would be remembered for millennia to come.

On the shattered plaza below, the war had changed. Tria tasted blood. Heard the sky howl. "You're safe now, Captain," someone said again. She didn't respond. Because she knew the truth. They had just kicked open the gates of hell. And hell was fighting back.

Chapter Eleven:
CONSEQUENCES FOR DISOBEDIENCE

"Every commandment ignored plants the seed of its own reckoning."

The Holy Terran-Orion Bible - The Book of Knowing, 8:1

The sky of Venus blazed like a rose-gold fire, the sun refracting off towering dark spires like shards of eternity. Beneath the massive golden Gates of Gadd, hundreds of High Lords knelt upon the obsidian floor, heads bowed low. The wind tugged at their gilded robes, but it was not the wind that made them tremble. It was the weight of Divinity.

Upon the living hovering dais of light stood the Holy Duality. The God Emperor and God Empress, veiled in their own starlight, radiant and terrible, absolute and wonderful. Beside them, their first born, their twin children: Theldren'Ra, the Prince Transcendent, eyes burning like the most powerful stars; and Veshdren'Ra, Princess Transcendent, haloed in sorrow and storm, a storm of mystery and secrets. Their combined presence bent the air itself.

When the Empress spoke, her words were not just heard by the ears but felt deep down, a tide surging through marrow and soul alike.

"It was written when the Empire drew its first breath, one of our most important commandments. Carved into the foundation of our creation: no engine of war shall ever bring ruin to a sanctified world. Yet you broke it. You rained fire upon Venus. You slaughtered billions without a thought. Umbers and Unders and Uppers alike. They are all our children, as you are. And now Justice itself cries out against you."

The Emperor's voice followed, vast as thunder rolling through eternity.

"You gave the order to desecrate cities bearing Our name. Whose voice defied a commandment of Heaven?"

One of the High Lords dared raise his head, voice quivering. "Holy Gods, Divine Majesties, forgive us. The rebellion infested the holy cities—we thought it necessary—"

"Necessary?" Theldren'Ra's blade of living flame hissed into being, its light slicing the courtyard. "You set your fear above Heaven's law? The sanctuaries are not yours to scorch. The faithful are not yours to slaughter."

Another Lord stammered through tears, "We feared that Venus would fall to heresy like Mars, without swift—"

"Silence." The Empress' word cracked like a star's death. The air itself froze. Her voice carried both mourning and wrath, each syllable a weight of aeons. "We do not grant our children leave to butcher the innocent along with the guilty within our holy places. Fear is no shield for your heresy. It is cowardice dressed as faith."

The Emperor stretched out His hand. A projection bloomed above the kneeling Lords, cast across the Dominion to every world and every soul. It showed the atrocity: burned temples, once pristine grand cities reduced to rubble, pilgrims and heretics charred to silhouettes on sacred streets. There would be no hiding, no excuses.

"Who gave the order?" the Duality demanded as one, Father and Mother joined in a single storm of judgment.

At last, a woman's voice broke from the farthest row: "It was Lord Halvros! He commanded the fleets. We—we only obeyed—"

All eyes turned. Halvros shrank back, gilded robes rattling like a shroud. "I—acted to preserve the Dominion! I thought—I believed You would—"

"You thought wrong. You thought as a coward and heretic."

The Emperor's gaze locked upon him. Halvros screamed. Not from pain, but from the terror of being utterly known. The sun above dimmed like an eclipse. Atoms trembled. And then, he was gone.

Not slain or struck down by blade or bolt. He was unmade. Atom by atom unraveled, dissolved into a scattering of dust, erased from creation itself. The silence that followed was heavier than any scream.

The Empress' voice fell upon them like a funeral bell for an entire age:

"Let this be a reminder that no one forgets. Let it stand eternal: No holy world shall burn by the fire of a Dominion war machine. To harm even a single sanctified soul is to war against Heaven."

Theldren'Ra lifted his flaming sword high; its light flooded the empire-wide broadcast.

"The Duality remembers. The Duality shields. The Duality does not forgive unrepentant heresy."

Veshdren'Ra's voice came softer, but it carved just as deep:

"All of you deserve death today. But mercy has been given to you. Remember that mercy is not weakness. It is the grace you've been granted this day. Do not waste it." And to the trembling Lords, the Princess Transcendent gave the final sentence: "You will be cast out to the outer colonies, to the soil you scorned. You will till the dust with your hands and bring life to places where there is none. Birthing gardens where there is drought. This is your sentence, until, if honor still lives within you, it is reborn."

Beneath the blazing banners of the eternal empire, the Holy Duality and their royal entourage advanced into the next courtyard, their radiance spilling like a second dawn over the assembly. Thousands of Dominion soldiers knelt in trembling silence, their armor reflecting the terrible light of judgment.

These were the crews. The ones who had fired the weapons that had shattered Venus, whose hands had loosed the wrath of warships upon the innocent and guilty alike. The air itself quivered as their voices broke into desperate pleas, a chorus of anguish and repentance that echoed against the obsidian walls.

"Forgive us! Have mercy, Divine Mother! Divine Father! We obeyed! We obeyed!" they cried, faces pressed to the stone, tears mingling with the dust of their shame.

The God Empress, her eyes like suns burning through the void of their souls. At her side stood the God Emperor, and behind them their two radiant children, silent witnesses to the reckoning. The Empress raised her hand. Not in blessing, but in finality. Her voice thundered across the courtyard, carrying the weight of law older than stars.

"You commanded fire upon the sanctified. You spilled the blood of our children. Justice demands its due."

Thirty names were spoken, their identities laid bare for all to hear. The commanders who had relayed the orders without hesitation, without conscience or guilt. The Empress extended her hand, and with a gesture like the tearing of reality, the thirty figures dissolved into white fire and dust. No screams escaped them; their bodies turned to ash and light in an instant, scattered into the winds. Silence fell heavy as a tomb.

The rest shook with terror, waiting for their fate. The Empress lowered her hand, her voice softer now, yet no less terrible.

"You obeyed in fear, beneath the yoke of duty you were blinded, not thinking. We give you the mercy of life. But you shall live in service for the rest of your days. You will be sent into the lowest under-cities of Venus, among those who you so heartlessly slaughtered. You will serve the Umbers and the Unders. There, you will spend your remaining days laboring with your hands in the dark places, serving those you wronged. Only then may you seek the faintest hope of honor's return."

A great sob rippled through the courtyard. Not of despair, but of awe and salvation, for even mercy from the Gods came wrapped in the fire of justice. The Duality turned, their children following, as the soldiers remained kneeling, broken and bound to their new fate, the holy judgment echoing in their souls forevermore.

Chapter Twelve:
HEALING THE BROKEN

"Where the Duality steps, the wounded rise from the ashes of their despair; the lost, long wandering through shadowed corridors of hopelessness, find at last a home; and the night itself, once heavy with sorrow, is drenched in a light that shatters darkness and turns grief to song. A new rebirth. A new cycle of existence. A new life begins."

3rd Codex of Faith, Testament of Gelanma Kelranni Elmas

Bells of gratitude rang from the surviving cities of Venus, carried on the warm, still sulfur-scented winds in the aftermath of the conflict. The faithful poured into the avenues, their voices rising like a storm of prayer:

"All glory to the Holy Duality! Mercy upon mercy! Light of our salvation!"

The God Empress and God Emperor stood at the heart of the gathered masses, their radiant forms shimmering like living suns. Their two divine children, resplendent in garments of starlight, followed closely behind as the royal entourage moved toward the scarred wastelands.

The devastation was immense. Mountainous heaps of collapsed towers, molten rivers where streets once lay, the stench of burned metal and blood still lingering. Without hesitation, the Duality ascended, their forms expanding, becoming titanic beings of compassion and judgment. Three hundred and thirty-three feet tall, their eyes glowed like twin stars as they floated above the ruins.

A hush fell over the crowds as the air itself vibrated with divine power. The God Emperor raised his hand, and reality bent. Cracked foundations knit themselves whole, shattered streets reformed into shining marble. With a whisper of the Empress's voice, the fires hissed out, replaced by gardens of emerald and gold. Beneath their holy gaze, rubble shifted and entire districts rose anew.

Then came the muffled cries from distant rubble, that no one except the divine could hear. Young children. An Umber school, buried deep. The Duality turned toward it.

"Beloved ones," the God Empress's voice rolled across the wasteland like a gentle thunder. "Fear not. The Light sees you."

The God Emperor stretched out his hand, and with a pulse of divine force, the mountains of wreckage peeled away. Slabs of steel and broken walls lifted into the sky, dissolving into dust as if they had never fallen. Beneath, the children huddled. Thousands of small, trembling souls with dust-streaked faces and tear-filled eyes.

The Duality descended, shrinking, until they stood only six feet tall. Flesh among flesh, yet still radiant. Their masks disappeared into air, revealing faces sculpted by eternity: chiseled yet warm, stern yet kind. The children gasped, awe-struck.

One tiny voice quavered, "A-are you really here? Are we safe?"

The God Empress knelt, her golden hair catching the rays of the fading sun. She gently placed her hand on the child's cheek, and the bruises vanished in a shimmer of light. "Yes, little one. You're safe. None who call to us shall be forsaken."

Another child sobbed, "But... our homes are gone. We have nothing."

The Empress smiled gently, lifting the child into her arms. "Then you shall have a greater home, one built of light and love. Look around you."

The children turned, seeing the newly raised spires gleaming, the healed rising from their stretchers, the land reborn beneath the Duality's mercy.

The God Emperor stepped forward, his deep voice steady and kind. "You and your families will live in our palaces, under our protection. No storm, no fire, no heretic shall ever harm you again." The Emperor continued his declarations, his voice echoing across the skies, "From this day forth, Venus will not remember its wounds but its salvation. And you, little saints, will dwell with us in joy."

The children pressed close to them, touching their garments, their tears turning to laughter. In the distance and throughout the empire as this was being recorded and shared on every world, the faithful knelt and raised their hands, their voices a tidal wave of devotion:

"Glory to the God Empress! Glory to the God Emperor! Eternal Light, Eternal Mercy! Eternal Power, Eternal Truth!"

The Duality bathed in their worship. Not as tyrants, but as beings fulfilled in their sacred duty to those under their charge.

"Come," the Empress whispered to the children. "Your blessings await, and your future begins."

The Duality stayed with the children for a time until they felt safe and secure one again. Then they sent them to a newly built divine palace, on Venus where they could live their new lives.

Beneath the once shattered splendor of Venus that was now remade, where sunlight never reached and the air hung heavy with dust and grief, the Holy Duality descended. Their passage was choked with ruin; entire avenues of the largest of the undercities lay buried beneath the wreckage of fallen towers.

Behind them they were still followed by their radiant children, Theldren'Ra and Veshdren'Ra, clearing the path with waves of transcendent light, disintegrating debris into vapor, lifting entire collapsed bridges and beams with a flick of their hands. The royal entourage trailed close. Other Tribunals robed in cosmic silk, The highest of the High Lords of Divine Will, Royal Heralds carrying the banners of eternity. Yet even their magnificence seemed pale in the presence of the Divine.

Before the Gods, the Unders crawled from the wreckage, broken and bleeding, their gaunt faces streaked with thick soot and flowing tears. They fell prostrate, voices hoarse with desperation, crying out for mercy, for rebirth, for life itself.

"Save us!" a mother screamed, clutching a child no older than two.

"We're dying." whispered an elder, too weak to kneel.

"Have you forgotten us? Are you punishing us?" sobbed a boy, his ribs showing through torn flesh.

The God Empress knelt among them, the starlight of her robes cascading over their wounds. "No," she said, her voice reverberating with a combination of infinite tenderness and wrath. "Never. We have heard your cries. We have seen your pain. And you will never know need again."

At her touch, shattered bones knit, torn flesh mended. With a sweep of the Emperor's hand, fountains of food erupted from portals: fruits and meat from blessed worlds, breads of the finest celestial grain, rivers of sweet drink flowed and poured out. The Empress broke the loaves and meat and they multiplied endlessly, spilling across the streets like a miracle reborn. The sick were healed, the blind opened their eyes to see Divinity itself; the starving feasted until they wept.

Through the smoke and rubble, the Duality pressed on, until they reached the heart of the undercity: the black pyramid, the central temple, like the one in the undercity of Antica. This one was split and broken down its spine. Its sacred pools lay dry; its walls, defiled by reckless, unrestrained warfare. The Unders continued to wail out cries, seeing their sanctuary ruined. But the Holy Duality raised their hands as one.

The pyramid groaned as if the stone itself remembered its true purpose. Cracks sealed; shattered obelisks rose. The temple grew higher, wider, reshaped into a vision far beyond its former glory, exuding out a golden light, infused with the power of the Gods. It was now a living monument to the divine will of the Duality.

The Unders' cries softened, their hearts still trembling with awe, convinced that the Divine gifts had reached their zenith. They dared not imagine that the mercy, the splendor, could stretch even further. But the God Empress and God Emperor's eyes glimmered with untold purpose, and Theldren'Ra and Veshdren'Ra's hands glowed with the fire of renewal.

From the broken dust of this once dark city, the Duality lifted chosen souls, pilgrims who had crawled through fire and famine, who had held faith when all hope had abandoned them. One by one, the lowest of the Unders, the humblest of servants, the most devoted and loyal, were drawn closer into the light of the Gods. Their faces, etched with years of sorrow, were bathed in radiance they had never truly known until this day.

"You have lived in shadow and endured when the world turned its back," the God Emperor intoned, voice echoing like the pulse of creation itself. "You have prayed without ending and we have heard. You labored when none cared, and loved when none returned it. Today, you rise."

The God Empress touched the first of them, a trembling woman who had carried the orphaned children of this undercity for decades. Her skin shimmered, her eyes brightened, her very bones seemed to hum with new life. "From this day forward," the Empress declared, "you shall be a High Lord of Divine Will of the Undercities of Venus. You will protect, guide, and prosper these people in our name. Your life will be long, your power unshaken, your judgment tempered by devotion."

The Duality spoke as one to the new High Lords of Venus "Our blessings has been granted, but it carries a covenant. Serve with your hearts, as you were served today. Protect the weak, uplift the fallen, honor our Divinity in every breath you take."

Tears streamed down faces young and old, old sorrow and new joy colliding. The Unders, once bowed by suffering, now rose with heads high, hearts alight with worship and devotion. They fell to their knees, praising the Duality, their voices blending into a thunderous hymn that shook the undercity and reached even the heavens above.

Then across the Dominion, the Pools of Seeing within every temple flared to life. Holographic light bathed millions of worlds as the faces of the Holy Duality appeared in every sanctuary.

"All who bear faith," thundered the Duality, their voices rippling across the stars, "come to Our temples. Come, children of the light. Bear witness to Our divinity. Bear witness to rebirth and a new life."

And when the faithful gathered. Countless upon countless kneeling in awe across the galaxy. The Holy Duality levitated above the black pyramid. Their forms swelled with incandescent fire. Their children flanked them, blazing like twin seraphs.

"Unders of Venus," the Duality declared, as one, their words rolling through the cosmos, "Unders of every world. Hear us. You are not the forgotten. You are the faithful. You are our true children. No longer shall you crawl in shadow while others bask in stolen glory. Today, we lift you into the light."

With that, the miracle expanded. Across every Dominion undercity with a great temple. On millions upon millions of planets. The largest undercities started to erupt in golden radiance. Crumbling hovels of twisted recycled metal melted into palaces of living golden light. Mansions more glorious than current High Lords' estates rose for those who once lived in squalor. Gardens blossomed from barren stone; rivers of crystal water carved through the darkness.

Royally crafted Dronekind by the millions swarmed forth from portals, gifts from the Gods, bound to serve and love the Unders forevermore. Tribunals descended to remain among them, guardians and teachers, ensuring none would ever be abandoned again.

Cries of grief became hymns of ecstasy. Across the Dominion, the lowest of the low wept and sang as one.

"You were cast aside," said the Empress, her voice breaking with both wrath and love. "But never by us. You will never hunger again. You will never thirst again. This is your inheritance, your new dawn, your rebirth. Your resurrection from the shadows into the light."

And in that moment, the central undercities of almost every single Dominion city world ceased to be slums. They became golden sanctuaries, cities built by the hands of Gods. The Dominion trembled, not from fear, but from adoration and thanksgiving, as love and power intertwined in a miracle no age would ever forget.

Chapter Thirteen:
OUTCASTS AND HERETICS

"The outcast bears the scars of a heretic and the dreams of a saint."

— Old Edgeworlder Saying

Amarax moved through the underbrush like a shadow. Silent and deliberate. The jungle greeted him with a stillness that felt all wrong. The humidity clung to his armor, masking his heat signature beneath layers of flora-dampened camouflage. Every leaf, every root, every breath of wind across the canopy. He knew them all. These jungles had been his youthful companion, they had trained him, scarred him.

So when something cracked that shouldn't have, he stopped cold. No birds scattered. No animals hissed or fled. That meant the intruder wasn't natural. It was cloaked, tech-quieted, moving with military precision. But it wasn't good enough.

He vanished behind the curved roots of a massive mutated tree, his armor seamlessly blending with the mottled green-black bark. He waited, listening. Another step. Closer. Then a faint, nearly imperceptible distortion in the air. Like heat shimmer, but colder.

Amarax struck. His hunting blade plunged forward, hissing through the jungle mist. A scream erupted from the empty air as metal bit into armor and flesh. Cloak tech glitched and fizzled out, revealing a Peacekeeper, a heretic. Standard silver armor with blue tech intertwined throughout and overlapping plating. Modified and tuned for stealth insertions. Similar to the kinds used at the battle of Antica.

Before the body hit the ground, another attacker lunged at his back. Amarax pivoted, grabbed the second Peacekeeper mid-leap, and rammed his elbow into their jaw, driving his blade upward under the rib plating. Another cry. Another body.

He grabbed the first one by the chest plate and slammed them against the tree. "How did you find me?" he growled, voice low, rough from disuse. The Peacekeeper coughed blood, eyes wide with terror behind their visor. But gave no answer. Then he heard it. More branches cracking. Dozens of steps. A squad. Maybe more.

Amarax vanished into the foliage. They didn't see him. They never would. He began to hunt.

One by one, he picked them off. Silently, surgically. For every tripwire they disabled another hidden tripwire activated, nets of spiked vine-arms.

Two disappeared into a marsh that wasn't a marsh. It was a carnivorous sink-creature. One was lured into a clearing where the massive jaw of a thorn-beast clamped shut like a temple door. The Peacekeepers died not on a battlefield. But in his domain. They weren't trained or prepared for this. Amarax was. By the time the last of them died screaming in the mouth of a bio-engineered predator, Amarax was already gone on his way again towards the nearest city. The forest behind him steamed with blood and he didn't care.

It took him hours to reach the city, running through the thick. He crested the final ridge before the city and the great walls that held back the jungles. He saw the city on fire. Once a vertical crown of Dominion order. Now, it burned like an open wound. DAS-plasma still raged and was spreading in blue-purple arcs across spires, melting whole wings of municipal towers. Civilian housing zones were collapsed into craters. Smoke curled in great clouds that filled the horizon.

He sprinted across the scorched ridge and down into the ash-choked outskirts and climbed the damaged walls at the perimeter, breathing heavily through his helmet filters, anger started to well up within him. As he entered the ruins of the city, the sound of metal boots and servo motors echoed through the abandoned streets. Dominion robotic patrols. Four-legged recon walkers. Bipedal sentries. And flying drone packs overhead.

The first one spotted him. "Heretic. Heretic. Heretic," the synthetic voice repeated as it opened fire. No implants. No Legion genetic tags. No identity codes. To them, he wasn't Amarax. He wasn't even a citizen. Just another insurgent ghost.

Dark matter bolts sliced past him. He dove into cover behind a collapsed hovertram, rifle in hand. His shots were precise. Head, knee joint, thorax. Machines sparked and dropped, but there were more. His boots kicked up sparks as he moved and slid from place to place. Never staying in one place more than three seconds. One robot got too close; he lunged from behind cover, driving his knife up beneath its optics with a snarl. White fluid sprayed. The bot twitched and collapsed.

But then. That sound. Peacekeeper weapon fire. The shriek of heretic energy. One hit nearby. Blue tendrils of concussive force rippled out, disorienting him. There was great pain. But he was still alive.

He crawled behind a broken column that was laying on its side, fired blind over the edge, ducked back. He wasn't just fighting for the empire anymore. At this moment he was fighting to understand. What had happened to Mars? It didn't make any sense. But he didn't have time to really find out. The ground quaked. A massive thud followed. Then another. Something huge was coming.

Another Dominion sentry. But this one was three stories tall. It stomped into the ruins like an iron deity. Twin rotary cannons spun to life at its shoulders, flanked by rows of arm-mounted plasma bore. It scanned for targets. And it found him. Amarax fired again and again. The bullets might as well have been pebbles against its metalic hide. The machine stepped forward. Slammed a metal fist into the building he sheltered in. Everything collapsed. The roof cracked, then the floor gave way. Amarax fell into darkness, surrounded by dust, rubble, and the groaning wail of a city that had turned into a tomb.

Amarax gasped awake. His lungs pulled in the sterile, cold air as if he'd just risen from drowning. A dull ache permeated his entire body. His head pounded. He opened his eyes to the blinding white glow of new crystal walls. Smooth and angular, too perfect just like his former cell. The same strange, unnatural prison as before.

The same synthetic chill in the air. And the same white, seamless bed and new clothes. Only now he was in a different room, he could tell he wasn't on Mars any longer, he could feel it. Besides the base on Mars where he had been imprisoned had been completely destroyed.

A new cage without chains surrounded him. He clenched his fists. And then he saw her. Tria. She stood nearby, dressed in blue civilian wear. A simple tunic over dark leggings, unarmed. No armor. No command presence. Just her. Staring at him like she was trying to read his thoughts before he could weaponize them. He sat up slowly as she spoke.

"You've been busy. Single-handedly destroying a Peacekeeper base. Taking out mutiple squads. Fighting your own robotic forces. Very busy."

Even though he wanted to yell at her he kept his composer. He re-centered himself and thought about all the work he did to deceive them, he had to be careful in his words.

"I only did what I had to do."

"You had to destroy an entire base?"

"I didn't destroy any base. Your own people destroyed it. They're stupidity and ignorance destroyed it."

"What are you talking about?"

"Stop pretending that you don't know what happened. It's an insult to my intelligence."

"I'm not pretending anything. You were the only one who made it out alive from the base on Mars. Which would suggest that you were the cause of its destruction."

"Well, I wasn't. The base had a self-destruct. It activated when your experiments got loose."

"What experiments?"

"The Beasts of Mars, they were twisted and turned into things more hideous than they already were."

"I have no idea what you're talking about."

"Then maybe you should go ask your superiors about it. Your scimancers on Mars were creating abominations. Twisting the Beasts of Mars into weapons of war."

"That's impossible. It's not allowed."

"It doesn't matter if you believe me or not. It's the truth."

Tria ended her holographic projection and stepped off of the hologrid sensor array. Standing alone in a pristine room of

Tria deactivated the holographic projection and stepped off of the hologrid. She stood alone in a pristine room of polished metal and softly glowing panels, Tria let the silence settle around her. The same quiet hum of the Peacekeeper secret Venusian base filled the gaps where no answers came, and she pressed her palms to the smooth surface of a console, the coolness grounding her racing thoughts.

Frustration coiled in her chest. Every inquiry she'd made. Every file requested, every whispered question, had been met with the same response: "You don't have clearance. You're only a captain." The barriers were not just digital; they were built of hierarchy, secrecy, and deliberate obfuscation. Her patience, once vast, was wearing thinner and thinner by the minute.

Tria let out a long breath and straightened. There was only one person who might pierce the veil of secrecy: Ari'Ella Dunesky. If her friend's powers of clairvoyance could be applied, perhaps she could uncover the truth—but only if Ari'Ella was willing to help.

She made her way to the Hangar Bay, the hum of starship engines and distant machinery echoing around her. A small shuttle waited, sleek and unassuming, designed for a single passenger. Tria checked the systems and launched, the world around her folding and stretching as the warping spacetime tunnel within the jump gate swallowed her.

Moments later, she emerged near a hidden Peacekeeper space station at the heart of a nebula. Sensors glimmered on the shuttle's display, showing the complex in the swirling gas clouds like a jewel in shadow. She touched the controls starting up the jump drive, plotting her jump: Arakia'Thuun. In an instant the desert world drew closer, its ochre sands and jagged mesas filling the viewport. She descended down through the thick atmosphere and landed in the capital city, where construction crews and automated drones still worked on the rising structures of the new administrative hub.

Tria navigated the streets, moving through half-finished plazas and scaffolding, until she saw a familiar figure: Maris Solvannis. Her heart stuttered. He was alive. She ran to him, arms outstretched, and pulled him into an embrace.

"I had no idea," she breathed heavy and joyfully. "I thought, I thought you were killed. How?"

"It's a bit of a long story. I can tell you later. I'm guessing you have something pressing to deal with."

"Yes, I do. But I need to know how you made it out. That's more important."

"It can wait. There's plenty of time. You do whatever it is that you need to do first."

"Alright if you say so. I'm looking for Ari'Ella. You wouldn't by chance know where she is would you?"

Maris nodded. "High Temple of Light. She's been meditating there all day."

Tria hugged him again, relief washing over her. "I'm so glad to see you alive. I won't be long and then you can tell me all about what you've been through."

"Of course. Just whenever you're done."

Minutes later, she had a hover bike under her, engines humming as she lifted into the fading light. The temple loomed atop a high desert mesa, carved directly into the rock, ancient and commanding. Ari'Ella levitated in the center of the grand inner chamber, legs crossed, eyes closed. A soft glow from within the temple walls framed her like a halo, and the desert stretched out endlessly beyond the mesas.

Tria approached respectfully yet with a sense of urgency. "Ari'Ella... I need your help. I need to know what happened on Mars with Amarax and the truth. Have scientists of the Republics experimented with the Beasts of Mars?"

Ari'Ella's eyes remained closed. "It's good to see you too. I'm a little busy at the moment. Why didn't you ask the Messengers?"

"They're in a resting cycle," Tria replied, voice tight. "It'll be weeks before anyone can see them. I can't wait that long. I need answers now. Please... help me."

Ari'Ella inhaled deeply, a faint wind stirring around her robes. "You understand what you're asking. The truth is not gentle, Tria. Once seen, it cannot be unseen."

Tria met her friend's words with unwavering conviction. "I need to know. No matter the cost."

"You aren't ready to know the full truth of the secrets that are kept from you. It would tear you apart inside and you're still healing from the revolution on Mars. You're still struggling with that artificial relief. I can't tell you everything."

"Please, I need to know. I can handle the truth."

"No. You can't. I will tell you. Amarax spoke the truth. He wasn't the cause of the destruction of the Peacekeeper base on Mars. He barely made it out alive. Experimentation has been done and it's still ongoing. You need to stop digging. You can't stop what they're doing. You'll just be put into prison to silence you and keep you out of the way."

"If that's true. We have to stop it. We have to. I might not be able to stop them, but you can. Please, help me stop them, this can't be allowed to continue."

"Tria, it's not so simple. Though of course I have the power to stop it. I have responsibilities here. I have to remain on this world.

My people expect me to be here. I can't go on some personal crusade."

"Jankking hell. Ari'Ella, I need your help."

"I know. But I can't."

"You can."

"No. I can't."

"You have the power to help and stop this madness. And yet you're unwilling to. Why?"

Ari'Ella Dunesky levitated down and stepped onto the floor, walking over to Tria, looking into her friend's eyes.

"It's complicated. Far too complicated for me to explain it all. But you can be assured of one thing, these experiments won't destroy the Republics. These experiments might actually save the Republics."

"How? How would creating biological weapons save the Republics?"

"That's a good question, one that you will answer on your own in time. I need to focus on my meditations for now. I need to keep this world hidden. You know, it takes a lot of focus to keep an entire planet invisible. We can talk later. I'm sure you want to catch up with Maris. Go and see him. I should be done by this evening."

Tria thought about what her friend had said and knew that she was stubborn, once she had made up her mind on something, it was made up. She nodded her head and walked out. As she sat on the hover bike ready to head back to the capital city she thought about what her friend had said. She considered every word in detail. Ari'Ella had never led her down a lie before, she tried her best to trust in her judgement in not telling her even though it was getting under her skin.

Somewhere between trust and fury, she chose to believe that her friend knew best... but belief, she knew, would not be enough for long. And so began her descent into the inner places of doubt and confusion, where friends became prophets, truth became poison, and silence was the only answer provided.

Chapter Fourteen:
DISLOYAL DAUGHTER

"There is no rebellion without resolution. No resolution without a reckoning. No reckoning without retribution."

— From The Book of Ashes

A hidden throne room was carved into the cliff-side of a frozen world, buried beneath thick glacier sheets so vast they seemed eternal. Pillars of black stone rose like fangs, their surfaces etched with Dominion runes that pulsed faintly, casting ghostly light over the vaulted chamber. Beyond the golden obsidian balcony where Maris Solvannis and Tria Oberon stood, an abyss of machinery stretched out into the dark. A city of war built in secret.

Factories exhaled streams of chilled vapor into the cold, colossal hangars brimmed with sleek warships of every single kind imaginable, from every corner of the Dominion to every corner of the New Earth Union, a fleet conglomerated from a variety of places.

Massive war machines of the most dreadful kinds stood like colossal statues along the edge of the hangars. A sleeping grand jump portal beckoned them to enter it.

Barracks the size of mountains churned with endless ranks of soldiers. A variety of clones, and armored dronekind stripped of their original purposes and turned into weapons of war. They moved with perfect synchronization, silent, unthinking, bound only to one will. Veshdren's will. Thousands of legions. Billions of Legionaries, awaited command. It was a kingdom within a kingdom, a blade hidden in the ribs of the Dominion, sharp enough to bleed it from within.

Maris leaned forward on the balcony rail, his eyes wide, his lips parted in a mix of awe and dread. "I've fought in wars across half the galaxy," he whispered, "but I've never seen power like this. Not hidden. Not waiting." His voice faltered. "This... this isn't just a simple rebellion or heretical uprising. It's apocalyptic in its design and breath."

Tria's gaze didn't waver. She watched the marching legions as though staring into the abyss itself, her hand tight around the hilt of her deactivated Singublade.

"She's been planning this for longer than any of us guessed. If Veshdren truly commands all this… She could shatter the Dominion from within. If we're able to somehow subdue the Duality and circumvent Earth's defenses this would probably be enough to crown her empress. But I don't know how long her reign would last. I don't know if it'd be worth it."

Maris turned sharply, his voice edged with a deep rooted panic. "And what then? Another tyrant seated where the old one fell? You know what kind of power it takes to keep something like this hidden. You know she's most likely spilled a lot of innocent blood to keep her deeds secret."

But Tria shook her head slowly, her tone quieter, heavier. "And yet… this changes everything. If even half of this force is real, if she unleashes it, the Dominion will feel it. The balance of the empire will break. Especially if she publicly reveals her intentions to the entire galaxy."

A silence stretched between them, broken only by the distant thrum of engines and the marching cadence of cloned boots. Then, as though the sight below wasn't already unbearable, Maris spoke again, softer this time, his words laced with disbelief.

"The Duality…" he swallowed, almost unable to say it. "They descended into the undercities themselves. They walked among the filth and the forgotten. And they blessed them. Do you realize what that means? The Unders who we were going to free… they've been lifted up. Some raised to High Lords. I never thought I'd ever see the day. Maybe we're wrong to continue this rebellion, maybe we are heretics."

Tria's face hardened. "I never thought they would either. Never believed they would stoop to the depths. But they did. And now every undercity bleeds with fire and hope. They've given the forgotten a crown."

Maris's voice trembled slightly. "Recruiting them won't be just difficult, it'll be near impossible. The Unders believe themselves chosen now. Saints forged out of shadow and hunger. We'll be asking them to choose between the Duality's hand and our words. Between lordship and our promises of a better world which has already been given to them. Between Gods and heresy."

Tria finally turned, her eyes burning with something that was not fear but a quiet, razor-sharp resolve. "Then the question isn't if they will fight," she said. "It's who they will fight for. If they believe they are fighting for their Gods. Can we make them believe that the Duality has fallen? Somehow trap them somewhere and let Veshdren become the new ruler, bringing the unders and umbers into our ranks once again?"

And as her words lingered in the cold chamber, the vast throne at the end of the hall remained empty. Yet its presence weighed on them like a storm waiting to break.

The chamber darkened as the doors opened. A hush swept through the vaulted hall, as if the very ice above had bent low to listen. Veshdren'Ra entered with the certainty of a whirlwind contained within flesh, her every step measured and deliberate.

Twelve Tribunals flanked her. Towering figures clad in midnight armor, their helms carved like obsidian masks, each radiating the cold finality of judgment. They moved in unison, their heavy tread echoing across the crystal-veined floor.

Veshdren did not look at Maris or Tria at first. Her eyes a shifting dark crimson and golden fire, blazing like captured suns, swept across the vastness of her throne room, the secret empire she had built beneath the ice. Only then did she turn, fixing her gaze on the two heretics as though measuring the weight of their doubts before they could even speak them.

"My guests," she said, her voice carrying the velvet edge of authority, "have you seen enough to understand what true unbroken power can forge? Or do you want to see more? I have so much to show you. I have many worlds under my control. Over a million Tribunals under my command, birthed from my blood. Unknown to my parents."

The Tribunals formed a perfect crescent behind her, silent and immovable, their presence alone a reminder that she did not come alone, and she never would.

Maris swallowed, his throat tight, but he did not bow. Tria's gaze sharpened, steady, though her heart pounded with the question she had not yet spoken aloud: Was this power salvation. Or another mask of tyranny?

Tria stepped forward, voice steady but razor-sharp. "You have spoken of reform, of tearing the Dominion from within. But I've seen promises like yours before. I've seen them die in silence. Prove to us that your intent is real. Show us that you are not just another mask hiding ambition beneath it."

Veshdren'Ra's crimson eyes blazed, her voice low but vibrating with fury as she stepped forward. "You think freeing Maris from the chains of the Dominion was nothing?" Her words cut like jagged plakinsteel. "I could have left him to rot in the dark, forgotten. But I shattered his prison, burned their wards, and let him walk into the light once again. And still you demand more?"

Tria did not flinch. Her jaw tightened, her hand hovering near the hilt at her side. "Yes. One man is not enough. You could be playing us for Muggbrained fools. You could be wearing another mask, another lie. If you're sincere, then prove it. Not with whispers of rebellion or empty promises. With an act that shakes the very foundation of the empire."

Before Veshdren could retort, the air thickened. A shimmer of light split reality open, and from it stepped Ari'Ella Dunesky, robed in flowing desert cloth, her dreadlocks shifting as if caught in a wind only she commanded. Sand spilled from the edges of the portal, hissing as it scattered across the stone floor. Her presence was a storm contained in flesh.

Veshdren'Ra's breath caught for the briefest of moments. She felt it. Power, ancient and unyielding. The pulse of Ari'Ella's spirit was like standing at the edge of an abyss carved by the oldest of fire and the most ancient sun.

Ari'Ella's voice rolled like a low deep crakling thunder over dunes. "Tria doesn't ask for much. She asks for the impossible. But only through the impossible will your sincerity be proven."

Veshdren's hands curled into fists, her nails like claws biting into her palms. Rage swelled within her, but beneath it, something else: the desperate hunger to be believed, but also the agravation of being challenged, she had always been treated as a God among mortals.

"You continue to doubt my intentions. I don't have to prove anything to any of you. Especially not you Dunesky, you hide and wither on your hidden world. I could rise up and make my own empire if I deemed it so. But I'm here. I want something new. A new beginning for all of us. I want unity, not division."

Dunesky saw through the words. Knowing a deeper current of the princess's emotions and feelings.

"It's fear that makes you want unity. You know that even with these grand armies and a million Tribunals loyal to you, it's still not enough to win. You can't defeat your parents and you know it, that's why you want us. You know we have what you don't."

The princess Transcendent became even more frustrated by Ari'Ella's words.

"And what would that be? Your armies are faltering. The Peacekeeper assaults have ended. The empire is more united then ever before. The unders, umbers, and uppers are more filled with adoration and commitment to the Dominion than they've been in millennia."

Tria gave Veshdren and answer.

"You have Tribunals, titles, legions that march at your command. But all of it is bound. Every choice, every action, every triumph is shackled to the expectations of the throne and people, to the dictates of your lineage and those who worship you, to the eyes that watch you from above and below. You cannot create or rule freely, for even great power carries numerous chains that can't be easily broken. We, however, move unbound. We build without fear of reprisal, without the weight of pretending divinity pressing on our shoulders. We shape what must be shaped, strike where the worlds expect restraint, and forge futures no dynasty could ever decree. That is what you lack. And that is why you want this secret alliance, that is why you need us."

"It's simplistic and basic. You don't know anything, Peacekeeper."

Ari'Ella became annoyed by the Transcendent princess.

"Then why are we here? Stop playing games. We don't have time for games."

"It's true, I need you. But I could continue to build my strength and bide my time. Maybe in another thousand years I could rise up against my parents, but I don't want to wait that long. I want to bring a new empire into this galaxy now. Are you with me or not?"

Ari'Ella, Tria, and Maris shared glances between each other, a slight pause to ponder Veshdren'Ra's words.

Every second of silence was crushing. Tria's lips pressed into a thin line, practically unreadable. Ari'Ella's dark eyes studied Veshdren, weighing her soul. Maris stood silent, contemplating their actions, still considering the fact that they might be making a mistake. And Veshdren stood strong but trembled deep down. Not with fear, but with the feral resolve of one who had set her own fate ablaze.

Chapter Fifteen:
REVELATIONS OF HERETICS

"We must hide from the Dominion and rebuild a free society that one day might be able to rise up against the darkness that's spreading throughout the galaxy."

Aleron Corbin-James Knight, First President of the United Free Republics of Earth, circa 3,110 AD

Weeks bled into months. Tria and Amarax had many more conversations and debates. Tria hoped for the best, seeing slight changes. Yet Amarax remained steadfast in his deeper commitments to the Dominion and his Gods. Locked in a silent war of questions that kept coming, challenging his beliefs. His mind was torn between duty and doubt. Still, his resolve held firm. He would break free again. He would have his revenge on the heretics who caged him like a common Mugg.

Then, one day, amid his new routine, a sound like molten rock churning through stone shattered the silence. His cell wall, once crystalline and seamless, began to shift. A fissure widened into a doorway, spilling forth an almost blinding light.

From within that radiance, Tria emerged. No longer just a projected hologram, in the flesh. She wore her Peacekeeper battle armor. A flowing blue cloak draped over her shoulders. Identical to the one she had worn in the battle of the undercity of Antica. No helmet hid her face, and her armor, shined with sleek elegance, it surpassed even Dominion crafted tech. She spoke first.

"These months have flown by too fast. It's time to go to trial. It's time to face judgement Amarax."

"You have no right to judge me. I'm a Grand Marshal. Only a Tribunal or High Lord can judge me."

"You're our prisoner. We'll go by our rules. You will be judged. I don't know what they'll decide. It's not up to me. Let's go."

Beyond the threshold lay a vast white chamber, stretching for miles. Multi-leveled, lined with cube-like cells identical to his own. Towering white pillars rose to a ceiling of shifting blue, an artificial sky. Tria led the way, flanked by three Peacekeeper security bots, their tall close metallic presence grating on Amarax's nerves.

"Are these really necessary?" he asked, irritated.

"I don't think so. But I don't make the rules. All prisoners in the Republics require at least a Peacekeeper or a security bot. The prison administrator decided you needed extra after your previous prison break."

Amarax bit down his frustration. He wanted to tear them apart, but for now, he played the part.

"If it's the rule, so be it. I have no argument against laws meant to protect your people. I'll do my best to respect your codes. It's not what I'm used to, but I'll try."

As Amarax strode through the vast chamber, his gaze swept over the scene. Hundreds of armored rebel soldiers patrolling high platforms, watching over a recessed commons where thousands milled about. Men, women, and hybrids, all clad in white like himself, engaged in various activities: reading Holopedias, watching holograms, exercising, speaking in hushed tones. All prisoners like himself.

Dominion citizens, perhaps? Or Judicators from Antica, taken before the battle in the undercity? The reports had spoken of entire garrisons vanishing. If these rebels had captured so many, their goal was clear. Extract information, or worse, twist them into heretics. It was a chilling sight to his still mostly faithful mind.

Amarax's instinct screamed to rally them, to incite a revolt. But strategy held him back. Even if he could stir their hearts with words, what good would it do? Their neural implants were likely removed just like his were, severing the Dominion's mental web. And without weapons, breaking free from this fortress would be suicide. No, not yet. He had spent too long earning their trust to waste it now.

Ahead, Tria stepped onto a raised hexagonal platform, a marvel of technology. Silver metal gleamed beneath an azure lattice that shimmered like a sea of stars. An MTN pad, the Republics' Matter

Transfer Network. Its artistry clashed with the Dominion's stark utilitarianism, an alien elegance to Amarax's rigid mind.

A perimeter of heavily armored guards stood watch, their Dark Matter Rifles poised. A force field surrounded the platform, crackling with unseen energy. As Tria stepped forward, the barrier flickered away, granting passage without a word. Amarax hesitated only a moment before following. For now, he played along. Until the moment came to strike.

Amarax stepped onto the platform. Tria, with practiced ease, pressed a sequence of buttons on her wrist control panel. A tingling sensation coursed through his body, followed by a flash of bright light.

When his vision cleared, he found himself standing on another identical MTN platform. But this time, he was no longer in the prison. Instead, he looked out over a sprawling, lush valley, bordered by ancient, genetically-engineered jungles and towering pines reaching for a breathtaking sky. The landscape stretched endlessly, a vibrant mix of colors beyond even Mars's wildest flora. In the distance, megalithic golden towers rose, forming an ancient yet timeless city. Their ornate, spiraling shapes seemed to whisper stories and emotions, reaching skyward like living things.

Every few miles, massive white pillars spiraled toward the heavens, wrapped in vines. The ceiling above seemed to stretch into infinity, a perfect day with clouds drifting lazily by. Far off, snow-capped mountains rose beyond the city, a sight that reminded him of Mars before the decline. This was nature as it was meant to be. Wild and unspoiled.

A stark contrast to the smog-choked Upper Earth he had known, where even the royal gardens no longer had room for true wilderness. The cities had swallowed the land, cramming countless people into dark, uninspired skyscrapers that scraped the sky and stretched into orbit.

Amarax gazed, awe-struck, at the multi-layered beauty before him, his mind racing with the disparity between this world and the suffocating one he had left behind.

Tria's voice broke the silence. "It's stunning, isn't it? I've lived here my whole life, but sometimes I still can't believe it. This is Unum, the capital of the United Free Republics of Earth—thousands of years old, still standing, still growing."

Amarax's tone carried a note of envy. "Yes, it's... remarkable. The Duality would envy what you've built. It seems impossible. But where exactly are we? This doesn't resemble any undercity I've seen."

"We're deep within Earth's mantle, near the outer core. You could say we're at the heart of the planet. Our seclusion has shielded us from prying eyes, and the Duality remains unaware of our existence. We intend to keep it that way. For now."

"How long do you think you can hide all this?" Amarax's words dripped with skepticism. "After you attacked my legion and destroyed the Holy Temple in Antica, after abducting citizens from the upper industrial zones, the Duality will surely send legions to crush you."

Tria's gaze hardened. "After the collapse of Antica, the government ordered a halt to our offensive. The Duality likely believes that we've been defeated, since we haven't struck again. But the true fight is not against the machines of war or the Legions of the Dominion, it's against the madness that twists the innocent. The true fight is for the minds of the people. All the Dominion citizens we seek to free. Our fight is to liberate them from their mental and physical prisons. We were able to free billions in Antica, one small step to the ultimate victory we seek: to free all from Dominion slavery."

"How did you manage to help so many? This place is vast, but billions? There must be no space left. Your cell isn't matter-compressed, is it? So your quarters...?"

"It wasn't easy. They're not here, they're on another world, a free world, they're seeing a real sun, a real sky, breathing fresh air. It took a lot of effort. That's one of the reasons why I had to leave for a time. But it was worth it, the once-subjugated slaves of Antica are free. Free of the Dominion's control devices, free from poverty, and free from their forced worship of false gods. An entire undercity liberated, a temple destroyed. It's just the beginning, though."

Amarax nodded, feigning agreement, but inwardly, fury burned. Her heresy and utter disdain for the Dominion's Godhood tore at him.

"That is a lot of progress," he replied, masking his disgust. "Defeating a Diviniterra Legion is no small feat. Destroying a temple? Muggjankking mind-boggling. No temple's been destroyed in over a thousand years. Except on alien worlds. Never on Terra."

His blood boiled at her casual pride. The destruction of a temple was unforgivable blasphemy. But he masked his rage, continuing the ruse to gain her trust, listening as she spoke again.

"The defeat of your Legion wasn't all us. The Emperor did most of the damage. He destroyed the upper districts to try and wipe us out. We intercepted a transmission from his flagship. Trillions likely died. But we did our best to save as many civilians and legionaries as we could."

Amarax was stunned. Her words didn't add up. Why would they save legionaries?

"Why save legionaries? You were fighting us. What use are they to you?" He shook his head, still processing. "I saw my legion. They were left lifeless in the undercity. The Emperor wouldn't collapse a district, not with so many still there. It doesn't make sense. He could have sent reinforcements for the same result."

"We don't kill, Amarax. At least, we try not to. We use lethal force only as a last resort. Most of our weapons disable, not destroy. None of your soldiers died at our hands; your Legion still lives, imprisoned like you. If they prove they've shed their warlike conditioning, they'll be free. The Emperor ordered the destruction of the upper districts, and his son carried it out. That's indisputable."

Amarax rejected her words outright. No civilization used non-lethal force in war unless they sought slaves or high-ranking prisoners. The idea felt like some absurd nonsense. He agreed, eager to end the conversation, unwilling to accept her so-called moral superiority.

"I didn't know you could intercept the Duality's communications. If you can do that, I can't argue with your assessment. So, what other wonders do you have to show me?"

Tria turned around and gestured. Amarax turned around as well. Ahead was a multi-leveled intricate hovering platform, that stepped up, each receding level more intricate than the last, hanging gardens flowing over the edges and waterfalls flowing with serenity, atop the tallest level was a grand twisting silver spire that rose majestically, more intricate and ornate than any Dominion treasure.

Its hundreds of stained-glass windows told stories through their weavings. Every curve of the tower spoke of perfect symmetry, blending culture with art. Below, pillars and metallic statues rivaled the grandeur of the Duality's palace. The spire soared, its peak disappearing into the air, the lower platforms that it was built upon were connected by stone-like walkways that were floating in the air with ease.

In the courtyard ahead that centered in front of the grand tower, amidst statues and artistic installations, at the entrance to the structure stood a larger-than-normal towering silver replica of the Statue of Liberty, an ancient symbol of freedom, overshadowing and outshining everything around it.

As they crossed a floating causeway, hundreds of heretic soldiers—Peacekeepers—stood sentry, their battle armor gleaming. Foot traffic was a blur of motion, people moving between entrances and hexagonal platforms, disappearing and reappearing at a rapid pace.

Amarax couldn't shake the unease that gripped him. Heretics on Holy Terra, free and powerful, thriving in a society independent of the Dominion. It was an abandonment of the duty owed to the Duality. The constant flux of people disappearing and appearing across all the floating platforms unsettled him. It seemed more advanced than even the Dominion's portals.

He tried to break free of what felt like a delusion, but nothing changed. He was forced to admit. This was no illusion. It was real. And in that moment he didn't know what he would do next against this tide of heresy, he just knew that he had to do something.

Chapter Sixteen:
MY TRUTH IS OUR TRUTH

"Doubt is the cage; conviction is the key. I have broken free."

— *Orava Dran,* Reflections on the Infinite Path

Vaulted ceilings stretched like the ribs of some colossal beast, and the polished obsidian floor reflected the princess in fractured shards of light. She sat upon her throne, poised and imperious, draped in silks that whispered of power and command. Her eyes, sharp as sharpened blades, followed the approach of twelve figures stepping from the shadows.

Each was an embodiment of absolute loyalty and discipline, their armor blackened steel with golden filigree marking their rank. These were Tribunals, handpicked by the princess herself, warriors and advisors who had sworn their lives and souls to her alone.

First among them, Jorathak Malvekath, the eldest, bowed deeply. "Princess Transcendent," he began, voice low and reverent, "we come with grave concerns. Your recent... alliances with the Peacekeepers and other heretics have unsettled us. We are confused by your choices as of late."

Another stepped forward. Seralythan Veyorkor, a Godblade slung across her back. "We swore loyalty to you, not to those who openly defy the deepest and most important traditions of our Dominion. Their philosophies are twisted and corrupting. To bring them into your council risks polluting the truth of divinity itself."

From the shadows, Korradda Dalenne, his armor scratched and dented from centuries of service, added, "We have fought and bled for purity, for the order that sustains the Dominion. To trust outsiders who have burned what it means to have duty to the divine, is... unthinkable."

Veshdren'Ra leaned forward, her gaze unflinching, voice calm but cold as plakinsteel. "And yet, they stand with me, ready to act where even my Tribunals hesitate. They are my means to a future none of you have the vision to see."

Another, Talysadda Korrin, narrowed her eyes. "Princess, we serve you. That is our oath. But aligning with heretics risks everything we hold sacred. You court chaos, not unity. Can you not see it?"

Veshdren'Ra's lips curved into a faint, sharp smile. "I see clearly, Tribunal Korrin. I see a Dominion unchallenged, stagnating under the weight of its own sanctimony. I see the outer worlds that could flourish beyond imagination. I see galaxies beyond our own ready to be colonized, if only we dared to step beyond fear, beyond dogma. You fear dilution, disorder, doom. I fear nothing, except stagnation."

Jorathak Malvekath let out a tight, controlled breath. "We swore fealty to you and you alone. We expected guidance, wisdom, strength. Not... alliances with those who would see our faith broken."

Veshdren'Ra rose from her throne, her presence magnified, commanding, unyielding. "Then let me remind you why you swore loyalty. Not to doctrine. Not to comfort. Not to purity. You swore loyalty to me. And as your Transcendent Princess, Grand Master Tribunal of Orion, heir to the Godly throne. I decide the path we take, the enemies we strike, the alliances we forge. My truth is our truth. Do not mistake loyalty for consent."

The room went silent for a heartbeat, the tension so thick it could be cut with a Singublade. The Tribunals exchanged glances. Some tight-lipped, some simmering with barely restrained fury. But none spoke. One by one, the twelve turned and left. Their faces were grim, their displeasure palpable. Veshdren'Ra watched them go, unmoved, her mind already turning to the next step, the next move that would force her vision into reality. Whether her Tribunals understood it or not. A storm was coming, and even those sworn to her could not stand in the way of what Veshdren'Ra intended to do.

Chapter Seventeen:
THE POWER OF HERETICS

"The Earth Civil War shattered not only nations but the very concept of unity. From the ashes, as the Dominion spread its iron grasp, a different fire began to smolder. Small enclaves of rebels, thinkers, and warriors who refused extinction and the end of a free humanity. History records two names above all others in this resistance: Zoephiria and Maxamas Hendrix. Without their vision and unyielding will, there would be no New Earth Union today."

— New Earth University, Department of History, 'The Rise of the Union'

Amarax could no longer deny it. What he was seeing and feeling was too real. This was no illusion. The heretics had somehow mastered the impossible: instantaneous matter transport. He knew that only the divine power of the Holy Duality and the twisted forbidden knowledge of the Zeetarians had ever wielded power that came close to it.

The jump drives of the armadas of the Dominion and all other galactic major powers were much larger and more complicated than the technology these heretics possessed, their complex engines, required time to fire up, to lock onto their coordinates, and usually needed at least five hours to cool down before another jump would be possible.

But these heretics had achieved something that no one else had. This technology far surpassed anything the Dominion had, more advanced than the portals throughout the empire. Or the jump gates of the New Earth Union, both of which needed a very noticeable amount of time to align their quantum links and connect to another gate and the travel through the sub-dimension taking some time..

He didn't marvel at their achievement; instead, thoughts of stealing this technology and delivering it to the Duality danced in his mind. The reward would be great, but those thoughts had to wait. He needed to focus on the task at hand: his deception.

Amarax and Tria entered the grand silver tower, weaving through the crowds that bustled about their business. Inside, a magnificent lobby stretched upward, adorned with colossal crystals that sparkled like stars. Cascading waterfalls, towering hundreds of feet, fell from rock formations, while ancient trees stood proudly by the water's edge. Lush greenery softened the stone, and flowers bloomed in random bursts of color.

Between waterfalls, grand staircases rose, endless streams of people ascending or descending. Transparent tubes, like ancient Hyperloops, shot people upwards at lightning speed. The silver stair steps, lined with gleaming jewels, were etched with sayings of freedom. Reminders of a history that had survived Earth's fall. Some of these words had endured since before the Earth Civil War.

Tria led Amarax up one of these grand staircases. She avoided maglevs, nauseated by their motion, preferring to walk or use matter transfer. At the top, they entered a hallway lined with mesmerizing artwork. Amarax stopped before a painting that caught his eye: Zoephiria and Maxamas Hendrix in radiant power armor, their faces unmistakable. He'd seen enough recordings of them to recognize them immediately.

"That's Maxamas and Zoephiria Hendrix, right?" he asked.

Tria walked back to admire the painting. "Yes, two of the most pivotal figures in our history. In humanity's history, really."

"Do you really put them on such a pedestal?"

"They gave us freedom. Without them and their leadership, I wouldn't be free to choose my worship, my path, or even to become who I am today."

Amarax paused, trying to digest her words. "I still can't understand how there's so much freedom here. You haven't told me about your faith, your beliefs. What do you worship?"

Tria smiled, her gaze distant. "There will be time for that later. There's too much to do today. That is, if your case goes well."

"My case?" Amarax frowned with anger. "What do you mean?"

"A case, like in any court system. Ours is a bit different. Your case is... unique. I'm not sure which way the judges will go."

"Well, let's hope they make the right choice."

"I hope so, but we can't waste time on art. We need to get to the courtroom. They're waiting."

Tria started walking again, but Amarax lingered, still curious about the armor. He hadn't asked about it before because he wanted to seem more interested in the history than in their weapons.

"One more question about Zoephiria and Maxamas," he said.

Tria stopped, turning back. "I suppose we have time for one. What is it?"

Amarax studied the painting, mesmerized by the radiant armor. "That armor. It looks beyond powerful. I've never seen anything like it. Where did they get it? What is it made of?"

Tria glanced at him, then back at the artwork. "According to their personal logs, it was a gift from a friend."

"A friend? What kind of friend bestows armor fit for gods?"

"I've wondered the same, but that was always their answer. Nothing more." She exhaled, then motioned forward. "Here I want to show you something else before we go to your trial."

With a final glance at the painting, Amarax nodded and followed her down another corridor.

They moved into a vast corridor where the walls themselves breathed with memory. Holographic crystal slabs hovered in the air, each glowing with shifting scenes of the past. This was the Hall of History, dedicated to Zoephiria and Maxamas Hendrix.

Amarax slowed his pace as towering projections ignited around them. Battles where Zoephiria's voice rang out like a clarion call, cities rising from ruin under Maxamas's command, and the haunting moment when they saved the Messengers of Light from Dominion annihilation.

The chamber was immense, the ceiling lost in a haze of radiant mist, as though history itself had no end. Tria's eyes shimmered with quiet reverence, but Amarax stood rigid, jaw tight, as though every image stabbed at his doubts and loyalties. The legends of Zoephiria and Maxamas were carved here not as myth, but as undeniable truth—etched into the very walls of Unum like the heartbeat of a people who didn't want to forget where they came from and who they owned so much to.

Tria greatly admired the heroes of the Republics, the Hendrix's were here role models, even though they lived three thousand years ago. After a few minutes of walking the corridor Tria relized they were late.

"Let's go we can't keep the judges waiting. Judges aren't known for being patient. We've been here too long. But that's my fault, I get caught up in this place, the history and importance of it."

"I completely understand. Lead the way."

As they started heading again to the courtroom, the image of the armor lingered in Amarax's mind. It wasn't just protection; it was a symbol of something more. The "friend" who had given it to them wasn't a simple ally. This was a promise, a guiding force for a greater destiny.

He felt the subtle shift inside him, a quiet realization settling like dawn breaking over dark waters. The past, the battles, and the weight of what had come before weren't just stories. They were preparing him for something. Something he would no longer be able to ignore.

By the time they reached the threshold of the next corridor, something stirred within him, a knowing he couldn't quite grasp. The fight ahead felt larger than him, older than his understanding. A thread, unseen yet undeniable, seemed to weave through his very being, and though he couldn't name it, he felt it pull him forward, urging him along a path he didn't fully recognize but couldn't resist.

Chapter Eighteen:
HEIRS TO THE THRONE

"From my essence, they are shaped for glory. My blood my power reside within them both. May they know only a future of perfect peace."

— God Empress of Humanity, at the birth of her first born twins

Sigils of power and divinity covered the grand ceilings of the Duality's throne room on Holy Terra, their luminous forms pulsating faintly, as if watching the heirs who dared tread beneath them.

The room had emptied after the Duality issued a new decree, the courtiers, advisors, and priests departing in hushed awe. Only the two heirs remained: Theldren and Veshdren, Ra. There was no warmth between them. No affection, no camaraderie. They were rivals, predators circling a throne that both coveted.

Theldren'Ra's gaze was cold, piercing through the half-light as he stepped forward, the air itself seeming to recoil at his movement. "The decree was made," he said slowly, deliberately. "Yet I see you moving in ways even this chamber cannot contain. Secrets, sister... and I suspect they are not meant for my eyes."

Veshdren'Ra's violet eyes narrowed, a quiet storm brewing in their depths. She did not flinch, though the weight of her plots pressed against her like iron chains. "Do not mistake caution for secrecy, brother. Every move I make is measured, every plan deliberate. You, too, are learning the lessons of restraint. Or do you fancy yourself ready to seize what is not yet yours?"

He smiled, sharp and dangerous. "I have always been ready. Unlike you, I do not hide behind shadows. But I can see yours, weaving and curling, hiding truths that try to reshape this Dominion. You are ambitious... but ambition alone does not guarantee survival."

Her voice was soft, almost a whisper, but it cut through the silence like a blade. "And yet, it is my ambition that moves beyond mere survival. You cling to titles and appearances. I wield power in the dark. Unseen, shaping events that even you cannot predict. Every secret I keep, every alliance I forge, brings me closer to the throne. And when the time comes, brother... nothing you do will stop me."

Theldren'Ra's eyes glimmered with calculation. "And when the shadows you cast become too heavy, will they crush you, or will they crush everything else first? Secrets are dangerous, Veshdren. Even the most loyal Tribunals can falter, and even the most hidden armies can be turned. One mistake... and the throne will belong to me."

Veshdren'Ra let a faint, cruel smile curve her lips. "Perhaps. Or perhaps I have already laid the groundwork for a future in which mistakes no longer matter. You underestimate the weight I carry and the lengths I'll go to bend the future to my vision."

Theldren'Ra took a deliberate step closer, the shadows of the room twisting unnaturally around him, as if sensing the tension. "Then let us see, sister. Let us see whose vision prevails. For the throne of our parents is no prize for the timid or the cautious. It is for those willing to wield every secret, every weapon, every allegiance... to claim it as their own."

Veshdren'Ra's eyes glinted, a storm coiling beneath her calm. "Let us see indeed. But know this, Theldren: I've already begun. And when the time comes, the Dominion will bend, not to your will, nor mine, but to the designs I have carved in the shadows, where you will not see them... until it is too late."

Theldren'Ra paused, studying her as if weighing her words against the divine architecture of their bloodline. Then he turned, leaving her alone in the obsidian cathedral for the Duality's thrones. The echo of his steps faded within moments. But the tension between them lingered with the deep division between them, heavier than any decree, more dangerous than any army either could field.

Veshdren'Ra exhaled slowly, letting the silence absorb her, her mind already plotting the next moves in a game that neither ally nor enemy could fully grasp. The throne was within reach, but the path was treacherous. And she alone bore the full weight of the secrets that would decide who would ultimately sit high in dominion.

Chapter Nineteen:
THE COURTROOM

"In doubt, we find forgiveness; in pain, we find strength. Though the path may twist and the weight of our burdens grow heavy, we must press forward. For in the darkest corners of the universe, it is our light that must shine brightest. Guiding the lost, offering justice where there is none, and restoring order to a broken reality. Even in the face of insurmountable odds, we are the ones who must bring hope to the weary, the lost, and the forsaken souls trapped within the Dominion."

Maxamas Rivenborne Hendrix,

Captain United Resistance Front, Personal Journals, circa 3,115 AD

Each step carried them further into the heart of the building, the silence growing more oppressive with every turn. Then looming just ahead was a pair of massive silver doors, their presence commanding and final. With a soft hiss, they parted, revealing the chamber. It was simple yet imposing, its stillness filled with the quiet anticipation of what was to come.

Tria and Amarax both kept walking down the hallway and turned down a smaller hallway and then another and then through a pair of guarded large silver doors that opened into a chamber. It was a simple and yet still ornate chamber. There were dozens of intricately shaped chairs on a raised pedestal in front of them, shaped in a half circle around the back end of the room.

The room was circular in shape. One giant soothing light was projecting from the ceiling and a series of smaller lights were built into the walls. Sitting on the chairs were robbed humans, of all genders. Some robes were simple and humble, others a little flamboyant. Along the edge of the room were armed Peacekeepers in their battle armor. Tria addressed the group of sitting Judges.

"Honorable judges of the Free Republics, I ask the court today for a free roaming pass for Amarax Mirvega, a former Grand Marshal within the Dominion and current prisoner of war of the Free Republics."

One of the humbly robbed judges, who had a simple robe of dark grey and black lining gave Tria the first reply.

"Why should the court show such leniency so soon to this prisoner? The Dominion troops that survived the recent battle in the undercity of Antica have only been here for a matter of months. That seems like a very short amount of time for recouping from years and years of brainwashing."

"He has shown a lot of progress in that short amount of time and wants to be free from the Duality's control. I believe that if he's allowed to roam our great Republics and see who we are as a people. That he'll be able to fully shake off the chains of the Duality and the Dominion."

"That's a big if captain. I'm not convinced of Amarax's good intentions, and I don't think the other judges are either. You were assigned to his case because of your meritorious service and clear thinking, but I think in this case you may be wishing for the best in him when he is most likely still struggling with the trained evilness that has been pushed upon him for so many years."

Amarax stayed silent. Even though he wanted to rip them all to pieces he kept as quite as a stone. Knowing that that was the best strategy at the moment. That by letting Tria continue her dialogue with the panel of judges, he might find a way to complete his plans.

"Your honor I am not wishful in this instance, I know that he will change one day. I feel it deep inside my gut and I am never wrong when it comes to my gut."

The judges whispered and quietly chatted among themselves, one of the judges, the most flamboyantly attired and pompous looking, their robe covered in golden inlays and jewels addressed Tria and Amarax.

"Captain, we are the deciders in this instance. Your gut means nothing to this court. The laws are clear. Any prisoners of war who are guilty of war crimes to the extent that Amarax has committed are to be sentenced to life imprisonment in solitary confinement without any chance of parole. The law is crystal clear, Amarax will be in prison for the rest of his natural life."

Tria didn't like the pompous attitude of the gaudy judge and snapped back.

"The law is not clear; this is not so cut and dry! Amarax and the rest of the Dominion are brainwashed. They are implanted at birth against their will with mind control devices. Punishment and pleasure modules are installed within them, and they are genetically engineered to be predisposed to violence and servitude to the Duality's evil whims. It is madness to think that they in their brainwashed and controlled states are totally responsible for what they do without regard for the controls that have been pushed upon them since their births."

The pompous judge snapped back with his own self-centered refutations.

"I do not appreciate your tone of voice Captain. I am a judge of the United Free Republics of Earth. Remember that before you raise your voice again in this court of law. We as a body of judges must rule as precisely as possible within the boundaries of what is known to be our laws. We cannot simply create new laws at our own discretion. Especially not laws and verdicts based on emotion and feeling. Amarax must be punished for all that he has done throughout his conquests in his service to the Duality and to the Dominion."

"Emotion has nothing to do with this case. Amarax is a victim plain and simple. The entire Dominion is a victim. All continually receiving unjust treatment and forced commands from the Duality and their children. We must be better in every way. We need to be the light that erases this blight of oppression. If we can't help a single former soldier of the Dominion than we won't be able to help all those subjects that we freed in the undercity. They still aren't giving up their worship and adoration of the Duality, but I believe in time they will, just as I believe that in time Amarax will completely choose to reject the darkness of the Dominion. It is logical to do everything we can to erase this influence once and for all in any way that we can. Even if we are revolted by the evil they have committed in the past, we must turn a new page in the story of humanity's fate."

All the judges whispered and discussed among each other again for a few minutes, in deep quite debate. Then they all became silent except for one judge who was dressed in a purple robe and lined with sparkling silver.

"Tria, what makes you really think that Amarax is breaking free?"

"He has been very interested to know all about our history and especially about Zoephiria and Maxamas Hendrix. He has read many of their books and watched hundreds of hours of their recordings and journals. I really think that he is stepping away from his former life and I just have these gut feelings that just won't go away."

Once Tria had finished speaking the judge turned to Amarax.

"Amarax, what do you say? Are you changing?"

Amarax was taken a bit off guard by the judge addressing him, he thought for a moment and did the best he could in such a brief time, but they were just more memorized lies.

"I would be lying if I said that I was completely free of my Dominion training and brainwashing, but I know for a fact that what Tria and you have done for me is working. I feel more freedom every single day. I know that it's going to be a long journey to fully break free, but with Tria's help I know that I can. She is a good teacher. I know that with her guidance and in time that my mind will be as free as yours."

The judges again discussed amongst themselves and the pompous judge spoke up.

"I think that we should follow the law precisely, without reservation or sullied interpretations. If we give pass to this monster, we will have betrayed the Republics, we will have betrayed everything that we are as a body of law keepers. We must stand firm in the originality and perfection of the words of the law. Those words should remain as our beacons and guideposts to lead us forward, so that we can keep the Republics as safe and secure as possible for future generations, we canno…"

Tria spoke up, interrupting the judge.

"Excuse me, but you are not the one and only decider of what law means. If yo…"

The pompous judge interrupted Tria's interruption.

"How dare you, interrupt a judge! This is a courtroom, not a barracks! I hold you in contempt of court! Peacekeepers get her and Amarax out of my sight!"

The Peacekeepers in the room didn't move one inch and the pompous judge stood up and yelled at them.

"Do you hear me? Get them out of here, now! They both need to learn respect for the law! Arrest the Captain now!"

One of the judges who was sitting close to the center stood up and addressed the pompous judge with a slightly raised and annoyed voice.

"Sit down Brodious! Stop making a fool of yourself! Did you already forget that we are in a joint session of all the high courts? None of us can make any unilateral decisions here! So sit down and let the proceedings continue!"

The pompous judge slightly raised his voice.

"I don't answer to you Darian, I have a right to voice my disgust of the Captain's disrespect!"

"Yes, you do, but you don't have a right to have her forcefully removed from these chambers or arrested. Now please, stop this nonsense and let the captain have more time to make her case. We are here to listen and learn. If we don't learn we cannot come to any reasonable judgements."

"Fine, I'll retract my previous statements, have it revoked from the record."

"Thank you, Brodious."

The two judges slowly sat back down as they stared at each other. Judge Darian Wang-Lee Ngalula, the judge who had challenged the emotional judge Brodious Fairchild Gates spoke to Tria in a much calmer voice compared to her counterpart.

"Please, continue what you were saying before. I'm very interested and I think all of the other judges are interested in learning more of your prospective on Amarax. This is the first case of a Dominion Grand Marshal being brought to any court of the Republics."

"Thank you, your honor, I'd be more than happy to continue. As I was saying before, the law is ever-changing. As you all know, our perceptions of law change over time. Our system has changed greatly over time, in the past our ancestors allowed the death penalty. Now we realize that that's a barbaric mistake. Just a few short years ago this very court decided to show leniency to the Cultists of Kronos, even some who had attacked the Republics. You forgave their crimes knowing that they weren't fully capable of understanding their actions. We must put Amarax in the same category as those cultists. He was not fully aware of his actions. We must continue with that same proposition as we go forward and help others who are controlled within the Dominion."

Judge Darian Wang-Lee Ngalula thanked Tria as she finished.

"Thank you, Captain Oberon for your passionate opinion, I am inclined to agree with you. I even thi—"

Judge Brodious Fairchild Gates piped in right as Judge Darian Wang-Lee Ngalula was about to continue to explain her thoughts on what Tria had said.

"I am inclined to disagree, completely and utterly disagree. Let us stop this farce and send Amarax back to prison where he belongs."

Judge Ngalula, spoke up again.

"No, we cannot abandon our principles. We must consider more."

She turned to Amarax and asked him a direct question.

"Amarax, would you be willing to share your memories with the court?"

Amarax was again taken off guard by such a question and responded with a bit of confusion.

"My memories? What memories exactly?"

"Whatever you feel willing to share. Our memory reading devices can only show what memories the individual wants to show. Are you willing?"

"I am willing to show some of my memories, yes."

Judge Gates raised his voice again.

"No, that would be a mockery of this court. He is a Grand Marshal. A servant to the Duality and their vile empire. We cannot allow this."

The judges conversed with each other for a moment and the primary judge in the middle spoke.

"Amarax, should be allowed to share what memories he would like to share, so that we can understand him better."

A small metallic pedestal like table appeared in front of Tria and Amarax with a Holoviewer on it. Almost identical to what he had used when looking up battles of the past. A holographic projector was also on the table in front of the Holoviewer. After the table appeared the primary judge spoke again.

"Please Amarax, put the Holoviewer on and share what memories you're willing to share."

Amarax looked at Tria with a bit of hesitation in his eyes and she nodded with reassurance and gave him a slight smile. He sighed deeply with a deep feeling of not wanting to do it, but he forced himself and put the Holoviewer on. Once he did, he found himself among the clouds again. The Holopedia voice spoke to him.

"Welcome to memory sharing, you can share any memories you wish to. Please just think it."

Amarax didn't want to give away any military secrets, but he couldn't help but to think about war because those were the strongest memories in his mind.

His first mission as a commissioned officer within the Holy Grand Army of Terra popped into his head. He was given command of the 8th Battalion within the 801st Terra Legion of Luna. It was a mission to an Askar world. The world of Asmakar'Assarakara. He remembered his three close friends: Handoro, Modoora, and Addarias. They were also newly commissioned officers after they had all graduated at the same time from the Great Holy Institutes of War on Orion. They had all become officers at the same time and were all sent on this mission together, each commanding a separate Battalion.

He remembered how the mission did not go as planned, the Askar had abandoned the world long ago and it had been occupied by various human colonists. He remembered his friends again just like it was yesterday. They were killed by fellow Legionaries in front of the commanding Grand Marshal of the Legion for strangely breaking their oaths as junior officers in the Grand Army.

She had ordered them to kill all the colonists. For some unknown reason Amarax's friends were hesitant and pretended to kill the colonists, but had actually let most go. The Grand Marshal was furious and had them killed for disobeying direct orders.

The memories of his friends being killed were chipping away at this rocky heart. Without the drugs and implants controlling him, he was free to feel. He didn't want to see his friends dying, not while he felt like this, so he thought about the Askar. His memories of his friends disappeared and memories of the Askar campaigns were projected all around him and within the courtroom itself. He could see the wars and devastation that he had been a part of.

Memories of more war and devastation flashed, fleets clashing and shattering above dozens of different worlds. The killing of so many heretics and rebels and insurgents and innocents alike, in massive battles. Cities burning and starships falling from the skies, but there were also memories of times when Amarax saved lives and lied to his superior officers above him just like his friends who had been killed for doing just the same thing. But Amarax didn't even know why his friends did what they did, he only broke the rules occasionally to honor his friends.

Then the memories focused again, this time onto the first time he met an Askar face to face. They came in the dark. Always in the dark. Amarax remembered the first time he heard them. Deep in the ruined forests of Kurnash IX, where the trees had long since twisted into blackened bonewood and the air stank of rot and old blood. The Legionary advance had gone quiet that night. No birds. No wind. Just static in the holocomms and that awful feeling... like something watching. Then the howl.

It wasn't just a sound. It was a wound. A primal scream that tore into the mind like claws through flesh. A thousand notes of hunger, rage, and something worse: joy. These Askar weren't soldiers or warriors. They were hunger with bones.

Werewolf-like, yes—but that word was too human, too tame. These Askar were taller than battle mechs, their limbs longer and crueler than common Askar, bodies slick with pulsing muscle and wet fur that reeked of ammonia and copper. Their eyes glowed violet beneath bony crowns, and their jaws unhinged wider than any predator Amarax had seen in all his campaigns. Teeth like shattered obsidian, gnashing in excitement.

They didn't rush in. They played. Like predators that already knew their prey was easy picking.

He remembered a Legionary named Ravia. One moment he was at Amarax's side, muttering prayers to the Duality. The next he was gone. Dragged backward into shadow, his scream cut off with a crack and a spray of red mist that painted Amarax's visor. All that remained was his hand, twitching, fingers still gripping his rifle.

A pack-mind. Hunting minds. They moved with terrifying coordination. One tore through a flamecaster team before the gunner could scream. Another pulled a heavy trooper into the trees. The sound that followed. Wet, crunching, final.

It wasn't war. It was slaughter. The plasma fire barely slowed them. Their hides could take a hit. Sometimes two. Amarax had seen one Askar run on a broken leg, blood spurting from a cauterized gash, just to tear out the throat of a downed soldier. And they didn't fight to win territory. They fought to feed. The field became a feeding ground.

The Legions had burned down the entire forest by midnight. Flames chased shadows. Screams echoed through the black. The Askar didn't retreat. They vanished. Slipping through the smoke like ghosts incarnate, their howls fading, as if mocking the Dominion for thinking fire could banish them.

When the sky finally cleared and the sun had risen, over a thousand Legionaries were dead. Ripped apart. No burials. No honor. Amarax stood over their remains. Scattered limbs, crushed armor, half-eaten torsos. And made one quiet vow:

"Next time, there would be no forest. No dusk. No darkness. Only light and fire from above."

Because the Askar were not gods. They were monsters. And monsters burned.

His shared thoughts went to the second time Amarax Mirvega met an Askar, there was no forest. No blood-soaked soil. No war cries. Only the cold, metallic stillness of a Dominion command ship. The Divine Claw, high above the orbit of Mycareth Prime.

And this tall Askar... spoke. He wore no chains. No muzzle. No restraints. He strode through the central war chamber with the ease of a seasoned noble, dressed in ceremonial war robes fused with Dominion-adorned armor, black trimmed with crimson steel. His fur was silver like starlight, and though the jaw was lined with fangs, his amber eyes carried deep calculating thought. Poise and absolute control.

Amarax had been summoned to the chamber for a commendation. A rising officer, a newly blooded commander from Orion, baptized in flame and the screams of Kurnash IX. But instead of a human, he found himself face to face with High Lord Veyrask, an Askar of royal lineage, now sitting as a powerful and important High Lord of Divine Will.

Something in Amarax broke. Before words could be exchanged, his hand flew to the hilt of his blade. Sparks shrieked from the floor as he lunged, steel humming with fury. The image of his fallen brothers. Mauled and devoured. Flashed in his mind. The smell of bonewood sap and burning meat still clung to his memories.

But his blade never reached its target. A crack of energy. Then shooting pain. Then darkness. He awoke in a prison cell buried deep within the ship's underdecks. Cold polished black walls. No windows. Just silence and failure.

Amarax sat up on the edge of the metal cot, rage boiling under his skin. They'd locked him away. For doing what any sane soldier would have done. He whispered the names of the fallen under his breath. An unspoken prayer for justice.

Hours passed. Maybe more. Time meant nothing in the dark. Then the door hissed open. He stood immediately, fists clenched. But what stepped through was not a jailer, nor an officer. It was Veyrask.

The High Lord's claws clicked softly against the metal floor. His golden eyes studied Amarax. Not like prey. Not like predator. Like a teacher sizing up a child who didn't yet understand the fire he played with.

"You have a fire in you, Legionary," Veyrask said, voice deep and calm, tinged with the weight of age. "But fire must be wielded with precision and discipline. Not flung without reason."

Amarax trembled beneath that truth, jaw tight. "You're one of them."

"I am Askar," the High Lord said evenly. "But I am not one of those beasts you fought with in the wilds of that forsaken world."

"You expect me to believe you're different?" Amarax spat. "They slaughtered my Legion. They fed on our dead. They—"

"I know," Veyrask interrupted, eyes narrowing. "I've fought them many times. My people have long been divided. Feral blood runs through some like a plague. But not all of us are beasts. Not all of us are mindless monsters. I serve the Holy Duality, as do many of my kind. I have given my blood, my name, my soul to the Dominion. You would be wise to remember that."

The silence that followed was suffocating.

"You just graduated from the war academy on Orion," Veyrask continued. "You have potential. But you're blinded by fear and rage. I would hate to see a rising star be torn down before he had a chance to redeem himself."

Amarax swallowed hard. The truth seared through his anger like a hot blade. He wasn't facing a beast. He was facing a warrior. An equal. A superior. And worse… he was absolutely right.

Amarax dropped down to one knee and bowed his head in respect.

"I was wrong," Amarax said, voice hoarse. "I let the past speak louder than my present. My error in judgment will not happen again. I apologize… High Lord."

Veyrask stared at him for a long time. Then, he turned toward the open cell door.

"Good. Because this is your one chance at redemption." He paused in the doorway, eyes glowing in the dim light. "It can never happen again."

Then he was gone. Amarax rose slowly, the cold bite of shame buried deep in his gut. But something else, too. A sliver of clarity. The Dominion was not built on prejudice. It was built on strength. On loyalty. On service. And if even an Askar could rise beyond blood, so could he. He left that cell a different man. And he never forgot the look in the High Lord's eyes. Not beast. Not monster. Something far more dangerous: A believer.

Experiencing all these memories like they were happening all over again was starting to become too much for Amarax to handle. They were all becoming so clear and present. Especially now without the implants that had always brought him a sense that he was doing good. Now he strangely felt shame, but the mental programming was still there inside him. Even with this new shame and disgust he was feeling, he still felt a loyalty to the Godly Duality and the Dominion, but he was keeping that to himself.

The memories were flashing faster and faster and faster. A cycle of chaos in his mind unfolding, unraveling the mess of war and pain that he had brought to so many worlds. A face, the face of a child kept replaying within the jumble of images, the face of the child he had killed in a battle on a distant battlefield. Amarax felt the guilt welling up inside of him as he saw the child's face over and over again and started yelling in anguish. The Holoviewer turned off, unable to lock onto his emotionally broken, now unwilling mind. He ripped it off his head and threw it onto the ground.

Amarax fell to his knees and started yelling "No" in repetition. Tears of sadness rolled out of his eyes. Tria went down on her knees as well and tried her best to try and console him in his grief of all the terrible pain he had caused. As this was happening the judges started to discuss again and they activated their neural connectors that allowed them to share a few momentary thoughts and ideas very quickly.

After a few minutes of this exchange of ideas, the judge in the very middle of the large curving c-shaped table stood up. She pushed her chair back as she stood up, it was the largest and looked like an ancient piece of art. It was intricately carved wood with deep etchings of historical significance covering it.

Even though she looked aged and white hair covered her head she pushed back the large chair with ease. Her robe and hood were both midnight black, but as it moved it sparkled like a million distant stars. The trim around the edges was a tint of shining silver. A bit of glowing technology was around her wrists. There was also technology on her old, but still youthful-looking face, that was illuminated by the tech, projecting out shades of blue light from their technological workings.

She stood there for a moment in silence and closed her eyes. After a moment she opened her eyes again and proclaimed to Amarax and Tria in a projecting tone of leadership and experience the court's decision.

"The court has decided the fate of Amarax. We will show leniency in this case and any cases to come as it is deemed necessary when concerning individuals who have been forced into service or worship to the Duality or their Tribunal children or the many Lords within the Dominion. There must be a new precedent if we are to stop the Duality and their Empire. We must bring these lost souls to find a new freedom. Forced controls like those in the Dominion are an affront to everything we hold dear. Both mental and physical slavery are abominations, they always have been and always will be. You must understand though that Amarax has committed many more crimes than the average soldier. If he fails, just one more time while roaming the Republics he will be sent again to solitary and this time forever. Another thing, he must always be escorted and because you have already been an integral part of his recovery it should be you. If he commits any serious crime while under your watch and it's discovered that you did not report it than you will lose your position within the Peacekeepers. If Amarax shows any signs of recidivism you must report it to us or the Justice Administrators immediately, but we understand that we cannot be too hasty in our expectations of his recovery. Small infractions of the law or misunderstandings of local code will be forgiven. At least for the time being. Also, you should probably take Amarax to the Messengers first before bringing him to too many places. I'm aware that you're good friends with one of them, maybe they can help Amarax with his memories and relieving, some of the pain. I pray that you both have safe travels as you roam our Republics and may the truth guide your way."

Amarax was still on his knees as the judge finished what she had said, and Tria was still trying to console him. Tria could tell that he was suffering a great deal. That he finally had to emotionally and psychologically come to terms with what he had done. But in that moment, she felt sorry for him, even though she knew some of the heinous things that he had done, she still felt compassion, her upbringing and beliefs guided her to show compassion even to those who didn't deserve it.

She activated the Medheal setting on her arm module and injected Amarax with some of the Nano-Feelgood-Biogels (NFB) the Goodgel that Tria was addicted to. The medicine relieved the debilitating anxiety and traumatic memories he was experiencing. The medicine helped numb some of the traumatically piercing, guilt-filled feelings that were stabbing into his mind and soul.

Uncontrolled tears stopped flowing. As the feelings of guilty conviction subsided and he stood up, he met Tria's gaze with a faint, grateful smile. She saluted the judges, and they stepped out, ready to journey through the vast expanses of the Republics.

The road ahead was uncertain, his redemption a distant hope, but the first steps had been taken. Tria bore the weight of guiding him, a burden she welcomed. No words were needed. Only the quiet understanding of what time, regret, forgiveness, and mercy might forge.

Chapter Twenty:
BONDS SEALED IN BLOOD

"Fear has no place among Gods, it leads to division, division brings chaos, chaos births extinction."

— From The Creed of Godhood

Beneath the glacial skin of her secret frozen world, the hidden citadel of Veshdren'Ra pulsed like a buried heart. The command chamber was vast, its vaulted ceiling intricately carved from black stone and golden plakinsteel. Every surface was alive with the reflecting glow of hologrids. Dominion sectors, war routes, and planetary strongholds shimmered in spectral light, casting ghostly shifting shadows across the faces of those gathered.

At the head of the war-table stood Veshdren'Ra, regal even in her current state of slight weariness. Her armor shined with a dark radiance. Her hands were pressed firmly against the shimmering steel rim. The faint stain of blood marked her robes, remnants of recent battles fought in the crusades with her parents. Her eyes were steady, her voice controlled, but beneath the surface tension coiled like an eager predator.

Around her, the rebellion sharpened its plans. General McMaster of the Peacekeepers traced glowing routes through the map with his wrinkled worn finger, each motion precise, like a surgeon opening veins.

"Here. Here. And here. If we strike these bases before reinforcements arrive, the Dominion will bleed before it knows that it's been cut. Timing is everything. If we fail, the worlds we mean to free will be ash before we set foot on them. We must create diversions and misdirection wherever we can. We must scatter their gaze before the hammer of their fleets fall." His officers murmured assent, shock-lances gleaming faintly in the glow.

Ari'Ella Dunesky, the edges of her desert robes flowing like living fire, leaned into the light. Her dreadlocks swayed as she raised one hand above the projections, fingers crackling with restrained energy. "We need swiftness. We need precision. We need to strike not where they're strong, but where they cannot imagine we would dare go. That is how the outer colonies will rise. Their chains will break. We will give them a new hope."

Veshdren'Ra nodded slowly, her eyes bright with the conviction of what they were doing.

"Our plans are sound. This is a step in the right direction. We will triumph, we will find resolution in this conflict. The empire will be reborn. By our actions a new dawn is coming."

A hush settled over the chamber. Maris Solvannis leaned heavily on his staff, both hands gripping the polished steel as though to steady the weight of ages. Around the table, cautious smiles passed between the gathered figures. Fleeting sparks of hope, fragile but genuine.

And then, without warning, the light in Veshdren'Ra's expression faltered. Her lips parted in a sudden, sharp gasp, her body shuddering as if struck by an unseen force. Pain carved itself into the features of her face. Raw and unmistakable in their intensity.

The next heartbeat tore the silence apart. A thin blade engulfed in flame, spectral and cruel, burst through her chest, piercing straight through her armor and puncturing her heart. Gasps and raised voices erupted, chaos broke the fragile calm.

It was no outside assassin. No shadow at the door. The hand on the blade belonged to one of her own. Seralythan Veyorkor stepped forward and grabbed onto Veshdren'Ra with her left hand, her eyes cold, twisting the Godly Duality-forged weapon in a deliberate motion that wrenched a cry of agony from the Princess Transcendent. The betrayal was absolute.

Before shock could harden into paralysis, Ari'Ella surged forward as the traitor threw Veshdren to the ground. Lightning met God steel, light clashed against shadow as she struck at the betrayer. They

117

screamed with fury, their movements a terrible tempest. For a few breathless moments, the duel raged with un-contained ferocity. Fast, brutal, and unrelenting.

Then Ari'Ella forced Seralythan back and dropped to her knees beside the fallen princess, her hands glowing with desperate healing light as the other Tribunals who were still faithful moved as one against the one who had stabbed their sister Goddess in the back.

Black cloaks flared, chains of command and authority cracking like thunder as their divine seals ignited. Power seared the air, ancient words and forgotten names falling like hammers upon the traitor. The assassin, her Godblade still humming with spectral fire was overwhelmed and disarmed, her wrists were bound by spectral Tribunal shackles before she could strike again. Her body was seized, bones grinding under the sheer weight of the collective wrath of the fellow Tribunals.

As she rested in Ari'Ella's arms Veshdren'Ra's gaze wavered, her voice breaking with the weight of disbelief.

"I... wasn't expecting that. I should have... seen it coming."

The grand ice cavern shook as if the planet itself sought to bury the dying secret within it. But it was the traitor who had made plans of dismantling the secret armies. Explosions thundered through the ice, shattering ancient frozen walls into avalanches of shards and jagged spears that rained down. The command chamber splintered beneath the weight of the collapsing tide of frost, and Ari'Ella clutched Veshdren'Ra tighter, the crimson life of the Grand Master Tribunal, Princess Transcendent, heir to the throne, staining her arms as it spilled across the frost covered floor, the Godblade had done its job and Ari'Ella couldn't heal the damage.

Veshdren's lips trembled, her voice a ghost against the storm of destruction. "My sister... she cut deeper than any blade ever could."

Portals snapped open in the chamber like wounds in the fabric of reality, spilling light and shadow all at once. Out stepped divine warriors. More Tribunals clad in the cold fire of exacting retribution.

Their Singublades humming like streaks of lightning coiling around each other.

These weren't just any Tribunals. Their faces carried the lines and echoes of the betrayer's bloodline. Her children. Her heirs. They came not for conquest alone, but for retribution against a shattered oath. In defense of their mother who had carved her own sister's heart with betrayal.

Their eyes fixed upon Ari'Ella and the fading Veshdren cradled in her arms. The room became a crucible of chaotic conflict, ice chunks crashed down, stone split and shattered, lightning arcs seared the air with every swing.

The cavern convulsed, ice crashing down as faithful and disloyal Tribunals tore the chamber apart. Lightning split stone, Singublades screamed, and divine blood stained the frost and bodies piled up. These Tribunals loyal to the traitor were weaker and less trained, but their numbers continued to sweal and grow with every passing second.

Ari'Ella clutched Veshdren'Ra, the wound beyond healing. The princess's breath faltered as the chamber buckled. Ari'Ella rose, eyes burning, and split reality itself. A portal flared open, revealing the spires of a small hidden Peacekeeper base beyond on a far off world.

"Now!" she commanded. McMaster led the way as wounded Peacekeepers helped each other through. The faithful Tribunals held the line alongside Ari'Ella and Maris. Once everyone had escaped Ari'Ella and Maris used their combined powers to hold back the attackers as they retreated, carrying Veshdren'Ra into the dim light of this other world as fire and ice continued to devour the once grand secret citadel that Veshdren'Ra had spent centuries building.

A final flicker, and the portal sealed as quickly as it had formed. Almost complete silence followed for a few moments. Only the hum of Peacekeeper machines in the distance remained. The bloodied and broken survivors collected themselves, burdened with the fallen princess and their fractured hopes that might never be mended again.

Chapter Twenty-One:
ROAMING THE REPUBLICS

"Each Republic names itself free, yet every citizen carries chains: some forged of duty, some of greed, others of faith, and some of hope."

Zoephiria Vergaragas Morganvale Hendrix

Captain, United Resistance Front, Personal Journals circa 3,118 AD

Tria and Amarax left the courtroom together. As they exited the chamber, he felt like screaming in angry pious indignation, but held his mouth shut. He wished that he had a dark matter rifle so that he could punish the court right here and now for their role as figureheads within the Republics, leaders of heretics. For their role in imprisoning him for months. But his greater mission was more important, he had to focus on total victory over all the wayward lying vile deceivers who were trying to twist his mind and his fellow Legionaries towards their beliefs.

He had to focus on absolute total triumph. If he was ever going to return to the Dominion with his honor intact. And the possibility of endless future glory awaiting him once he was able to completely defeat all the heretics was too much of a reward to risk for a little momentary pleasure.

The thoughts of glory started to swirl in his mind and then thoughts of stealing the matter transporter popped into his conscious mind again. He slightly salivated at the thought of all the privilege he would receive if he were able to bring it to the Holy Duality. His Gods would be so very thankful that they might even bestow an important and high-ranking regency.

Amarax liked the idea of being a regent, especially a respected and feared one. A whole planet or sector under his own rule. Maybe his homeworld of Holy Mars, he liked that thought or even better Holy Orion. He pondered the possibilities, proclaiming it in his mind, Amarax Holy Regent of Mars or Amarax Grand Holy Regent and Lord Protector of Orion. Yes, he liked that much better.

He would love to be regent over Orion. It was one of the Duality's throne worlds and the secondary capital of their expansive empire. It was an especially important world, second only to Terra itself. Amarax thought that that would be the most glorious thing ever and those thoughts were clouding his vision, he saw himself on a throne in robes and armor suited for a regent.

In his distracted state of mind Amarax bumped into a group of three children, accidentally knocking them down onto the floor as he was imagining his reign on Orion, not paying any attention to where he was walking. He proceeded to slightly yell at them in his still pompously self-centered nature. Letting his true self show for a slight moment.

"You little Muggrats, how dare you run into me, do you have any idea who I am? In the Capital City you would be sent to the Holy factories for a month for such Muggbrained incompetence!"

The children who had fallen to the floor immediately apologized. Each expressing words of courtesy and kindness in their own way. The oldest expressed it first and then the second oldest and then the youngest.

"We're very sorry, we didn't mean to bump into you. Please forgive our rudeness."

"Yes, we're sorry."

"Very sorry."

They were deeply sorry for hitting into him even though it wasn't really their faults. But they had all been raised to be kind. No matter what. After hearing their innocent sounding apologetic filled voices Amarax refocused and realized he had failed in his feigned newfound personality of goodness and kindness. He knew that he needed to fake harder, hoping that he could recover from this verbal blunder and that Tria would overlook it. He reached down and helped the children up by gently holding their hands and forearms.

"No, no, I'm the one who should be sorry. Please pardon my shameful rudeness. I don't know what got over me. I hope you can forgive me for my lack of manners. I'm trying to be a better person, but none of us are perfect. I come from a very bad place and these wonderful people here are trying to help me."

121

One of the children replied after slightly brushing off her clothes with her hands, she looked like the oldest of the group, probably nine or ten years old.

"Of course, sir. All is forgiven, no worries at all. Hope you have a good day and good luck becoming a better person, just keep trying and never give up. Sorry, but we have to go to school now, we're already late. Goodbye for now, let the truth be your guide."

Amarax was a bit befuddled by the politeness of the child as they walked away. Not a single scream or yell. Just pure kindness and it was his fault to begin with, he had knocked them over. He appreciated the kindness even if he didn't fully grasp the full concept yet. Little seeds of this new way of life were slowly being planted into his heart and subconscious. Amarax asked Tria about the children.

"Tria, I was wondering about those children, they were so kind, very odd for children to be so disciplined and collected. What kind of education do they receive? I bet you must have powerful neural inhibitors for them to be so controlled in their words and emotions."

"Amarax, I've told you before and you should know this by now. We don't allow any implants for control in the Republics, not even for prisoners. It is contrary to our laws, our codes of ethics and against the very idea of freedom in general. We outlawed control implants and any neural inhibitors that could be used to force people to act in any certain way altogether at the foundation of the Republics in the time of Maxamas and Zoephiria Hendrix. You should know that. You read many of their books, I would think that you'd remember our United Republics Constitution."

Amarax didn't really memorize those books or anything that he had seen, he didn't want to memorize it, but he tried to distract Tria from her questioning of his state of mind with more lies.

"Oh yes, I remember now, there is just so much information. It's hard to keep it all straight in my mind. Thank you for the reminder, I appreciate all the help you're giving to me, and I have given you nothing in return. It's very kind of you to be helping a former Dominion Grand Marshal."

With a slight nod of welcome Tria responded to Amarax.

"You're very welcome Amarax, I only strive to do what's right. What I hope others would do for me if I was in their place and in their same situations."

"That's a very enlightened way of thinking."

Tria nodded again as Amarax complimented her and they walked for a few moments until Amarax asked more questions about the children, because their free roaming by themselves fascinated him. In the Dominion children would almost always be escorted by some kind of adult, at least in the Capital District above and especially in the Holy Palace.

"I'm also wondering. Why would these children be in a courthouse in the first place? Why are they allowed to be in a court of law? It seems very impractical and unwise to let them roam the halls of justice freely."

"Everyone is free to go as they please, there are no restrictions on where citizens can go. The only exception to that rule is Peacekeeper defense installations. This place is not just a courthouse. It is practically everything that helps keep our society unified. It is one of the primary centers of our Republics. The courts of course, as you know, but also the United Congress and many of the main institutes of research are here as well. The national museums where we store our most precious relics and historical artifacts. The great archives of knowledge. All of humanities known history is here and another thing, probably one of the most important things for our society is the Temple of Religious Freedom, but to answer your question about the children, they were most likely headed to a research institute to learn from the scientists, to see them carrying out their experiments and to actually get to know the scientific method first hand. Our system of education is very free, our children learn from everything around them. It's a fluid way of learning. We don't just instruct them within the walled confines of a regular classroom. We've generally gone beyond that simplistic system."

"That's an interesting way of raising your youth, the Dominion is very different. I remember my short youthful education. I was always required to wear my cadet uniform within that dusky pillar lined classroom. All of us chanting our daily praises to the Duality and learning for three straight years with barely any rest. We didn't stop for even a single day. The main subject of course was the Holy Terran-Orion Bible and the Holy Chronicle of the Duality. I had to memorize both from cover to cover. If I forgot a single word in my chanting of those verses a daily spinal buzz would be administered from my neural inhibitor for days after any forgetting mistake. It was the same for all the other students. Our headmaster was not merciful, not one bit, she was very dedicated to the Dominion and the Duality, but that's in the past now, I'm pleased to have the chance to move on and focus on the future."

"I am so sorry that you had to endure that kind of torture. One day no other child will have to face that ever again. I know that one day the Dominion will fall, and their hideous backwards way of teaching will fall with them. I have faith that one day darkness will be defeated and that the light will reign supreme."

Amarax wanting her to trust him more agreed with her, speaking softly with a tone of total acceptance even though in his heart he hated what she had said.

"We can only hope, but it's going to take a lot of sacrifice and determination to see it through to the end. You seem ready to lead though. I'm sure that one day you'll get the task done."

"Not me, I'm just a captain, not a general or the president. I don't think I'll be accomplishing any sweeping victories on my own. But I intend to do everything that I can."

Amarax nodded in acknowledgement to what she had said and the two of them continued walking out of the majestic tower as they finished their conversation. Tria started heading over a different causeway from the one they entered from to another hexagonal MTN platform and Amarax followed. Once they were standing on it Tria activated her arm module control again as she did before, but this time in an entirely different combination.

After a few moments of waiting on the platform the same momentary flash of light occurred again. They were transported to another matter transfer platform that was identical to the one they were just standing on, but this one was hovering high in the sky like an observation deck in a different cavernous area. Amarax was shocked by what he saw, a city made of what looked like crystal in the distance. Shimmering and sparkling. Seemingly beaconing them to come.

A strange alien-looking jungle stretched for miles and miles. It blossomed in various directions all-around, twisting up around jutting rock faces. The plants and foliage were so varied in color and shape that it looked like a work of art. It was mesmerizing. Tria turned to him and spoke.

"This is the Republic of Peace, one of the eight Republic's within the coalition that is our United Free Republics of Earth. I come here often; this is probably my favorite Republic to visit. It's so serene and peaceful. The people here choose to live lives of contemplation, focusing their minds on the spiritual things. Exploring every metaphysical theory and idea that has ever been thought, experienced, or felt. They are an amazing people. They are the prime example of what I wish all the Republics stood for, they are so centered on nonviolence and serenity. An interesting fact about their political system, they have none locally. They just send representatives to the United Congress as needed and those who do serve in that capacity only serve for a month and are chosen by random ballot. They don't want to even entertain the possibility of corruption or greed infiltrating their society. Especially within politics. They think it distracts from the truly important things. Many of the most wonderful moments of my childhood come from this place, my family has owned a villa here for generations."

"Your family is blessed to have a villa in such a place. The existence of this place is a fascinating concept to accept. A whole society without a structure of government. How do they get anything done? Who enforces the laws? Who decides how the resources are divided among the people? I have so many questions and their city, it's definitely a sight to behold. I've never seen anything like it before. It projects majesty and splendor. How did they build it?" Amarax smiled slightly and said one last thing before letting Tria answer his many questions. "Seems like I'm overflowing with questions. I hope you don't mind."

Tria smiled and responded.

"Not at all, I don't mind at all. The details I can tell you later, I don't really want to get into it at the moment. Their way of doing things can become complicated to understand pretty quickly. Maybe it might be better if you read a book about them. There are many books about their way of doing things. It's not an easy lifestyle for everyone. There are many people throughout some of the other Republics, that mock them for their extreme pacifism and borderline obsession on rejecting worldly systems of doing things. But I like their way of doing things. Let's go I want to share another Republic, the Republic of Faith, somewhat the same as here, but a lot of difference in other ways."

They took the MTN to the Republic of Faith and Tria led Amarax through the shimmering gates of the Republic, her fingers brushing against the cool, polished stone that seemed to hum with quiet devotion. The air was thick with incense and the soft murmur of prayer, yet it carried a serenity that made even the harshest thoughts in Amarax's mind falter. Towering structures of glass and gold and thick polished stone rose like beacons, each one a testament to centuries of faith carefully woven into the very bones of this place.

"Every step here carries a deep history with it," Tria whispered, her voice reverent. "Not just of the people who call this place home, but of every soul that has ever sought meaning, guidance, or forgiveness."

Amarax's eyes scanned the city in awe. Mosques, synagogues, churches, temples, of every imaginable faith and creed, all standing in harmony, their bells, chants, and calls to prayer weaving together into a single, powerful symphony seeking the supernatural. The people moved with purpose but without haste, their eyes calm, their gestures deliberate. It was disciplined and purposeful, yet no one seemed oppressed or forced in their actions, they seemed happy, smiling, joyful, laughing.

"Does it… ever cause conflict?" Amarax asked, struggling to reconcile what he saw with the chaos he knew humanity could breed with relative faith and the fracturing of belief.

Tria shook her head slowly. "Debate exists, yes. Sometimes passion runs high. But here, faith is a guide, not a weapon. Each disagreement is a bridge, a chance to learn and grow. Everyone has come to understand that morality, justice, and compassion are stronger than fear, stronger than domination and forced faith."

A small child ran past them, carrying a basket of flowers, scattering petals along the marble walkways. Amarax's chest tightened at the simple act, something so ordinary yet so full of grace.

"You... live like this?" he asked, his voice low, almost breaking. "All your people?"

Tria met his gaze, her eyes soft but firm. "We try. We know that perfection is a myth. But even in imperfection, we choose harmony. We choose hope. It's not easy, and sometimes it's painful, but it's always worth it."

Amarax swallowed hard, feeling a rare vulnerability tug at him. His visions of conquest, of glory, of regency and dominance. All of it seemed hollow against the quiet power of this realm. A realm that did not command reverence and love for the divine through fear and power, but through the living truth of its principles.

Tria's eyes found his again, grounding him. "One day, maybe you'll see that strength is not always forged in war. Sometimes, it's forged in trust, in mercy, in understanding. Perhaps... you can carry a piece of this with you."

And in that moment, Amarax felt the weight of every battlefield, every victory, and every command he had ever carried in the name of the Duality and their holy empire. Against it, the gentle rhythm of this Republic's heartbeat was almost unbearable in its purity. And almost impossibly beautiful in its simplicity.

Even as his voice and outward attitude remained calm and collected, Amarax's mind roared with conflict. He imagined bending this heretical Republic to the will of the Holy Duality, as he had done with countless others. Yet the laughter of children, the devotion of worshippers of various beliefs, the gentle sway of a many different faiths coexisting without destruction. This free bloom of unbound hearts stabbed at him, a strange, painful awe.

Part of him longed to crush it all, to impose certainty and order, while another, forbidden part trembled with wonder, humbled and enraged at once. Desire and duty. Feelings and thoughts of domination and reverence for these heretics tore through him. Leaving him balanced on a knife's edge between control and surrender.

Chapter Twenty-Two:
TWILIGHT OF VESHDREN

"The dead rise again and again. In memory and in cause."

— From the Peacekeeper Codex of Peace

On the Peacekeeper outpost world of Ganduron III, Veshdren'Ra's body lay suspended in a Peacekeeper glass coffin, her form still radiant even in death. The chamber was cold and sterile, silver walls etched in intricate patterns. Light from the overhead strips washing her features in pale silver. She looked less like a fallen godly princess and more like a weapon sealed away, like her armor had been polished by eternity. Her face remained deceptively serene.

Around her, silence reigned. Peacekeepers stood at the perimeter alongside the faithful Tribunals, they all kept a respectful vigil with heads bowed, their once-brilliant seals were now dim and cracked. For numerous centuries, Veshdren had carried herself as untouchable. Now she was gone, and the rebellion itself felt as though it might unravel beside her.

Ari'Ella's hand rested on the coffin. Her palm trembled faintly against the glass, her breath fogging its surface.

"She was going to change everything," she said at last, voice hoarse but steady. "Every target, every Dominion weakness, every hidden route. We only knew them because she gave them to us. She carried knowledge that none of us can replace."

Maris Solvannis stood beside her, his staff planted firmly, both hands gripping it as if it were the only thing keeping him upright. His eyes traced the lifeless face within the coffin, then shifted away.

"Without her, the rebellion loses its sight. Its teeth. She was the one who was going to make the Dominion bleed. Now…" He trailed off, shaking his head.

"She was the rebellion's blade," Ari'Ella whispered. "And now it's broken."

The faithful Tribunals ignited their Singublades and raised them into the air towards the coffin as they spoke in unison.

"Eternal she remains. Our Goddess has left the now realms into the forever realms. Her light will never fade."

After the vigil was over, everyone left the mausoleum and sealed it shut, not yet sure of what to do with the body of the princess transcendent. The Tribunals stood watch over the tomb of their fallen divine princess. The Peacekeepers returned to their duties. Ari'Ella and Maris made their way through the base to a high lookout.

Maris drew in a slow breath. "We can't tell Tria. Not now. She's bound to Amarax, and their bond is the one thing that can anchor what's left of our movement. If she knows this truth, that Veshdren was struck down by her own blood. It would fracture what hope she has left."

Ari'Ella's gaze hardened. "You'd shield her with lies?"

"Not lies," Maris answered firmly. "Silence. A silence that keeps her path clear. She must build a future, not drown in what is already lost. If she falters, Amarax falters. If he falters, Tria falters. I can't see everything, but I do see that their path and journey is important."

The words hung between them, heavier than chains. "You're right. She needs hope more than ever. That's the only thing that can outlast this darkness."

They both stared at the horizon for a time and Maris broke the silence again, his voice low and heavy with foreboding. "We stand at a turning point. So many things are coming together. Something vast and destructive is coming, but I cannot yet see its shape."

Ari'Ella's eyes did not leave the horizon. "Then we prepare for the shadows that will come. And pray that the children of tomorrow can survive them."

They stood side by side, yet each carried their grief in solitude. The stars above did not comfort them. The rebellion's path was narrowing, and the light ahead was as fragile as a glass cup in the hands of impatient giants.

Chapter Twenty-Three:
MEETING THE MESSENGERS

"To glimpse love that can never be yours is to taste the full bitterness of a broken existence."

— Ari'Ella Dunesky, Personal Journals

Amarax and Tria headed back to the nearest MTN platform and Tria again pushed a sequence of buttons on her arm module and they were transported to another place. This time to a MTN platform that was on a rocky plateau surrounded by huge crystals. Gigantic and small crystals of various sizes and different shades of every color. The crystals were everywhere. It was a sea of crystalline magnificence.

Tria walked out into the field of monolithic crystals that almost looked like graceful angels to an imaginative or discerning mind, depending on how the viewer saw it. Amarax followed Tria as she walked through the forest of crystals; it was beyond amazing. He had seen crystal forests before, but nothing like this. These crystals almost seemed alive.

He could hear a strange sound that almost sounded like singing and vibrating music that seemed to be emanating out from the crystals and he thought he saw some of the crystals move and shift in structure. But he realized that wasn't likely. He was probably just seeing things. Crystals can't be alive, but the more he tried not seeing them move, the more he saw it.

Amarax had an expression of shock and apprehension, and Tria could see that. She tried to calm his tension with a little lightheartedness.

"Don't worry, they won't bite." She smiled and said a few more things. "Don't worry, you're not losing your mind. They're alive. Sentient living crystals. I use the word crystals to make it easier to understand, but they aren't really crystals in the typical sense. We don't exactly know how they do the things that they can do or even how they're alive, but they are absolutely sentient. There are many who accept that they're even smarter than we are."

"Crystals, smarter than humans? That seems like a Muggbrained theory if I ever heard one. You're probably just testing me. I would bet all my credits that this is just an optical illusion. A game of shadows and reflection."

"Like I said before, we don't trick people into believing false things. It's against our codes to be tricking people. It would cause mental pain and we don't want that. The only justifiable times to use illusion is in combat. Only in combat."

"Come on Tria, tell me the truth. This is a Muggjankkin trick, right?"

"No, not at all. These crystals are a part of the Republics, and we are a part of them. We call them Messengers of Light or just Messengers, and they've come to like the name. Zoephiria and Maxamas Hendrix saved their kind from Dominion annihilation ages ago and in return they have given us many gifts and assisted us in so many things, too many to tell you right now. But I'd like you to meet one, if you're okay with it. They might be able to help you."

Amarax thought for a moment and gave Tria a response, hoping that he could glean more knowledge and information to enact his plans.

"Of course. I would be pleased to meet one of these Messengers."

Tria walked through many thousands of dense crystal-like entities on small paths that seemed to be treaded down and compacted over thousands of years. As they walked many of the Messengers seemed to reach out towards Tria in what looked like expressive displays of adoration and affection. They seemed to retreat from Amarax in fear and fright. Amarax could feel their emotions as he walked by them, they seemed to emanate with an unnerving strength. After a few minutes they came to a circular crystal glen and at the center was one giant crystal that shifted all the colors of the rainbow.

Amarax felt a strange energy coming from this crystal. And was confused by it. There was an obvious power, a power that was a bit overwhelming. Tria walked up closely to the crystal and closed her eyes. Crystal branches came out like welcoming arms and seemed to hold onto Tria as she then held onto the extended arm like crystals and smiled. After a little while she opened her eyes as the crystalline

131

arms slowly and gently retracted and then she turned to Amarax and spoke.

"Tel'Mor'El would like to commune with you. If you're willing."

Amarax was intrigued, he walked up to Tria and responded as he walked.

"Of course. I would very much like to."

"I have to warn you. Communing with Messengers can be jarring. They sometimes show us things that we don't want to see. Sometimes they speak to us through people we know or knew, dead and living."

"I understand. I think I'll be alright. What do I need to do?"

"Just come closer and put your hand onto the surface."

The moment Amarax touched the surface of the crystal he found himself on the bridge of an Eternal Dominion Doomstar. It was definitely a jarring experience to find himself in such different surroundings so quickly. For a moment Amarax thought that he might have dreamt up the heretics and his captivity. Being there on the bridge of the Doomstar seemed so real.

He looked around the large bridge and didn't see anyone at first, it seemed to be empty, but after looking for awhile he saw a single person standing at the front of the bridge looking out into space down to a strange alien planet that seemed to be connected to other alien worlds in a giant technological web like structure that seemed to be holding the planets nearby each other. The person was wearing a Dominion Fleet Admiral uniform. Amarax walked up to them and as he got closer, he recognized who it was. It was his dead father. His father spoke as he approached, still looking out at the planet.

"You are confused, my son. A war rages on inside you."

Amarax stepped forwards until he was right next to his father who was most likely Tel'Mor'El the Messenger simply using the image of his father. Amarax responded to what he thought was a cryptic thing to say.

"You're mistaken Tel'Mor"El. There is no war raging on inside of me. I'm clear and free."

"You might be able to keep up your lies with Tria and her people. But lies will not work with me."

"I don't know what you're talking about."

"Yes you do. You know very well. Tell me, why do you keep lying to Tria? Why not tell her the truth about your still dedicated heart to your Duality and their Dominion?"

Amarax wanted to lie more, but he felt like he couldn't anymore in this singular moment. It was almost like he was being compelled to speak the truth.

"I need to keep lying so that I can have victory over these heretics. The Dominion must be supreme over everything and everyone. We cannot allow treason and heresy to ferment and flourish within Holy Terra, it would rip the empire apart, it would lead to our destruction."

"I can feel your hesitation. You're starting to question everything. Why not just give up your loyalties to the Duality and the Dominion right now? Why not join Tria? I can feel that you want to. Deep down you want to."

"I can't. It's not possible. I'm a Holy Grand Marshal, she's a captain of heretics. She's an agent of chaos and cataclysm. I am an instrument of order and of the ordained. I can't do as you say, even if I did want to."

"Your rank is a meaningless title in the grand fabric of the universe. Your Duality has forced upon you the use of words in such a childish way to justify the enslavement of souls and minds to something that is no longer beneficial for humanity."

"You sound just like Tria. You're just another heretic. This is probably a fanciful simulation to drive me to the end of my sanity and break me. It won't work. You cannot break me."

"I don't have to do anything. You're already breaking yourself. You're already shattering the walls of control. I can see into your soul and future. I see that you'll do great things in the time to come and change the very foundations of the Republics and the Dominion."

"Your sageful heretic words will not sway me. I am who I am. I will not change. I will never change."

As Amarax finished what he was saying he found himself somewhere else, he was no longer on the bridge of the Doomstar. He found himself in a place of darkness and then suddenly he started seeing so many strange things. Things that he couldn't understand. Many of the things that he had seen in his previous strange dreams he was seeing again now, but with more intensity.

He saw himself living a life he had never dared to dream. Quiet, unburdened, achingly normal. In that vision, he walked through golden fields at dusk, his hand entwined with Tria's as laughter rang out around them. Four children. His children, ran ahead, their voices like bells in the wind. Two of them bore the same faces as the young ones he had nearly collided with moments earlier in Unity Tower, as if fate itself were mocking him with glimpses of a future that could never be. Time unraveled before him like a tapestry woven from light and memory. He did not merely see it; he felt it. Every heartbeat, every tear of joy, every quiet evening spent under starlight. In the space of a blink, Amarax lived an entire lifetime, as though eternity had been poured into the cup of a single instant.

Time didn't pass; it opened. It spilled out before him like a tapestry of light and memory, every heartbeat its own eternity. He felt the weight of his youngest clinging to his neck, the warmth of Tria's lips brushing his cheek, the ache of joy so fierce it hurt. And beneath it all, the other truth. The one that tore him in two. This life was possible... but only if he turned his back on everything he had sworn to be.

Duty clashed with desire in a silent war within him. The soldier who had been forged in fire and obedience screamed that love was weakness, that destiny had already written his role in blood. But the man. The man buried deep beneath the armor. Begged to believe that mercy could be stronger than wrath, that one impossible choice could rewrite the stars. For the first time, Amarax did not know which side of himself would win. And that terrified him more than any battlefield ever had.

And then it shattered. The communion with Tel'Mor'El snapped like a thread pulled too tight, leaving him reeling. He staggered back, the crystalline glen spinning, his heart hammering with equal parts wonder and fury. How dare this being show him such a life? A life he could never claim, a love he could never hold without betrayal. The weight of those phantom years pressed upon his chest, and a storm of anger and grief rose inside him, complicating everything he thought he understood about himself.

Without a word of explanation, Amarax turned to Tria, his voice remained low and slightly unsteady. "I'm ready to go," he said firmly, though deep down his soul trembled. Tria looked at him, her brow furrowed in quiet concern. There was something different about him now. An unspoken wound behind his eyes, a question burning too deep for words. He wore his anger like invisible armor, but beneath it, there was a strange and silent longing. For a moment she considered asking, but the crystalline glen whispered with an otherworldly stillness, and she let it go.

Perhaps she was simply misreading him. Perhaps not. Either way, Amarax said nothing else, carrying his unanswered questions and unspoken ache like a secret fire, as they stepped away from the Messengers' realm and into the uncertain light of what may be waiting for him beyond his twisting doubts and pains.

Chapter Twenty-Four:
PRIDE BEFORE THE FALL

"Thou shall have no pride of oneself or your own thoughts that deceive, it is the death of any civilization, for pride belongs only in the divinity of the Holy Duality."

— Sixth Holy Commandment of the Duality

Above the world of Hallanor, a Throneship of the Duality loomed like a cathedral of eternity, its spires seemingly wreathed in fire and shadow, overlooking the carnage of fleets breaking against one another in the distance. Within the Grand Sanctum, the Duality stood gazing upon their warships advancing against rouge hives that had recently infested this part of the empire. No thrones needed, for They Themselves were throne and dominion over all, light and abyss entwined in one infinite form.

The Tribunal, Seralythan Veyorkor knelt before Them, forehead pressed to the cold obsidian floor, her voice a brittle deep whisper against the silence of the grand room.

"My Gods… My parents… I must tell you what I've done. But I have done it for you. For your truth. Your divinity. I have killed the Princess Transcendent. She had aligned herself with heretics. She had planned a campaign against you with a secret army that she had built over centuries."

The confession carried like a curse. For a long moment, only the thunder of the distant war filled the chamber reverberating the shields of the massive Godly warship. Then the Duality's gaze fell upon her. Two eternities converging, brighter than flame, darker than void.

"We knew of Veshdren's secret treachery," the God Emperor said, voice resonant as a collapsing star. The God Empress spoke next "We knew of her army that she had bred in the shadows, her defiance that was coiling like a virus. But it was not your place to act. She was Ours. A sanctified firstborn, one of the holy twins. You spilled blood that was not yours to spill and for that you must pay the price of your grave mistake."

The Tribunal pressed her face harder to the floor, trembling. "I thought it justice... I thought it duty to your will. Veshdren was following the lies of heretics. The heretics of Terra, of Venus, of Mars. The false Prophet of Mars, Maris Solvannis, was among her ranks."

The God Empress raised her voice in angry frustration at the Tribunal's justifications for her actions.

"We know. Do you think we are fools? Do you think we are simple mortals?" Her words cut like scripture broken. "You struck her down because of your pride. You struck her down, thinking it would bring you closer to the throne. The throne will never be yours. It was never going to be yours."

"No, I serve you. I did not do it for mysel—"

The God Emperor interrupted the quivering Tribunal. "Lies. Do you think we can't sense your deception. For this transgression, you shall be stripped of all Tribunal grace. No seals of power, no light of divinity, no mantle of honor will remain to you. You will not walk among the faithful again."

A low rumble echoed through the sanctum. The Godblade that she had been gifted long ago by her parents, the same one she had used to kill Veshdren'Ra vanished from her back and the obsidian floor beneath her began to open like a rip in the fabric of space, its glowing seams widening into a jagged circle. Light and shadow tore apart in the gap, and from within, a howling void rose. A chasm of energy leading to a world of the forsaken, where no Tribunal gift could survive its oppressive shifting energies.

The Tribunal's eyes went wide. She dared to lift her head, but before a plea could leave her lips, the floor beneath her completely gave way. With a cry swallowed by the abyss, she fell, her body vanishing into the seething black of a dark world. The portal sealed itself in an instant, the floor smooth once more, as though she had never existed.

From the edge of the chamber, Prince Transcendent Theldren'Ra surged forward, fury blazing across his face.

137

"You knew that Veshdren planned to betray you and you did nothing? She was raising an army against you and you did nothing? How is that Godly, how is that balance, when you banished me to die in the darkness against monsters and fake gods of torment. How is it balance and truth? How is it right to send me to my death for the smallest of failures and yet you did nothing to punish Veshdren for her planned betrayal against your power and authority?"

The God Emperor raised his voice louder than before, but spoke clearly and calmly.

"The balance is ours to weigh. Not yours to demand. Do you think we don't know about your own treachery, your own plans to take the throne from us?"

"I have no plans to take to the throne."

The God Empress opened a portal above the Godly Prince and out fell a dead twisted servant of the old gods of torment. Theldren jerked back surprised that his mother would bring such a grotesque and hideous thing into one of their inner sanctums but it was also a slight tremble of his guilt. The God Empress spoke.

"We know that you swore an oath to the old gods of torment to save yourself. We know that you didn't even try to kill any of them. The dead you brought back are clones. Duplicates of the same pretend god. You didn't even try to fight. You're a coward and liar. You're unworthy of the throne."

"You both gave me an impossible task. I would have died. It couldn't have been done. I wouldn't have lasted even a day. The oath I gave and the deal I made with those pretenders was out of necessity."

The God Emperor again raised his voice as he stepped towards his son.

"You wouldn't have died. We were keeping watch. It was a test and you failed. You failed entirely. We wouldn't have allowed you to die. Do you really think we don't love you? After all these thousands of years do you really think we would have left you to die? Are you that blinded by petty distractions and your own pride that you can't see the truth?"

"It was an unfair test. A test that should have never been given."

"And that's why you failed. You limit yourself. You think you know more than us? You're our son. You come from our blood. You're not above us. Have you learned nothing?"

"I've learned what I need to know."

The God Empress raised her voice as well as she walked closer to her son, annoyed by his pride-fullness.

"No, you haven't. You act like you know nothing. How could you be so weak, so distrustful? Your father and I love you. You should have known that. And yet you were willing to sell yourself and the future of our empire to those galactic snakes. You were willing to stab us in the back for promised power. You thought you could take our place so easily?"

"Maybe you're not worthy of the throne any longer. Maybe you need to step aside. If Veshdren and I both planned to betray you, what does that say about you?"

"You're an ungrateful, twisted child. Your weakness couldn't keep the empire together. Your father and I have kept order on billions of worlds. Can you not understand that? The responsibility of it. The burden of it. Can you not see that your words are childish and narrow-minded? Do you really think you could take our place?"

Theldren hesitated for a moment, but only a moment.

"Yes. I could. The empire is self-sustaining. It practically runs itself. You're just figure heads. Nothing you do actually matters on a cosmic scale."

The Emperor was getting angrier by the second. But he simply laughed at the arrogance of his son and then spoke.

"You see yourself equal to us. So be it. A test of your abilities then, to rule an empire."

The God Emperor looked to the God Empress and they smiled at each other nodding in agreement as they shared their thoughts between their minds and then the Empress spoke.

"Yes. A test of your abilities. You will be given another chance to prove yourself. All the outer colonies. All our bases and outposts in the CAD regions. Make an empire of it. Make it thrive. Make it powerful. If you could run our empire. You could make your own

139

empire. Go and make an empire for yourself. Show us what you're capable of and then maybe we will consider you worthy."

Theldren'Ra spat, a sound without joy. "I will not be an object of mockery," he said, dropping the facade. "If you wish to test me, test me here and now. Not by banishment to the border. I will not prove my worth by playing governor to worlds you deem expendable."

"Are you afraid you will fail? Are you scared you can't rise to the task? Are you incapable of creating an empire?"

Theldren'Ra's jaw tightened, his voice low but trembling with rage. "Afraid? No. I despise the insult. You dress exile as opportunity. You think me too blind to see the truth? The CAD regions are a graveyard, a wasteland of broken colonies that face enemies beyond number. You don't give me a test. You hand me a corpse and expect me to resurrect it." He stepped forward, daring to meet the Duality's gaze. "If I succeed, you will claim it as your own. If I fail, you will cast me into shadow and say it was my destiny. That is not a test. It is a slow execution."

The Emperor stepped forward closer to his son until he was face to face with him, his divine features thunderous.

"You are an ungrateful..." The God Emperor clenched his teeth, a deep anger exuding out with enough force to shatter stone into dust. "You were given eternity, power beyond stars, and you throw it back at us like a spoiled infant! We have loved you for thousands of years and this is how you repay us..." The emperor's hand raised, lightning gathering at his fingertips. "Perhaps we should end you now, before your arrogance rots the throne further."

Theldren met his father's rage without flinching, ready to accept fire or exile, but never an ounce of shame for his own pride. The God Emperor closed his eyes and closed his hand, the lightning and energy dissipating as every tense second passed. He lowered his hand and spoke again after a few moments of silence.

"You will go to the CAD regions whether you like it or not. You will make a new empire of the outer colonies. Do not return to us without increasing the holdings of the Dominion in that region ten times what it is now. Your mother and I could achieve it within a matter of months. I don't care how long it takes you. You will do it. If not don't bother coming back to us. Do you understand?"

The Prince Transcendent's jaw clenched. "If you want measured victory, I will achieve it on your terms." He leaned close, voice low and lethal. "But know this: every colony I rebuild, every world I conquer, every civilization I assimilate, will carry my mark and my mark alone. And when I return, the throne will sit differently. I will not beg for your blessing. I will command it." He left with a vow that tasted like a poisonous deadly winter, cold and calculated, frigid and fanatical.

"He will learn," the Empress said flatly. "And she will learn as well. In the end one will prove themselves worthy of the crown we want to give them."

The Emperor gazed out again at the battle raging, voice low. "Their empires will collide, and only the stronger throne will rise from the ruins. Until then, we watch and wait."

Chapter Twenty-Five:
GOING TO THE MARKETPLACE

"In the marketplace, entire planets whisper their bargains through the hum of jumpdrive engines; starships dock like living creatures, their hulls glinting with stolen treasures, forbidden relics, and whispered promises. Every vibration of the recycled air carries rumors of alliances forged and betrayals waiting to ignite. Here, commerce is war, and war is commerce, and the pulse of the galaxy beats in every neon-lit alley, every hovering stall, every desperate plea for survival."

— Tales of the Celestial Bazaar

From the crystal glen, they took the MTN to the marketplace next. The marketplace was filled with thousands of busy business storefronts down many streets going out from the main square that was designed in a hexagonal shape just like the matter transfer platforms and the technology that adorned Peacekeeper armor. Towering stone and glass-like buildings that were covered with golden intricate weavings of artistic and architectural lines surrounded the square and streets. It was a busy scene of activity.

All the streets looked ancient. Oversized hexagonal stone pavers and lots of healthy moss between the cracks of the large hexagonal stones. Each piece was carved with a saying of wisdom or freedom. There were countless numbers of colorful stalls throughout the square. The whole marketplace was bustling in dense pedestrian traffic and numerous flying cars were whizzing above every few seconds. Amarax was confused by the fact that Tria had brought him here and asked her what they were doing there.

"What are we doing in a marketplace? I thought you would be taking me back to my cell by now. The court verdict said you would lose your position if I broke any serious law. Are you willing to risk your military glory and reputation for me? In your own words, I'm an evil Dominion Marshal."

"You deserve a second chance at life, a real chance, a life where you're free to make your own choices without the threat of death and punishment. I believe that anyone can change. It might take a very long time, but I have hope. Should I be worried that you'll break our laws? I thought you said you would try your best to abide by the ?"

"You have nothing to worry about, I will try my best. I'm just still confused by your willingness to help me. It just seems like a potential risk on your part. Most officers wouldn't risk their rank and glory for an enemy."

"I want to do everything I can to assist you in your recovery. I know that it's going to take a lot. It's going to take a whole lot of soul-searching for you to really change. But I'm willing to risk my career if there's even a little chance for you to break free of the Dominion and the Duality. If it's possible to help you, it's possible to help anyone in the Dominion."

"It still seems like a fantasy that an officer would be so dedicated to a mission of trying to change a Grand Marshal."

"It's personal to me. I want to rid the Earth of false gods. My two brothers were murdered by cultists of another supposed god and I never want anyone else to suffer as my parents and I have suffered. I will be with you Amarax until you shed all of your darkness. Maybe you'll be instrumental in stopping the Dominion and ending the Duality's rule. I know that's a fanciful notion, but I like to think positively about the future."

Amarax continued his agreeing fakeness, but there was a hint of rising sincerity deep within his heart that he would not allow to take hold in his mind.

"Darkness can make people do terrible things, I'm very sorry that you lost your brothers to a false god, I wish I could reverse time to bring them back for you and your family."

Tria slightly tilted her head down, remembering her brothers and their deaths, Amarax seeing her pain continued talking, wanting her to forget it in the moment. Even in his still Dominion-centered mindset, he didn't like seeing her in pain. With the Dominion implants out, he had a new sense of emotional caring that was slowly forming. He was also falling in love with her, especially after living a whole life with her in that vision that Tel'Mor'El had projected into his mind, but even with that powerful vision he still wasn't ready to accept his true feelings.

"I'm very grateful that you'll be the one to help me through my journey out of evil and into a new way of being that's centered on life without the chaos of the Duality and their twisted darkness. I know that you'll be a powerful guide for me to reach towards the light that you speak of."

Tria raised her head from thinking about the death of her brothers and slightly smiled at Amarax and his words of encouraging goodness. Even though they were mostly hollow words coming from a still mostly hollow heart, it still meant a great deal to her in the moment. Once he saw her smile and he smiled back he asked her a question about his current state of freedom.

"This new freedom here in this strange new world is definitely something to be celebrated and thankful for. I am filled with gratitude that you're risking so much for me. I will try and do my best to change. This roaming pass as you said in court, am I really free to roam as I please, is it true roaming, true freedom of travel anywhere?"

"Yes you'll be totally free to roam anywhere that you'd like to go as long as our robot chaperones and I are with you. I'm sure this concept of freedom after imprisonment is probably hard to comprehend, but you'll get used to it. Now let's go get you some new clothes. That's why we're here at the marketplace. I figured you could use a new set. We can't be letting you go around in a prison uniform. I don't think my fellow citizens would appreciate it for very long. Now come on, let's get you something, there's a fine shop just on the other side of the square."

Tria started walking towards a shop on the far side of the marketplace, Amarax followed very close behind and his three assigned security robots followed him through all the commotion and trading chaos, it was such a lively place, full of life, wares and goods of all varieties were being bought and sold, everyone was wearing an endless assortment of intricate and simple clothing, an endless array of culture was being displayed all around. It looked like people were wearing their feelings.

It was a very strange place for Amarax to be. It was very different from any market he had ever seen anywhere in the Dominion. Throughout this lively and festive market there was not a single announcement about military victories or daily prayer reminders. Not one list of the glorified dead or hovering holographic ads for God Empress and God Emperor Memorabilia following subjects around like vultures ready to attack just like all the other markets he had ever been to in the Dominion. Here, Amarax could only hear the chatter and laughter of contented sounding people.

The cheerful buzz of thousands bartering and laughing jarred his senses. With the Dominion implants gone, Amarax was beginning to think freely—and in that fragile new clarity, he wondered if these people truly were heretics. They didn't seem like it. But they had to be. The Holy Terran-Orion Bible, the Chronicle of the Duality, even the Prince Transcendent had declared it so. To question the Duality was heresy. That truth had been drilled into him since birth.

As they moved through the crowded marketplace, doubt crept back in. Maybe these people weren't heretics at all. He quickly shoved the thought away. The holy books said otherwise, and Terranism demanded obedience. Any feelings of sympathy were lies—lies planted by enemies of the Empire. He had to stay focused on the mission.

But the scents—spices, herbs, aromas he'd never known. Nearly broke his control. The air was thick with wonder, and for a moment, he wanted to chase each smell and breathe it in again and again. He restrained himself. Tria moved ahead quickly in her power armor, unfazed by it all. She had grown up here. To her, the magic of it was just routine.

After a few moments they reached the other side of the marketplace and Tria walked into a storefront that was in a building which was futuristic art deco in style and looked like it had been there for over a thousand years. Its silver like exterior with multiple artistic figures jutting out was faded, but still breathtakingly artistic in their design. Amarax followed her inside, there were all kinds and styles of clothing on display, the various designs were being holographically projected in a continuous changing loop. Far more variety than the average and most common wear in the Dominion: grey, black, and red tunic style suits that practically everyone wore most days.

These clothes of the heretics were so varied in style, it was hard to choose. Amarax asked Tria to pick something out for him, he wasn't used to these styles or what was customary to wear in the Republics. She looked for a few moments and chose an outfit, a dark blue outfit, with different shades of blue and a brown leather looking jacket, with a pair of black stylish boots.

She gestured to the changing rooms that were in the back of the store and told Amarax what was there. He went back to the rooms to change and as he went in a robot voice asked him if he was ready to change and he said "Yes" a scanning array came down and his prison uniform came apart and disappeared without so much as a rip or tear, the cloth just coming apart like a conglomeration of connected magnets and vanishing into thin air. Then his new clothes started to appear on his body in the same way. A smooth almost seamless transition. Once their task was done, the scanners and matter transfer projectors disappeared back into the ceiling.

The intricate outfit was loose at first, but after a few seconds it adjusted by itself and formed precisely around his body to feel perfectly comfortable. As Amarax walked out of the room in his new attire Tria complemented him.

"That's much better, definitely a thousand times better than that old prison uniform. It suits you very well. I hope that you'll like it."

"Thank you very much Tria, I appreciate it. It's very comfortable. I do like it. There's nothing quite like it in the Dominion. It's nice to have something new and out of the ordinary."

"I'm glad you like it. If you're okay with it, let's head to my parents' house. They've agreed to be part of your rehabilitation. You can stay with us until you have fully acclimated to your new life here and hopefully one day be allowed to be on your own, without the need for any extra security constantly following you around."

"That would be fine, I look forward to meeting your parents, I'm sure they're both amazing people."

Amarax and Tria headed out of the store. Tria thanked the robotic store attendant on the way out and the robot reciprocated in return. Thanking her in return for the purchase, wishing her a fine day. The two of them walked down a store-lined street for a couple of hours, chatting about all the sights and landmarks in the city.

Tria explained a few of the basic facts about the city and its history. Telling Amarax about the current festival and celebration of "Freedom and Liberty" that's why the markets were so busy and bustling with activity. The celebration was once a year and lasted for weeks. Focusing on and appreciating the liberty of the Republics and the relatively overwhelming freedom that everyone enjoyed.

The celebration was important to help everyone appreciate what they had in the present and what had happened in the past to bring them to this point. It was an important part of what made Tria's home what it was. Which was a vibrant and diverse majority human society that treated everyone with dignity and respect. At least compared to galactic standards.

Especially when compared to the Dominion, or the chaotic anarchy of the CAD Regions, and the Edgeworlders who lived without any formal laws, their chaotic society relying on fluctuating codes that changed with the whims of every changing leader.

Within the entire Milky Way Galaxy, the only other power that could even come close to any comparisons to the United Free Republics of Earth would be the New Earth Union and some of its member states, but they had their obvious and silent flaws as all civilizations do.

Amidst the laughter and vibrant light, the world felt vast and uncharted. A quiet hum of possibility rippled through the air, beneath the pulse of celebration. For the first time, the future seemed not like a distant threat, but an open horizon. No promises, no guarantees. Just the breath of freedom, a call that stirred the spirit. The past was respected but it didn't hold anyone prisoner; this was a place where choices could be made anew. In the midst of it all, something shifted. Fragile, uncertain, yet undeniably real.

Chapter Twenty-Six:
RISE BEFORE THE DAWN

"Every beginning trembles beneath the echo of endings."

— Zeetarian Proverb

Maris Solvannis leaned over the holomap, tracing the star systems of the outer colonies with a measured finger. The glow of distant worlds cast faint reflections on his stern face. Ari'Ella Dunesky stood beside him, arms crossed, dreadlocks swaying with the subtle hum of the Peacekeeper base's ventilation.

"The rebellion is ready," Maris said, his voice low but certain. "Once we hit the first few supply depots, the Dominion won't know what hit them. Our forces in the outer colonies are trained, supplied, and... most importantly, loyal to the cause."

Ari'Ella's eyes narrowed as she scanned the projection. "Loyal, yes. But disciplined? Focused? The Dominion's outer colonies are fractured, but the people are wary. They've seen too many false promises. One mistake, Maris... one misstep, and this new effort to free the people from the Duality will collapse."

He nodded. "We've accounted for almost all possibilities. We have operatives in every sector ready to finish what we start. Communication lines are already secured. What could go wrong?"

Before Ari'Ella could answer, a sharp alarm shrieked through the command room, echoing across metal halls like a blade scraping stone. Red lights pulsed along the corridors. Both of them instinctively drew closer to the console.

"Movement detected," the automated voice announced, "Mausoleum Sector. Unauthorized presence in Veshdren'Ra's resting chamber."

Maris's eyes flickered to Ari'Ella. "That can't be... the area is sealed. No one should be down there."

"Let's go see what it is," Ari'Ella said, already moving, her tone brisk but tight with unease.

The two of them, were joined by a contingent of Veshdren'Ra's still-loyal Tribunals, and they moved through the silent halls of the mausoleum, unlocking bulkheads as they proceeded. The air was cold, unnaturally so, and carried a faint metallic tang. The walls of silver carved metal reflected their determined faces, as though it was watching their approach.

They reached her chamber at the center. Veshdren'Ra's glass coffin gleamed in the dim lights, untouched, pristine. Her body still lifeless, her hands folded over her chest like a statue. The Tribunals lowered their heads, reverent, silent.

Ari'Ella's hand rested on the glass. "Nothing," she whispered. "There's no one here..."

Then a voice. Soft, measured, but unmistakably Veshdren, broke the silence.

"I'm not going to let myself die so easily."

Every eye snapped toward the sound. The glass shimmered. Shadows bent unnaturally, and a figure emerged from the other side of the coffin. Not the original Veshdren. But another Veshdren. Identical to the one that was dead in the glass coffin but alive, vibrant, her eyes alight with the same icy fire. The contours of her face were perfect, but there was a subtle unnaturalness in her movements, a fluidity almost too perfect.

Maris took a cautious step forward. "What are you?"

Veshdren. This new Veshdren. Smiled, a thin line of defiance curling at her lips.

"I couldn't allow my legacy to end with a single betrayal. I have prepared for this moment long ago. I cloned myself. I inhabited a new vessel. My untimely death... was never going to be the end of me."

Ari'Ella's brow furrowed, and she glanced at the loyal Tribunals. Their faces were taut with tension, awe, and confusion. "You... this body..." Ari'Ella began, voice steady but incredulous.

Veshdren stepped forward, hands brushing the glass coffin as though paying silent respect to her previous self. "This body," she said, "is mine. But my mind... my will... my plans are eternal. I refused to be buried by the sins of a single traitor. The revolution, the vision, it cannot fail."

Maris's jaw tightened. "Is it actually you, or a basic fake copy of the original? How can we trust you?"

Veshdren's eyes glimmered like shards of starfire. "In time you'll come to trust me again. I will not wait for the universe to decide my relevance. I will continue to carve it from the flesh of existence myself."

Ari'Ella's fingers brushed the coffin again, a faint tremor running through her hand. "Then we have a new problem... or perhaps, a new ally. Time will tell which."

Veshdren's smile widened, the air around her seeming to hum with power. "Indeed. But remember this... nothing, not death, not betrayal, not the Duality... will stop me from ensuring my vision comes to pass."

The mausoleum, once silent and cold, thrummed with a new energy. Glass sparkled, shadows danced, and in the center, the reborn Veshdren'Ra stood, alive, calculating, and still as infinitely dangerous as she had always been.

Ari'Ella and Maris exchanged glances. Both knew the future had just grown a little bit more complicated. For they both knew that if this secret was kept from them, what other secrets did Veshdren'Ra have up her sleeves.

Chapter Twenty-Seven

A SHATTERED PEACE

"A single flame of division alone isn't harmful, but when that singular flame becomes a raging fire, it can lead to the downfall of an entire society. We cannot allow the little single flame of division to turn into a raging fire that will shatter the Republics, we must remain as one."

Zoephiria Vergaragas Morganvale Hendrix

Captain, United Resistance Front, circa 3,125 AD

A blast rippled through the quiet street where Tria and Amarax were walking, abruptly ending their conversation. The shockwave knocked Amarax and his three security robots to the ground, and even Tria, in her powered Peacekeeper battle armor, was viciously thrown to the ground, landing her flatly on her back.

The shockwave came from a nearby Qmatter bomb. They could see that it had decimated several buildings a few blocks away. Many of the once regal structures had been turned to rubble in a matter of seconds. While on the ground trying to regain their senses from the ear ringing explosion, they could hear multiple detonations of other Qmatter bombs in the area and even Darkmatter-Antimatter-Shiftmatter (DAS) Plasma bombs.

Tria was the first to get up and as she looked around the rubble filled street, she saw many people bleeding and injured, she was furious with the callous nature of the attackers.

"Those evil Jankking devils! Inbreeded Muggjankking terrorist trash! Muggjankkin degenerates!"

Amarax slowly stood up as well and looked around at the same scene of devastation that had shaken Tria's heart. But it didn't really bother him as much as it had bothered her. He was drenched in the art of war and had experienced and been a tool in mindless and brutal killing for the majority of his life. Death was a second language to him. A few dead bodies and dying people around him didn't faze him much, at least it hadn't before this moment, but unexpectedly now he was feeling some pain within, seeing the suffering.

At this moment his surface thoughts were still mostly as callous as the terrorist attackers. In the moment of seeing devastation a part of him even wished he had more DAS-Plasma bombs and Qmatter explosives to blow up a few more heretics, just like these terrorists had done. Whoever these terrorists were, he was somewhat twistedly grateful that they had displaced and most likely killed many deniers of the Dominion's Godhead. It made his future job of destroying the rebel heretics just a little bit easier.

Those callous thoughts of total heretic annihilation were being challenged within his mind and heart. Inner thoughts of being wrong had already seeped into his subconscious mind many times before. Those dreams of regret and death were pressing harder and harder upon his moral compass.

These feelings of the moral light were even now starting to seep into his conscious and there was a battle raging within. Even though all of these thoughts were rolling around in his mind he allowed the darkness to win for now and focused on his mission of deception and tried to show feigned sympathy and caring for the heretics.

"Are you alright, Tria? What kind of Muggjankkers would do such a despicable thing? It's such a travesty that this could happen at all. They're cowards for not showing themselves. They're Muggrotten filthy snakes for killing the defenseless."

"Yes, I'm fine. It's most likely the sadistic and inhuman Cultists of Kronos, the same devils who murdered my two brothers years ago. They are a constant thorn in our side. They relentlessly attack us for no reason besides blind faith in their fake warlord god."

Tria didn't say anything else, her training kicked in, she rushed over to the other side of the street to an injured woman and her children, all bleeding heavily and near death, pieces of metal and stone sticking through their body. There was no time to wait for medical help or transport them to a Tranquility Center—they wouldn't survive that long. If something wasn't done immediately, it would be too late.

She quickly activated her Nano-Healing-Biogels or Nanohealgel or more simply Healgel (NHB) within her wrist module and injected large doses into them. She chose to help the children first. They were the most injured. She waited for the NHB to work and as she waited a strange sensation washed over her.

An eerie feeling that she was being watched. Her gaze instinctively shifted to the entrance of a nearby alleyway. An old-looking man stood there, dressed in a dark blue robe and a thick hood covering some of their face. His eyes fixed on her. His stare was unsettling. His face was unfamiliar. But his eyes seemed strangely familiar. She couldn't place where she had seen them before, but the recognition sent a shiver through her, as though his gaze was tormenting her.

Compelled to confront him, Tria stood and moved toward him, but the man quickly turned and disappeared into the alleyway, vanishing from sight. Tria hesitated for a moment, the lingering unease clouding her thoughts. She tried to refocus, but a burning sensation flared in her mind, sharp and invasive, like a Gravnail driving through her consciousness. She forced the feeling aside, turning her attention back to the injured.

After a few more minutes their wounds started to heal. The blood-covered skin dried and dissipated, flaking off like a snake's skin. All the burn marks covering their skin started to fade as new skin was formed and replaced the once damaged. Eventually, all of their injuries entirely disappeared.

Within just a handful of minutes, there were no longer any signs of injury. There was no evidence that they were so close to death besides their burnt and partly destroyed clothing. The mother thanked Tria and helped her children up, they walked away without a scratch.

Tria then used her Holocomm within her other wrist module to contact her parents to make sure they were alright; she was worried for their safety. They lived on the other side of the city in the Green District, but she was worried that their district might have been attacked as well. They answered Tria and assured her that they were alright. They were more concerned for the safety of their daughter, telling her to be safe and careful. She assured them back that she would be as safe as possible and would be home as soon as it was possible. She asked them to stay home, knowing that that would probably be the safest place from any possible future attacks.

Before they were able to say their goodbyes communications abruptly stopped. Tria tried multiple times to reconnect but was unable to re-establish the connection. She then tried to contact Peacekeeper Headquarters through main channels and then she tried various emergency channels, but was unable to connect to anyone, she knew this wasn't a normal disconnection. This must be a part of the cultist's attack, a disruption of the entire network. Tria was disturbed by this and verbally expressed her frustrations.

"Muggjankking great, the entire hologrid network is down, Muggjankking cultists."

Amarax knowing that she was annoyed by the current situation tried to reassure her, still wanting to grow a closer bond of trust.

"I'm sure that we'll get those cowards. They can't hide forever. We'll find them and stop them."

"Thank you Amarax, I hope so."

Even though Amarax was trying to grow the trust between them he couldn't help himself from asking Tria a question about this healing ability she had. He was somewhat in shock that Tria was able to heal others in such a miraculous and divine way, only the Holy Duality and their prodigy were able to heal like that. A part of him again felt like he might be having a delusion, but it was no delusion. What he saw was real and factual. It was yet another proof against the Duality's claimed divinity.

Amarax didn't want to think about what he just saw. He knew deep that the God Empress's and God Emperor's divinity was unquestionable. Maybe Tria was part of the Holy Family, it might be possible that she was partly a royal divine by blood. The God Emperor and God Empress both had many illegitimate children over the eons. Yes, she had to be a part of the divine bloodline. With those thoughts swirling in his mind Amarax brashly and uncunningly questioned Tria on what just happened while she continued to try to help others who were nearby.

"How in the galaxy did you save that woman and her children? Are you a descendant of the Duality? That's the only possible and logical answer. You must be a descendant of the Duality."

"No! Muggjankking no! I'm definitely not related to the Emperor or Empress, at least I hope not. It's just technology, it's a simple thing to us. We've had this knowledge for at least a couple thousand years now. It's saved many lives and can heal very serious wounds, but it can't bring us back from the dead. Even though I wish it could."

As Tria continued helping other injured people around them, injecting them with the Nano-Healing-Biogels (NHB) Amarax continued his shocked questioning.

"I don't know Tria, it seems fantastical and almost unbelievable that your people have this ability. The Duality and their children are the only ones that I know of that can heal so quickly and in the way that you just did. In the Dominion only a select few of the Duality's children and their descendants can directly heal those needing lifesaving intervention and they only heal within the Holy Temples. There is no healing outside of the temples except for the rare occasions during combat. Are you sure you aren't controlling my mind and showing me a shadow of reality?"

Tria became slightly annoyed and angry at Amarax and responded with a tone of slight disgust in the stress of the moment as she continued to help those around her.

"I can assure you; we're not controlling your mind in any way. We totally detest control. If you haven't already Muggjankking grasped that simple concept about us. Then start grasping it. Control is the downfall of humanity; only free choices will allow us to find peace. I'm sure the Duality will always only want control. If they really wanted to have this kind of healing technology their Scimancers could have invented techniques as advanced as this ages ago and it could have been used to help the masses throughout the Dominion, but the Duality is not interested in helping the masses. They use religion as a way to warp the minds of countless people for blind servitude. Religion, when wielded for evil purposes, simply to gain more power, more control, can become a tool of hell, solely interested in the subjugation of the free. When faith is freely chosen, it usually becomes a powerful tool for self-growth and discovery, guiding individuals toward deeper understanding and personal transformation."

"Yes, that's all fascinating, but I'm more interested in these powers you have. The power to stop death from coming. How does it work, and can anyone use it? It just seems like a magical and divine ability. I still think that you must be a descendent of the Emperor or Empress, a child of one of their children, you must be a Tribunal, this is all a mind game, maybe you're a descendent of one of the minor gods of Orion, these are the only possible answers."

"It would take all day to really explain how it works precisely through science and engineering, but this isn't the best time right now. I have to focus on my duty. I must help my fellow citizens. This attack has most likely injured many more people. The cultists haven't attacked this ruthlessly for centuries. There's just no time for me to explain it right now. There's no telling how many innocents have died. We need to head to the nearest Tranquility Center, I'm sure they'll need all the help they can get, come on let's go."

Tria and Amarax went to the nearest Tranquility Center, on the way there they saw so much destruction and death. The terrorists had carried out a terribly successful attack and precisely used the bombs to cause the most damage. It was total devastation. It looked like a great majority of the market district had been blown to pieces.

Almost every window was shattered. People were laying in the streets screaming for help, Tria and Amarax assisted anyone along the way as needed. It was a heart-breaking sight for Tria, she couldn't believe that they were able to do this, it seemed impossible that they could accomplish such a large strike. She had believed the reports that the terrorist threat was contained, this attack proved that theory of safety to be wrong.

The terrorists must have more sympathizers than what was previously thought. Tria began to come to the realization that The Republics needed to reassess the threat. The cult centered terrorists, had to have help to commit such large and catastrophic violence. She tried to understand who could have betrayed the Republics, but she was left without any definitive answers. She couldn't accept that anyone of high ranking within the Republics could betray the people in allowing such a horrendous attack.

After many hours of walking through ruble and helping countless victims of the attack along the way they reached the Market District Tranquility Center. It was badly damaged just like almost every other building in the area, but it was still mostly intact and currently being used entirely for the injured, as an ad hoc hospital.

Tria walked into the center with a compassionate determination to help in any way that she could. Amarax was right behind her in his typical callously pensive mindset. Focusing on betrayal and power, but even in that vicarious misalignment of spirit he continued to follow reluctantly and assist as many people as he could because he knew that it would allow him to gain more trust.

His plans of total conquest and victory over the heretics of these morally wayward Republics were still reeling in the back of his cerebral cortex. But he needed to wait for the right moment and now wasn't it. He wouldn't have any chance at all defeating the heretics at this moment in time, he needed an army.

In the once peaceful center, a place for community gatherings and happy celebrations, there was now children and adults screaming in pain, there were no moments of silence. Every room was filled to beyond overflow. Injured people laying on the floor on emergency mobile beds, some individuals leaning on walls holding their stomachs or faces or limbs in suffering. The attack left a horrendous amount of agonizing affliction for so many. It was a soulfully frigid and frightening sight to behold.

At almost the exact moment they walked into the center a medical doctor noticed them and implored Tria for her assistance, waving for them to come over.

"Oh, thank goodness a Republics Peacekeeper! Please come quickly. Do you have any Nanohealgel left?"

"There's not much left, but yes I do. I still have a little. Around 8 milliliters."

The doctor spoke quickly once she had heard that Tria had some Nano-Healing-Biogels, speaking so fast that they were almost bumbling over their words.

"Good, good. We'll need every single drop of it. I need you to administer just a tiny bit to everyone in the lobby and hallways,

0.0367 milliliters each. It's not going to fully heal them, but hopefully it'll stabilize them long enough until more supplies come. We're completely over capacity, this place is not a hospital, I have barely enough staff to help those who're already here, and I'm sure there will be many more. Please help them."

Without another word, Tria jumped into action to assist the people around her. Injecting single minute drops into each person's neck, having her injection system dispense the exact amount that the doctor had told her. The neck was one of the best and quickest routes of entry for the Biogels to begin the healing process. People stopped screaming as she injected them and as the doctor had said it started to stabilize them, but they still had noticeable injuries. After she had gone around the entire room and injected everyone the doctor expressed her gratitude for Tria's help.

"I'm so very thankful that you were here. We ran out of Biogels over thirty minutes ago. We're expecting more in a hospital transport that's on its way, but it won't be here for another fifteen minutes. They need to stop at other centers that are in greater need first. I just wish that the matter transfer systems weren't down. They've been disabled throughout the city. I heard through emergency channels that the attack has completely destabilized the entire matter transport grid, so I'm glad that you got here when you did. You saved a lot of lives today."

"Thank you very much doctor, I appreciate it. I was just doing my duty. I just hope this is the last of the attacks, I would hate to see more innocents suffer at the hands of these Muggjankking fiendish psychopaths."

"We've lost all connections to the Holocomm grid. Have you heard any word from Republic Peacekeeper Command on what's happening? I would think they would need every Peacekeeper searching for the culprits of this heinous crime."

"I haven't heard anything either, I've lost all connections too. But I'm sure that we'll catch these vile criminals before the end of the day. They won't get away with this unconscionable act. The Peacekeepers will find every last one of them and bring them to justice."

"I very much hope so, good luck in finding those evil sickos and thank you again for your assistance, it really has made a difference,

I'm sure that the rest of the victims here will be fine until the emergency shuttles arrive. Thank you again. Peace and prosperity to you."

"The same to you doctor, stay strong."

Tria and Amarax left the damaged Tranquility Center which was filled with so much suffering. But Tria hoped with all of her heart, that all those people she had used the last of her NHB on would make a full recovery, especially once they received full doses of the healing substance. Amarax and Tria continued through the rest of the damaged and sometimes in ruins market district that was still smoldering and on fire, continually helping whoever they could in whatever way they could, but many times it was useless without NHB.

Helping the many people she crossed paths with was becoming emotionally and physically straining, Tria was beginning to feel exhausted. On top of the strain of trying to handle and fix this chaos and death, the added exhaustion from her extra hard and grueling Peacekeeper training over the last few weeks was catching up to her. No one was expecting something so horrible to happen, and Peacekeeper Command had ordered new training above and beyond normal, trying to stay prepared for the Dominion.

By this time many other Peacekeepers and emergency personnel of the Tranquility Corp were flooding into the district to assist the injured and repair what they could.

Amid the chaotic response, an emergency android dusted Amarax off, mended his attire, and moved on—efficient, indifferent, as the emergency operations raged on. Attending to the next person, with the same efficiency.

Dedicated teams of passionate engineers were frantically trying to repair the many damaged areas and structurally reinforce areas that seemed to be a danger. They brought in mobile matter transfer pads for anyone who needed quick evacuation and or anyone that may need to leave the area to another district for personal reasons. Personal and commercial hovercars weren't allowed anywhere near the district until an investigation could be completed.

All the hard-working teams would continue to do their duty for as long as was required of them, Tria especially wanted to do everything she could, but even Peacekeepers need breaks from time to time. Tria wanted to stay and help, even to the point of collapse, but was cordially and understandably ordered to leave and get some rest by a Tranquility Commissioner, who noticed the exhaustion affecting her performance.

Knowing that she wouldn't be much help in her current condition and understanding that she couldn't do it all on her own. Having the reassurance of the Commissioner that she had already done her duty as best as she could she agreed with them, not putting up a fight or disagreeing, she left with Amarax and the bots. They used one of the mobile matter transfer pads, they teleported to the Green District, where her family home was.

Their journey, once guided by a hope for new beginnings, had been shattered by mindless violence against the innocent. What lay ahead now? The peaceful path they sought felt like a distant dream, eclipsed by the harsh reality that had torn through Unum. Could anything ever return to the way it was? Or had the world of this once idyllic place changed irreparably, leaving them to navigate a new, uncertain future? The silence around them spoke more than any words ever could. Shattered, oppressive, and saturated with the ache of all that had been lost.

Chapter Twenty-Eight:
THELDREN'S CRUSADE

"There was no promise of paradise, only proof of power."

— Koradon Proverb

The void shuddered as millions of Dominion banners unfurled across the CAD regions, banners not of royalty or Duality, but of conquest and war. Warships and Legions once scattered in disarray, their admirals and generals content with fractured command, now bent to the will of one voice. Theldren'Ra. His decree from his Throneship had been simple, thunderous, and undeniable to anyone who heard it.

"All fleets, all legions, converge to me. All power is mine to command. My Holy Conquest begins today! Stars will be silenced, defiant worlds will burn, all heretics will pay for their evilness with their lives! Transcendence wills it!"

Once he was done sending out his orders, fleets began to jump around his Throneship. Then the secure holocomm link flared across the Throneship's bridge, a Grand Admiral's seal pulsing insistently. A connection was opened and the console projected a holographic image: Grand Admiral Raal Meros, carved by centuries of command in this forsaken part of the galaxy, eyes sharp and unyielding, one of the best within the Dominion admiralty.

"Prince Transcendent," he said, voice firm despite the tension, "I cannot obey this order. If I move my fleets from their designated defense positions to join your conquest, hundreds of colonies will be left undefended. Outposts, citizens, supply lines, they'll be vulnerable. I will not trade their lives for glory. My fleet must remain in reserve to continue their role in defense of the colonies."

A tense silence followed. Then the air on the Admiral's bridge shimmered, bending as if reality itself gave way. Theldren'Ra stepped through a slit of shadowed golden light, presence folding into form like golden silk. He did not speak immediately; at first he only looked.

"You refuse a direct command of an heir to the Godly throne? You would dare to question me?" His voice was calm, low, and lethal. "Loyalty is not argument. Obedience is not optional."

Before Meros could respond, Theldren'Ra raised a single hand. The Admiral's protest died mid-word. There was no blood, no fire. Only a thin wisp of vapor and dust where the man had stood. The bridge convulsed with stunned silence. Officers dropped to their knees, eyes pressed to the steel deck, hearts hammering against the weight of absolute authority.

The Prince Transcendent's gaze swept the bridge. "The next officer in line will take command of this fleet. Serve me well in loyalty. Or share the same fate as the admiral."

A tense hush filled the room. Fear and obedience intertwined, ensuring the fleet would now follow without question.

Theldren's crusade began like a storm breaking over brittle glass against anyone who refused to join his empire. Edgeworlders were the first to face his fury. Ragged ununified fleets, patched from centuries of salvage, met him in the burning haze of the Ravelin Nebula. They fought with desperation, each vessel a family's last hope. But desperation was nothing against Theldren's tide, their fleets fell in a matter of hours. The nebula ignited, its clouds painted in flame and wreckage.

When it finally cleared, not a single Edgeworlder remained unaffected. Names, bloodlines, histories. Many were erased, their ashes scattered into the void. The Edgeworlders scattered and retreated to their strongholds or surrendered and became servants to Theldren'Ra's will.

From there, the crusade spread like a wildfire across the cosmos with no horizon or end in sight.

Various pirate empires, which had ruled large parts of this broken chaotic part of the galaxy like feudal kings of ash, fell next. Fortresses hollowed into asteroids were cracked open like eggshells. Fleets of stolen vessels became graveyards of twisted hulls. Theldren made a spectacle of their downfall, broadcasting the executions of pirate lords across every frequency: their crowns of rust and bone torn from their heads before they were cast into the void. His words echoed like judgment.

"This is what awaits all false sovereigns. There is room for only one sovereign in the CAD regions."

Numerous cult enclaves came soon after, the zealots of shattered faiths chanting as fire consumed their sanctuaries. They welcomed death, but Theldren'Ra denied them any glory. Their idols were ground to dust, their sacred texts burned, their followers scattered and silenced until not even their names could cling to memory.

Scattered corporate zones, swollen with luxury and decadence, thought credits and mercenaries could buy survival in the wilds of this unruly region. But their wealth in the end meant nothing if they didn't submit to Theldren's rule. The towers of those who denied his divinity toppled into seas of fire. Factories became furnaces filled with screaming workers as Theldren'Ra ordered them burned alive inside the machines they once tended. He did not ransom their wealth. He salted it, burned it, until there was no longer any doubt of his power.

The CAD regions bled. Within a matter of days thousands of systems became a theater for Theldren's wrath, each conquest more brutal than the last. What had begun as a consolidation of power twisted into an orgy of annihilation, his fleets moving with fanatical precision, his Legions with the fervor of zealots drunk on fear and triumph. Dark zones, where navigation itself was a gamble, were no refuge. Theldren's legions hunted down any heretic who thought shadow could shield them. Whole stations were dragged from orbit, their screaming inhabitants chained together and hurled into the star they once worshiped as life. No mercy was granted, no bargains struck with any who denied his divine authority. His word had become absolute law, and defiance was erased like a blemish from heavenly stone.

On the most remote farthest Dominion colony world of Veylosiana, whose people had begged for neutrality in this galactic conquest, he descended in person with his thousands of fellow

Tribunals who were absolutely loyal to him. Theldren'Ra walked the capital's streets with his golden cloak trailing ash, and by a mere gesture of his hand the city's heart erupted in molten ruin.

"Neutrality," he said to the survivors crawling in the rubble, "is heresy in disguise." Then he ordered the surviving citizens bound to their own spires and set aflame, their screams rising higher than the towers as the flames consumed them.

Everywhere his legions tread, his banner replaced shattered sovereignty into a single entity, no protectorates or independent zones were allowed under his rule. Yet it was not conquest that lingered in the whispers of survivors. It was the cruelty, the deliberate spectacle of Theldren's campaign. Pirate crowns shattered on public broadcasts. Cult prophets tortured in chains. Corporate magnates drowned in their own vats of luxury wine. Entire world split in two, shattered at their core, their husks exploding into fragments, before the holofeeds cut to static.

Word spread faster than his fleets could burn: the Prince Transcendent was no longer a beloved heir, but a tyrant; not a savior, but the living embodiment of everyone's darkest nightmares.

And still, Theldren was unsatisfied. In the temple of his Throneship, surrounded by the glow of dying worlds cast upon holoprojection screens reflecting against the golden glory of massive statues of his parents, the Holy Duality, that stood in front of him, he spoke with quiet deep venom.

"You think me unworthy. You dream of another heir. I will show you what worth truly is. I will build an empire in blood, one that no God can deny. And when I return, you will kneel to me."

Theldren raised a hand towards the golden effigies and golden bolts of lightning consumed them, shattering and collapsing in a storm of shards that rang against the temple floor. Theldren'Ra stood still, dust clinging to every fold of his robes. He lowered his hand, breath sharp, voice colder than the void.

"I will not live as a reflection of your rot. I will reign forever as your replacement."

Chapter Twenty-Nine:
SILENCE BRINGS SILENCE

"Do not let yourself doubt that the future holds both pain and lies, joys and hope, all colliding into madness and clarity."

— Luminarian Proverb

Across the central table of the command center of the Peacekeeper base, the holomap pulsed like an open wound: red expanses spreading inexorably where once fragile constellations of blue had marked living networks of assets ready to fight for independence. Each extinguished light was not merely a failure of communication but the obliteration of the revolution itself.

Veshdren stood motionless at the map's edge, her palms anchored to the alloy surface as though holding back the weight of inevitability. Her silence had the gravity of time; when she spoke, it was with a precision that cut away all pretense.

"They aren't simply quiet. They're erased. Entire cells, entire systems, wiped from existence. This isn't cosmic energy interference or raids by maniacs. This is planned."

The pronouncement reverberated. Ari'Ella, angular and severe, inclined her head toward the bleeding holographic cartography. Her words were scalpel-sharp.

"Then it's not entropy we face, but design. A singular hand reshaping the CAD regions, with neither hesitation nor limit."

Maris leaned forward into the light, its red glow casting his scarred features into a brutal relief. His voice was low, almost angelic in tone, but thrummed with restrained fury.

"These weren't just allies. I have come to know many of them. Their voices, their faces. Now there's no trace. No echo. We have to stop whoever is doing this, or everything we've done will fracture into dust. The outer colonies was our next best choice to ignite the revolution for a better future, but now, what do we have?"

An older Peacekeeper general, commander of the base, Kendol Raios, spoke next, his voice scarred as his skin.

"If the freedom fighters in the CAD regions are dead, then we must hide again and take our time to reorganize before we're consumed whole. Survival demands it. If even survival remains possible."

The response came immediately and visceral in its intensity. Braxxan Lume, the Umber leader of Venus who had miraculously survived the High Lords wrath and was extracted to safety. His eyes raged like burning coals against the Raios, he spat words of anger.

"Survival? That is cowardice draped in strategy. To crawl into the shadows is to endorse our own extinction. Better to burn the stars themselves than to vanish unheard. Revolution is not choice; it is our obligation now to the dead."

A sharp intake of breath from Sirius Malvak stirred the room. Her voice was deliberate and ascetic, offering an Edgeworlder counterpoint like frigid cold steel.

"Revolution without knowledge is Jankking ritual suicide. To march blind against what we cannot yet name like Muggjankking Muggrats into an acid bath will bring us the silence we dread. Strategy against the unknown demands patience, not Jankking theater. I jankking won't lead my fellow Edgeworlders into the jaws of death for the possibility of nothing. You're all Muggbrained Jankking fools if you think we Edgeworlders are that stupid."

Tarin Vos, the youngest among them, a Dominion colonist who had joined the cause of independence trembled but pressed forward, his words desperate, almost prayerful.

"Silence is already defeat. If death is certain, then let it be loud enough to rattle the fabric of existence itself. Let our ending be remembered for all time. Sirius I would think you'd want to rescue your fellow Edgeworlders. We've lost all contact, is it logic or fear that drives you?"

Sirius Malvak responded in anger.

"Go jankk yourself Tarin, I don't fear anything! You're just a child! I jankking have lived through more than what you could ever jankking imagine! So muggfrakking jankk yourself!"

Tarin responded to Sirius with an equal amount of anger.

"No! You go jankk yourself! You jankking muggrat!"

Sirius lunged toward the young colonist, but was held back by her fellow Edgeworlders. General Raios was reserved in his tone but agreed with her.

"Please, we can't be fighting like this. We have to focus on the challenge at hand. I still think we need to be patient and take out time. Send some robotic surveys."

Braxxan Lume hit the holotable and yelled out in fustration.

"Robotic surveys? We're not on a scientific survey! We need to send all out forces into the CAD regions and hopefully save some! Maybe there are some survivors! We must go now with everything we have!"

Ari'Ella said.

"It's not wise to commit everything we have. We should send just a small contingent."

Maris spoke next, agreeing with Ari'Ella.

"Ari'Ella is right. We can't send everyone. It would be unwise. We might be sending all of them to their deaths."

Tarin said.

"You're all jankking cowards! You're all muggrats!"

The command center vibrated under the clash of ideologies, as argiuments erupted. Survival against sacrifice, calculation against fervor. The voices collided like tectonic plates, each grinding against the other with sparks of conviction and despair.

Veshdren'Ra raised her head at last. Authority emanated in the stillness that followed, as if even the holomap's crimson pulses paused in deference.

"Enough."

The chamber fell into an absolute hush. Her gaze traveled deliberately from one leader to the next, her silence binding them in judgment before she finally spoke again, her tone slow, deliberate, inexorable.

"Anger is a hollow shield. Despair a coward's refuge. What has happened in the CAD regions is not chaos but orchestration. A powerful will has moved there. Systematic, merciless, beyond the scale of any insurgency. We are not witnessing collapse. We are witnessing the birth of a new empire."

Ari'Ella inclined her head slightly, her voice taut.

"Then truth becomes our only weapon. Its face. Its hand. Its weakness. Without it, we collapse as swiftly as the others."

Veshdren'Ra raised her voice to affirm the truth of her authority.

"My Tribunals and I will go to the CAD regions and discover what has happened. I will ensure our path forward is clear."

A new resolve had replaced debate, a truth sharper than any declaration. Veshdren would lead the way through the darkness ahead. Silence fell like stone. What had been argument now bent toward Veshdren'Ra, for her word was no longer counsel but law.

One ship. A chosen few. No spectacle, only purpose. Her seal struck the holotable, and from her thoughts her Throneship was called, its approach flared like a scar across the screen, final and irrevocable. Within minutes her Throneship hovered in the sky above the base.

The leaders who were gathered bowed or nodded in silence, rage and grief bound by inevitability. The crimson map pulsed on, indifferent, as the stars beyond gave no witness. The mission was not hope, nor vengeance. It was a blade being driven into the unknowing dark. And the dark would answer.

Chapter Thirty:
TRIA'S CHILDHOOD HOME

We cannot allow our home to be controlled by darkness. Earth has become the cradle of a new free humanity. Thriving in secret. Far beneath the rule of tyranny above. We cannot allow that newly created cradle to be twisted into a vile place. We must continue to nourish these new Republics, until the Emperor and Empress are defeated. We must protect our home. We must protect our children.

Zoephiria Vergaragas Morganvale Hendrix,

Personal Journals, circa 3,116 AD

The Green District of Unum was peacefully serene compared to the practical warzone that they had just come from on the other side of the city. People were walking their pets and families were spending time together in the parks all around. The sounds of joyful birds sang in the air. A gentle rush of waterfalls could be heard in the background. Scents of fresh flowers of every kind filled the air. The intense aroma of the most lavish garden seemed to permeate every square inch of this district.

Long winding lanes of wide overgrown and yet manicured boulevards went out in all directions. Curving over and around the lush, forested rolling hills, the thoroughfares seemed to embrace the land, leading travelers through a tapestry of majestic towering trees and soft, undulating terrain that tickled the senses.

Homes of palatial grandeur peppered the hilltops in elegant art-deco neo-futurist neo-gothic facades reflecting the golden light of the artificial setting sun. Each gated estate was a masterpiece of architectural grace, a testament to the human need to express itself, statues and artistic installations surrounded the palace-like homes with gentle expression. The Green District seemed to be a practical utopia.

In the valleys, grand artistic installations were woven seamlessly into the landscape, blossoming with vibrant colors and shapes. Sculptures and fountains almost seemed to dance with the rhythm of the wind and water. Trees stood as silent guardians along crystalline streams, and the air itself seemed to hum with the promise of possibility and evident prosperity.

The Green District was filled with a harmonious blend of beautiful nature and creative design, where innovative creativity and natural beauty coexisted effortlessly. It seemed as though it was a practical utopia.

Tria's family home was one of those palatial estates and wasn't that far. As they were walking and talking at around the designated time of dusk a loud announcement was projected throughout the city, a deep commanding voice.

"This is President, Wasuta Elamoor. I apologize for addressing you this evening in this uncommon manner. I would like to convey my deepest and heartfelt condolences to everyone who has suffered the loss of a loved one. All the lives that were lost today will never be forgotten. I can assure you of that. Once we know for sure who all the victims are, we will have a vigil in remembrance of their lives and their spirits. This terrorist attack by Kronos cultists will not go unanswered. I have ordered the best of the Peacekeepers to hunt down and bring these cowards to justice. We will find these vile monsters and they will pay for their crimes. I swear to you all my fellow citizens; justice will be served. Again, I apologize for bringing these announcements to you in this manner, but the main connections to the Hologrid network are currently still too damaged from the attack to fully uplink to all citizens. We're doing everything we can to repair all systems as soon as possible. Thank you all very much for your continued patience in these trying times. Peace and Prosperity to all of you and our great Republics, may they stand for all time."

The announcement ended and Amarax asked Tria a few nagging questions that were bugging him.

"Tria, I think we have time now. I was wondering if you could answer a few questions that have been gnawing at my mind."

"Of course anything. Go ahead."

"What is this Kronos Cult, exactly? I don't really know anything about them, I just know their name, but I don't know the details. Tell me about it. I've never heard of them before being here in the Republics. Kronos is a planet near Orion and was one of the ancient fallen Gods of Orion. He was the God over the planet of his name and a part of the Orion Ascendancy until the Emperor killed him and took his title and throne. Does this cult have anything to do with the dead pretender god?"

"This Kronos Cult has nothing to do with that old superstition of Orion. None of those supposed deities are anything close to Gods. They're most likely just another ancient offshoot of humanity. They may have powers, but I'm a hundred percent sure that they're not actually Gods. There are many legends and postulations of why they have power like the Duality, but there is no defining scientific truth that we know with a hundred percent accuracy. There are many different theories, but I'm pretty sure that their powers are not divine. They're simply not understood."

"So, this Kronos Cult has nothing to do with the fallen fake God of Orion, so what does it have to do with then? Why would they have the same name?"

"The cult is a religious faction that rose to power here within the Republics a few thousand years ago. Its leader and founder is a maniacal lying piece of Muggjankkin sludge. He calls himself Kronos. His followers say he was resurrected from the dead thousands of years ago and is the messiah of humanity. He claims to be the one and only God of the underworld, reaper of souls, and creator of all life. Just like your Holy Duality, Kronos is a fraud. It is a little concerning that we don't know how he's lived as long as he has. His followers say that he has been with them for three millennia. I just wish he would die already."

"He does sound like a Muggjankking fraud if he's taking other God's names, even if they are false fallen God's. But followers usually have a reason to follow. It seems incomprehensible that they would follow a blatant lie without any evidence for their beliefs. You said that these cultists are responsible for murdering your brothers. What happened?"

Amarax was practically still a hollow shell with barely any emotional consideration even after all that he'd been through. He still didn't know how to ask questions gently, he was just blunt and to the point without thinking, his question of Tria's two brothers being murdered brought tears to her eyes as she thought about it in detail. Recalling what had happened to them was heartbreaking. Tears started pouring out as she was barely able to get her words out. It was painful to recollect the memories.

"Yes, they are the cultists that murdered them, they have no hearts to speak of none at all. My brothers were NAXV Bible believing Christians. They believed so strongly in their convictions that they traveled to proselytize to the followers of Kronos within Kronos's realms, planning to go to his citadel. Our parents told them not to go. Many of my fellow Peacekeepers advised against it as well, their pastor even told them to stay. I tried my best to convince them not to go, I begged them, but they were both stubborn fools sometimes. They were there for only three days until their bodies were discovered in many pieces at the far edges of the borderlands between Kronos realm and the Republics."

She wept, controlled but trembling, her voice failing as she struggled to speak of her brothers' fate.

"Jonothon was decapitated, his head mounted on a spike. Daniel... they only found pieces. Their NAXV Bibles were torn apart, scattered for miles through the under tunnels, the pages soaked in their blood. They didn't deserve this. Daniel was so young, the kindest soul I've ever known. And for what? Nothing. Proselytizing to these cultists was a total waste, it was a guaranteed death sentence. Jonothon believed in the cause. Enough to drag Daniel into it."

She stopped again for a moment. Needing to recollect herself in the emotions of losing her brothers, she still felt an extreme anger and sadness, that felt fresh in her heart, even though she had lost them years ago. The emotions and feelings had a powerful hold upon her, like it would have on any loving sister.

"I will never forgive those evil monsters for what they did to my brothers. And even though I know that they're both in Heaven right now. Those cultists don't deserve one bit of forgiveness. They don't have one shred of humanity within their twisted minds. They can't be redeemed. They don't deserve redemption. Sometimes I wish we could just wipe them out. Deep down I know that's not right. But sometimes, I just can't help thinking that it's justified."

Amarax, still hardened, tried to make an effort to apologize, unsettled by the weight of her grief.

"I'm sorry for asking. I hope you find peace one day. This Muggjankking false god Kronos needs to be taught a lesson. Maybe, one day, I'll kill him for you."

She wiped her eyes but held firm.

"I won't deny I'd like him dead, but we don't kill unless there's no other way. Not even those monsters who murdered my brothers deserve to die without recourse. Jonothon and Daniel would never have wanted revenge. They swore oaths of nonviolence—they wouldn't even swat a Muggfly biting them. I appreciate your intent, but vengeance would dishonor them."

Amarax exhaled deeply, nodding.

"I'd never want to dishonor their memory. But leaving Kronos in power over a bloodthirsty cult? That seems like insanity. I'd have thought you or the Peacekeepers would've dealt with him long ago."

She let out a bitter sigh.

"Many of us wanted to. But the Congress of the Republics has bound our hands. Over two thousand years ago, after centuries of war and millions dead, the Republics signed a noninterference treaty. The cultists have broken it time and again, but Kronos himself has never led an army against us. And as long as that remains true, Congress refuses to act. They fear another war, though I can't see why—we have far superior equipment. But after recent events... I don't know if we could win."

Amarax scoffed.

"What kind of government allows attacks of this scale to go unanswered? The Duality would never tolerate such defiance. Any enemy who harms a Dominion citizen is either wiped out or enslaved to atone. You may think it's brutal, but it works. There hasn't been a single terrorist attack against Dominion citizens in millennia. And yet your Congress would rather wage war against the Dominion than deal with Kronos?"

She breathed deeply, thinking for a moment before responding.

"It is a contradiction. But violence to prevent violence is still wrong. No matter what future bloodshed it avoids, it only adds to the sins of a shattered world."

"That's Jankking Muggwash, considering you led the attack against me and my Legion in Antica. Looked like violence to me."

She hesitated again, looking away.

"I know. Sometimes we act against our own beliefs. It was the only logical choice. But not the moral one. I broke my oath of peace. I don't know what got into me... it feels like I lost a part of myself. But at least I'm not like the Muggjankking Duality, slaughtering millions over a fistfight. Their so-called Holy Lords demand blood for the slightest offense. That's not justice. That's just cruelty."

"The Duality and their Ascendancy can be extreme, but it's all in the name of protecting their people. Your Congress, on the other hand. That's an even deadlier extreme. This path they've chosen looks like self extermination. Do they not see the cultists will keep attacking until there's nothing left of your way of life?"

She exhaled sharply. The deep truth of what Amarax had said cutting deeper than she wanted to admit.

"I know. The cultists are already at our door. They strike again and again, yet Congress has shackled the Peacekeepers for millennia. Instead of acting, they try to integrate so-called defectors, only for many to betray us from within. It's beyond Muggjankking frustrating. We fight to keep our people safe, and Congress ties our hands."

"You know, but still you don't rise up. Are you and your fellow Peacekeepers not capable of rising up against the dictates of insanity?"

"We all have free will. We're just unwilling to possibly break apart the Republics. We all have given an oath to protect and preserve the Republics no matter what, to uphold the constitution and be guardians for what it represents, that includes the government, even if we hate their choices."

"That doesn't make any sense. You've told me that you rely upon truth and logic, upon what is right and good and yet you follow madness into destruction."

"None of us are perfect. It might be an imperfect system, a broken system even, but it's better than other systems that have been tried before. It's better than the system that the Dominion relies upon."

"It is? Can you justify that statement with facts?"

"I think I could, yes."

"Well go ahead. How is this system of madness and insanity better than the system that has kept the empire together for three thousand years."

"Longevity is not an important factor in proving if something is better than something else."

"I completely disagree. It has everything to do with it."

"Maybe, but it's not entirely the case."

"Go on, elaborate what you mean. I want to understand."

Their conversation carried on, circling the same maddening truths and disagreements. The Kronos Cult thrived, the Republics faltered, and the Congress, paralyzed by fear, stupidity, or incompetence, refused to act. Meanwhile, the Duality's iron yet measured grip throughout their Dominion never wavered for millennia and their empire continued to thrive in size and number and power.

Joshua, Tria's father, heard their voices. Heated yet restrained. As he stepped outside to water some of his plants at the front of the estate. Tria's voice was unmistakable. Following its pull, he strode down the hill, eager to see his daughter, grateful beyond words that she was safe. And curious about the guest who would soon share their home.

Beyond the grand silver art-deco gate, Amarax and Tria stood locked in debate. The moment Joshua reached them, he pulled his daughter into a tight embrace, her armored frame making it awkward, but he didn't care. She was alive.

"Thank the stars you're safe. Your mother and I were worried sick. When the bombs exploded, we feared the worst. You were in every one of my meditations today. I petitioned the universe that the Peacekeepers could stop those vile Muggrats before they could destroy any more lives."

Releasing her, he turned to Amarax.

"So, this is our guest?"

Amarax inclined his head before Tria could answer.

"Amarax Mirvega, Grand Marshal of House Mirvega. A pleasure to finally meet you. I've heard much. I'll try to be a pleasant guest. Despite my station, I assure you, I can be quite civil in the right company. And I believe I'm in the right company."

Joshua chuckled.

"A Grand Marshal under my roof. I never thought I'd see the day. My library is filled with books on the history of the empire, the Duality, and their Dominion. I imagine we'll have many fine arguments. And I do love a good argument."

Tria sighed, stepping between them.

"Father, please. Not tonight. It's been a Muggjankking horrible day. I just want to rest."

"Of course, of course," Joshua conceded, his tone gentle. "It's been a long day for all of us. Let's go inside."

Together, they ascended the stone path next to the wide driveway up toward the estate. It was nestled atop a green hill, wrapped by strange trees and fragrant, alien flora. As they passed through the now-opened gate, its steel surface shimmered in the fading light. Beyond it, the towering silver fence stretched along the perimeter— not just a barrier, but a masterpiece. Strength and elegance entwined in its design, each curve and rivet whispering a silent truth: to protect is an art, and the right to defend what you love is sacred.

The three of them and the three robotic guards headed up the artistic stone pathway to the estate which was on a high green hill that was surrounded by all kinds of strange-looking trees and foliage, the smell of exotic plants filled the air, which brought some needed serenity.

They stepped through the now-opened steel gate, its polished surface gleaming faintly in the subsiding sunlight. Flanking the entrance stood a towering silver metallic fence, stretching along the property's perimeter like a vigilant sentinel. The fence was more than a mere barrier, it was a masterpiece. Its intricate design wove patterns of strength and elegance, each twist and curve telling a story of peaceful protective purpose. It wasn't just a fence; it was a narrative in metal, a tale etched into every beam and rivet, whispering of the right to protect what you love.

Mature and healthy ivy of multiple varieties was growing up all around the old dwelling. Their home was a mix of neo-futurist art deco and neo-Gothic, it was a very inspired design for a home. Every detail looked like it was meticulously crafted to tell the feelings or life story of those crafting it. It was very much opposite to the Dominion's mass-produced, assembly-line cities. Most of the buildings within the empire were dreary and dark compared to this vibrant-looking home, that looked alive. Like it had a soul.

Compared to the Dominion's Romanized neo-punk, cyberpunk Brutalist in their primary expression, with their usually obsidian black exteriors and red ascents in color. In comparison to the empire's typical designs, the Oberon family home was a timeless-looking masterpiece. Almost beyond description, giving a feeling of timelessness which would naturally lead to feelings and thoughts of eternity. Gazing upon every curving piece of metal wrapping around the façade was a journey all on its own.

Tria's childhood home was an adobe suitable for a Regent or Planetary King. As they walked into the grand home Amarax was amazed by all the art that was everywhere. On every single wall, there were grandiose paintings. The foyer was filled with twisting metallic statues that looked breathtaking, they stretched up into the high cathedral-like room with an almost divine elegance.

There was a clearly hexagonal theme to the foyer. The floor was made with hexagon-shaped tiles mixed with old and yet polished wood. The ceiling had a hexagonal design to it as well, with multiple stepping levels. There was even an open elevator which was shaped in a hexagon. It seemed like the hexagon was the cherished symbol within the society of the Republics. The shape was almost everywhere. But Amarax didn't yet know why that was or what exactly its true significance was.

Like the Dominion and its red Rhombus, the Radara which represented the Holy Duality and their power. The hexagon was very important to the Republics. He was somewhat fascinated by its obvious importance. But didn't feel the need to ask about it.

The interior style of the Oberon estate was futuristic and artistic like its exterior. But it also looked ancient. It looked at least hundreds of years old if not much older. Tria was the first to say something as they went inside together.

"I need to get out of this armor. It's killing me. I don't know why, but it is. I'm starving though, is there any dinner already made?"

Tria's father responded to what she had said.

"Yes, of course. Your mother and I were waiting for you and Amarax. It was started right after you were done with your conversation with your mother. It's already done and ready anytime you both would like to have it."

"That's great because I'm really ready for some home cooking for a change. Eating at the Peacekeeper headquarters just isn't the same as being back home. I appreciate it. Do you mind if Amarax stays with you in your library so I can change into something more comfortable?"

"I know the feeling of missing home-cooked meals. I felt the same way when I was your age about eating at Peacekeeper HQ. It's definitely not homey, that's for sure. I'd be more than happy to keep Amarax company until you're finished. I'm sure we'll get along splendidly."

"Just try not to ruffle too many of his feathers the first night he's here, he'll be here a long time. There's going to be plenty of opportunities for you to challenge his knowledge. Okay?"

"No promises, you know I can't help myself sometimes, but I'll try my best to be good. Just this once though. Now go ahead and get out of that cumbersome armor already, I think your mother is upstairs, I'm sure she'll be overjoyed to see you."

Tria smiled and nodded and then headed upstairs and her father gestured Amarax to follow him through their home to the library. As they went through the long hallways of the huge manor Amarax asked about the various paintings and sculptures that were throughout the massive home.

"These pieces of art are fantastic. Many are almost as amazing as the pieces in the Holy Museums and the Palaces of the Lords. How did you obtain all these pieces and what do they all mean? I don't recognize any of these scenes, what are they about?"

"Thank you Amarax, I'm very thankful to have such a fine collection. Most of the pieces have been passed down through my wife's family, but also my family as well. The pieces focus on the birth of the Republics, on humanity hiding from the Duality and the Dominion. Freedom is everything to us and many artists recorded that passion for freedom and our beginnings. Even though many are abstract in nature, they have deeper meanings about our beginnings. All these pieces within our home are heirlooms. One day we hope to continue the tradition and pass them down to Tria."

"That's nice to keep it in your family, I'm sure many others are jealous of how big of a collection you have. I'm sure that there are many Muggbrained simpletons that want these pieces, just so you don't have them. I hope to one day have such a fine collection so that others would be jealous of me. I never really had a chance to build up my personal possessions. I was always on a crusade fighting for the glory of the Duality and the Eternal Dominion."

"I don't think anyone is really jealous of my collection. Many others have just as fine collections, our neighbors actually have more pieces than us, but I am not at all jealous. I do enjoy analyzing some of their pieces. But I'm never jealous. Most of their pieces are even more fascinatingly abstract than my own. Many are ancient, from the mid-twentieth and twenty-first centuries. They're spectacularly preserved, it's amazing to think that we have so much here in the bowels of Earth."

"It seems highly unlikely that no one feels jealousy of what you have. I would think everyone would be jealous of your great wealth and your apparent high standing in society. This manor alone is fit for a king or regent."

"Jealously has long been theorized to stem from need and scarcity. But there is no scarcity in the Republics. No one is left to fend for themselves. No one is left on the streets to die alone. If someone has a need their need is met."

"Need is one thing. What about want? I'm sure everyone has a want for more and more."

"If people want things, more than their need, they can serve the Republics in one way or another. Maybe as scientists in the science institutes, or caretakers of the monuments and historical artifacts, many choose to be teachers or librarians, yet others choose to be Peacekeepers and others choose to be artists, musicians, writers, entertainers, and many other things. Any and all service to society allows a person to gain credits for their wants. The Republics guarantees income if a person works. That's still the one pitfall of our society and practically all societies. Money. But it's a necessity for long-term stability. Humanity is flawed. Even in a free and almost Utopian society, not everything is perfect. We're still human beings. And people love to buy and sell things. But I probably would never sell these pieces, not for all the credits in the Republics. I like them too much and they're family heirlooms. I've given a couple away though, to friends who really really wanted them."

"That seems reasonable, but I think it's silly to provide everyone the means to live. If you're too lazy and weak to survive then you don't deserve to live a prosperous life. At least it seems logical, it helps people to be self-reliant, strong, and independent to keep society moving forwards and growing."

"That's a disturbing and messed-up view of life. It has been a common belief throughout history. But it's wrong to make people struggle and suffer for no reason. Sadly ancient Earth had the same views that you have. Nation states would let their own people die, for nothing. Left to rot in the streets like discarded trash. It's a heartbreaking truth of humanity's past and even present on many worlds and undercities."

"It could be wrong. I'm still working through the morality of life in general. The morality of right and wrong, but there's an interesting few verses in the Holy Terran-Orion Bible, it says 'Survival of the fittest is the will of existence, the very cosmos proclaim the life and death of the weak and the strong. We must be strong to spread throughout the universe. Humanity must be supreme to overcome all who oppose it.' That's just the Holy Terran-Orion Bible though, it might be wrong."

Amarax believed it to the depths of his still twisted mind and that's why he couldn't help himself from sharing his thoughts, but he tried to word what he was saying in a way that would continue his pretending deceptions. Tria's father, challenged his shared verses.

"That's interesting, very reminiscent of beliefs held by humanity for a very long time, very similar to the beginnings of the theory of evolution, survival of the fittest, your Duality must have taken it for their own. It's an interesting idea, but at the end of the day it's short-sighted. We cannot allow the weak to die just to make room for the strong. My view and the view of many others is that the meekest and weakest among us makes the rest of us stronger. Another thing. Strength is just a word. What is true strength? Is it just physical or spiritual? Is it brute force or our state of intelligence? Is strength the ability to take or to give? They are all very deep questions that we all must ask as individuals and as a society."

Even though Amarax disagreed completely with Tria's father, he tried to be kind in his words and not reveal his still remaining darkness.

"I agree, it's very complicated. They're definitely not easy questions to answer, but I hope to one day find the truthful answers to it all. To see the light and goodness. I hope to one day be filled with overwhelming peace. The same as all of you."

"That's good. Keep searching, there is so much to existence. It would be a shame to not search and look for truth. Seeking out the truth of it all is all any of us can really do. Seeking out that peace is so important. Even though we might fail in the attempt, the trying is the important part."

Tria's father gave a subtle, knowing nod, his gaze steady and purposeful as he guided Amarax deeper into the heart of the estate. Each step they took seemed to stir the very air, which was thick with the weight of centuries of history.

The floors, polished to a mirror's sheen, reflected their movements as they passed beneath towering arches, the intricate carvings along the walls whispering echoes of forgotten legacies. The light from distant intricate sconces slightly flickered almost like soft flames, casting fleeting shadows that danced along the stone like spirits of the past.

As they neared the end of the great hall, an amber glow began to seep from underneath the great library doors ahead, bathing the space in a warm, almost otherworldly light. The doors themselves were yet another masterpiece, adding to the brilliance of the home. Their metallic surface was etched with gods in battle, creation clashing with ruin—stories of a world both ancient and untamed, the story of the human struggle to seek out and find paradise in an uncaring universe.

Amarax felt his pulse quicken, the air around him almost crackling with anticipation. What lay beyond these doors was not mere knowledge, it was a representation of everything that the Duality and their servants hated, the freedom to know the truth, and the wisdom to accept it.

Chapter Thirty-One:
JOSHUA'S LIBRARY

I am the God Empress, I am the Way. I am the beacon that guides you through the infinite dark. You, in your fragile mortality, seek answers, but only I can illuminate the path you walk. My heart beats with the rhythm of the cosmos, and in that heartbeat, you will find clarity. Every thought I have is a ripple in the fabric of existence, a whisper of truth that transcends time and space.

The Holy Platitudes of the Holy Duality

Platitude, III

A vast expanse of shelves stretched before them, each row laden with the weight of untold stories and forgotten histories. The library was expansive its shelves stretching endlessly with tens of thousands of books. Each spine gleamed. Some golden, some silver, others iridescent like the armor of Maxamas and Zoephiria Hendrix in the painting Amarax had seen in Unity Tower. There were books with spines that shimmered like crystals, each one a beacon beckoning to be opened. As they entered, Tria's father broke the silence.

"So, Amarax, I hear you've become quite the reader. Tria mentioned you've tackled Maxamas Hendrix's first book. That's rare, even though it's part of the school curriculum. Few actually finish it."

Amarax nodded. "Yes, it's a dense book. There's so much knowledge packed into it. I'll probably need to read it again. It all blurred together. But I remember the feeling it gave me. Freedom is what I felt."

In truth, Amarax hadn't read a word. He was just playing along, weaving his web of deception carefully.

"I feel the same. I've read it and his wife's countless times. So much wisdom. They accomplished so much despite their trials. It makes me grateful for the safety we enjoy."

Amarax continued his charade, keeping his emotions guarded.

"It's heartbreaking, what the Duality has done. The Hendrix family is just one example among trillions who've suffered. I'm ashamed to admit I followed them for so long. It's painful to think how blind I was."

Joshua nodded, his voice steady.

"We all have our struggles. Our stories aren't written in stone. We can still change, if we choose wisely. It's never easy, but it's always possible."

"I'm trying," Amarax replied quietly. "I want to find the right path, away from the Duality and my Dominion programming."

"Books are a good start," Joshua said. "Knowledge leads to enlightenment. There's no wrong way to seek it."

Amarax gave a small smile, a slight and yet meaningful deception within it.

"With guides like you and Tria, I won't fail. I hope one day to repay you for your wisdom and for helping me see the truth."

"You want to grow, and that's all any of us can do," Joshua said, his tone warm. "True enlightenment isn't easy, but the effort itself makes all the difference. If you don't mind me asking, did you memorize the Chronicle of Terra and the Holy Terran-Orion Bible? Or the Platitudes? What parts spoke to you the most?"

"Yes, I've memorized most. Its required for Every Dominion subject to learn the Chronicle and Platitudes and Terran-Orion Bible by heart. Their words were drilled into me, day and night, waking and sleeping, even when we did our daily hygiene. The precepts of the Duality, the decrees of their Children, their Deacons and Prophets, their Lords of Divine Will, an unending tide of doctrine that never ceased. Why ask? I'd assume, like Tria, you'd find the books repulsive."

"I don't believe in them, but I'm not repulsed. They're just books. Dangerous, deceptive, yet still just books. No matter how false, no text revolts me. I've read all three, and what fascinates me is their power, their grip on humanity, even on those not indoctrinated. To understand a thing is to overcome it. But I've never heard the words of a true believer, only echoes from ancient texts. I want to know what faith is like within the Dominion, here and now?"

"It's not simple. The Emperor and Empress shape all minds differently. As the Chronicle declares, 'I am there for all worlds, the flame that warms, the torch that guides to paradise under my eternal reign.' The first platitude says, 'I am the dawn that breaks the eternal night, the voice that speaks where silence binds. Through My grace, the lost shall see, for wisdom flows from the depths of My heart, and in its tide, the blind awaken. Know this: The path is Mine to carve, the veil is Mine to lift. To deny Me is to slither in shadow; to follow is to walk in light.' The Terran-Orion Bible proclaims, 'The universe moves by their hands; nothing is chance, all flows by their will.' The story that is woven is intoxicating. It's hard to refute a faith upheld by three thousand years of unbroken reign with their Demigod offspring and endless Legions enforcing their dominion across the galaxy."

"All powerful words. And their longevity is a mystery. Their power unsettles the senses of any logical mind—like the fallen Gods of Orion. Many beings claim divinity. But which do we follow? All, one, or none?"

"None wield power like the Duality. They alone have slain a so-called Supreme God of Orion. They have cut down dozens who claimed divine right—Dark Gods, Abyssal Lords, cosmic tormentors, all fallen to their blades. Their crusades have swallowed empires with ease. Even the Gods of Orion now bow. Baal, Kronos, Ares, Osiris, Zues, Marduk, El, Anu, Dagon—all dead by the Duality's hands. Isis, Athena, Ishtar, Aphrodite—wives to the Emperor. Apollo, Poseidon, Thor, Horus—husbands to the Empress. If gods kneel, were they ever gods at all?"

"Agreed. A true god does not fall. Dominion faith intrigues me— their rituals, their evolving creed. My knowledge is drawn from old texts. The Republic fixates on military intelligence but neglects the soul of the Dominion. Tell me—how does faith thrive in their empire today?"

"The Duality binds its subjects through more than just faith, it speaks to them. Every day, without fail, it addresses every temple in the Dominion through the Sacred Viewing Portals, vast gateways that pierce space-time. For over two millennia, these portals have adorned every temple, drawing the faithful in throngs to witness the divine presence in person. The moment They appear, a wave of rapture washes over the crowds, a transcendence beyond words."

"Fascinating. That explains the Dominion's fervor. Daily, tangible communion with their gods. An ever-present force reinforcing loyalty. I assume temple attendance is mandatory?"

"Of course. To be a true Terran, to be a faithful Dualinite and Terranite, one must heed the call every single day. Even during Holy Crusades, the Duality has never missed an oratory visitation. How does one reject Gods who stand before them each day? They are present, near, real. And the Dominion adores them for it."

"It makes me wonder, how do you sever such a grip? The Republics may plan to overthrow the Duality, but can we truly unshackle minds conditioned for over thirty centuries? It's probably going to take generations. If it's possible at all."

Amarax said nothing. He merely nodded, eyes drifting over the shelves until they landed on a line of tomes, war and strategy. His interest piqued. Politics did not concern him, but tactics did. Knowing the enemy was the first step to defeating them.

One title caught his eye: The New Art of War: Strategies of Multi-Dimensional Warfare. He reached for it, but the cover would not budge. Intrigued, he turned to his companion.

"Multi-Dimensional Warfare? Sounds like fighting across the multiverse. I thought your people were against war. How do you justify this?"

"We abhor war, but we are not fools. History shows that some conflicts cannot be resolved with words alone. Still, we have evolved beyond killing. We fight, we resist, but we do not take lives. Others do, even our allies still cling to the old ways. We've tried to dissuade them, but sometimes the pull of vengeance is too strong to ignore."

"That's absurd, Tria told me the same thing, but I don't believe either of you. War without death? Victory without some annihilation? Mercy may grant temporary leverage, but only total conquest ensures lasting peace."

"We once killed in war, but we learned long ago that victory need not come at the cost of life. With our technological superiority, we can usually end battles without bloodshed, but sadly it's not always the case. To take a life when it can be spared is not conquest. It is malevolence."

"The Dominion, too, is mighty. Our technology rivals any, our armies are vast. But victory without punishment feels hollow. If our enemies lose nothing, they learn nothing. Fear is the forge of obedience. That is what I was taught at the Great Holy Institutes of War, on Orion."

"That's what makes the Dominion so evil. They do not stop at victory—they punish, they torture, they break. They call it unification, but it is ruin. They strip beautiful freedom from worlds, replace it with fear, and call it paradise. You may still believe the Duality will bring salvation, but it's all Jankking Muggwash."

Amarax exhaled, slow and measured, calculating. "I am trying," he forcefully admitted without inner conviction. "I fight against the chains in my mind. Against everything I was raised to believe. But I will break free. I just need to keep listening to reason and logic—to you, to Tria, to your ideals."

Tria's father nodded in quiet approval. Amarax returned his gaze to the book in his hands. Once more, he tried to pry it open, subtly and carefully. Nothing. No crack in its sealed pages, no glimpse into its guarded secrets. The knowledge within could turn the tide of war, reveal the Peacekeepers' strategies. With such knowledge, he could crush the hidden Republics. He could claim victory for himself.

The Duality would reward him. Perhaps not just with a planet, but with a kingdom. The Holy Protectorate of Mirvega. The name rang sweetly in his mind. But first, the Republics had to fall.

As his thoughts swirled in ambition, a scent drifted through the air. Graceful, delicate, mesmerizing. The metallic doors of the library slid open. Amarax turned.

Tria entered. An elegance beyond description. A casual perfection that couldn't be truly explained. She wore a layered ensemble of deep gold and blue with soft grey, patterned in labyrinthine designs that shimmered as she moved.

Silence lingered between them as he took her in, awestruck. Then, she spoke.

"How are you two getting along? No Muggling yet, I hope, Father?"

Her father smirked and spoke. Then Amarax added his thoughts.

"Not too many."

"We're just fine. Your father was curious about the Dominion's religious stance. We had quite the discussion on the Duality claiming divinity above all other gods."

Tria sighed. "Glad he didn't cause too many waves. He can be... relentless when he thinks he's right. A riotous, walking Holopedia."

Her father was momentarily amused, then bitter.

"You exaggerate. I'm not that much of a know-it-all—only about things that matter. Your brothers and I debated for days on end in this very library. They welcomed it. I miss those times... I miss them."

Tria, though she shared the grief, had grown weary of the past weighing on the present.

"Can we not dwell on this today? Let's focus on our guest."

"I don't mind conflict. If things need to be said, say them. This is hardly a fight by my standards."

Tria's voice sharpened. "There's nothing left to say. My father rehashes the past almost every chance he gets, we all mourn their loss. But he mourns my brothers while diminishing me. Now, with these new attacks, it'll only get worse."

Her father stiffened, not wanting to accept anything within himself, his own faults, his shortcomings, or his failures as a father.

"I don't want you to be like them, Tria. I just don't want to forget them. They were great. And they're gone. I'll never see them again. That breaks me, every single day."

She softened but only slightly, she knew his words were deceptive in a way, he did want her to be like her brothers, he had told her that on many occasions.

"I know you miss them. I do too. But if they were right about the afterlife, we will see them again. I know it."

Her father's self-absorbed frustration finally broke loose.

"You know I don't believe in that Muggjankking Jesus Christ salvation nonsense! Your brothers rejected science for superstition. They were tricked like so many others! They're gone. We'll never see them again, except in memory."

Tria's eyes burned with anger. She understood the truth, the truths he refused to accept and internalize.

"That's not true, and you know it. You're just angry and lost in your regrets. But don't you dare dishonor them. We go through this time and time again. You're the hypocrite—you once believed the same things they did! They believed because of you! Maybe if you hadn't encouraged them to seek God the Omega to the point of practically brainwashing them, they'd still be here."

Her father's voice cracked under her words.

"It wasn't my fault they went proselytizing to maniacs. Who spreads love and forgiveness to the Kronos Cult? I begged them not to go. I prayed. But Alpha Omega never answered. Because He doesn't exist. My sons died for nothing."

Tria's jaw tightened even more.

"You're only lying to yourself and to everyone who hears your words. Daniel and Jonothon's beliefs mattered. It mattered to you once, too. Just stop being a hypocrite. Stop lying." She breathed deeply and exhaled deeply, closing her eyes for a moment seeking meditation and focus, her voice softening. "Can we stop this? Mother is waiting for us. She's probably tired by now."

Amarax stayed silent during Tria and her father's exchange, knowing nothing he said would earn their trust. The three walked to the dining hall in uneasy quiet, the ancient walls bearing witness to a deeper and more intense emotional conflict than they wanted to accept.

If faith was a fire, then doubt was the wind, and somewhere between the two, they stood, unsure whether to burn or to be extinguished. They stepped through the threshold of the library, hearts weighed down by the impossible burden of knowing too much and understanding too little. The reasons for their sorrows and convictions were a complex interweaving dream of memories, sometimes too painful to discern.

Chapter Thirty-Two:
AMARAX COMES TO DINNER

Meals of the mouth come and go like the wind. But the meals of the mind can stay for an eternity. I hope that the meal of truth within my mind will be with me forever and never spoil like the fruits on our family table.

Zoephiria Vergaragas Morganvale Hendrix

Personal Journals, circa 3,114 AD

An air of quiet sophistication greeted them as they stepped into the dining room. The elegant surroundings were a perfect reflection of history and legacy.

As Amarax entered the dining area, flanked by Tria, Joshua, and the security robots, he couldn't help but marvel at the room's meticulous design. Subtle yet intoxicating elegance. Tria's mother sat at the large, silver dining table, its surface alive with intricate carvings, each stroke telling a story, each scene flowing into the next. The table was set for four: polished silverware gleamed in perfect symmetry, and cups sat neatly beside them, their delicate rims catching the light. Four chairs encircled the table, but the space was massive, it could easily welcome dozens more without losing its intimacy.

Everyone joined Tria's mother at the table. After they were all seated, golden robotic assistants with designs almost like the house brought in dinner and set a single large plate in front of each of them, each plate was filled with delicious-looking exotic fruits and vegetables. A rapturous odor emanated from the food, making Amarax's taste buds start watering in anticipation.

The varied foods on the table were nothing that was at all familiar to Amarax. All of this produce was genetically engineered and created within the Republics: Red, Blue and Purple Fundaberries of various geometric shapes and sizes. Some of the multi-colored Gracous root, which looked like alien tentacles spun into weaved forms of artistic excellence. A thick multi-layered pyramid-like dish of Drakka, a finely made dessert that looked like it was for kings or gods, a golden flaking leaf covering its surface was sitting at the center of the table.

All the food seemed fit for royalty, but within the Republics, they were all eaten regularly as a daily staple. After dinner was served by the golden robots, Tria spoke to her mother with a forced polite respect, even though she did love her parents as all children do, deep down she was still upset with her father and mother for their years of childhood emotional turmoil and neglect.

And now their constant comparison to her brothers and always wanting her to do what they wanted her to do, wanting her to carry on the Oberon legacy, lead the Republics, become a politician, wanting to live through her, wanting her to achieve greatness. Also, the constant incessant annoyance of wanting her to settle down and have a family that she wasn't ready to have, but she controlled herself.

Although she was emotionally scared and had inner turmoil's she had found a tempered inner peace in her life now, she forced a kindness that felt bitter, her meditations and Goodgel giving her control over her emotions.

"Mother I want to apologize for not being here more often. I'm sorry that I haven't been over in such a long time. I promise you that I'll try better in the future. Especially now. It feels like the whole world could end at any moment. These attacks are making me think more about how brief life is."

Tria's mother held her hand and responded with reassurance and thankfulness, she was overjoyed that her daughter was alive and well. Tria was the only child she had left.

"It's fine. I understand my love. I'm just glad that you're alright. It's a blessing that you were able to make it through these horrible attacks alive and well. It's a blessing that we're all alright. Let's not focus on regrets or the past. Let's think about the future and all the goodness that could be awaiting us. So much is possible."

Thoughts of family swirled in Gema's mind. She wanted a grandchild so badly. She had even tried arranging Tria with multiple suitable partners over the years, but it never worked out. After responding to Tria she turned to Amarax.

"I wanted to thank you Amarax, for assisting my daughter during the attacks. Tria told me how you were helping so many people. I appreciate that. The Republics appreciate it."

Amarax responded to Tria's mother with a fake sincerity.

"You're very welcome. I'm trying to do my best to make up for a lifetime of darkness. I'm attempting to take one step at a time towards being a better person. Making the necessary changes to be the person I should be. I don't want to be a brainwashed drone my entire life. I want to be free and filled with this passion for liberty that all of you possess. And your daughter has already saved my life, I was obligated to return a simple gesture of goodwill."

Gema said in response.

"That's an understandable point of view. Not wanting to be a drone, not wanting to be controlled. I can't imagine what it must be like being under the rule of tyrannical rulers touting false Godhood. It must be a horrendous burden on you to walk away from it."

Amarax's blood burned with fury at Tria's parents' blasphemy against the Holy Duality, the supreme gods of humanity. Yet, he swallowed his rage, maintaining the ruse, though every word against his God-Emperor and God-Empress sickened him. This sacrilege would not go unanswered. One day, he would have his vengeance. One day, in the name of his gods, he would crush these heretics.

"No mortal should endure such a burden. The Dominion's control is maddening, a prison under a false Godhead. I am only grateful your daughter freed me when she did. Without her, I would have spent decades more in service to the Duality, committing horrors in their name. She saved me from that fate."

"She is a dedicated Peacekeeper," Tria's mother said warmly. "Her father and I prayed for children who placed others before themselves, and we were blessed with three."

"From what I've seen, it's no wonder they grew to be so virtuous. Your home is built on truth and honor. May your lineage endure for generations."

Both parents smiled, expressing their hope for exactly that. Amarax, still playing his part, pressed further.

"Forgive my rudeness—I never asked your name. You know mine, yet I do not know yours."

"My name is Gema."

"You and your husband have strong names. It is an honor to dine in your home. If I may ask, what do you do here in the Republics? Joshua, I know you once served as a Peacekeeper—do you still?"

Joshua shook his head as he took a sip from his drink.

"No, though I miss it at times. I gave sixty-five years to law and order. Now, in my golden years, I build instead of protect. I serve in the Republics Building Corps—this is my seventy-fourth year. Hard work, but it sustains our people."

Amarax raised an eyebrow. "Sixty-five years as a Peacekeeper and seventy-four as a builder—that's one hundred thirty-nine years of service. You don't look a day over thirty. If you don't mind me asking, how old are you?"

Joshua chuckled. "I don't mind. I'll be two hundred thirty-two this year. A good diet and daily vitality supplements keep me young. Here in the Republics, the average lifespan is three hundred years."

"Incredible. Three centuries for the average person... I'll be lucky to reach fifty. But that's the price we pay in the Diviniterra legions—unless the Duality grants us more years."

Gema turned to him, curiosity in her eyes. "If you don't mind me asking, how old are you?"

"Eighteen. Nineteen soon."

Her brows lifted.

"Eighteen—and already a Grand Marshal? How?"

"Childhood of a Diviniterra Legionary is brief. Four years at most, usually much less. From birth, we train. Quantum links infused into our newly born minds, starting the downloads right away. We're molded into warriors. By five, I had the body and mind of a grown man. I never knew the luxury of a slow, gentle youth, but at the time, I didn't mind. My lineage is one of warriors, and I was expected to continue the tradition, as all in my bloodline have."

Gema shook her head, disbelief etched across her face.

"I can't imagine a life like that. Dying at fifty—it feels almost obscene. Even less advanced civilizations live longer. Why so young?"

Amarax answered without hesitation.

"The Duality's blessings grant us strength, but mortals can't endure such power beyond fifty years. Unless we transcend into War Saints or High Lords. Without transcendence we are consumed in the power of the Duality."

Joshua scoffed. "Sounds less like a blessing, more like a curse."

Tria cut in, her voice edged with truth.

"They aren't blessings—far from it. When Diviniterra Legion soldiers pray, their implants don't channel divine power; they siphon their very lifeforce, burning it away to fuel their war rage. The Dominion calls it a gift, but it's a slow execution. Their own essence is the price for their strength, their bodies sacrificed for borrowed power. Life withers away quickly. Some don't even live to fifty. Some within the Diviniterra die much younger."

Amarax dismissed her words, unwilling to entertain the doubt creeping into his mind. He shifted the conversation.

"Gema, what do you do in the Republics?"

"I lead research at the Ruth-Mosen-Delarue Memorial Institute of Advanced Mathematics. Named after the pioneers of matter transfer. I've spent over two centuries in this field, working across academies and institutes."

"Impressive. You oversee all matter transfer research?"

She smiled, a bit of ego rising, but she tried containing it.

"One of many. There are hundreds of institutes. I lead one. My work is important, but so is everyone else's. No scientist stands above another."

"A rare humility. I should take notes. Dominion leaders are raised to be ruthless, to boast of our 'divine' standing. Humility—it'll take me a lifetime to learn."

"You're kind, but I'm as flawed as anyone. We all falter. I simply try my best every single day. Though I fail time and time again."

"Still humble," he mused. "If I may ask, what are you working on?"

"It's no secret. We're focused on miniaturizing matter transfer technology. Dozens of teams tackle different aspects, but mine studies the math—how to keep matter waves untangled across dimensions. Eighty years, and I feel like we've barely scratched the surface. We may solve it tomorrow or we may never solve it, but perhaps we'll leave stepping-stones for future minds."

Amarax offered a pleasant smile, feigning interest. "I hope you find your answers in your lifetime. Your Republics must value your work." In truth, he cared little for scientific discovery, but he knew he could exploit it. Knowledge of technology, especially advanced technology, was power, and power was all that mattered.

As the conversation flowed, Gema spoke with fervor about mathematics, Joshua reminisced about his Peacekeeper days and his role in the Builders Corps, and Tria shared stories from her own service. Amarax answered each of their questions with careful calculation, threading himself deeper into their web of trust. Hours seemed to slip away as they wove their stories together, each conversation a thread of understanding that was bringing them closer, especially Tria and Amarax.

As the old clocks struck midnight they all agreed that it was getting late and retreated to their rooms. The conversations lingered in the air long after their footsteps had faded. In the solitary silence that followed, Amarax sat awake thinking, contemplating, scheming his next moves. Tria wanted to forget her pains and worries. She injected herself with more doses of Goodgel, and some Sleepgel to make her sleep better.

In the stillness of the night there was an unspoken promise, a flicker of hope that perhaps, in the tangled threads of their shared pains and truths, they had begun to stitch together the fabric of a future that could be brighter. It was a fragile thing, this hope, woven from the moments of understanding they had discovered between the scars of their pasts. Something was shifting. An uncharted path had begun to form, one where their collective fates might give rise to a world more compassionate, a place where the pain of today could give birth to something beautiful tomorrow.

Chapter Thirty-Three:
SILENT DESIRE

"In the shadow of the world's judgments, where every law is a cage and every oath a chain, hearts may still reach across the impossible. Forbidden love becomes the forge of courage. An unyielding fire that bends steel, shatters fear, and defies every hand that would bind it. Even the mightiest armies, even the strictest laws, fall before the quiet, relentless truth that binds two souls, unbroken and eternal."

Forbidden Garden, a poem of the Seekers

The hollow of Unum slept, but within Amarax's room, the night was alive. Shadows clung to the corners, trembling as if aware of the heat that hung in the air. Tria moved like a phantom through the dim light, her presence impossible to ignore, her steps silent yet echoing through his chest.

Amarax's security bots were nowhere in sight and Tria stood at the edge of his bed, eyes locked on his, fierce and unflinching. No words were needed. Everything unsaid pulsed between them in an instant, urgent and dangerously evident.

"Amarax," she whispered, a tremor beneath the steel of her voice, "I can't deny what I feel any longer, I love you, I need you, I want you."

He stirred, alert and trembling deep down. Not from fear, but from the gravity of her nearness. Every instinct screamed to resist this heretic's temptations, yet every heartbeat dragged him toward her, deeper into the forbidden.

She walked towards the bed and sat beside him leaning in closer. When their lips finally met, it was not gentle. It was fire and restraint colliding, a force that neither could deny. The world outside the walls ceased to exist. Time folded in on itself, leaving only the electricity of stolen breath, the brush of hands, and the dangerous truth of their desire.

In this moment, Amarax and Tria were no longer soldiers, no longer bound by oaths. They were something far older, far more volatile: two hearts igniting in defiance of the world.

Some desires, once awakened, cannot be silenced. And some nights leave marks that linger long after dawn.

Morning came slow, pale light creeping through the cracks in the curtains. Amarax stirred first, the warmth of Tria pressed against him lingering like a brand. She was awake too, eyes tracing the lines of his face, lips curved in a soft, almost teasing reassurance.

He pulled her close, letting the comfort of her presence anchor him. Words were unnecessary, yet he whispered anyway, voice low and hoarse. "I fear what comes next. Your people, my people, they'll never forgive us for betraying our oaths. Your people see me as a monster and my people see you as a heretic."

Tria's fingers threaded through his hair. "Let them think what they want. Let them come. Today is ours. But when the storm hits, we'll face it together. They can't take away what we have."

They rose, dressing in quiet harmony, and stepped out into the gardens of the estate. The air was crisp, carrying the scent of blooming nocturnal flowers, the shadows stretching long beneath the Art Deco, advanced technological lanterns. Dawn draped itself over the landscape, painting everything in shades of gold and violet as they walked through the gardens.

Days past in their shared secret passions. Keeping it hidden from the world. Those few short days seemed like an eternity.

For those fleeting moments, Amarax walked unguarded and free, hands brushing together, hearts tethered. And then the world intruded as it always does. Multiple squads of Peacekeepers emerged from the hedgerows and walkways, disciplined and unyielding, their weapons leveled with merciless trained precision.

"Captain, Tria Oberon," the lead officer intoned, voice slicing through the evening. "You're under arrest for treason against the Republics. You've broken your oath."

Tria held her head high, eyes meeting Amarax's. "You have no proof," she said evenly, voice steady, but the truth was cold in her bones.

"We have enough proof," the officer replied, voice ironclad and unbroken in its conviction.

Amarax's body reacted before his mind could catch up. A rifle discharged blue energy, but it arced wildly as he grabbed it, harmlessly sizzling against the ground. With superhuman speed, he seized it, yanking it from the Peacekeeper's grasp. He tried the trigger, nothing. The weapon refused him; it was bio-linked, only firing for the soldier it was bonded to.

He swung it like a heavy club. The stock smashed against the nearest attacker's skull, sending him sprawling into the undergrowth. Momentum carried Amarax forward, a whirlwind of muscle and precision. Fists collided, legs swept enemies off their feet, and every strike sent shockwaves through the ranks. He used the bodies of those who fell as shields, spinning and crashing into the next wave before they could react.

Tria moved beside him, her breaths sharp in the evening air, refusing to strike at her own people. She dodged, weaved, and kept herself out of harms way as best as she could, her above normal nanobot infused strength giving her a little edge, eyes wide at the unstoppable force he had become.

"What have you done?" she shouted, voice trembling. "I was prepared to face the consequences!"

Amarax's eyes met hers, fierce, controlled. "Then come with me!" he growled, grabbing her hand and pulling her close.

They ran, crashing through the ancient genetically engineered pine forests of Unum. Roots snagged their boots, branches tore at their sleeves, and the scent of resin and earth filled their lungs. Behind them, squads of Peacekeepers and support Mechs barreled after them, relentless.

Amarax fought as they ran. Every punch, kick, and grapple sent soldiers sprawling, bodies slammed into each other or into trees, rifles and logs were used as bludgeons. Sparks flew as metal hit metal. He twisted, ducked, and spun, continuing to use fallen attackers as shields to push through the swarm. Tria stayed close, whispering in between evasive movements.

"What have I done?"

Branches snapped overhead, energy bolts and weapon fire streaked past, and the forest shook under the relentless chase. But the numbers pressed in, circling them. Hundreds of Peacekeepers and Mechs formed a tightening ring, weapons raised.

Amarax grabbed Tria's hand, eyes scanning the encirclement, muscles coiled for the impossible fight.

"Enough," Tria said, voice trembling but resolute. "I can't fight my own people. I... I won't."

The forest, the soldiers, the machines. Everything blurred. The world tipped and fell away...And then he awoke.

Sheets tangled around him, pale moonlight spilling across the Oberon estate room. The three security bots stood silent and ever-watchful. Night still reigned outside. His hand reached the empty space beside him. Tria absent, but her presence lingered, electric, impossible to ignore. Silent desire, he realized again, refuses to be contained.

Chapter Thirty-Four:
MORNING MEDITATIONS

"To walk the path is not to seek the destination, but to become the journey itself. The river does not ask where it flows, nor does the mountain question its height. Commit not with the mind that wavers, but with the soul that knows."

Kaelinshu Chang'Lee Naddura, Reflections on the Infinite Path

Night still clung to the sky, refusing to surrender to the coming sun. Amarax sat up, running a hand through his hair, feeling the cold stare of his mechanical wardens upon him, his nightmares still haunting him. He let out a deep exhale and turned toward the large arching window that covered almost the entire wall. His senses were being drawn by the quiet rhythm of movement beyond the glass.

The heavenly gardens stretched over the rolling hills beneath the night's lingering embrace, a sea of obsidian and silver, where dew clung to marble paths like fallen stars. And within that expanse, moving like a shadow given form, was Tria.

She was a phantom in the twilight, her breath steady, her body was coiled and fluid, shifting between strikes and ancient meditative stances with a precision that defied the stillness of the world around her. Each motion carved a path through the darkness—her footfalls were light upon the large stone that she stood on, like she was being held up by angelic wings, her partially closed fists slicing through the cool air with a force that bent the mist around her.

Amarax had seen warriors train before. He had seen Legionaries break themselves against steel, had witnessed the brutal regimens of soldiers honed by war and conquest. But this was something different. This was not violence for violence's sake. This was discipline woven into every fleshly action, motion crafted into meaning.

Her arms flowed like liquid, wrists snapping at precise angles, fingers striking unseen pressure points in the air. As if she fought an opponent that only she could see. The silk of her blue tunic whispered with every movement, its dark fabric blending seamlessly with the night, the faintest sheen of sweat catching in the cold projected starlight.

Then came a turn. A pivot on the ball of her foot, a deep stance, a breath held at the edge of motion—before she drove forward, a single, sharp strike that cracked against the quiet like whispering distant thunder. A blow powerful enough to shatter bone. Yet there was no rage behind it, no recklessness. Only calming purpose and focus on the inner struggle.

Tria stood for a moment, still as stone, her breath misting in the cool air, her gaze fixed beyond the garden walls towards the snow-capped mountains along the horizon. Amarax studied her through the glass, his eyes narrowing. This routine of hers was fascinating and beautiful in a deep meaningful way and it was moving him to love her even more. The visions that her friend had given her were still pressing upon his thoughts like an unending torrential rain.

As he tried to understand who she was, really was, he could sense that there was a silent war within her, one that had nothing to do with duty, titles, nobility, or the weight of bloodlines.

The stillness held her like a whisper of the night itself. Tria stood unmoving, the echoes of her movements still lingering in the cool breath of pre-dawn. She was carved from years of discipline and meditation, sculpted by conviction and trials as a Peacekeeper. In this moment, she was neither noble nor an heir of empires—only a soul bound to a path that few could walk.

Amarax exhaled, pressing a palm against the cold glass. Something in her stillness called to him—not as a warrior drawn to battle, but as one soul that was being pulled to another, standing at the edge of the same abyss. He rose, the hum of his security drones shadowing him as he made his way through the quiet halls of the Oberon estate.

The grand doors to the garden parted with a soft hiss, and the air met him like a ghost, crisp with the scent of wet stone and distant flowers. Tria did not turn as he approached. She had sensed him the moment he had stepped beyond the threshold.

"You rise early," he said, his voice low, as if the stillness itself demanded reverence.

"You rise later than I expected," she replied, her breath steady, gaze still fixed upon the mountains beyond. "I thought warriors did not waste the morning."

A faint smirk tugged at the corner of his lips. "I am a guest. And besides captives tend to rest lightly."

She turned now, slow and deliberate, eyes searching his, as if peering through layers unseen.

"Do you feel like a captive?"

He glanced at the three robotic sentinels behind him, their cold metallic presence, an ever-present reminder of his situation.

"Do you?" he countered, gesturing to the estate, the weight of expectation that clung to its very walls.

A flicker of something passed across her face, a crack in the marble of discipline, but it was gone before it could settle. Instead, she exhaled, the breath shifting into a deeper stillness. Then, without another word, she lowered herself into a meditative stance, legs folding, hands resting lightly on her knees.

Amarax watched her, the way she settled upon the stone as if she belonged to it and it belonged to her, as if she had carved a sanctuary within herself that no force could breach. He hesitated only a moment before stepping forward. With the precision of a soldier, he mirrored her, lowering himself onto the cold stone. His security drones standing guard, uncertain what was going on, their logic faltering in the face of something that could not be measured in commands and protocols.

For a while, there was only breath, only silence. Then, softly, she spoke.

"You fight wars with steel and fire. But tell me, Amarax Mirvega... have you ever fought a war within yourself?"

His gaze did not waver. "Every day."

She nodded, as if she had always known the answer.

"Then you understand," she said, closing her eyes. "The greatest battles are never waged among the stars. They are fought here." She tapped one of her hands lightly to her chest. "In the unseen. In the silence. And the only victor is the one who refuses to yield to the whispers that try to shatter our hearts."

Amarax watched her for a moment longer before closing his own eyes, letting the silence settle over him like a weight he had long carried but never acknowledged. The war within him had already begun. And in this quiet, in this moment shared between two souls who carried burdens unseen, a part of him wondered if he had found something greater than what he had always known.

The sun rose slow and golden, peeling away the shadows that had clung to the world like remnants of a forgotten dream. The cold breath of night faded into the hush of morning, and with it, the stillness between them shifted—not broken, but evolving, like the quiet before the first steps of a long journey.

Tria rose first, the disciplined grace of her movements untouched by exhaustion. Amarax followed, slower, his body still waking, though the meditations had steadied something within him. His security drones stayed nearby, almost hovering, their cold vigilance an echo of the invisible chains that still bound him to the dictates of these heretics.

"Follow me."

She said, then led him through the gardens, past the ornate bridges and marble fountains, where water ran like liquid crystal over sculpted stone, reflecting the first embers of dawn. The scent of blooming nightshade and star lilies still lingered in the cool air, remnants of the estate's midnight hush. At the garden's edge, beneath an open circle of towering pillars entwined with ivy, a matter transfer pad hummed softly, its runic engravings pulsing with ethereal light.

In a breath, the world shimmered, and they were no longer among the sculpted beauty of the Oberon estate but in the raw, untamed embrace of the wild. In front of them where civilization faded into something older, untouched, a forest older than the founding of the Republics stood. The towering pines stretched up like silent sentinels for the pure and unaltered states of nature, their branches woven together high above, filtering the light into shifting streams of gold and shadow.

The moment they stepped beneath the canopy, the world changed. The air thickened with pine and damp earth, the hush of wind through the needles replacing the distant hum of technology. The weight that hung over Amarax—over both of them—seemed to settle, as if the forest itself understood the burdens they carried.

"You walk like a soldier," Tria said, glancing over at him.

Amarax smirked. "I am a soldier. I'm a Grand Marshal of a Diviniterra Legion."

She shook her head. "Not here. Here, we're just… people. People searching for the truth. People wanting to find paradise. People hunting the illusions of perfection."

He exhaled, running his right hand across his temple towards the back of his head, trying to contemplate the meanings of Tria and her people. Not grasping the depth of what she was trying to say to him.

"I can tell that you come here often, you seem as one with this place. I would say almost symbiotic." he noted, feeling it to be true.

She nodded. "Yes, I come here. When I need to breathe deeper than what is possible in the capital. When I need to remind myself, what peace feels like."

Amarax glanced up at the towering trees, their roots gnarled and deep, their scars from storms past still visible in the bark. "Does it work?"

She gave a small smile. "Sometimes."

They walked in silence for a time, their footsteps soft against the moss-covered path. The deeper they went, the denser the forest became, until the world of steel and duty felt like a distant memory.

Finally, Amarax spoke. "I was raised for something greater than myself. Duty. Discipline. Service. We believed peace could only exist beneath the heel of order and the Divine." He let out a slow breath. "Now, after being with you. I wonder if that was ever peace at all."

Tria stopped, turning to face him. "You were a slave, a slave to ideas that weren't your own. But now you have a chance to find something better." It wasn't a question, just the obvious things that she felt to be right.

"I'm starting to think that your right." His voice was even, but beneath it, something wavered. "I fought for a cause I thought was just. I gave everything to it, killed for it, slaughtered for it. And now that my eyes are opened... I can see what I was. A monster."

She studied him for a long moment, then reached out, pressing her palm against the rough bark of a massive pine.

"You see this tree?" she asked. "It's been struck by lightning. More than once."

He frowned, unsure where she was going with this. "And?"

"And yet it stands."

She ran her fingers over the deep grooves, tracing the scars left behind by the programmed created storms of the ancient systems. No matter how many scientists tried to change the ancient Atlantean code, it didn't want to change. It wanted to instill and preserve the reality of what the ancient Earth was like at one time.

She continued.

"It didn't break. It didn't fall. It kept growing, shaping itself around what had tried to destroy it."

Amarax crossed his arms still uncertain of what Tria was trying to say.

"Are you saying I should keep growing around the horrors, the butchery, the reality of what I am, the monster?"

She turned back to him, her gaze unwavering in its deeper beliefs, but also becoming a little impatient.

"I'm saying you're not dead yet."

Silence stretched between them, thick as the air before a storm. Then, she smirked.

"Come. There's a clearing ahead. When the sun rises over it, the light sets the ground on fire."

Amarax glanced at his security bots annoyed and distracted by their overbearing presence, then he looked back at her. Her presence was more intoxicating than the finest of wines in the Dominion. For the first time in a long time, the weight on his chest didn't feel quite as heavy.

"Lead the way."

When they reached the clearing, the first true rays of the sun had broken through the horizon, spilling gold and amber across the earth. Dewdrops caught the light, igniting the strange almost magical grass in a shimmer of seemingly liquid fire, each blade a flickering ember of a timeless morning.

The world around them was silent, but not empty. A sacred hush, as if the forest itself held its breath in reverence of the light.

Tria exhaled slowly, stepping forward. "See?"

Amarax said nothing at first, only watching as the glow touched her face, her eyes reflecting the brilliance like molten metal. There was no battle here, no war to fight—only this fleeting moment, this quiet peace carved from time itself.

"It's beautiful," he finally said, his voice quieter than before.

She glanced at him. "It's a reminder."

"Of what?"

"That the world keeps moving, no matter what we carry." She looked back at the golden-lit clearing. "That even after the longest night, the sun still rises."

Amarax took a breath, deeper than he had in a long time, letting the weight of her words settle over him. He had lived in the shadow of war, of orders that demanded blind obedience. But here, bathed in the light of a new day, something in him shifted. Just slightly, just enough.

For a long while, they stood there, neither speaking, neither needing to.

Then, as the sun climbed higher, Tria turned back toward the path. "Come on, we should be getting back," she said, a knowing look in her eyes. "The estate will be waking soon."

He hesitated for a moment before nodding. As they retraced their steps, the forest seemed softer, the weight of the world just a little lighter.

At the edge of the woods, beneath the ivy-wrapped pillars, the matter transfer pad shimmered once more, waiting to return them to reality.

Before they stepped onto it, Amarax glanced back at the towering pines, the clearing now hidden beyond their embrace. The moment had passed, but the fire of it remained.

He turned to Tria. "Thank you."

She tilted her head. "For what?"

"For this." He exhaled. "For reminding me that there's more than what I was."

A small smile touched her lips. "There's always more."

Would this moment linger, woven into the fabric of something greater, or would it vanish like breath on glass? Were they merely two souls passing through the vast tide of time, or had fate drawn them together for reasons neither could yet see?

The universe was endless, its stars burning with stories long before they were born and long after they would be gone. But here, in this fleeting space between dawn and duty, something unspoken took root. something neither of them named, yet both felt.

And as the transfer pad hummed to life, the golden light of morning wrapped around them one last time before the world faded into a shimmer of stars.

Chapter Thirty-Five:
PASTIMES AND PHILOSOPHY

"A little laughter can untangle the greatest knot, turning trials into threads of beautiful memory rather than chains of despair."

— From *Finding the Joys in Life* by Anton Blanc

Time seemed to slip by so quickly as they spent the rest of the morning together, the weight of duty and war held at bay by the quiet simplicity of shared moments. The estate's grand halls, so often filled with the formalities of noble life and the ever-present hum of obligations, became a sanctuary. If only for a little while.

They sat in one of the sunlit lounges overlooking the gardens, the scent of freshly brewed coffee curling through the air. Tria poured them each a cup, her movements measured, precise, almost ritualistic. Amarax watched her, noting how even in something as simple as pouring a drink, there was a quiet discipline, a steadiness that spoke of a mind that rarely rested.

She took a slow sip, exhaling softly before glancing at him over the rim of her cup. "Do you ever play Jaxabract Chess?"

Amarax smirked, setting his coffee down. "I've played it, yes."

"Good." She reached for the ornately carved board, its pieces already set in their opening positions. "Then I won't have to go easy on you."

The game began, the smooth clink of pieces shifting across the board punctuated only by the soft strains of Mozart playing from the room's classical archive. The music wove through the space, lending an air of timeless elegance, as if this battle of minds had played out countless times before across history, in different places, under different stars.

Amarax studied the board, calculating his next move. Jaxabract Chess was unlike traditional chess, its ever-shifting board, powered by micro-gravity plates, caused pieces to subtly change positions every few turns, demanding constant adaptation. He moved his

Knight forward, only for the board to hum softly, shifting the ranks ever so slightly.

Tria arched an eyebrow. "Bold."

He shrugged with confidence. "Calculated."

She countered swiftly, her strategy unfolding with a fluid grace that mirrored her movements in the training grounds. Each piece she moved was deliberate, a step in a dance only she could see the full shape of.

The board shifted, the micro-gravity plates humming softly beneath their hands, warping the positions of the pieces ever so slightly. Jaxabract Chess was a game of strategy, yes, but also of adaptation, of recognizing that the board itself was never truly stable, never truly fair.

Amarax exhaled, his fingers hovering over a rook. Across from him, Tria studied the game with quiet intensity, her eyes moving not just over the board, but through it—seeing the patterns yet to unfold, the inevitabilities taking shape in ways he had yet to grasp.

"This game," he deeply murmured, "it reminds me of the galaxy."

Tria tilted her head slightly. "How so?"

He finally moved the rook, fortifying his side of the board. "It never stops shifting. Empires rise, empires fall. Gods ascend, Gods are cast down. The moment you think you've mastered the field, it changes beneath you."

Tria smiled again ever so slightly.

"Then the mistake is believing the field can ever be mastered." She slid her queen forward, forcing him into a defensive posture. "The Holy Duality, the Tribunals, the fallen pantheons before them, they all believed themselves inevitable. And yet, none of them are eternal. Eventually, all fade away."

Amarax narrowed his eyes at the board. "The Duality would disagree."

"They can disagree." Her fingers hovered over her next move. "But it won't change the truth."

He looked up at her. "And what truth is that?"

She tapped a pawn, shifting it forward, just a single, calculated step.

"Power is never truly owned. It's only borrowed from those willing to let you rule over them."

The words hung between them, heavier than the game itself. In a few final moves of luck and skill Tria defeated Amarax. A service android came around to refill their coffee. And then Tria spoke to Amarax.

"Oh, there's another game that I think you'd enjoy. I can guarantee you, that's you've never played it before. It was created right here in the Republics."

She tilted her head back and looked at an intricately made quantum computer module on the fireplace that was connected to the estate's AI, speaking to it as if it were a person.

"Ayn, could you please retrieve a game of NOR for us?"

A warm and inviting voice responded.

"I'd be more than, happy. Here you go."

"Thank you, let's start at a beginner level."

The Jaxabract Chess set dematerialized from the table and a new circular board appeared in front of them, a Nexorbact board, but everyone just called it NOR, it was much simpler to pronounce. The board's intricate design was like a piece of art that took centuries to craft. Its uniform grid, split the board up evenly. Little golden walls projected out into the center. A few pieces appeared on its surface and Tria explained the complex and yet simple rules to the game.

Nexorbact, like Juxabract Chess, required skill and strategy, but also luck. The Republics were enamored with games of chance and finding ways to beat the odds. The unique thing about this game, it could be played in many ways. There wasn't a single way to play. Sometimes there were different rules for every play-through.

The pieces on the board moved with urgency, each one trying to carve a path toward the center, toward the core where victory would be claimed. Unlike the shifting chaos of Jaxabract, this was the Nexus, Orbit, React game—steadier, but more unpredictable in its own way.

Amarax watched as his pieces moved in careful arcs, their every advance disrupted by the unpredictable nature of the Nexorbact, the game's unique rule. As they drew closer to the center, their roles changed, what was once a knight became a rook, a pawn became a queen. The pieces took on new purposes, forced to adapt and redefine their meaning with every turn. There was no rhyme, no reason beyond the sheer flux of their movement.

He paused, looking at Tria. "Do you think that's how power works? Always shifting like this, never truly stable?"

Tria moved one of her pieces, watching it transform in the same unpredictable way with the current ruleset that they were playing with.

"Power is like a Nexus piece," she said quietly. "It runs to the center, but will never reach it without trials. The trials never stay the same. We have to evolve and power needs to evolve, it has to take on new roles depending on who controls it, what is required of it in the moment. You may think you've mastered it, only for it to change into something else entirely. Something you never anticipated."

He moved one of his pieces, watching it shift and change, now a rook where it had once been a knight.

"Then what is the point of trying to control it, if it can just change form?"

"Control is an illusion," she replied, her voice low but firm. "Control isn't about holding onto something. It's about knowing when to release it. When to let it become something else. That's the mistake of the Duality, the mistake of the Tribunals—they held onto power too long. They don't see that power's true nature is to grow, to change. To flow like water, not stay stagnant like stone. Not to be as stale as dead bones."

Her queen shifted form, becoming a knight with no warning. The sudden change made her smile.

"It's not about the destination," Tria continued, her gaze never leaving the board. "It's about how you adapt, how you evolve with it."

Amarax studied his pieces as they reshaped themselves, and for the first time in a long while, he understood something deeper. Power wasn't something to dominate, it was something to ride with, something to be one with, like the ebb and flow of a tide, the ups and downs of waves on water worlds.

He moved his piece again, more intentionally this time, embracing the uncertainty of it.

"Then maybe it's not about winning the game. Maybe it's about the game itself."

Tria's eyes met his, a knowing look passing between them. "Exactly."

And with that, the pieces continued their dance, ever-changing, ever-evolving. With luck and a bit of strategic guess work, attempting to anticipate the unguessable, Amarax beat Tria, by eventually bringing two Nexus pieces to the center.

"I think you've taught me a lot today. It's definitely going to stay with me for a long time."

"I would hope so."

They smiled in their moment of carefree logical competition and went out to the gardens again enjoying the afternoon sun. Taking a walk through the peaceful maze of art and manicured nature, discussing life, philosophical conundrums, the history of her family and his, sharing more about their lives, the little details about their childhoods.

As they wandered the serene pathways, their conversation wove between reflections on history and the quiet details of their pasts— childhood memories, fleeting moments that had somehow stayed with them through the years. The sunlight filtered through the sculpted trees, casting shifting patterns along the marble walkways, the scent of blooming star-lilies carried on the breeze.

Then, a soft chime echoed from Tria's wrist. Her steps slowed as the module on her arm pulsed with urgency, she pressed a finger upon the pulsing light and the incoming signal threaded directly into her mind. Her holonet connection flared to life, projecting the message within her vision, a seamless overlay of information against the world before her.

Amarax noticed the change in her expression, the way her eyes grew distant as she processed the unseen.

"What is it?"

She remained silent for a moment, watching as the emblem of the Presidential Office unfurled in glowing light, followed by a solemn-faced figure addressing the capital. The President's voice was calm but heavy, weighted with grief and sorrow, but also with the resilience expected of him.

"Tonight, we will gather in solemn remembrance of those lost in the recent attacks, mothers, fathers, brothers, sisters, precious children, innocent lives taken in the cruel shadow of malevolent violence. I hope to see all of you tonight. We stand together, united, unbroken. Let this vigil be more than mourning; let it be a promise. That we will not yield. That we will not forget."

The words faded, replaced by the city's official crest, with information of time and place. The vigil would be held at 'The Grand Cathedral of Unified Faith of Unum and of the Republics' after the information remained for a few moments, the message was gone.

Tria blinked, her gaze refocusing. The gardens remained serene, unchanged, yet the air carried a newfound weight, subtle but undeniable, like a silent ripple spreading through still water.

She exhaled with burden and sadness upon her face. "A vigil tonight. For those killed in the bombings."

Amarax's gaze drifted toward the horizon, where the sun dipped lower, casting the gardens in a solemn glow.

"They call it a vigil," he said, his voice quiet but firm. "But it's more than mourning. It's a ledger of loss…and a reminder that the debt is never truly paid."

Tria let his words settle between them, like fallen leaves caught in the hush of the evening air. The weight of the message pressed against her, an ache she couldn't quite name.

"I believe it to be more of a vow, not of debt, but of faith—a promise that we will carry their light forward, knowing that in their unjust loss, we are made stronger, and their memory will guide us toward justice." She paused for a moment looking at the mountains in the far distant horizon "We should go. If you're comfortable going, I'd like you to come."

With a still calculating, planning mind, Amarax gave a simple and yet darkly patient answer.

"Of course, If you want me there. I'll go."

They walked on, back towards the manor, unhurried, their steps quiet against the stone paths. Neither mentioned dinner—neither felt the need. What was a meal when the night itself carried the taste of sorrow?

The estate's halls were quiet as they moved through them, the usual warmth of the grand corridors dulled by the weight of the evening ahead. The soft glow of wall sconces cast elongated shadows across polished marble floors, their reflections stretching like silent specters bearing witness to the moment.

Tria's pace slightly quickened with purpose. She did not want to be late. More than that, she wanted to be early. To stand beneath the towering spires of the Grand Cathedral before the throngs arrived, to let the silence of that sacred space settle over her before it was filled with the echoes of grief.

Once all of them were ready they descended through the estate, past the gilded archways and towering windows, until they reached an open-pillared chamber where a matter transfer network pad awaited. The MTN hummed softly, its surface etched with shifting patterns of light.

Tria stepped onto the pad first. Amarax, his robot guards, and her parents following closely behind her. With a silent command, the sequence engaged, and the world dissolved into a cascade of luminous filaments. For an instant, there was no motion, no sound. Just the weightless sensation of localized existence unraveling and reforming. Then, with a whisper of energy, they reappeared at their destination. The transfer ended, but the true crossing had only just begun.

Chapter Thirty-Six:
THE COVENANT OF THE REPUBLICS

"After a century of bloodshed, we stand not as victors, but as survivors, bound by the scars of war and the resolve to heal. The time for vengeance has passed, and with it, the shadow of destruction. Today, we choose to walk into a new day, where peace is not a concession, but the greatest of all triumphs. This treaty is not the end of our struggle—it is the beginning of what we were always meant to be."

Jovanak Halladan Duran

President of the United Free Republics of Earth, at the Signing of the Peace Treaty, At the end of the War of Kronos, circa 3,273 AD

Past a long and intricately kept plaza, The Grand Cathedral rose before them, an indomitable presence against the twilight sky. Its argent spires caught the dying light, gleaming like celestial spears piercing the heavens. The vast stained-glass windows, dark for now, stood as unseeing sentinels, waiting for the vigil's flames to breathe life into their stories once more.

The Grand Cathedral stood as a testament to eternity itself, hewn from carved white marble and light grey granite, its countless spires reaching skyward like prayers frozen in stone. A masterpiece of Art Deco grandeur fused with Neo-Futuristic ambition and the solemn grace of Neo-Gothic reverence, it bore the weight of divinity in every line, every arch, every towering pinnacle. Statues of ancient saints and heroes of the Republics stood in silent vigil alongside sacred figures of every faith, their solemn visages carved with devotion, their watchful eyes cast toward the heavens as if bearing witness to the eternal light.

Beyond the plaza, the city's restless hum had dimmed, as though the very world outside had bowed its head in reverence to the sorrow of the night.

Numerous people had already begun to gather, their footsteps soft against the polished stone, their hushed voices lost beneath the distant murmur of prayer. The faithful came in solemn procession, draped in dark robes or the formal attire of mourning, some with hands clasped in silent devotion, others carrying the weight of grief in their weary eyes.

Saints and martyrs stood in their silent watch, carved from white marble and dark granite, their faces solemn, their gestures frozen in acts of mercy, battle, and sacrifice. Some raised swords, others torches or open palms—a pantheon of the devout, the fallen, the redeemed. They bore witness to the unbroken cycle of faith, to the tides of power that lifted and shattered the faithful, to the price paid in blood for the right to believe in their individual supernatural convictions.

Peacekeepers stood like living statues throughout the plaza and along the cathedral steps, their armor reflecting the amber glow of the lanterns. They did not speak, did not move beyond the slow, measured turns of their heads—watchful, unwavering, guardians of the sacred and the grieving alike.

The great cathedral doors loomed ahead, immense and carved with visions of creation and destruction, of divinity and sinners, of angels and demons. The massive rectangular doors did not wait for hands to push them open—at their approach, the hexagonal seals pulsed with ancient authority, and the doors swung inward with a slow, resonant groan.

Vaulted ceilings soared above them, a masterpiece of celestial design, where mosaics of forgotten deities and triumphant saints shimmered beneath the flickering glow of suspended lanterns. Light poured through stained glass, casting shifting patterns of crimson, gold, and deep sapphire onto the polished floor, like the fractured remnants of a thousand prayers.

Rows and rows of pews in a descending terraced hexagonal pattern stretched down into the vastness. The countless seats were quickly being filled with the mourning and sorrowful. Some knelt in silent supplication, their lips moving in whispered devotion. Others sat in solemn stillness, eyes fixed upon the grand altar at the heart of it all—a towering edifice of marble and light, where the names of the lost would soon be spoken into the fabric of eternity.

Tria moved with quiet reverence, Amarax at her side, her parents close behind, the three security bots constant chaperons of their every action. They took their place among the gathering, sitting towards the front in the center, next to other Peacekeepers and government officials, all keeping reverent abidance beneath the cathedral's vast embrace.

Soon, the bells would toll. Soon, the vigil would begin. Once the cathedral was filled to capacity a priest of the unified faiths stepped forward to the center in front of the alter and gave a heartfelt dedication to those who had died.

"In the Good Book, the NAXV Bible, it is written, God said, let there be light, and there was light. But what is this light? Is it merely the glow we see with our eyes or the warmth we feel upon our skin? No, the light that God created is far more profound than what we can perceive with our senses. It is the very essence of life itself — the divine spark that resides in each of us, the eternal flame that connects us to our Creator and to each other.

My parents taught me, and I now believe with all of my heart, that this light is not simply what shines in the physical world. It is found in our actions, in our love, in our joy and in our sorrow. This light is the spirit of compassion that moves us to help one another, the laughter that fills our homes, the tears that bind us together in our grief. It is the light of the heart, the light of the soul, the light that transcends time and space, for it is rooted in God, in the Omega.

Yesterday, the lights of many of our loved ones, was taken from us. Their hearts, once so full of life, now rest in peace. And yet, even as we mourn their loss, we know this: the light they carried has not gone out. It has not vanished. It has been transformed. The love they gave, the kindness they shared, the joy they spread — that light lives on in us. As long as we remember them, as long as we hold their memory in our hearts, their light continues to shine.

It is easy, in the face of loss, to feel that the darkness has swallowed the light. The absence is overwhelming, and we may wonder where the light has gone. But I say to you, my brothers and sisters, the light is not gone. It cannot be extinguished. It is eternal. It lives on in the love we continue to give, in the lives we touch, in the way we carry the lessons they taught us. Their light is now part of us, woven into the very fabric of who we are.

In our sorrow, we are not lost. In our grief, we are not abandoned. The light that we carry is not our own; it is the light of God, the light of all who have come before us. And as we hold their memory close, as we continue to walk in their light, we honor them. We keep their spirit alive by reflecting the love and light they gave to us.

The darkness may feel heavy, but it will never overcome the light. The light is always with us, guiding us, comforting us, leading us through the shadows. It is in the moments of grace, in the quiet acts of kindness, in the love we share with one another. And it is in the remembrance of those who have gone, whose lights continue to shine brightly in our hearts.

So let us not fear the darkness. Let us trust in the light, knowing that it will always find its way back to us. For in the end, the light of those we love — the light of our Savior — will lead us home."

The words of the priest lingered in the heavy silence, filling the vast cathedral with a reverent stillness. His voice, rich with sorrow and hope, carried through the sacred space, each syllable imbued with the weight of the day. The mourners sat in stillness, absorbed in the depth of what he had said, as the light of the eternal flame was invoked in their hearts.

For hours, they stayed in the solemn vigil, their grief a shared blanket of quiet reflection, each face illuminated by the flickering light of candles placed throughout the cathedral. The names of the lost were read aloud, their memories etched into the stone of the ancient walls. The cathedral, once a place of reverence and joy, now held only sorrow and remembrance—yet, there was something powerful in that.

Tria, sitting between her parents, her hand resting lightly on her knee, felt the sanctity of every prayer, every whispered hope and cry of anguish. Her mind was a whirlwind, yet there was peace in this place, a comfort in knowing that for all the darkness, the light would always remain, never fading because of persecution from forces that only wanted control and the blind dedication to a god that was callous to the core.

As the final echoes of the bells faded into the night, Tria and her family stepped out into the solemn hush of the plaza, where clusters of Peacekeepers and officials—General McMaster, General Gatalan, and the President of the Republics—stood in quiet conversation, their faces etched with the same grief and resolve that weighed upon them all like the last embers of a dying fire, glowing with quiet endurance, even when they go out, reigniting again and again.

The Oberon family joined the conversations that were being had, exchanging common courtesies and greetings. General McMaster giving Joshua an especially firm handshake, both of them reminded by the years of friendship that they shared. McMaster was the first to speak after their pleasantries.

"Right now, we mourn, but tonight, we act. The enemy believes our sorrow makes us weak—they will learn it only the opposite. We will make them pay for this."

General Gatalan, spoke next.

"The names spoken within those walls will not be forgotten, nor will their forced sacrifice go unanswered. Vengeance alone will not suffice—we must ensure this never happens again. We must act, as McMaster suggests, we have to bring these monsters to justice, the sooner the better."

President Wasuta Elamoor, was the next to speak.

"I feel as though, we stand at the edge of history, and history demands choices that are thought out and mindful. Do we yield to despair, or do we rise above all the hatred we hold? I trust we all know the answer."

Joshua, quickly added his opinion.

"The light of those we lost must guide us, not blind us. Justice, not wrath, must temper our course. But we must act. I know I'm no longer a Peacekeeper, and I have no say in this matter, but I fully agree with the Generals. We can't be waiting around, we have to act, and act soon."

The president, responded.

"We cannot act without first understanding the complicated reasons behind the attack, we will bring justice, but we need to be patient. A military action when carried out in haste risks becoming a story of revenge rather than a resolution, and I will not let our grief drive us into a putrid war of revenge. Especially one we're not prepared or able to finish at the moment."

General Gatalan, greatly disagreed with the President and expressed his disdain for the slowness that Elamoor was suggesting.

"Our people need more than words; they need assurance, they need the action of the Peacekeepers. The Republics cannot afford hesitation. You must order us to attack the cultists. We have to put every last one of them into confinement. If we don't we can't be sure that the threat would be eliminated."

Elamoor was very upset at Gatalan's words, and snapped back.

"Hesitation is not in my nature, General. But every step forward must be precise. Missteps now could cost us more than lives. It could cost us the soul of the Republics themselves. Many cultists have renounced their former god and have found true peace here, I will not shatter their newfound freedom, for our safety, I cannot strip away the liberties of the few to give the assurance of safety to the many. This situation is not so simple, it's not just black or white, if we blame all cultists, current and former, violent and peaceful, we will create a feud more horrible than we have ever seen. I will not be responsible for any further bloodshed. I cannot stomach it any longer."

Tria, added her own devoted thoughts, to what seemed to be a conversation that could come to an argumentative ending.

"Then let it be justice that moves us forward. But let the enemy tremble, for we do not stand alone. I know we are spread thin, that our forces are weaker than they've been in a long time, but we have allies. We can ask the Messengers to help, and I know that they will help. I just know it."

The President was moved by Tria's words, he hadn't thought about the Messengers. Elamoor let out a slow breath, his gaze drifting toward the towering cathedral behind them as if searching for wisdom in its silent spires.

"The Messengers…" he murmured, the weight of the idea settling upon him. "If they stand with us, we may yet find the strength to prevail. But if they refuse, then we must seek another path—If our requests to the Messengers goes unanswered. Then I intend to send diplomatic envoys to Kronos. A new peace must be forged, no matter how much our inclinations tell us no."

The hearts of the entire group peeled and reeled from the President's words. Another peace treaty, another deal to continue the slow death of the Republics, death by a thousand cuts of peace-seeking pens. Death by the slow degradation of reasonable defense.

Tria gave the president an answer.

"I understand sir, I'll go to them right now. I'll report to you when I have the answer."

"Good, go as soon as you can. I'll be in my office in Unity Tower. Best of luck to you Captain, best of luck to us all."

The President walked away, the Generals and staff following him. McMaster gave a quick handshake again and a friendly strong hug to his old buddy Joshua before the group left. Saying a quick uplifting word to each other.

"Stay strong old friend."

"I will. And same to you."

Once the group had left, Tria's mother Gema turned towards Tria and spoke to her with words of kindness, but also with worry.

"The people may say that they seek justice, but I know that their hearts burn with anger and hatred. I agree with Elamoor, we cannot allow the hatred we have for these lost souls to control us, to warp us. You must be careful not to let that fire consume your reason, your love. Stay vigilant Tria, I sense that a storm is coming, stronger than it has ever been. I wish I could solve all these problems with math calculations, it would make it so much simpler, but I can't. I wish I could do more to help."

Tria paused, looking at her mother with a quiet intensity.

"You've helped more than you know. Every word. Every choice that you've made is a reminder to dig deeper, to never let assumptions cloud our vision. The mind is a well that never runs dry, and it's in the digging that we find our truth. We must stay anchored to the facts, no matter how stormy the waters become. Only the facts, the truth, can guide us forward. You made that possible. You've done more than enough."

They hugged and exchanged their pleasantries as they parted ways, her father nodding with agreement and approval. Her parents went back to the estate and Tria headed to the Messengers, Amarax right next to her, a part of him now trying to understand the extreme devotion of these heretics. He still didn't understand them, but was now wanting to know what gave them their conviction, they were almost as dedicated in their beliefs as the most faithful Dualinite to the Duality.

Chapter Thirty-Seven:
SEEKING CONSUL FROM TEL'MOR'EL

"Every step forward is an agreement with fate: to risk, to endure, to remember."

— *Old Edgeworlder Saying*

The journey to the crystal grove felt heavy with anticipation. Tria walked with a sense of urgency, though her steps were deliberate. Amarax followed, his skepticism still lingering, though now tempered by a reluctant but wanting curiosity. The weight of her task was clear to both of them. This was not a simple search for enemies. It was a search for deeper truths. And truth, Tria knew, could be both a weapon and a curse.

Once they reached the center of the grove, the heart of the crystal forest, the Messengers again greeted her with caring affection. But still feigned from Amarax, only slightly this time, less abrasively running from him, but still retreating from his presence. The crystalline formations rose like ancient monuments ready to be studied, their light shifting and pulsing with an intense sentient rhythm. Tria stood before the largest of these crystals, Tel'Mor'El, a gleaming pillar that thrummed with energies older than humanity, its surface rippling as though it were an organ.

She took a deep breath and closed her eyes. "Tel'Mor'El," she whispered, her voice steady, but filled with a quiet urgency. She reached her hand out "I need to know. The cultists responsible for this pain within me—where are they hiding? The Republics are in danger, and time is running out. Please, I need your help."

Tria opened her eyes and found herself in a world of shadow—a phantom reality where pillars of black stone stretched endlessly into an unseen sky. The air was thick with an eerie stillness, and the space between the towering monoliths felt suffocating, as if the weight of unseen forces pressed against her very soul.

Wisps of darkness slithered along the ground, moving like living echoes of something ancient and forgotten. Her heart pounded in her chest as unease crept up her spine, a silent whisper of warning that she was somewhere she wasn't meant to be.

She turned in place, searching for any sign of Tel'Mor'El.

"Why have you brought me here?" she called out, her voice cutting through the stillness.

The sound barely carried, swallowed by the vast emptiness stretching around her, the thunder and lightning crackling as judges in the ominous sky above. A cold wind stirred, carrying with it something else—something familiar, yet deeply, unbearably wrong.

A figure emerged from the shadows, stepping forward with deliberate slowness. Tria's breath caught in her throat as she saw his face—her brother, Daniel. He looked just as he had the day he died, the same sharp eyes, the same confident smirk, but there was a hollowness behind his gaze, an emptiness that chilled her to the core.

"No," she whispered, shaking her head. "Why would you come to me as my brother. Today of all days. Coming to me as Daniel. He's dead. Why Tel'Mor'El? Why, make me feel this pain right now?"

Tel'Mor'El's expression softened, the hollow gaze flickering with something deeper, something ancient yet heartbreakingly familiar. When he spoke, it was not with Daniel's voice, but with something greater, a voice that carried through the void, reverberating like a forgotten melody in the halls of eternity.

"Because, Tria," he murmured, stepping forward, "I feel your hatred. It coils around your soul like the shadows that dance in this place. Whispering false promises. Feeding a fire inside you. If left untamed, it will not only burn your enemies, it will consume you and everything you hold dear as well."

His words wove through the air like a quiet hymn, reaching for her, pleading with her to listen.

She clenched her fists, her breath sharp and uneven. "What would you have me do?" she demanded, her voice trembling between grief and anger. "They murdered my brothers, my people. They left children to die in the streets, they—" Her voice cracked, and she swallowed hard, forcing herself to stand firm. "You want me to forgive them?"

Tel'Mor'El shook his head, his form wavering like a dream barely held together. "No, child of light. I do not ask you to forgive, nor do I ask you to forget. I ask you to see. To look beyond the hunger for vengeance that gnaws at your heart."

He stepped closer, and though the illusion of Daniel that stood before her, she felt something else behind his presence, something boundless, something impossibly vast.

Tria turned her gaze downward, her breath hitching. "I don't know how," she admitted, the words barely above a whisper. "How do I let go of this dark fire inside me when it's all I have left?"

Tel'Mor'El reached out, and though he did not touch her, she felt warmth radiate from him, a presence like the echo of a forgotten dawn.

"You are not meant to let go of the fire, Tria. You are meant to temper it. To wield it with wisdom, not wrath. Let not the embers of vengeance dictate your path, for hatred is the language of the lost, the blind, the broken." His voice softened, a quiet sorrow threading through it. "I do not want you to feel pain. I want you to think. To stop. To breathe. Let the thoughts of revenge be washed from you like dust carried away by the rain."

She closed her eyes, and for a moment, she allowed herself to listen, not to the anger, not to the agony clawing at her heart, but to the quiet beneath it. And there, in the stillness, she heard it, the echo of something deeper, something stronger than rage. A whisper of reason, of purpose.

The storm above rumbled, distant and fading, as if the judges in the sky had turned their gaze elsewhere. She allowed the moment to wash over her. It was as though a burden was being lifted from her shoulders. She no longer felt the pulling ropes of retribution tugging upon her consciousness. Thoughts of all her pains began to splinter within her mind's eye. Tel'Mor'El walked even closer and put a hand upon Tria's shoulder.

Tel'Mor'El's touch was the hush of dawn before the sun's ascent, the ghost of warmth in a winter's breath, intangible, yet unwavering. His eyes, veiled in the borrowed face of her fallen brother, were not mere reflections of memory, but mirrors to something greater, something boundless. Within them lay the weight of ages, the sorrow of all things lost, and the quiet, enduring promise of all that could still be found.

"The road ahead is carved from sorrow." his voice a ripple through the fabric of the void, neither forceful nor faint, but almost with eternal reassuring solitude. "There will be moments when grief clings to you like a phantom, when rage coils around your heart and whispers the comfort of vengeance. But listen well—light is not the absence of shadow, nor is it its conqueror. It is the defiant spark that refuses to be swallowed. When the abyss rises to claim you, when the fire within you starts to wander towards darkness, you must choose to reignite who you truly are."

Tria opened her eyes and now stood before Tel'Mor'El's crystalline form within the center of the forest of Messengers. The meanings within meanings of his words still settling in her chest. The storm that had once raged inside her, fueled by vengeance, now felt distant, as though it had been washed away by a quiet, undeniable truth, yet a whisper of the darkness remained in the recesses, waiting patiently for the chance to strike.

She took a steadying breath, grounding herself in the calm that had replaced the tumultuous fire of vengeance. The light of the Messengers seemed to pulse softly around her, a reminder that she was not alone, that there was purpose beyond her own storm. Tel'Mor'El's form flickered faintly in kind regard to their connection, his presence was another confirmation of the path she had chosen, she had to stop the cultists before they had a chance to destroy everything she held dear.

The whispers of the cultists, of Kronos, were now clear in her mind, their location burned into her thoughts by the Messengers' cryptic guidance. Turning away, she found Amarax waiting for her, his steady gaze locking onto hers.

"I've seen it. The location. The cultists responsible for the bombing—they're hiding in the Republic of Peace," she said, her voice firm yet strained with the gravity of her next step. "I need to see the President. We have to stop these fanatics before they can hurt anyone else. We need to put an end to this madness."

"I understand. You have to make them pay for what they've done, I understand that well. I could come and be a great asset. I am highly capable in combat."

"That's not possible, Amarax. You're still a prisoner of war. I think the Peacekeepers can handle it this time."

"If that's what you think is best, of course."

"Yes, it's just what it is. I'm sure we'll have the element of surprise and it'll all be over soon. Hopefully they'll never see us coming? I'm sure your security bots will be good company while I'm gone."

"Right. Because these security bots are known for their sparkling social etiquette, and overwhelming charisma. We're going to have a spectacular time together. Maybe we'll even have deep philosophical debates."

Tria couldn't help herself but grin at Amarax's words. His sarcastic charm was starting to rub off on her.

They parted ways as the winds of fate carried them in opposite directions—one toward duty, the other toward uneasy quiet solitude. Tria headed to Unity Tower using the MTN to transfer directly to the Peacekeeper wing of the grand building. Her recently granted Presidential clearance allowed her to bypass all the security protocols, walking through checkpoints and scanners without a moment wasted.

Each step through the towering halls echoed with the importance of what Tria was bringing with her, the information they needed to bring justice. Her mind sharpened with singular focus as she approached Peacekeeper Command and Control, where the President and command staff waited for her.

When she entered the massive control center, the atmosphere was taut with urgency. The President sat at the head of the elongated elegant table, surrounded by the highest-ranking generals and politicians of the Republics. Their eyes turned to her as she walked forward, her presence alone enough to command attention. Without hesitation, she placed her hands on the table's polished surface, the fire of conviction burning behind her gaze.

"I have their location, Mr. President," she announced, her voice unwavering and with absolute conviction. "We have to strike now, before they vanish into the shadows again. We cannot afford to delay any longer, we have to bring these monsters to justice, and we need to do it now."

The room fell into tense silence before the President stood up and gave a slow nod.

"Then I authorize Operation Nightfall Covenant. Captain Oberon, I want you to lead the mission. Bring justice to the Republics. We end this tonight."

"Yes, sir. I'll get it done. You have my word."

Within the hour, the Republics war machine surged into motion. Inside the Peacekeeper Command Center, holotables flared to life, painting the room in cold blue light. Tactical maps projected the jagged peaks of the Republic of Peace's northernmost mountains, where a once-sacred refuge had been corrupted into a den of zealots.

A remote Temple of the Unified Faiths, a sanctuary of harmony had fallen into the hands of the cultists, its once peaceful purpose now defiled beneath the hands of unseen horrors. No one had noticed. Until now when they were looking.

Tria stood at the heart of planning, eyes locked on the shifting data, of the building, they couldn't do current scans of the building, they might be detected. They had to plan based on the construction schematics alone and plan for any contingencies that might arise.

The plan had to be exact and ruthless in its efficiency. MTN platforms would take them to the Republic of Peace undetected, but from there, they would move on foot, their cloaking systems concealing them from prying eyes. The temple's assumed defenses would have to be bypassed, its desecrated halls reclaimed before the cultists could slip away into obscurity and hiding once more.

Another Peacekeeper officer approached; helmet tucked under his arm.

"Captain Oberon, the teams are assembled. We await your command."

Tria took a deep breath of meditation and then exhaled, her hands resting on the edge of the holotable. The cult had thrived in the shadows, believing themselves untouchable, believing their false god would shield them from justice. They were wrong.

"Good. Let's get it done."

She walked with the fellow officer to the Peacekeeper staging area. Multiple battalions awaited in formation, Alphathorn, Eagleborn, Phoenixwing, Dragonspear, and Freedomshield, all ready to do their duty. Her gaze swept back and forth over the gathered forces, their silent dedication to the Republics an unspoken promise of their loyalty to the greater good for all. Tria stepped up to a raised platform in front of the ready Peacekeepers. Her voice, steady and unwavering, carried across the assembly, as sharp as the morning thunder across the plains.

"You stand here not as soldiers, but as the guardians of justice. You are the shield that stands between the innocent and the darkness that seeks to swallow them whole. Tonight, we move with purpose, driven by something far greater than the call of duty. We move as one, united in the belief that the light of the Republics will never be extinguished, no matter how deep the shadows grow.

We strike with precision, with speed, and with resolve. We will be the storm that tears through the lies, the avenging angels that will bring justice to those who have been left to suffer in silence. The cultists believe they can hide. They believe they can escape the consequences of their twisted deeds.

But they're wrong. Very wrong. We will show them that there is nowhere in this world, no corner they can flee to, where the will of the Republics cannot reach them. We are the reckoning. We are the ones who will bring them to justice. And when the dawn breaks, this plague will be nothing but ashes in the wind.

We fight not only for those who stand beside us, but for the children whose laughter still echoes in our hearts, whose dreams must never be marred by the darkness we now face; for their future, pure and unbroken, is the light we must protect at all costs.

We fight for the Republics. We fight for the innocent. We fight for what is right. Tonight we put an end to their terror."

The air crackled with the burden of their mission, every Peacekeeper standing as an unyielding testament to the cause they bore. Tria's words hung like a clarion call, and in that moment, they were not mere soldiers—they were the storm, the harbingers of justice.

With every step, they moved as one, each footfall, a promise that the darkness would no longer go unpunished. Tonight, they would erase the cult's shadow that loomed over the Republics. From the ashes of their terror, they would pave the way for a future built upon the promise of protecting the innocent.

Chapter Thirty-Eight:
OPERATION NIGHTFALL COVENANT

"They call it the end of suffering. They call it peace. They say this treaty is the dawn of something new. But I know better. A new day? A new beginning? No. This is a veil. A thin, fragile veil over the festering wounds we've been forced to ignore. When the President signed that Muggjankkin treaty, I could barely keep my hands from drawing my weapon. She spoke of healing, of unity, as though a century of bloodshed could be wiped away with words. The ink hasn't even dried, and already I can taste the bitter aftertaste of her cowardice. I fear for the future of the Republics. But what can I do against the will of the people."

Kaeleron Lanastar Vortane,

General of the Peacekeepers, Personal Journals, circa 3,273 AD

Like invisible ghostly specters, the Peacekeepers emerged from the MTN in the deep mountainous forests of the Republic of Peace, their mission was the only thing on their minds, all focused on the task before them. The mountain's dense forest swallowed their great numbers whole. The air was dense with the ancient growth around them. The very breath of the wilderness clinging to them as they pressed forward in complete silence.

Each and every step was deliberate, each movement a finely tuned rhythm, a ghostly presence that moved in perfect harmony with the darkness. There were no drones, no engines, no hum of technology to betray them. Only the quiet murmur of their boots against the forest floor, the pulse of an entire mission carried in the steadiness of their advance.

The world outside had disappeared. Only the temple ahead remained, its silhouette rising like a silent monument to the corruption it now housed.

The temple itself, once a place of unity and peace, now stood warped and twisted by the hands that had claimed it. Its broken spires reached up like accusing fingers, grasping at the night sky. The techno lanterns at the entrance cast feeble glows, their light fragile against the crushing cursed surrounding it. This temple, hollowed out by the poison of the cultists' rites, had become a sanctuary for depravity. A place where the light of self-determination and freethought had long since been extinguished.

Tria's eyes locked onto the structure, calculating, assessing. Time was fleeting, but the plan had been laid to perfection, each move deliberate, every angle covered. It had to be. There could be no failure tonight. With a single, swift motion, she raised her hand. The signal. A cold, sharp command that cut through the air like a Singublade.

Without hesitation, the Peacekeepers surged into motion, their actions were seamless, like water flowing through cracks in the earth. Their translucent forms melted into the shadows, fanning out along the temple's perimeter with lethal precision. Every piece of armor, every step, every breath was part of a singular, unbroken rhythm. They were not soldiers. They were instruments of fate, slicing through the silence with purposeful intent.

Tria's heart thrummed in her chest, not with fear, but with the kind of electric anticipation that coursed through her veins every single time she was on a mission. But, this wasn't just another mission. It was justice, long overdue. The weight of every life lost, every soul stained by the cult's dark influence, pressed down on her. Every stolen breath, every broken spirit, every life torn asunder in the name of their twisted doctrine. It would all end tonight.

The cultists, consumed by their twisted rituals, remained oblivious to the silent force closing in around them, their fate was already sealed. The temple's walls pulsed with the echoes of their unholy chants, the air thick with the rancid stench of decay and old blood, as if the very stones had been steeped in suffering. Corruption seeped from within, stretching its vile tendrils into the mountain itself. But tonight, the darkness would be purged.

Like a thunderclap shattering the silence, the Peacekeepers struck. Explosive force tore through the temple's outer defenses as Tria led the charge, her power armor a blur of dark steel and fury. She slammed into the first cultist, her Singublade carving through his weapon before her armored fist crashed into his ribs with a sickening crunch. Another lunged at her. She sidestepped, driving an elbow into his throat, sending him gasping to the ground.

The temple erupted into chaos. Peacekeepers moved like phantoms, striking with ruthless efficiency, their impact batons cracking against flesh and bone, energy shields deflecting the wild, frenzied attacks of the cultists. Smoke and flashing lights filled the air as stun rounds burst against walls and flesh, sending dozens of robed figures sprawling upon the hard floors without mercy.

A twisted priest raised a dagger, shrieking a curse. Tria shot him in the knee, the force of her energy pistol dropping him instantly. Another rushed her, swinging a rusted energy chain, but she ducked low, sweeping his legs out from under him before driving her boot into his chest, knocking the wind from his lungs.

These cultists deserved far worse, but she and the other Peacekeepers controlled themselves just enough not to be lethal in their assaults, death would be far too easy for these fanatical monsters.

Through the swirling battle, Tria advanced, a force of raw justice, breaking bodies with precision, carving a path toward the inner sanctum where the true horror awaited.

The temple's corridors funneled the fight into a brutal gauntlet of flashing steel and shattering bones. Tria surged forward, her Singublade slicing through the air with terrifying speed, carving through cultist weapons before they could even swing, turning its power to max and bringing it back to a less lethal setting before impacting their flesh.

A robed zealot lunged at her with a serrated blade covered in the blood of innocents. She caught his wrist, twisted hard until she felt the pop of tendons snapping, then slammed him against the stone wall with enough force to leave a smear of blood as he crumpled.

Behind her, the Peacekeepers fought with relentless precision. Energy batons cracked skulls, boots crashed into ribs, and stun rounds sent cultists convulsing to the floor. Smoke curled through the temple halls, thick with the scent of burning incense and scorched fabric. Screams of panic and fury echoed through the ancient stone, the desperate wails of fanatics realizing their night of blood was ending in ruin.

A monstrous figure emerged from the shadows—one of the cult's so-called Boneknights of Kronos's Might, wrapped in layers of blackened armor and the skeletal remains of countless victims, the fanatic was wielding a warhammer crackling with a strange green energy.

He swung with the force of a landslide, but Tria was faster. She ducked beneath the massive strike, the wind of it whipping past her face, and drove her blade into his side, sending a surge of raw energy through his body. He convulsed violently, his hammer slipping momentarily from his grasp as he stumbled back. She followed through, ramming her armored shoulder into his chest and sending him crashing through a wooden partition.

The cultist crashed through the wooden partition, sending splinters flying, but he did not fall. Instead, he caught himself mid-air with a force that should have been impossible, his boots skidding across the stone floor as green energy pulsed around him. His warhammer, though momentarily lost, did not stay down, it lurched back into his grasp as if drawn by unseen hands, the sickly glow intensifying. Tria's eyes narrowed. She had read about this before. An ancient energy, erased from history. And yet, here it was, coiling around him like a living thing.

With a guttural snarl, he launched forward, his speed unnatural, his hammer blurring through the air in a strike that would have shattered bones on impact. Tria barely twisted out of the way, feeling the pulse of green energy sear past her like a breath of concentrated hatred. The stone floor cracked beneath the weight of his swing, deep fissures spider-webbing outward. He was stronger than she had anticipated, his movements were precisely dealt in an unnatural way despite his hulking frame. This thing was no mindless brute—this Cultist was trained and dedicated in their attacks.

She pressed the attack, her Singublade flashing as she aimed for the joints in his armor, testing his defenses. But each time her blade neared, the green aura twisted and coiled, intercepting her strikes with bursts of raw energy. One parry sent a shock-wave up her arm, numbing her fingers for a split second too long. That was all he needed.

With terrifying force, he backhanded her, the impact slamming into her helmet and sending her crashing into the stone wall. Her vision flickered as she rebounded, her boots scraping against the floor just in time to duck beneath another hammer strike that would have caved in her ribs. He came at her again, relentless, a force of sheer destruction.

Tria growled, shaking off the ringing in her skull. If her blade wouldn't cut through the energy, she'd have to find another way. She fired her energy pistol point-blank at his exposed shoulder. The bolt struck, but the green aura absorbed most of it, dispersing the damage. He grinned beneath his helmet—a cruel, knowing expression.

She didn't give him time to gloat. Twisting low, she kicked off the cracked stone and vaulted over him, her blade humming as she drove it straight into the back of his armor. He staggered, but the unnatural energy surged again, locking his muscles, keeping him from collapsing. With a furious growl, he spun, catching her by the throat mid-air.

The force of his grip was suffocating, the energy leeching warmth from her body. Pain flared through her chest, but she refused to let him win. She drove her knee into his ribs, once, twice, then braced against his armor and pushed off, breaking free. She landed hard, gasping, rolling to avoid the inevitable hammer strike that obliterated the ground where she had just been.

No hesitation. No fear. She surged forward again, this time with everything she had. The battle was far from over—but neither was she.

The cultist enforcer roared, his warhammer rising again, the sickly green energy swirling violently around him like a living storm. Tria barely had time to steady herself before he lunged, his hammer a blur of death. She sidestepped, but even as she did, the unnatural energy lashed out, a tendril of emerald fire slamming into her chestplate. The force sent her skidding backward, her boots carving deep grooves into the stone.

She grit her teeth, forcing herself to ignore the sharp ache in her ribs. Her Singublade hummed, charged with power, but it wasn't enough. This thing—this abomination—was beyond human, beyond anything she had ever faced. Worse than even the Raddak'Khazmar. The green energy shielded him, warped his movements, made him faster, stronger. Every strike she landed, every wound she carved into his armor, only seemed to enrage him further.

It came at her again, a relentless wall of destruction. Tria ducked under its next swing, but the energy snapped at her like a serpent, searing against her armor. She twisted away, firing her energy pistol at his exposed flank, but the green aura absorbed it, dispersing the shot like it was nothing. He lunged, swinging their Warhammer in a brutal arc. Too fast to dodge.

Before the strike could land, a flash of blue rippling energy cut through the air. The Bone-Knight recoiled as a searing energy blast slammed into his shoulder, staggering him for the first time. A second shot followed, then a third, then dozens of concentrated weapons fire. Tria barely had time to register what was happening before more Peacekeepers rushed into the fray, their armor gleaming under the dim temple lanterns, their cloaking systems no longer functioning. Standing in fire teams, sending controlled bursts at the thing.

Master Sergeant Gideon Elson of Alphathorn led the defensive charge to assist Tria, his rifle barking rapid bursts of precision fire at the enhanced cultist's face and then upon his chest.

"Captain Oberon, fall back!"

He ordered, but she ignored him, instead using the distraction to rush the cultist again. She struck low, slashing at the tendrils of green energy. The Boneknight howled in fury, his Warhammer swinging wildly as the Peacekeepers surrounded him.

Another Peacekeeper closed in, wielding a heavy impact baton. He brought it down hard on the Boneknight's knee, cracking their armor. The cultist stumbled, but before he could recover, another Peacekeeper—this one carrying a pulse spear—drove the weapon straight into his back, through a break in his armor. Energy rippled through the spear as it discharged, sending a violent shockwave through the Boneknight's body. Still, he didn't fall.

The green energy around him flared, pushing back the attackers with a pulse of raw force. The Peacekeepers staggered, some knocked off their feet. Tria dug her boots in, trying to keep herself steady, but the force was too great, she was knocked against the stone.

As she was picking herself up her eyes locked on the Boneknight's movements. His breathing was heavier now, the attacks were taking their toll—but the unnatural energy still fed him, still made him a monster.

"We need to cut off his connection to this energy!" she shouted, scanning for something. Anything. That could sever him from this forgotten power. But there was nothing visible. Whatever fueled him, it wasn't external. It was inside him.

The enforcer straightened, his armor cracked but his fury burning brighter than ever. He raised his hammer, the green energy around him pulsing wildly, coiling like an enraged beast.

Tria set her stance, her Singublade glowing in her grip. The Boneknight charged, his Warhammer crashing down like the wrath of a vengeful god. Tria leaped aside, barely escaping the seismic force that split the stone floor beneath her. The impact sent tremors through her boots, but she refused to stumble. She had no time to hesitate. No time to second-guess.

She couldn't hold back anymore. She couldn't allow her morality to hinder the success of the mission, there were still so many cultists to deal with and this one Boneknight stood in the way of justice.

Gritting her teeth she would soon abandon her moral high ground, she surged forward, her Singublade a streak of rippling lightning-hot energy. The Boneknight swung again, but this time, she didn't dodge—she deflected. The blade met the hammer mid-arc, the impact sending shockwaves through her arm, but she didn't falter. She twisted, ducking low, driving forward like a spear.

She saw a sizable crack in his armor—the weakest point in the unholy shell that protected him. A damaged gap between the overlapping plates along his side, right where Gideon and his squad's concentrated shots had done the most damage.

Tria hacked the controls of her Singublade in a heartbeat, overriding its safety limits, forcing the Reverse Singularity Core within it to overload. The blade surged with unstable energy, flickering erratically, its hum turning into a scream. She deactivated the blade and drove the now unstable hilt forward, shoving it as deep as she could into the gap of the Boneknight's armor.

Ducking away as fast as she could, the overloading reverse singularity core did not explode. It collapsed. The energy imploded within the Boneknight's body, warping the space around it, pulling inward with a violent force before suddenly releasing. A pulse of distorted reality burst outward, and then. Nothing.

A gaping hole had been left in the Boneknight's side, an abyss where his body had once been. The sickly green energy flickered, sputtered, and died. His Warhammer clattered to the ground as he staggered, looking down at the emptiness carved into him.

For a breathless second, he still stood. Then his body crumpled, what remained of his armor crashing to the temple floor, lifeless. The Boneknight. The monster that had withstood everything thrown at him was gone.

The temple still echoed with the Boneknight's fall, but there was no time to linger. Tria ripped out a spare Singublade from matter storage and led her fellow Peacekeepers towards the Sanctum. Around her, and through the various levels of the temple the battalions of Peacekeepers surged forward, their momentum unbroken. The fight was far from over.

They stormed deeper into the temple, carving a path through the twisted faithful. The cultists fought like rabid animals, shrieking prayers to their false gods even as they fell. The corridors became a bloodstained gauntlet. Blades clashed, pulse shots hissed through the air, and the heavy impacts of armored boots shook the ancient stone.

Then, the sanctum doors loomed ahead. Massive, towering slabs of obsidian, newly carved with writhing figures and eldritch symbols, depicting Kronos devouring his own followers, their bodies entwined in agony. The doors stood slightly ajar, and beyond them, something foul churned in the air. Thick, cloying, wrong. Tria felt it in her gut before she even stepped inside.

With a silent signal, the Peacekeepers breached. The inner sanctum was a place of madness. At its center, a grotesque effigy of

Kronos loomed. A massive stone head, eyes hollow yet somehow watching, its maw wide in a silent, endless hunger. Faint green mist curled from its lips like dying breath.

Beneath it, robed figures moved in chaotic desperation, their bone masks featureless save for the deep red slashes that marked their devotion. But one figure stood apart. Tall. Cloaked in obsidian silk. A mask of polished carved bone concealing their face. Detailed symbols of evil rites and runes across its contours.

Yet their eyes were familiar. Too familiar. Tria's breath caught, but there was no time to process. Those eyes were the same eyes she saw in the old man in the market before the bombing. But she didn't have time to think about it now.

The Peacekeepers stormed the sanctum, their assault swift and merciless. Pulsefire shattered the stone pillars, sending debris raining down. Cultists howled as they fell beneath the onslaught, their rituals broken, their faith turning to fear.

The robed leader raised a hand, and something unseen lashed outward. A wave of force slammed into Tria, hurling her back. She barely caught herself, rolling to her feet, her blade snapping up just in time to deflect a crackling bolt of green energy.

Whatever power this was, just like the Boneknight. It was ancient. Dangerous. The masked figure didn't speak. Didn't falter. They moved with inhuman speed, weaving through the carnage, striking with unnatural precision. Their weapon, a jagged staff laced with veins of sickly light, clashed against Tria's Singublade, sending a shock through her bones.

For every strike she landed, they countered. For every step she took, they forced her back. Then, as quickly as they had appeared. They retreated.

A low, guttural chant swept through the remaining cultists. They turned, not to fight, but to flee. The sanctum erupted into chaos as the zealots scattered like little Muggrats, vanishing through unseen exits hidden in the temple's walls and floor.

Tria wasted no time. "After them, hunt them down! We can't let them escape!" she commanded, already in pursuit.

The Peacekeepers followed, giving chase as the cultists disappeared into a labyrinth of tunnels. The air grew damp, thick with the scent of freshly carved earth and the decay of dead laborers. The walls narrowed, forcing them into tight formations as they pressed forward.

Then the traps began.

Hidden, bladed pendulums swung from the darkness breaking through the dirt, catching soldiers off guard. Floor panels collapsed, sending Peacekeepers plummeting into unseen pits. Walls closed in, crushing the unwary. Explosions of green fire erupted from hidden alcoves, searing armor, sending bodies flying.

Tria pushed through, rage fueling her. She wouldn't let them escape. Wouldn't let them vanish into the void. Not this time.

The tunnels grew more twisted, more erratic, each one splitting into several insane directions. The walls and floors were slick with moisture, treacherous for the unobservant. It was a maddening labyrinth that seemed to mock them at every turn, forcing the Peacekeepers into tighter formations, their movements restricted by the cramped, twisting corridors.

Tria led the charge, her pulse hammering, her instincts burning hot with the need to end this once and for all. But the deeper they pushed, the more it seemed the labyrinth itself conspired against them. And then without warning she was falling.

One moment, her boots had found purchase on the floor, the next, it was gone. The stone crumbled beneath her feet, and she was sliding. Fast. Into the depths below. The tunnel spiraled away, her body whipped down, hitting against the jagged tunnel walls, like a leaf caught in an unrelenting current, the cold air rushing past her as the darkness swallowed her whole.

Her attempts to stop her uncontrolled descent were unsuccessful. The walls did not let her take hold. The Nanotube Grappler within her arm module was malfunctioning, the most probable cause being battle damage.

She hit the ground with a sickening thud, her enhanced body and armor absorbed most of the impact, but it still hurt, it hurt a lot. Her breath caught in her chest, pain flaring through her side, but she fought through it. Her eyes snapped open, and all she saw was blackness. Utter, unbroken darkness. The walls of the deep pit stretched impossibly high above her, out of reach.

Her arm module was useless right now, her fingers scraped the stone walls, trying to find a grip. She saw a nearby ledge that seemed to go to another side tunnel, but it was hopeless, it was too high too. She jumped and clawed, just barely missing the edge of the ledge. The depths of the pit were endless, its silence was absolute around her.

A voice echoed through the emptiness, low and mocking. Coming from the side tunnel out of her reach. It cut through her like a blade, familiar yet alien. Deep, warped, like the whisper of nightmares.

"You thought you could stop us?" the robed figure's voice hissed, the mockery dripping from every syllable. "You thought you could be a savior? You and your kind are nothing. You will feel the judgement of the righteous coming. Kronos rises. Kronos will show you the path forward."

Tria's blood ran cold as the voice sent a chill down her spine. The mocking tone...the familiarity of it...It was maddening. Every fiber of her being screamed at her to figure out who this voice belonged to, but the more she searched her memory, the more elusive the tone and eyes became.

But there was no time to think. No time for doubts. The robed figure laughed. A hollow, taunting laugh that echoed around her like the death of hope.

"Your little operation has failed, I go to do my work," they continued. "no matter how hard you fight, no matter how many of you come, you will always be too late. Always too slow to stem the tide of blood that needs to flow to quench the thirst of Kronos."

Then, like smoke vanishing into the air, the laughter died, and the robed figure was gone, vanishing into the shadows of the unknown tunnels. Tria's heart pounded in her chest, but she pushed herself up, fighting the vertigo still ringing within her head and the exhaustion that had already begun to settle into her bones. She scanned the pit, desperation clawing at her, but there was no sign of escape. No way out.

From above, she could hear the faint echoes of the Peacekeepers still in pursuit. But they were too far away. And as the last sound of their struggle faded into the labyrinth's twisted passages, Tria realized that many cultists had escaped.

Operation Nightfall Covenant was by all metrics a strategic and tactical victory—the temple secured, the cult's lair dismantled, a Boneknight vanquished, but victory felt hollow with the true mastermind still at large. The Peacekeepers had crushed the enemy's forces, yet the mysterious robed figure, the mind behind it all, had vanished into the maze of tunnels, slipping through Tria's grasp like smoke.

She pressed a hand against the cold stone of the pit, steadying her breath, forcing down the frustration gnawing at her. The thoughts of incomplete justice pressing upon her. Above, the voices of her allies carried through the cavernous dark. They would find her soon and when she returned to Unum she would most likely be praised for this win and for her dedicated leadership.

But even as she waited, the mocking laughter of the masked fiend echoed through the abyss of the cultists tunnels, a cruel reminder that the conflict was far from over.

Chapter Thirty-Nine:
WHISPERS OF WANTING DIVINITY

"I have walked where angels feared to linger and where demons carved their thrones. I have bowed before saviors who bled and spat on tyrants crowned as gods. I have watched idols crumble, galaxies fracture, and prayers swallowed by the silence of void. I have traced the edges of eternity and touched the weeping wounds of creation. Countless names, countless faces, endless divinities clawing for worship. It all seems like a bad joke, but it's the reality of our existence."

Rendu Yelqura Telerana, Journal of Divine Encounters, circa 4,632 AD

What is God? Amarax had killed in the name of the Holy Duality. He had conquered, bled, and burned worlds beneath their banner. He had stood in temples so vast they swallowed sound, knelt before golden effigies that gleamed with the fire of a billion prayers. He had felt their power, hadn't he? He had known the will of his Gods like the beat of his own heart.

And yet... what is God?

The question gnawed at him as he strode through the endless halls of the Oberon estate's library. It was a cathedral of knowledge, its towering shelves stretching into the dimness of night, lined with tomes older than some empires. The scent of aged paper and fading ink filled the air, a stark contrast to the sterile data vaults of the Dominion. This place breathed. This place felt as though it remembered.

His three security bots followed in silence, their metallic steps softened by the thick, ornate rugs. They moved like shadows, always a step behind, ever watchful.

Everyone else had long since gone to sleep. The estate was quiet, wrapped in the hush of midnight, the distant hum of nocturnal winds the only sound beyond the library's walls.

Amarax expected to be alone, but then he saw him—Joshua Oberon, Tria's father, seated at a long wooden table, a massive book spread open before him. The old man barely glanced up, eyes tracing the ancient script. Amarax recognized the text, Divinity and the Infinite.

He stepped forward. "What is divinity?"

Joshua finally looked up. The dim artificial light cast flickering shadows across his face.

"That," he said, tapping the page, "is what I'm trying to understand."

Amarax did not sit. He let his gaze drift over the endless shelves, the silent wisdom entombed within. How many voices here had dared to question? How many had been silenced for it?

What is God? What is divinity? What is life? What is the meaning of existence?

The questions whispered like distant thunder in his mind, and for the first time in his life, there were no easy answers.

Joshua studied Amarax for a long moment, the kind of look a man gives when measuring the weight of another's soul. Then, he shut the book with slow reverence, the sound a hush against the vast silence of the library.

"You fight for the Duality, I would think you would have your answer." Joshua said. It was not a question.

Amarax's jaw tensed. "I fought for order."

Joshua leaned back in his chair, the old wood creaking beneath him.

"And do you know what that order truly serves?"

His voice was calm, but there was an edge to it, something ancient and knowing.

Amarax did not answer. He had no need to. He had fought too long, too brutally, to pretend that the Duality and their Dominion were forces of pure and gentle righteousness. It was power. It was control. It was divine undeniable will—wasn't it?

Joshua gestured to the book before him.

"This was written by a man who believed divinity was not something given or taken, but something sought with patience. Something glimpsed only by those who dare to question." His fingers traced the cover as if feeling the pulse of the words within. "He was executed for his thoughts. Burned alive by those who claimed to hold the truth."

Amarax's gaze darkened. That was the deserved fate of Heretics, blasphemers, dissidents—erased from history with the same ease that a boot crushes an insect.

"If you are truly asking what God is," Joshua continued, "then you must be prepared to walk a path that has no clear end. You must be willing to step beyond the fire and the sword and see what lies beneath it all."

A silence stretched between them. The security bots stood motionless, indifferent to the metaphysical philosophical meanings of the conversation.

Amarax exhaled slowly. "And what do you believe? You said you didn't believe in the God you used to believe in. So, you believe in no Gods at all?"

Joshua smiled faintly, a flicker of something unreadable in his expression.

"It's complicated, but Tria is right, I'm a hypocrite in many ways, I let my anger get the better of me from time to time. I once believed without a shadow of a doubt in the God of the Bible. But I don't know anymore. I have more than pressing doubts. And now I have come to believe that the greatest lie ever told is that God is a force that demands obedience above everything else. A true God—if such a thing exists—does not ask for unstopping constant worship and the following of endless creeds. Only understanding, only connection, only knowing."

Something in Amarax twisted at those words, something deep, something unspoken. A battle waged within him, though there was no blade, no blood.

"I don't understand, you believed in the Duality? The Gods of the Bible, The Holy Terran-Orion Bible?"

"No, no. There are many Bibles. The Terran-Orion Bible belongs to the Duality—it is theirs and theirs alone. I believed in the NAXV. But there are countless others. So many translations upon translations, each offering new insights, new visions, old revelations, and forgotten dreams. Yet the stream of divinity remains unchanged—something unknown, something powerful, something that lingers just beyond the veil of our understanding."

"I'm sorry, I misunderstood."

"It's alright. It's a common mistake. There are so many books to read and understand. I don't blame you for being confused by what I meant. You've had so much new information thrown at you that I'm sure you don't remember much of it."

"It is a lot of information to take in. But I'm trying to learn as best as I can. But your beliefs are very different than what I'm accustomed to."

Amarax let the words settle, feeling their weight in his chest like unseen chains tightening around his ribs. He had never questioned before—had never needed to. The Dominion had given him purpose, had shaped him into its instrument, had whispered to him the will of the Holy Duality since the day he first held a blade.

And yet...Joshua's voice was quiet, but it cut deeper than any weapon.

"You've spent your life serving what you thought was divinity. Did you ever try to understand it? Or truly come to find out what it all meant?"

Amarax felt the heat of old lessons rise in his blood, a reflex of defiance that had been beaten out of him a long time ago. Understanding is weakness. Understanding is hesitation. That was what he had been taught. A Legionary does not hesitate. A Legionary obeys.

His hands clenched into fists. "Understanding the divine is not my purpose."

Joshua studied him again, that same unreadable gaze. "Then whose purpose is it?"

The question struck Amarax harder than any blow.

For years, he had fought, had bled, had carried the weight of holy war upon his shoulders. He had silenced doubt with the roar of battle, drowned uncertainty in the screams of the dying. But here, in the stillness of the library, surrounded by books that whispered truths older than the Dominion itself, he felt something unfamiliar.

Fear. Not the fear of death. He had walked in its shadow too many times to tremble before it. This was something deeper, colder. The fear of standing on the edge of a precipice and realizing the ground beneath him was not as solid as he had believed.

Joshua leaned forward, resting his partly folded arms on the table.

"If you don't seek truth for yourself, others will give you a truth of their own making. And they will use you to carve that created truth into the flesh of the universe. In the end I believe that that will destroy humanity. The morally blind following the morally blind."

Amarax turned away, his gaze drifting to the endless shelves of knowledge, to the countless words penned by those who had dared to ask the same questions now clawing at the walls of his mind.

He had spent his life carving truth with the edge of a Singulari. But never before his time within the Republics had he really seeked the answers of what truth really meant.

Joshua and Amarax continued their conversation for hours through the night and into the morning. As the first beams of the projected sun came up and through the windows of the library they left the halls of learning, leaving their philosophical metaphysical debating to the hall of books.

The library around them seemed larger than before, the books heavier with even more meaning. Somewhere in the quiet, between that scent of that old paper and that hum of knowledge yet to be read and understood, Amarax felt more flickers of doubt and seeking come into his mind.

Not doubts of his strength. Not of his purpose. But of the very foundation on which he had built his life. The very base of his entire existence up until now. The doorway to the infinite was open, he only had to follow a new path.

Chapter Forty:
MASQUERADE BANQUET FOR HEROES AND SHADOWS

"A hero does not seek the battlefield, it is the battlefield that seeks them. The truly heroic do not measure their triumphs by the enemies they vanquish, but by the lives they defend when the world asks for everything. It is not the blade they wield, but the spirit that endures beyond the sacrifice. This is the true victory."

Maxamas Rivenborne Hendrix,

Captain, United Resistance Front, circa 3,111 AD

Preparations were now nearly complete within the grand halls of the Oberon estate, where a masquerade ball and feast of unmatched grandeur soon awaited all who would come.

The President of the Republics had declared a celebration to honor the heroes of Operation Nightfall Covenant—a celebration not just of victory, but of those who had risked their lives to protect the people of the Republics and bring the shadows into the light. The tables were set, the crystal chandeliers glimmered in anticipation, and masks were ready to adorn the faces of the most esteemed guests. The Republics, united in their triumph, now sought solace in the revelry, a collective exhale to try and bring back normalcy and joy.

Yet beneath the veneer of jubilation, Tria remained uneasy. The silent calm that had followed the operation felt heavy, unnatural. Weeks had passed in what appeared to be peaceful perfection. The Republics were alive with continuing festivities, filled with the renewed sounds of Liberty and Freedom ringing through the air. The yearly festival had resumed as if nothing had happened. But Tria could not shake the gnawing feeling that this was only the calm before the storm.

Though Tria had found many interesting moments in the company of Amarax, those moments were fleeting, like whispers lost in the wind. Their time together was not grand or extravagant, but simple, quiet. A quiet that only made the silence around them feel more profound.

They walked the streets of the eight Republics, their steps a journey of discovery, a journey of seeking, allowing Amarax to take in the world that Tria so adored. They visited monuments and museums, attended plays, watched street shows where laughter mixed with the sounds of vendors hawking goods; they explored quiet corners of cities that were barely seen, an endless tapestry of beautiful diversity.

In their time together they again went to see the Messengers on multiple occasions, seeking more wisdom, and understanding, but so many times the Messengers left their questions unanswered. Many times just giving each thoughts of their destiny together. But neither Tria or Amarax spoke of the things they saw or felt, just the unsaid tension of what might be.

This time of peace seemed fake. The cultists had retreated, yes, their numbers were diminished, their hidden stronghold had been shattered. but they weren't defeated. Kronos was still in command of vast armies within his domain and his fanatical zealots were still on the loose within the Republics.

She could feel them still, like the distant thrum of a storm waiting to break. The mysterious and yet familiar masked cultist haunted her dreams. His retreat wasn't surrender, but regrouping. The quiet might seem like victory, but Tria understood what this lull meant. it was a momentary breath before the next wave of conflict.

The day passed quickly, hours slipping away unnoticed as Tria's mind churned with thoughts she could not silence.

As the evening drew near, the estate seemed to shimmer in preparation, the air thick with anticipation. The Oberon halls, bathed in soft golden light, were lined with banners, elegant drapes of deep navy and light blues, gold flowing from the walls like magical waterfalls made by Midas. The soft notes of classical music swirled in the air as servant androids and organizers moved through the spaces, arranging the last of the details. And soon, the first of the guests began to arrive.

The masquerade was in full swing when Tria finally entered the grand hall. The laughter and chatter of guests: dignitaries, politicians, and elites from all the Republics, echoed off the high stone walls. The guests, all masked, danced and celebrated, their identities hidden behind intricate designs of gold and silver. The scent of lavish food filled the air, mingling with the sound of clinking glasses and soft music.

But Tria felt none of it. The masks, the music, the food. It all felt distant, as if she were floating above it all. She moved through the crowd, her mask cold against her skin, her eyes scanning the sea of faces, each hidden behind their own illusion. There was no joy in the spectacle for her. Only shadows.

She noticed Amarax standing at the far edge of the room, watching quietly. He wore a mask of polished black, the lines sharp and angular, hiding his features but not his presence, he was easy to pick out in a crowd, especially because of his unnatural height and his three robotic chaperons.

Even in the midst of the festivities, he was alert, watching, as always. Their eyes met for a brief moment, a silent understanding passing between them. Without a word, she made her way toward him.

As Tria made her way toward him, Amarax's eyes never left her. The faintest smile of affection tugged at the corner of his lips, a silent acknowledgment of her intoxicating presence. Despite the lively chatter around them, he stood apart, his posture as rigid and watchful as ever, his three robotic chaperons, sleek, silent, and imposing, standing at attention beside him.

"Enjoying the festivities?"

Tria asked dryly but with kindness as she reached him, her voice softly cutting through the ambient noise that surrounded them.

Amarax looked around at the crowd, his gaze sweeping over the sea of gleaming masks and painted smiles. "Oh, absolutely," he said, his voice dripping with sarcasm. "It's a real party, reminds me of the Divine Galas within the Palace of the Duality. The Tribunals always wanted to celebrate something. Your Republics would put them to shame."

Tria couldn't help but let out a little chuckle, though the sound was short-lived.

"I know exactly what you mean. All this revelry, and yet I feel like I'm at a funeral."

Her gaze lingered on the dancers swaying in the center of the room, their movements too smooth, too rehearsed. The spectacle felt hollow, as if everyone were pretending, playing a role in a script that had already been written.

"Maybe you just haven't had enough wine," Amarax suggested with a smirking joviality. "Perhaps that'll fix the atmosphere. I have to admit, it's not half bad. These Fundaberries are a true asset of your people."

She gave him a sideways glance, a larger grin pulling even more at her lips. "Maybe I just need a distraction. A real one."

"Good thing I'm here then," he said, a playful glint in his eye. "I'm the best distraction this masquerade has to offer. I couldn't tell you how many times I've had to answer fascinated question after fascinated question. Apparently, I'm a bit of a fascinating curiosity here in Unum."

Tria's eyes softened, though she tried to hide the warmth that was beginning to creep into her chest.

"I'm sure you are," she replied, leaning in slightly, her tone teasing. "A man of mystery and danger. What more could a girl ask for?"

Amarax raised an eyebrow, looking as if he might say something flirtatious, but then he glanced back toward the crowd, scanning once more.

"And yet, even with all the masked figures in here, I'm still convinced the most dangerous one might be the person standing beside me."

Tria arched a brow.

"Oh really? And who might that be?"

He tilted his head slightly toward her, another small smirk forming beneath his mask.

"The one who thinks too much even at a masquerade banquet arranged for their heroism. The one who doesn't know how to enjoy herself even when she's being honored."

"Someone has to stay sharp. Someone has to make sure all the masks in here don't hide more than just faces."

"Maybe," Amarax said, his voice low, a touch of seriousness slipping in despite the light tone. "But that doesn't mean you have to carry the weight of your world while doing it." He paused, looking at her closely, the humor softening in his gaze. "You deserve a moment to breathe. To just be...here. To have a single night of carefree unadulterated pleasures without over-analyzing."

Tria's smile wavered, her eyes flickering throughout the room and to the dance floor before locking onto Amarax once more. "I know," she whispered, admitting the truth. "I just feel like, this is all an illusion, that it will be gone in the blink of an eye."

Amarax held her gaze, his expression unreadable for a moment before a rare deep softness touched his features. He reached for her hand, leaving an open palm.

"Then live this illusion with me," he said, his voice low but firmly confident. "Even if it fades, let's make it real while it lasts."

Tria hesitated, her fingers hovering just above his, as if afraid that the moment itself might dissolve at her touch. The music swelled around them, a symphony of fleeting beauty, each note a whisper of something too perfect to last. Shadows danced in the golden light, flickering like memories on the edge of forgetting.

Her breath was shallow, the weight of unseen tides pressing against her ribs.

"And when the illusion shatters?" she asked, her voice barely more than a sigh, her words laced with a quiet ache.

"Then it breaks. Everything breaks eventually," he said, his voice a low murmur, rich with something deeper than certainty. "If what remains is lasting, then it was never just an illusion."

For a moment, she lingered, caught between the pull of dutiful perpetual vigilance or the placid temptations of the present. The pressure of unseen threats wrapped around her thoughts, whispering of battles yet to come. But then, with a quiet meditative breath, she reached forward, her fingertips grazing his. A simple touch, yet one that grounded her in the now.

"A few minutes of illusion than," she allowed, though the steel in her voice had not yet melted. "But don't think for a second I'm letting my guard down."

"Not even for me?"

Amarax's smirk deepened even further, a little challenge laced in his words.

"Especially not for you."

She countered, though the words carried less bite than she intended. Beneath the veil of their playful words, something unspoken lingered. An acknowledgment, a hesitation, a truth neither of them dared name, but was growing within them both.

Amarax tilted his head slightly, as if weighing her answer, but he said nothing. Instead, he lifted their joined hands, his grip firm yet careful, guiding her into the tide of masked dancers. The world around them blurred. Golden light flickering off polished marble, silk and shadow entwining in the swell of movement. The music curled through the air, haunting and hypnotic, the heartbeat of the masquerade.

Both were warriors, but while Tria knew the rhythmic meditative discipline of the Peacekeepers, Amarax had learned the dance of wining and dining with the most powerful in the Dominion, that was one of the responsibilities of his title as a lord of house Mirvega.

Amarax led for the first time between them, his touch gentle yet commanding, guiding her into the swirling tide of dancers. For a fleeting moment, Tria allowed him to take the lead, a rare surrender to his presence. In that exact second, she wished for the visions of their love to be true. The ones that danced in the corners of her mind, half-formed and full of possibility.

Yet, despite the warmth of his hand in hers, despite the way the world seemed to bend around them, doubt lingered in the shadows of her heart. She wasn't sure. Wasn't sure if the visions her Messenger friend had given her and what she had seen in her desert journeys were real. Or if they were just more illusions she allowed herself to believe in.

Her body moved with his, but her mind still held back, cautious. The music wrapped around them like a spell, but the Peacekeeper in her remained alert, unwilling to be completely consumed by the moment.

In the whirl of silk and shadow, they were two souls caught in the same breath, their bodies swaying with a passion that blurred the line between devotion and desire. Each step they took was a silent vow, their movements a dance of longing, their eyes locked in an unspoken truth. As the music swelled, their faces drew closer, hearts beating in unison, the space between them charged with the promise of something that had not yet come to fruition.

And in that delicate moment, where time seemed to hold its breath, they hovered on the edge of a kiss, their embrace a symphony of silent yearning, a promise neither was yet ready to fulfill.

Amarax's grip tightened ever so slightly, not in possession, but in something deeper. An unspoken plea, a tether to the truth they both feared yet longed for. Tria's pulse quickened, her instincts battling the pull of his presence, the visions that haunted her mind teasing her with what could be, but also the reality of his Dominion past.

A chime echoed through the grand hall, reverberating like a distant warning, but was only a bidding to the banquet area. The masked dancers hesitated for only a moment before resuming their movements, the illusion of revelry barely disturbed. But for Tria and Amarax, the spell had broken.

Tria inhaled sharply, grounding herself as the heat of their embrace faded into a cool air between them. Her heart still pounded, not from the dance, but from something far more dangerous. Something she wasn't ready to name. Amarax's fingers lingered against hers, his grip hesitant before he finally let go, his face betraying nothing under the warm chandelier light.

The grand hall's golden glow faded behind them as the guests moved in a steady procession toward the gardens. The night air was crisp, carrying the scent of blooming flowers and the faint, spiced aroma of the feast ahead. Artistic lights lined the garden paths, their purposeful flickering illumination casting long, shifting shadows across the manicured greenery.

At the heart of the gardens, a massive banquet table stretched across the open green, its polished surface adorned with gilded plates, crystalline goblets, and elaborate floral arrangements. Glowing orbs floated in the air around the table, giving a magical ambiance.

The table's vast length centered perfectly within the expanse of the lawn, as though carved into the landscape itself. Android servants and organizers weaved effortlessly through the gathering, pouring deep crimson wine into waiting glasses and setting the final touches upon the extravagant spread.

Tria and Amarax were led to their seats near the head of the table, placed beside her parents. A position of both honor and scrutiny. Just beyond them sat the figures who commanded the Republics: The political hierarchy, the President at the helm of the table. The Generals of the Peacekeeper Corps flanking the politicians, General McMaster looking ever watchful, his sharp gaze missing nothing.

President Elamoor rose from his seat with measured grace taking his mask off as he stood, the ambient glow of the overhead luminaires casting shifting gold along the sharp contours of his face. As the murmurs of conversation dwindled, all eyes turned to him, sensing the significance of what he was about to say.

He lifted his goblet high, the crystal catching the cool radiance of the hovering light orbs like a beacon, and when he spoke, his voice carried not just across the table, but through the hearts of all present.

"To those who stand when others fall. To those who face the darkness so we may live in the light.

Tonight, we do not simply feast. We honor the Peacekeepers, the guardians of our Republics. They do not fight for conquest or power, but for those who cannot fight for themselves. Their courage is not measured in medals, but in sacrifice, in the burdens they carry so others may know peace.

They are the shield that does not break, the light that does not dim, the silent watchers who ask for nothing and give everything.

While the rest of us debate and calculate political games, they act. While others build walls of words, they stand upon the battlefield and make the impossible choices. Again and again.

Among those we honor tonight for courage above and beyond what is expected of a Peacekeeper, Captain Tria Oberon, Master Sergeant Gideon Elson, and Lance Corporals Darian Mykos, Rhenza Caldrith, and Iskanderai Veymon. They stand as shining beacons as undeniable examples of the highest ideals we hold dear.

Let this toast be more than words. Let it be a promise. That we will not forget their sacrifice. That we will not remain idle while they bear the burdens of our survival. That their fight, their pain, their unwavering duty will not be in vain.

Let us toast these heroes of the Republics."

Everyone at the table stood up with their glasses held high in salute as the President finished his toast.

"To the Peacekeepers. To their courage, their honor, and the unbreakable wall they form between us and the darkness."

Everyone there agreed in unison as they lifted their glasses even higher and said in raised voices.

"To the Peacekeepers."

Conversations wove through the night like currents in a vast sea, flowing from war strategies to the uncertain future of the Republics. Some spoke of politics, others of home, while a few indulged in lighter musings to push away the ever-present shadow of the conflicts that plagued them.

Tria listened, engaging where necessary, but the unease in her gut grew heavier with each passing moment.

As the banquet ended, many lingered in the gardens, their laughter and conversations mingling with the ambient hum of artificial lights. Yet, beneath the revelry, something felt off. A shiver crept up Tria's spine. A warning she could not place. She turned, her instincts screaming, but before she could speak, the darkness beyond the gardens erupted.

Shrieking figures burst from the shadows. Ravenous cultists clad in tattered robes, eyes wild with fanatic fury. It seemed impossible. How had they breached the defense perimeter? But there was no time for questions. Chaos swallowed the night.

Guests screamed as tables were overturned, goblets shattered, and once-elegant decor became discarded debris. The Peacekeepers sprang into action, but none had weapons. Improvised arms became their salvation. Silverware turned to daggers, shattered chair legs became clubs, and serving trays were wielded as shields.

The Peacekeepers Holocomm calls for backup were left unanswered. Communications were being blocked.

With a defensive fury that she had never felt so strongly until this moment Tria lunged for a broken candelabrum, swinging it with brutal efficiency against those who were trying to kill her, as Amarax ripped a large stone from the ground, slamming it into a group of incoming attackers.

Blood splattered across the once-pristine banquet cloths as the garden transformed into a war zone. These seemingly more psychotically vicious Cultists, undeterred by pain, fought with a reckless hunger, their shrieks mingling with the sound of fists meeting flesh and bodies crashing into furniture.

The Peacekeepers fought like cornered wolves, their survival instincts razor-sharp, but the enemy was relentless. The night of celebration had become a desperate struggle. And Tria knew that they had to end this fast, or none of them would leave this place alive.

Amarax was a beast unleashed, a force of raw, unbridled destruction. This was the first time he had fought since his captivity in the Republics, and in the chaos, no one would be the wiser to the satisfaction he took in the carnage.

His strikes were monstrous, his strength terrifying. He wrenched entire sections of the stone banquet table from the earth, hurling them like battering rams into the cultists, reducing bones to dust beneath the crushing weight. Marble statues became weapons in his grasp, shattered and repurposed as bludgeons to break bodies and send foes flying to their deaths.

Weapons were torn from the hands of his enemies, with malicious pleasure twisting their own blades against them. With ruthless precision, striking time and time again, pushing the sharp blades through their armor. Flesh parted, arteries spilled their warmth across the trampled garden, and with each strike, Amarax moved faster, his instincts sharpened by the bloodlust roaring through him. Necks snapped beneath his grip, spines cracked with sickening finality. There was no mercy, only destruction.

Through the shifting bodies and flashes of battle, Tria caught a glimpse of something in the distance. A lone figure stood beyond the carnage, perched atop a raised pillar, robes flowing like ink against the dark. Their presence radiated something colder, more calculated than the maddened thralls swarming the garden. She knew, without question, this figure was the one who had orchestrated the attack, this was the same leader who had evaded her before.

She lunged forward, wanting to enact a bit of justice with her own hands, but the cultists closed in like a living tide, their bodies crashing into her, slowing her advance. She struck out, breaking past one, then another, but it was not enough. The figure remained just out of reach, watching from the shadows before disappearing into the night.

A surge of frustration boiled within her. Who were they? How had they breached the perimeter?

Before she could fight her way through and chase the leader down, the tide of battle threatened to turn against them. The Peacekeepers, though fierce, were unarmed and unarmored, no Biogel, no Boostergel, their movements slowing as exhaustion and injury took their toll. The cultists did not waver in their ruthlessness, it was as if they didn't feel fear, and their numbers seemed endless.

And then. The crack of energy weapons. The sharp bark of Peacekeeper weapons filled the air as reinforcements stormed onto the unlikely battlefield, their armor gleaming beneath the artificial lights. Bolts of stunning energy and precision rounds cut through the remaining cultists with brutal efficiency.

The bloodied, battered unarmored Peacekeepers fell back as the battle-readied took over, ending the engagement with cold, methodical precision. The enemy was neutralized in a matter of minutes. The last cultist fell, their limp stunned body hitting the blood-soaked ground with finality. Silence settled over the ruined banquet, broken only by the labored breaths of the surviving Peacekeepers and guests.

An acrid disturbing scent of scorched flesh and cultist plasma discharge hung heavily in the air, clinging to their noses like a leech.

Tria's heart pounded as she turned toward the distant shadows beyond the carnage. The robed figure was gone, vanished like a ghostly specter into the night. Her fists tightened, nails biting into her palms. They had orchestrated this massacre, breached defenses that should have been impenetrable.

A shiver crawled down her spine. Not of fear, but of revulsion, of agony, of the unspeakable horror she had just witnessed and participated in. The revolution on Mars was disturbing and heart breaking, but this fight was more personal, this was her home, her sanctuary. She had been able to avoid becoming a monster on Mars, but tonight she had fought like a caged animal against the cultists who had turned her family home into a war-zone. It would become a stain on her heart and mind, one she would never be able to entirely wash away, no matter how hard she tried.

This hellish onslaught would etch itself into her spirit, as an unhealable scar written in blood and vengeance. And Tria vowed at that moment, with unyielding conviction, that she would answer their cruelty with the cold precision of a righteous reaper, delivering the final toll against their malevolence. A requiem for the countless lives they had stolen this night.

Chapter Forty-One:
SEEKING PEACE WITHIN CHAOS

"Peace is not always found after the chaos, it's usually found within it."
— Peacekeeper Codex of Peace

Midday cast its indifferent light over the shattered estate, illuminating the ruin that had once been a sanctuary. Tria and Amarax moved through the wreckage, their hands busy, her heart heavy, his light. The gardens, once vibrant and full of life, were nothing more than a graveyard of broken stone and scorched earth. The damaged walls of her family home stood, but they no longer felt like shelter.

A day had passed since the attack, yet the air still carried the truth of destruction and loss. The android servants worked tirelessly, repairing and cleaning as best as they could, but their precision could not mend what had been lost. Tria tried desperately to restore some sense of normalcy, to bring the estate back to the way it was. But no matter how many fallen branches she cleared, how many shattered windows were replaced, the scars of the recent attack ran too deep.

The sight of it all filled her with rising rage. A slow, simmering fury that refused to fade, soon it would boil over if she didn't temper it. This place, once a sacred oasis for her, was now tainted by the blood of innocent victims and vulturous violence. She couldn't stay. Not like this. She had to find a place to center herself again.

Tria knelt beside a shattered statue, her hands stained with adhesive as she desperately tried to fit the pieces back together. The cracks were deep, the damage irreversible, but she refused to let it go. If she could mend this, maybe, just maybe, she could fix everything else.

"It's broken, Tria, I don't think it can be fixed."

Amarax said softly, watching her struggle to mend the shattered pieces into one. She pressed the pieces harder, her breath struggling and ragged from the force she exerted against the inanimate objects.

"Everything's broken! My family, my home—" Her voice caught, but she swallowed it down. "I won't let them take everything from me, I can fix it."

Amarax crouched beside her, his gaze steady.

"You don't have to stay in the ruins of this place to prove that."

She squeezed her eyes shut. She hated how right he was. The destruction of her oasis, the thoughts of failure, her inability to apprehend the leader of the local cultist cells, the failure to protect the innocent, they were all suffocating her.

"You're right. I need to leave. I need to get out of here and find some kind of peace once again."

"Where can we go to find that?"

Tria thought deeply, contemplating her answer.

"The Republic of Peace."

Tria paused for another moment and thought about it more before speaking again.

"Yes, the Republic of Peace. I have to go. Do you want to come?"

Amarax thought for only milliseconds, she was too interesting not to follow.

"Of course I want to go. We can find this peace together."

The decision was made. Within hours, her request for temporary leave from the Peacekeepers was approved and a Hoveryacht was chartered, prepared, and packed.

They'd have to go through air transport. The MTN was being greatly restricted since the attack yesterday, Peacekeeper leadership thought that maybe the cultists were using the teleportation network to their advantage, overriding safety protocols. For the time being only necessary government and Peacekeeper business was allowed through the matter transfer network.

Tria's parents, silent and grief-stricken wanted to go and find some peace as well. They had spent decades adding and preserving their generational home into something beautiful, something sacred, only to watch it fractured in an instant.

Her father had barely spoken since the attack, and her mother walked through the ruined estate as if haunted by ghosts no one else could see. Perhaps, in the Republic of Peace, they could all breathe again, without the shadows of destruction suffocating them.

The chartered sleek Hoveryacht lifted off from their front lawn, leaving the ruined estate behind, the androids still working below like tireless sentinels of a broken past. Tria sat beside Amarax, her fingers absently tracing the armrest as the thick artificial clouds and projected stars stretched beyond the viewport.

For the first time in days, she exhaled fully, starting to let go of the weight pressing against her chest, allowing herself to meditate on the trip to the peaceful Republic. In her meditations Tria drifted into uneasy sleep.

And then, the nightmare began. She was back at the Oberon estate. Or what was left of it. It looked even worse than how she had just left it. The walls were now broken. The grand halls, once filled with laughter and warmth, lay completely shattered and fractured, broken beyond recognition. The air was thick with the acrid stench of burning wood and something far worse.

It was a graveyard of loss. Masks, cracked and bloodied, lay discarded among an endless sea of dead bodies. The once-pristine marble floors were now slick with crimson, reflecting the flickering light of smoldering banners of the Republics. The faces of the dead seared into her eyes.

A distant mocking sob echoed through the ruins. Tria turned, her pulse hammering. This nightmare was a terrible curse, her sanctuary had become a slaughterhouse. And at the center of it all. Him.

The cultist leader stood at the top of the still partially intact grand staircase, looking just as she remembered. His tattered robes trailed in the blood of the innocent, and his skull mask, carved with grotesque symbols of devotion to Kronos, he tilted his body ever so slightly, as if mocking her.

"You failed them. You will always fail them." he murmured, his voice twisted and warped, yet smooth as silk and sharp as fangs stabbing into her mind.

Her hands clenched into fists as a Singublade appeared in her hand. She would chase him through the chaos, she would stop him, she would make him pay for what he had done and what he would most likely do in the future.

Tria started running up the grand staircase, her Singublade igniting in a searing arc of white violet light. The cultist leader merely spread his arms, welcoming the fight like a priest welcoming a sermon.

"That's right, come."

Their blades clashed. Light against shadow, fury against madness. Sparks screamed as energy met steel, the force of their strikes splintering the ruined banister even more. Tria pressed forward, striking with relentlessness, each blow fueled by a deep wanting vengeance, by a righteous wrath.

The cultist weaved between her attacks like a phantom, his blade an extension of the darkness itself.

"Is this all your rage amounts to?" he taunted, sidestepping a lethal strike before slashing toward her exposed side.

Tria twisted, her armor absorbing the glancing blow as she whirled into a counterattack. Her Singublade sang as it arced toward his throat, only for him to vanish in a blur of motion, reappearing in the sky above her, hovering, untouched, unfazed.

"You fight with fire, Tria Oberon," he mused, his voice laced with amusement. "A fire that cannot be put out."

A deafening crack split the air as the cultist burst into a beam of dark energies that broke the sky, forming a giant portal above. Shockwaves and clouds of lightning rippled everywhere. A deep, guttural hiss echoed through the air. A giant serpent descended down from the portal, its monstrous form twisting through the air. Its golden eyes locked onto her.

Its body was endless, its blackened scales shimmering like liquid night. Its many golden eyes burned with a cruel, ancient intelligence, its forked tongue flickering like a whisper of death. The great serpent coiled down around the remains of the Oberon estate, squeezing, devouring, as if feeding on the destruction.

Tria stumbled back, but there was nowhere to run. The serpent reared back, its fangs dripping with darkness. It struck. Swallowing her whole.

Tria screamed out, jerking awake in the Hoveryacht. Her breath was heavy and quick, her skin cold with sweat. The viewport beside her showed only the vast, indifferent fake stars. But inside her mind, the ruins of the Oberon estate still burned, and the shadows whispered that this would be the fate of her home.

The soft hum of the Hoveryacht's engines filled the air, and Tria's ragged breathing slowed. Amarax glanced over, his brow furrowed with concern.

"Are you alright?" he asked quietly, his voice cutting through the lingering remnants of the nightmare.

She wiped the sweat from her brow, her fingers trembling slightly as she looked at him, trying to steady herself.

"I'm fine." she said, her tone sharp, though the slight tremor in her voice betrayed her.

"Alright." Amarax said, with simple acceptance.

After the words had left her mouth, she could feel the jagged edges of her thoughts cutting into her. The disturbing images were a painful reminder of the darkness that surrounded her.

Another three hours would pass by before they reached their destination. Tria meditated again, this time making sure she didn't fall asleep.

The Hoveryacht soared through the skies of Unum past hover barges and Hovercars, then over the mountains, then over endless grassy plains that rolled like waves, little tranquil villages peppering the landscape, then reaching the boundaries of Unum, entering a network of massive, dark gilded tunnels that were ancient and strange looking, the expansive tunnels were illuminated by bright spotlights that pointed towards the walls, black stone carved with runes and symbols, statues of strange beings and apparent ancient gods lined the megalithic walls, almost evil in their design, almost looking as though they had been carved from darkness itself.

Amarax was a bit surprised seeing such a strange sight within the Republics, but the thought didn't linger, it probably should have, but it didn't. In that moment it wasn't on his list of priorities. Their peaceful journey toward the Republic of Peace would soon be over and he needed to be alert and take every piece of information in. He needed to keep his plan of deception intact; he needed it to come to completion.

Their Hoveryacht burst out of the tunnels like a phoenix rising from the ashes, dust and fog parting as it whizzed through. Then rising up into the clouds again. They were in the Republic of Peace. Paradise stretched as far as the eye could see and beyond.

After only a short time after leaving the strange tunnels they arrived at their destination. The jungle air wrapped around them as the Hoveryacht descended, landing with a soft thud on the grounds of their old family villa. The sweet scent of vibrantly healthy damp earth and exotically enticing flowers flooded Tria's senses as she exited out of the craft. A stark contrast to the smoke and charred remains of recent events.

The peaceful, Utopian villa of old-world design, a beautiful mixture of cultures and styles was itself nestled on the banks of a crystal-clear river that wound through the jungle like a liquid ribbon of tranquility.

Tria's feet slightly sunk into the soft earth as she walked off of the landing pad. She took a deep breath, allowing the chorus of nature to wash over her. The melodic calls of birds soaring high in the trees, the chatter of excited monkeys echoing from within the villa grounds. Cute little monkeys darted playfully through the lush greenery, their antics creating a stark contrast to the dark turmoil that was still raging in her heart.

It was peaceful here. But it was a peace she had yet to embrace again since the war began. Since Mars, since Venus, since the cultist attacks. But she was here to claim it and wash away the dark conflicts of recent days.

The elder Oberon's headed inside, to appreciate their old and long neglected villa, but it was theirs, that's all that really mattered. It was better than the damaged estate back in Unum. Many Dronekind helped unload all their things and assisted with anything else that was required of them.

Tria wanted to go to the river and Amarax offered to cook her something, this place kind of reminded him of his youthful years in the jungles of Mars. He liked the atmosphere of this wild domain. Tria settled onto the soft riverbank as he gathered and prepared the food with an android's assistance. Cooking it in an old style pot over an old-fashioned but efficient fire. No technology or high tech gadgets. Just the practical old ways.

The scent of wet soil and jubilant blooming flowers mingled with the fresh aroma of the meal Amarax had prepared. The food was simple but hearty. Some kind of roasted root vegetable soup, and a mix of local fruits. Sometimes Amarax was full of surprises, and Tria appreciated that.

As she lifted a small piece of fruit to her lips, a rustling in the foliage caught her attention. Before she could react, a small figure leaped from the trees and landed squarely on her shoulder.

On trained instinct Amarax's hands shot up fists clenched, his eyes narrowing.

"What the—"

But Tria let out a soft laugh.

"Well, well, look who's still kicking around."

She reached up to scratch behind the creature's ear. It was an old monkey, its fur streaked with silver, its expressive eyes twinkling with mischief and recognition. The creature nuzzled against her cheek, chattering softly.

"You know this thing?" Amarax asked, lowering his hands but still eyeing the monkey with suspicion.

Tria chuckled. "Of course I do. This is Ozlo. He used to sneak into my quarters when I was a kid and steal my food, we became good friends."

She broke off a piece of fruit and held it up to Ozlo, who eagerly took it with both hands, stuffing it into his mouth like it was the greatest treasure in the galaxy.

Amarax raised a brow. "You're telling me you had a pet monkey and never mentioned it?"

"He's not a pet." Tria shot him a playful smirk. "He's a free soul. Comes and goes as he pleases. And besides, it never seemed important to bring up."

Ozlo, now munching happily, reached out and patted her cheek with his tiny fingers. Tria's expression softened as she whispered.

"You've gotten old, little one... but you still remember me, don't you, Ozlo?"

The monkey let out a soft chitter, then climbed into her lap, curling up like a child seeking comfort. Tria stroked his back absentmindedly as she thought about her childhood, those days she wished she could return to.

Amarax exhaled and shook his head. "You're something else, Oberon."

She glanced at him, raising a brow and smiled, enjoying the moment. "Is that a compliment, Mirvega?"

He smirked deeply. "Let's call it an observation for now."

The peaceful moment stretched between them, the river whispering its ancient song as the jungle breathed around them. For the first time in what felt like an eternity, Tria let herself simply be in the moment, unburdened for this little time of serenity that she had been given.

That stillness lingered between them, the river murmuring its timeless hymn while the jungle exhaled in quiet rhythm. For the first time in ages, Tria surrendered to the present, shedding the weight of what was and what could be. In that fleeting breath of tranquility, she allowed herself to simply exist. Frailly unbound, and wholly alive within the embrace of a world older than her grief and regrets.

Chapter Forty-Two:
WHEN THRONES COLLIDE

"No throne is eternal; only the struggle to sit upon it."

— The Testament of Marath-Kai Alidon

In a dark system of the CAD regions, Veshdren'Ra's Throneship carved its way through the black ocean of outer space, its vast silhouette like a crown of fire dragging across the void. Silence clung to the corridors as though the ship itself were listening for the faintest echo of life. None came. Days of searching, and still nothing.

On the bridge, the eldest of her faithful Tribunals stepped forward, robes falling in heavy folds of crimson and obsidian. His voice was roughened by centuries of war, but steady as granite.

"Princess Transcendent," Jorathak Malvekath intoned, his scarred hand sweeping toward the planet below them, "it is the same as all the others. Dead. Ripped to pieces by Dominion weapons."

The world below lay shattered: oceans boiled to steam, cities erased into jagged wounds of glass and twisting metal. Its orbit was littered with frozen screams. Wrecks of freighters and warships alike tumbling endlessly to their eventual flaming ends.

Veshdren'Ra's dark eyes narrowed, reflecting the corpse-world below. Her voice was soft, but beneath it coiled a goddess of storm and anger.

"It doesn't make any sense. The Dominion was already committed to crusades across half the galaxy. Why would Dominion fleets be destroying forsaken worlds along with Dominion colony worlds?"

No one answered. Only the hum of the Throneship's heart filled the silence. She raised her hand.

"Prepare the next jump. Holmmadun Prime. If any world could withstand this senseless annihilation, it's that one."

The stars seemed to tear apart and reform in the blink of an eye. In a matter of seconds the Throneship emerged into the gravity well of Holmmadun, its massive moon Holmadu an important place for Tribunals in this part of the Milky Way.

And the galaxy seemed to shudder as the Throneship rippled into position. A fleet awaited them. Colossal, ordered, endless. Not scattered bands but a singular tide: Theldren'Ra's will made metal and fire. Battlecruisers in phalanx formation. Dreadnoughts like mountain ranges given thrusters. And at its heart, his golden Throneship its form eclipsing the starlight.

The holocomms flared. His voice carried like molten iron pouring into the bridge.

"Sister." Theldren'Ra's face shimmered into being, golden eyes alight with cruel amusement. "You're supposed to be dead."

Veshdren straightened, a cold smile touching her lips.

"And yet here I am. While you scavenge among corpses for a crown."

His laughter was not mirth but mockery, a sound like chains dragged across stone. "Then let us see which corpse the galaxy remembers."

His fleet activated their weapons and were prepared to fire when Veshdren began mocking her brother.

"I should have known you were too weak to face me alone. You need an entire fleet to defeat me."

"I don't need a fleet to defeat you."

"Then show me."

The holocomms deactivated and the two Throneships engaged each other. Holmmadun's atmosphere ignited as thousands of lances of plasma and megalithic beams of red energy tore across the void.

Above Holmmadun, the heavens themselves became a battlefield for gods. The two Throneships closed like colliding continents, their

273

vast hulls blotting out stars as though the galaxy itself had been narrowed to this duel.

Theldren's radiated gold fire, its spires and weapon arrays blazing with incandescent fury, every salvo painting the void in molten arcs that seared across space like the hands of vengeful seraphs. Veshdren's was darker, heavier, its silhouette jagged like a fortress torn from some primordial age.

Each answered with singularity cannons that bent light, tearing holes in space that swallowed barrages whole. Armor plating the size of cities shrieked and tore, entire battlements breaking loose and spinning into the planetary gravity below. Their shields flared and cracked in rhythms like the heartbeat of titans, each impact shaking decks where soldiers clung to bulkheads as though clinging to the bones of the universe.

Boarding lances streaked between them but were instantly incinerated, reduced to sparks in the churning storm. Between the two Throneships there was no room for victory, only attrition. Moons could have split under their blows, and suns dimmed by their fury, yet still they pressed closer and closer, locked in a deadlock that felt less like battle and more like inevitability itself.

The two Throneships continued to collide across the void like rival gods tearing at creation. Spires the size of mountains sheared away under cannon fire, shields flared like collapsing suns, and space itself rippled where singularity blasts tore rifts through the void.

Fragments of entire decks tumbled into planetary orbit like burning continents, while the clash of their weapons continued their thunderous chorus.

It seemed the galaxy itself was screaming. But neither vessel yielded. Each strike was answered in kind, each wound mirrored almost precisely. Until the duel became less a battle than the raw embodiment of hatred given form in steel and fire. It went on like this for hours upon hours. And no winner was anywhere in sight. In fact, there would never be a winner. Their warships were of the highest and grandest designs, self repairing machines fixing the most important systems, engergy shields recharging before being fully depleted. They were in an endless deadlock.

Veshdren'Ra was the first to break the attack. Again opening holocomms.

"It is evident that neither of us will gain the upper hand in this battle. We'll be here until the end of time. Let us fight in the old way."

"So be it. Meet me on Holmadu. At the grand temple."

They descended to Holmadu's surface in royal shuttles larger than some empires warships, heading to the most mountainous region of this rocky moon where jagged cliffs thrust upward like the teeth of great titans. There, carved into the stone at the mouth of a ravine so immense that you couldn't see the bottom, rose a grand old temple that was built millennia ago, by a civilization that had long been lost to time and madness.

It had been taken over by the Dominion and dedicated to the Duality, but it had again been changed, no longer a dedication to the Gods of Humanity, but now an edifice for Theldren. He had rebuilt it for himself. Pillars of gold-veined blackstone clawed at the heavens. Statues of his own likeness stood where the duel godhood once reigned. Flames of strange fuel burned in royal braziers, their smoke coiling into the sky like prayers turned into curses.

Lightning rippled across the horizon as the dark godly shuttles landed opposite each other on each side of the ravine in front of the temple. Theldren and Veshdren both lead small armies of Tribunals. Their strongest and most loyal, to an ancient stone bridge that spanned over the expanse of the ravine.

The bridge itself was a relic of another age, a forgotten age, older than the Dominion. Hewn and formed from stone so black it seemed to drink the lightning, it stretched across the abyss like a scar cut by forgotten gods. Winds howled through the ravine, tearing at banners and cloaks, carrying with them the scent of ozone, blood, and ancient dust.

Veshdren's armor pulsed faintly with argent veins and seals of power as she stood in front of her Tribunals, her presence a shadow that seemed to drink the light from the air. The faces of her chosen hidden behind helms inscribed with runes of loyalty and obedience, blades shimmered with barely-contained entropy.

On the opposite side, Theldren strode forth like a sun given flesh, golden fire wreathing his godly plate. His cloak of crimson and gold billowed in the storm, and his Tribunals followed in perfect discipline, their steps resounding like the march of war itself. Their weapons burned with radiant fire, casting the bridge in an amber glow.

The two hosts met upon the bridge, lines of power and will arrayed across the precipice. The wind shrieked louder, as if creation itself resisted what was about to unfold. The Tribunals on both sides held ready for battle a great variety of weapons, all eager to end those who opposed their transcendent heir.

Theldren lifted his blade toward Veshdren, the golden corona flaring against the storm.

"Sister. At last the galaxy sees the truth. There is room for only one throne. Mine."

Veshdren's voice cut through the thunder like a blade through flesh.

"No. It will see that madness dressed in self godhood is no less a shadow. And shadows can be broken. They can be ended."

"Don't throw your life away. Submit my rule and I will spare your life."

"I will never bow to you Theldren. I will rise above you. I will rule the empire. The Dominion is mine."

"Then your end is by your choice. I gave you a chance. I will show no mercy."

A few heartbeats of silence followed as they stared at each other. Every second seemed to stretch on forever. Then the abyss of their hearts roared and the Tribunals rushed forward around their heirs. Singulari ignited, energies crackled, and both sides surged forward in

276

a collision that shook the bridge as though it were alive. A clash of fire, sparks tearing holes into the storm itself. The youngest Tribunals were the first bodies to be hurled screaming into the bottomless ravine, their cries vanishing into an endless uncaring dark.

Upon the very center of the bridge, Veshdren and Theldren closed the distance. Brother and sister. Heirs of ruin. When their blades finally met, the world itself seemed to fracture. Shock-waves rippled out and broke the rock along the cliff face.

Groaning beneath the weight of their fury the bridge began to break, every blow between brother and sister cracking the stone and shaking the heavens above. Around them, their Tribunals continued to clash in a frenzy. Body after body fell to the most skilled among them. As the brutality of it went on the ancient masonry split apart. With a thunderous roar, the bridge finally gave way, crumbling into the chasm and sending the surviving warriors scrambling onto the jagged cliff faces, jumping from ledge to ledge.

The battle only grew more brutal there. Blades and power were exchanged between the warring Tribunals. Fighters slipped and fell to their deaths, their blood painting the rocks red. Veshdren and Theldren fought with the wrath that their transcendence demanded, each strike a storm, each parry a quake.

As most of their Tribunals fell and died, the most powerful rose from the carnage, defying gravity itself as they launched themselves into the air. As if they had wings. Running through the air. Their duels tore through the shadow of the ravine.

Veshdren and Theldren pressed each other with merciless rhythm, their strikes reverberating through the mountain like thunder rolling from within the stone itself. Sparks erupted in showers as their blades clashed, molten fragments carving scars into the cliffs. Each parry, each counterstrike, split the air with a violence that seemed to bend gravity itself.

The sheer violence of it dragged the heirs onward, step by brutal step, toward the temple carved into the mountain's heart. Its colossal pillars loomed in the storm-light, black-stone veined with gold, trembling beneath the weight of the carnage spilling ever closer. Each strike between brother and sister seemed to draw them nearer, until the ravine's chaos funneled into the temple's ancient threshold.

There, where gods had once been worshiped and forgotten, where time itself had preserved silence for millennia, the war arrived, ending the quiet serenity of this ancient place.

Their struggle crashed through the gates, the towering columns now began to shatter and splinter under their fury. Stone split, statues shattered, and sacred halls that had stood for millennia became an arena of destruction. Pillars fell like trees struck by divine axes as Veshdren and Theldren hurled each other through walls of stone. Each trying to gain the upper hand.

All the surviving Tribunals followed, dragging their battle into the temple's embrace. Blood smeared steps as warriors fell, one by one, their corpses thrown aside like broken idols to false prophets. Some fought up the walls themselves, running along the vertical stone as though gravity bowed to their wrath, striking from impossible angles to bring an end to their enemy.

Then, in a single chaotic moment, a massive statue broke loose from its base and tumbled toward Veshdren as she was fighting. Jorathak Malvekath, ever loyal, ever doomed, leapt between her and the falling carved edifice of Theldren, but he was weakened and had spent too much of his energy, now his power wasn't enough to stop it, he pushed Veshdren out of the way with all the power he had left and the stone likeness of Theldren impacted against him. Crushing him. His final breath was spent protecting his empress, his mother.

With a scream that shook the temple, Veshdren's rage grew, her strikes becoming wild, relentless, driven by fury and grief. Yet even that was not enough to gain the advantage, in fact it made her lose the initiative. Her uncontrolled and unfocused flurry of attacks couldn't break Theldren'Ra's poised defense.

Theldren realized that he had the chance to defeat her once and for all, he overpowered her, his blade finding a path to her arm. That one clear strike disarmed her, she dropped her weapon and Theldren picked her up with his power and cast her to the shattered floor and to the ceiling. Ripping her through the air and agaisnt the stone again and again until she no longer moved.

Bloodied and broken, defeated and defenseless, she glared up at him through eyes burning with hatred.

"I will have my revenge…" she hissed. "You will pay for what you've done…"

Theldren's expression was colder than the void of space, and with a serpentine smile he gave his dying sister a reply.

"I don't think so."

He raised his blade high and brought it down again and again against her until he was sure that not a single breath remained. A vicious barbaric fate. He had won. He had risen above Veshdren'Ra.

A deep silence followed, yet it was not true silence. Only the toll of ruin. Dust fell like ash. Each echo of stone a funeral drum for broken divinity. The temple, once a sanctum to the Duality, now lay as a tomb for their progeny. Every surface now reshaped in rage and blood.

Theldren'Ra stood in the wreckage of what little remained of his temple, his blade wet with the blood of his twin, breath heavy with eternity's weight. At his feet lay the lifeless broken form of Veshdren. Fallen, shattered, a star torn from the firmament. Even in death her eyes burned, unbowed.

For a moment he lingered, the victor over the vanquished. Two halves of one transcendence sundered by betrayal. Shadows curled through the ruins, whispering of oaths unkept, of bloodlines cursed to devour themselves.

Then Theldren turned. Every step deliberate and heavy with triumph and doom alike. Behind him the temple groaned as though mourning; outside, the ravine lay choked with corpses, eyes staring into eternity. Yet even in victory her words clung to him, venomous as a curse: I will have my revenge. He had slain her flesh. But not her shadow. Not her will. Not her vengeance. For even gods cannot kill what hatred has made eternal.

Chapter Forty-Three:
TRANQUILITY IN THE STORM

"Even in the eye of chaos, when the tempest swallows both flesh and stone, the soul that clings to The Light, the unshaken truth upon which eternity is anchored, becomes the stillness that breaks the storm."[1]

The NAXV Bible, Book of Restoration 1:1

Days passed in a gentle rhythm, the jungle villa becoming a much-needed sanctuary where time itself seemed to slow. The trials and tribulations that Tria had carried upon arrival began to loosen, unraveling like the river's gentle current washing away the past.

Each morning, she woke to the golden light filtering through the villa's open windows, the scent of dewy flowers and damp earth filling her lungs. Birds greeted the dawn with their symphony, while the mischievous Ozlo made it his mission to wake her by tugging at her blankets or dropping little pieces of fruit onto her head.

"Persistent little Muggling," she muttered one morning, swiping at him playfully. But she never truly minded, in fact she loved her old childhood friend being there for her.

Amarax, in contrast, struggled with the slow pace of their days at first. He was a warrior, built for action, for battle, for war, for charging headfirst into the next crusade. But even he couldn't resist the strange consuming charm of this place.

One afternoon, Tria caught Amarax by the river, guarded over by his robotic sentries. He was attempting to spear a Gracous root that was moving erratically through the water with nothing but a sharpened stick.

"That's...ambitious. Hunting Gracous root with a stick. I'm surprised your robotic wardens let you create such a dangerous weapon like that." She teased, standing on a smooth rock above the water, her arms crossed in a relaxed position.

"Don't start, Oberon," he grumbled, his shirt slung over a nearby branch, sweat glistening on his skin. "The last time I checked, you weren't exactly a Star Ranger yourself."

She grinned, rolling up her pants to her knees before stepping into the water. "Let me show you how it's done."

280

"Please. By all means, educate me," he said, smirking, thinking that she didn't have a chance catching the fast moving root.

With surprising grace, she reached into the water, staying still, so still that even the wind seemed to hold its breath. Then, in a single, fluid motion, she struck. A slimy green vine-like root flopped in her hands trying to escape, its strange bark glinting in the sunlight.

Amarax blinked. "What the—"

Tria ripped a piece from the larger whole of the moving root and tossed the chunk of Gracous root onto the riverbank. Then she gave Amarax a smug but confident look as he responded in shock.

"That was luck," he muttered, wading in deeper beside her. "I bet you a trillion credits that you can't do it again."

Tria arched a brow from his words, amusement dancing in her eyes and expression.

"A trillion Dominion credits? You're that desperate to believe I just got lucky?"

Without another word, she turned her attention back to the water, her movements effortless, practiced. A few heartbeats passed, then, swift as a striking serpent, she plunged her hand beneath the surface. Another writhing chunk of Gracous root was in her grip before Amarax could even blink. She tossed it onto the riverbank with a casual flick of her wrist, smirking.

"That's two. Do you want to make another wager? Or have you had enough? Because if you haven't you should probably start looking for a loan."

Amarax groaned, dragging a hand down his face. "You've done this before, haven't you?"

Tria chuckled, wringing water from her sleeve. "Once or twice. Maybe next time, you'll bet on me instead of against me."

She grinned even deeper. He huffed, but the corners of his lips twitched upward.

"Fine. But I'm still not convinced. Best out of five?"

She laughed, stepping back into position. "You're on."

They spent the rest of the afternoon like that, engaged in a carefree joyful competition, laughing each time one of them fell into the water, sometimes having to wrestle with the Gracous root.

When the sun finally set, they roasted their catch over a crackling fire, their clothes still damp, their laughter lingering in the warm evening air.

On another day, Tria found herself simply enjoying the villa's small wonders. The garden, overflowing with alien flowers and strange vines, little waterfalls and streams, it became a place where she could lose herself in joyful thoughts, reminiscing about her childhood. She found her old hammock tucked away beneath the boughs of two ancient trees and spent hours there, Ozlo curled on her stomach, his tiny snores blending with the rustling leaves.

One night, when the projected sky sent out its artistic beauty, majestically fake stars stretching endlessly above them, she and Amarax would sit on the villa's stone terrace, sharing stories over a bottle of something Amarax had found in an old storage room.

The fire crackled softly, its embers casting dancing shadows across the intricate stone terrace. The warmth of the day still clung to the air, though a gentle colder night breeze whispered through the jungle, rustling the canopy above. The world around them had settled into a peaceful rhythm. Just the quiet hum of nocturnal creatures and the distant murmur of the river.

Tria leaned back on her elbows, gazing up at the artificial sky, the holographic stars glistening like an infinite sea of scattered diamonds. She knew they weren't real, she knew that the sky above the villa was just a well-crafted illusion—but for a moment, she let herself pretend.

Standing on the other side of the blazing fire, Amarax swirled the last remnants of his drink within his intricately styled cup, before setting it aside. He exhaled, glancing over at her and up towards the sky.

"Not bad for a fake sky," he muttered, his voice quieter than usual.

Tria smirked. "It's convincing if you don't think too hard about it."

They sat in silence for a while, the kind that didn't need filling, where the presence of another person was enough.

Ozlo had curled up beside her again, his tiny chest rising and falling in steady rhythm. She absentmindedly ran her fingers through his fur, her mind drifting.

"This place..." Amarax spoke again, softer this time. "It's like stepping into a different life."

Tria turned her head, studying him. His gaze was distant, caught between thought and memory, something still unspoken resting just behind his eyes.

She hesitated, then spoke. "Do you ever think about what your life could have been like...if things had been different? If you had never lived in the Dominion at all."

He let out a quiet breath, rubbing a hand over his jaw and then his cheeks, rotating between the two in deep thought.

"Lately, yes. A lot. Much more than I probably should."

Amarax exhaled, slow and deep. The fire flickered between them, a quiet witness to things neither of them had spoken aloud before.

"Life slips through your fingers before you even realize you're holding it," he said finally, his voice carrying a raw edge that cut through the serenity of the moment. "You see a fellow legionary one day, fighting beside you, and the next...they're gone. Just like that." He snapped his fingers, the sharp sound cutting through the still night. "A shot. A blade. A bad step. It doesn't take much."

His gaze drifted to the holographic sky, to the stars that weren't real, and for a moment, he looked impossibly tired. "I've seen so many die with hope still in their eyes. Believing they'd make it home to their families. That there was something waiting for them after the blood and the screaming." He shook his head, his jaw tightening. "But war doesn't care about hope. It doesn't care about promises, or dreams, or the futures we tell ourselves we'll have."

Tria stared into the fire, its embers glowing like the last breath of something once fierce, now fading. She had lived this truth too.

Her mind drifted—unbidden, unwelcome—back to the night everything was almost taken from her. The night the cultists had come like wraiths, their voices slithering through the gardens and halls of her family's home before the killing began.

She remembered the coldness of the stone paths beneath her hands, slick with blood that wasn't hers. The cries of the dying, cut short by the ruthless efficiency of uncaring blades. The searing pain when the knife had caught her shoulder and throat, just a fraction off from her throat.

One inch. One second. That was all that had separated her from death. She had survived. But survival had never felt like victory. Only a cruel joke played by the universe. One that left her wondering why she was spared when so many weren't.

The fire crackled, dragging her back to the present. Amarax was watching her now, his expression one of listening.

"War doesn't just take lives," she said softly. "It takes everything. The people you love. The places you call home. The certainty that tomorrow will come." She swallowed; the words almost stuck in her throat. "And even if you survive, you never really leave it behind. You just carry it with you, every single day."

Amarax didn't respond right away. He reached for his cup, stared at it for a moment, then set it down again. When he finally spoke, his voice was quieter than before.

"There are nights when I wake up, and for a few seconds, I forget. I forget the wars. The battles. The faces of the dead who've died because of me." He exhaled, slow and bitter. "And then it all comes rushing back, like it never left. Because it never really does."

Tria nodded, because she understood their shared pain, they were both warriors, they had both been through different kinds of hell.

For a long while, they sat in silence, the firelight casting long shadows across the stone like whispers of their thoughts. The stars above them, false and artificial, shimmered with a beauty that neither of them could bring themselves to believe in.

That night, Tria dreamed. The ruins of her family's estate stretched behind her, charred stone and broken columns swallowed by the dark. Bodies lay scattered, her parents, her fellow Peacekeepers, the president, her friends. Blood slicked the ground like ink, seeping into the cracks.

The cultists surrounded her. Hooded figures in tattered robes, silent, unmoving, their presence a wall she could not escape. Their faces were lost to the shadows, but she could feel their eyes—cold, watching, waiting.

A flash of lightning split the sky. She was no longer outside. The walls of the inner sanctum loomed around her, the temple where she had led Operation Nightfall Covenant. The air stank of burning flesh and death. The fallen were everywhere, cultists and Peacekeepers alike, their bodies twisted and fractured beyond recognition.

And in the center of all the death, the leader that had escaped her stood alone. Silent. Motionless. Draped in the blood of the slain, their mask a blank, unfeeling visage.

Tria gripped her Singublade. She rushed forwards. The fight was brutal, fast, a clash of pain. She struck again and again, but the cultist leader gave no sound, no cry of pain, only the dull reverberating echoes of their Singublades meeting. Their silence was suffocating, a reminder of everything they had taken from her.

A rumble shook the temple, the stone beneath them splitting apart like dry earth. A deafening roar, ancient and primal, filled the sanctum. Then, the ceiling started collapsing. A massive serpent erupted through the large stone head of Kronos, shattering the stone god's face with its titanic force. It was the same serpent that she had dreamed of before, its scales darker than the void between stars. Dust and debris rained down as its gaping maw loomed above them.

The serpent struck, swallowing both her and the cultist leader in one merciless gulp. Darkness.

She gasped awake. A sharp inhale, her heart slamming against her ribs. Ozlo yelped, startled from his peaceful slumber beside her, but Tria comforted him and he fell back to sleep.

Tria ran a hand over her face, breathing deeply, trying her best to ground herself once again in the present. It was just a dream. Just another nightmare. But it felt suffocating, clawing at her mind with vicious intent. She couldn't let it consume her. She had to go back. Back to the temple. She had to see it with her own eyes, had to push away these lingering doubts, these fears that the cult's shadow still lingered.

Chapter Forty-Four:
RETURNING TO NIGHTFALL

"Forgiveness is the fire that quenches destruction, the river that washes chains away. Whoever grants mercy is greater than the ones who conquer worlds, for in the pardoning of transgressions lies the triumph of eternity."[1]

The NAXV Bible, Book of Restoration 2:1

Morning came with a pale, golden light. As the first light of dawn broke over the horizon, Tria and Amarax boarded the Hoveryacht, its engines humming softly as they lifted off. The sleek vessel cut through the skies, leaving behind the villa as they set course for the temple where she had led the Peacekeepers against the cultists of Kronos.

When they arrived, flying over it, the temple stood, not as a place of death and ruin, but of life and light. The once-broken sanctuary now stood whole. Its spires bathed in the daytime light. They landed on a nearby rocky landing area. When they exited the Hoveryacht they could hear the echoes of chanting prayers and the quiet murmur of those seeking solace.

The temple had been restored to its former glory, the scars of war had been wiped clean. The towering spires reached skyward, bathed in soft snowy light. The scent of incense curled through the chilly air, mingling with the distant sounds of chanting prayers. Monks and pilgrims alike were once again walking its sacred halls, voices rising in harmony, a melody of peace and searching. For a long moment, Tria simply stood there, staring, taking in the change, the revival of this place, it gave her some happiness seeing the temple return to its intended purpose.

Tria and Amarax stepped into the temple, it was peaceful, so peaceful, you could feel the sense of solitude and peace. They entered the inner sanctum, the air was thick with incense and whispered prayers. At the heart of the chamber stood the colossal head of Kronos, repaired and whole once more—a terrible reminder of what had transpired. Tria's hands curled into fists as anger surged through her.

"Why is this still here?" she demanded, her voice cutting through the solemn quiet. "It should have been removed, it should have been destroyed, erased from history."

The monks, draped in flowing robes of all different colors, turned to her with calm expressions, their eyes filled with understanding rather than reprimand. One stepped forward, bowing his bald head slightly.

"We cannot erase what happened," he said gently. "To do so would be to deny the lessons we must carry. The suffering, the loss. It is part of this place now, part of us. To forget is to invite it to happen again."

Tria's jaw tightened, her mind warring between the weight of the past and the desire to move beyond it.

"You must accept it," another monk added. "Not as a wound to reopen, but as a scar to remind us. We must carry memory; not let it carry us. Only then can we truly be at peace."

She let out a deeply sharp breath, her gaze shifting back to the stone face of Kronos. The cracks were still visible beneath the repairs, a testament to what had been. As much as she wanted to reject their words, she knew there was some truth in them.

The cultists had already taken so much from her. She couldn't let them take her inner peace too.

Tria walked out in silence, the cold wind carrying the distant echoes of the chanted prayers as she and Amarax left the temple behind. She decided to take a walk into the mountains before heading back to the villa, the wide carved path they took wound through the jagged mountains, their sheer cliffs veiled in mist, their peaks crowned by the cold light of the sun.

The air smelled of stone and frost, crisp and ancient, as if the land itself had been waiting for this moment. For them, for their words, for the unspoken truths that lingered between them.

She expelled a deep heavy breath, watching the ghostly vapor of her breath vanish into nothing.

"To remember but not to be haunted," she murmured. "To accept but not to carry. How does one do that? It seems impossible."

Amarax, walking beside her, kept his gaze on the jungles in the valleys below and the colorful horizon beyond.

287

"I don't think anyone truly knows, the past is sometimes a blade—we can either wield it, or we let it cut into us, killing who we are in the process."

She scoffed a little, kicking a loose stone from the path.

"That's poetic, but what if the blade never dulls? What if the wound never truly closes?"

He stopped, turning to face her. The wind played at his dark hair, strands lifting like the dying embers of a fire.

"Then maybe the wound isn't meant to close," he said with deep conviction. "Maybe it becomes something else. A lesson to guide us into the future. But it should never become a cage. A prison that holds us hostage."

Tria frowned, looking out over the valley. The world stretched before them in a tapestry of mesmerizing colors.

She sighed deeply. "I don't want to be caged by it, I don't want it to become a prison," she admitted. "But forgiving...I can't do that either. Not yet. I can still see them when I close my eyes. The dead. They never leave me. I can't forgive the cultists for what they've done."

"They don't deserve forgiveness," he said plainly. "Not for what they did. Not for the lives they took." He paused, his voice steady and strong. "But if I've learned anything about you, Tria, it's that you want to forgive everyone. You want to find the goodness where there is no goodness, you want to plant the seeds of light even in a forest of hate and evil."

She scoffed, shaking her head. "That's not true."

"It is." Amarax's expression didn't waver. "You hold onto hope, even when it breaks you. Even when you think you've let it go, it's still there, clawing its way back into your heart."

Tria clenched her fists even harder, her gaze falling down towards the rough ground beneath them.

"Hope is a cruel thing sometimes," she muttered under her breath, then raising her voice again. "It makes you believe in things that aren't real. Makes you think that people can change when they never will."

"Maybe," he admitted. "But what's the alternative? To become like them? To let the past carve you into something unrecognizable.

Something hollow, something you could never bear to be?"

The wind picked up, carrying the scent of distant rain. Tria lifted her eyes to the sky, watching as soft clouds drifted across the endless expanse. She felt so small beneath it all, beneath the weight of history, of memory, of all the lives lost.

"I don't know," she finally said, her voice now a deep whisper. "Forgiveness, hope, they seem so distant. Like a shadow that you can never catch."

Amarax nodded, his gaze steady. "You don't have to forgive them. Not today. Maybe not ever. But you do have to live. You have to make your own peace, even if they try to take it from you. You have to live. I have come to see the truth that in the living is the hope."

She looked up at him, letting his words settle deep in her chest. He seemed so different now. He seemed like a new man. A changed man. In that moment of feeling she felt her affection grow. It was a long road ahead. A road paved with scars and ghosts and things she might never fully let go of. But she would walk it. She now felt that Amarax was being woven into her heart.

The days that followed passed in a quiet, golden peace. For the first time in what felt like ages, Tria's nights were not haunted by the screams of the dead, or by the cruel faces of the past. The ghosts that had once clung to her like chains had loosened their grip, if only just enough for her to breathe.

She spent most of her time wandering the mountains and jungles with Amarax, tracing old paths she had once walked as a child. There was something almost surreal about it. Bringing him here, into these memories, into a part of herself she had long thought lost. A healing was beginning to take form. It was as though the fabric of existence chose to sing a new song.

Chapter Forty-Five:
RESTORATION OF HOPE

"I did not find him in the grand halls of fate, nor written in the verses of prophecy. I found him in the silence between heartbeats, in the spaces where the universe held its breath. He was not promised to me, nor I to him—yet in his eyes, I glimpsed a love that had endured beyond ruin, beyond time, beyond the breaking of a thousand worlds. My heart is full, my life is now filled with uncontainable joy. I have found my eternal soulmate, in Maxamas."

Zoephiria Vergaragas Morganvale,

Captain United Resistance Front, Personal Journals, circa 3,101 AD

One morning as they were walking among the mountains and forests, seeing the sun pour down like liquid amber over the peaks, Tria turned to Amarax with an uncharacteristic lightness in her voice. She was feeling more at peace with him. His presence no longer felt like a simple duty to perform, but a joy to be fulfilled.

"There's a place I want to show you."

Amarax didn't know what to expect but followed her without question. The new path they took wound through the mountains, the air was filled with the scents of elegant pine and mossy wet stone.

Along the path carved into the mountainside was a small chapel nestled among old trees, its ancient stone walls covered in creeping vines, a silent witness to countless whispered prayers and forgotten vows.

Tria walked with purpose, her steps lighter than they had been in weeks, almost as if she were following the echo of her younger self. Finally, they arrived—a hidden crystal alcove, veiled by ancient trees and vines, where a waterfall cascaded down smooth, silvered stone into a crystal-clear pool below that was a giant crystal itself.

Tria breathed in deeply, smiling softly at the sight. "I used to come here all the time as a kid," she said, kneeling at the edge of the water. "Whenever things got to be too much, whenever I needed to think, this was my refuge. I had almost forgotten it. I can't believe it's been so long since I've been here."

Amarax stood beside her, taking in the scene with quiet reverence. The water shimmered in the sunlight, mist curling up like breath from the earth itself. The sound of it was soothing, steady—a rhythm older than memory.

"It's beautiful," he admitted. "It suits you."

She let out a breath of laughter. "You think so?"

He crouched beside her, dipping his fingers into the crystal cool waters.

"Yeah. It's peaceful, but there's something untamed about it too. Something that...I don't know...but it definitely suits you."

A quiet settled between them. The warmth of the artificial sun, the scent of fresh damp moss covered earth, the serene steady roar of the falls, the reflecting light upon the magnificent crystals. It all wrapped around her like an embrace of serenity.

For the first time in a long time, she didn't feel the weight of the past pressing down on her. Here, with him, in this place of old prophetic memories and new beginnings, she felt something else entirely. She felt free.

Amarax let his fingers drift through the water, his gaze lost in the endless dance of light reflecting off the massive crystal pool. The sight stirred something deep inside him. Something he had not expected. Thoughts and feelings that he had been trying to suppress. His breath caught as the shared memories of a life together with Tria surged through him again. The visions Tel'Mor'El had shown him. This place. This exact place was in those visions.

His mind's eye filled with the images. Tria standing here, not as she was now, but older, radiant, a warmth in her eyes that had softened over time. The sound of laughter echoed faintly in his thoughts. Children's laughter. His own laughter. The weight of a small hand slipping into his, the scent of the jungle mixed with the faint trace of something sweet. Tria's perfume.

He saw their home, nestled within the mountains, saw the nights spent beneath the stars, the quiet moments, the life they had built together. He saw her reaching for him, her fingers brushing his cheek with an affection that burned through his very soul. He felt a lifetime of love that seemed magically eternal and passionately everlasting.

The love he had not dared to fully acknowledge until now. The love that now overwhelmed him. His chest tightened harder; his breath uneven as he turned to look at Tria.

"Tria," he said, his voice rough and deep with emotion.

She lifted her gaze to him, something unspoken also flickering behind her eyes.

"Yes Amarax, what is it?"

He hesitated, pausing and swallowing hard, taking his time to say what he had to say.

"Have you ever…seen the future?"

Tria's expression shifted, her body stilling as if she already knew what he meant. Her lips parted slightly before she nodded.

"Yes."

His heart pounded harder with the single word that she spoke.

"And in those visions… did you see us?"

She exhaled slowly, her fingers trailing across the surface of the water.

"I did," she admitted, her voice barely above a whisper, but with deep feeling behind it. "I've seen… love. A love that endures, that shapes the future. Our future. Our children's future."

A breath of wind stirred the air between them, carrying the scent of fresh rain and blooming life. Amarax reached for her hand, his grip firm but gentle.

"Then let us live it," he said, his eyes locking onto hers, a knowing assured gaze. "Let us live this love. And no longer allow it to be just a shadow."

For a moment, the world stood still. Tria searched his face, as if trying to find the hesitation, the doubt. But there was none. Slowly, her fingers curled around his, and for the first time in years, she let herself believe.

Every molecule between them shimmered with anticipation, a force stronger than time, stronger than fate, love had been found. The crystal-clear water mirrored their reflections. Two souls entwined by a love destined before time began, standing at the precipice of something eternal.

Amarax lifted his free hand, his fingers tracing the curve of Tria's cheek, as though mapping the lines of a future that they had already lived. She closed her eyes, leaning into his touch, her breath shallow yet steady, as if she too felt the universe shifting around them.

Then, as though drawn by an unseen gravity, he rested his temple against hers, his breath mingling with hers, the heat between them more powerful than the artificial sun above. They held each other and pulled each other close as they shared an affection that was timeless. The moment stretched, almost endless, sacred, until finally, finally, their lips met.

It was not a timid thing, nor hesitant. It was fierce, a collision of souls that had waited too long to find true love, a fire long kindled now set ablaze. Their arms wrapped around each other, pulling each other close as if they could bind their very beings together. She melted into him, fingers threading through his hair, clutching him with a desperation that spoke of lifetimes lost and found again.

The jungle around them blurred into insignificance. The distant hum of cascading water became the rhythm of their shared breath. The world itself ceased to matter, for in that instant, they were everything.

When at last they parted for a breath, Amarax cupped her face in his hands, his thumbs brushing over her flushed skin.

"I don't want to waste another moment," he murmured, his voice thick with conviction in their found love.

Tria searched his eyes, her own brimming with something unshakable.

"Neither do I. Let us join together as husband and wife. Let us make the dream real."

"The chapel we passed, there must be a priest or priestess who can marry us."

"Yes, let's go."

And so, in agreement, hand in hand, they made their way back to the chapel they had passed along the path in the mountains. But before they arrived Tria made sure to hack into Amarax's three security bots and deactivate their recording systems. Then erase and replace what they had just seen. The luminescent flora they passed cast ethereal shadows as they walked in silence, they seemed to sing to them as their fingers continued to tightly weave together.

The chapel was just ahead, its small crystal spires stretching toward the heavens, an ancient sanctuary where time seemingly bowed before divine universal love.

Inside, they found a lone monk, robed in ivory and gold, kneeling before a sleek hexagonal blue crystal altar praying to Omega. As he heard them enter he stopped praying and stood, looking at them with seeking eyes that had seen long centuries. An old knowing expression settling over his features.

"We wish to be joined as one," Amarax said without hesitation.

The monk studied them for a long moment, then nodded.

"You seek union not by law, but by spirit and soul?"

"Yes, we do. We love each other very much. You could say we've loved each other for a lifetime." Tria affirmed, a loving faith in her words.

The monk smiled and looked at them again, shaking his head in agreement.

"Then step forward."

They did, standing before the altar as the monk raised his hands in thanksgiving, thanking Omega. The chamber filled with a quiet hum, the very air vibrating with something unseen.

"What are your names?"

"Amarax Mirvega."

"Tria Oberon."

The monk placed his palms over their joined hands.

"From this moment forward, your paths are one. Not bound by decree, nor by duty, but by the unbreakable force that is eternal love." He turned to Tria. "Tria, do you love Amarax with every fiber of your being? Do you promise to love and protect, over all else. In sickness and in health, for better or for worse?"

"Yes. Yes, I do. Always and forever."

"Amarax, do you love Tria with every fiber of your being? Do you promise to love and protect, over all else. In sickness and in health, for better or for worse?"

"I swear it. I swear it with everything that I am."

The monk continued the private exchange of vows.

"Tria, repeat after me. I Tria, take you Amarax as my husband, forsaking all others forever and all time."

Without a single doubt in that moment she spoke the words with all conviction.

"I Tria, take you Amarax as my husband. Forsaking all others forever and all time."

"Amarax, repeat after me. I Amarax, take you Tria as my wife, forsaking all others forever and all time."

Without a single hesitation he repeated the words allowing his heart to rule just this once. No deceptions in this moment. His mind was clear in wanting this love to be fulfilled.

"I Amarax, take you Tria as my wife. Forsaking all others forever and all time."

After they had finished the monk finished their outward commitment to each other.

"It is done. You are both now one. Let your souls walk together, through fire and storm, through shadow and light. May Omega bless your marriage. May Omega be your strength."

A warmth spread through them, the significance of the moment sinking deep into their hearts.

Tria turned to Amarax, her eyes luminous.

"We are one." she whispered.

"We always have been. We always will be." he answered.

And in that sacred space, beneath the watchful glow of eternity, they were bound. By love, by fate, by something greater than either of them could comprehend.

They slipped from the chapel with joy deeply woven into their faces, then they vanished into the embrace of the waiting forest. The scent of earth and rain-kissed leaves flowed through the air. The luminous flora shimmered with an ethereal glow that seemed almost knowing, as if the very land bore witness to the vow they had just spoken.

Without hesitation, Amarax pulled Tria into his arms, holding her as though he had spent lifetimes yearning for this single moment. And perhaps he had. She melted into him, feeling the strength in his embrace, the warmth that had always been there, waiting for her to claim it as her own. The Peacekeeper in her faded away entirely for a moment to appreciate what they had been given, the visions of a life together was becoming real. A love that seemed impossible had become their reality.

They moved together like whispered winds over a midnight river, their touch tracing the unseen lines of fated affections that seemed to draw them together. Every caress spoke of longing fulfilled, of silent promises that they kept within themselves now unbound. Their shared connection was now something deeper than words and secret hidden feelings. Their love, once restrained by war and duty, now unfurled like blossoms that only dared open beneath the pretending twin moons' glow.

Time unraveled in the hush of the forest, lost in the spaces between their breaths. Their fingers wove together, lips meeting in the quiet urgency of a love unchained. The world outside faded; in that moment, nothing else existed. Only them.

As the night deepened, they made their way back toward the villa, moving like shadows through the corridors of stone and time. With the grace of ghosts, they slipped past the robotic sentries at the perimeter, their hushed laughter dissolving into the stillness.

They both were careful not to be seen or wake anyone in the villa. Tria led Amarax into her room, turning off the lights and shutting the door behind them as if sealing themselves away from all but each other. She turned, eyes aglow with love, hands reaching for him. And in that moment, there was no hesitation, no restraint. Only them, only this.

They came together in a rush of passion and devotion. Their love, once an unspoken prayer was now made flesh. Their hands explored, learning every curve, every breath, branding this night into memory and touch. Each kiss, each whispered word, was a promise renewed, a vow sealed not by law but by the unbreakable force that had drawn them to each other.

The soft glow of the moons cast long shadows that danced upon the walls, bearing silent witness to the fire that burned between them. The night stretched endlessly, time-bending beneath the gravity of their embraces, the barriers of past and future dissolving in the sacred space between their entwined souls.

And when dawn's first light crept through the curtains, they lay tangled together, breathing slowly, hearts steady.

Tria traced soft patterns over Amarax's skin, a tender smile conveying her acceptance of their love.

"We lived our love tonight," she said with deep meaning. "Tell me Amarax Mirvega, all the wonderful things that I mean to you, tell me that you love me, tell me that we won't ever lose this."

He leaned close and held her hand with his own affectionate acceptance of their love, pressing a kiss against it and then pulling her closer.

"I love you, with all of my heart, I love you Tria Oberon. We will have these moments forever, no matter what happens, we will have this."

They held each other in embraces of infinitely expressed passion for the rest of the morning, their visions had finally come to fruition. The spark of shared destiny, a new beginning for both of them. The weeks that followed were stolen in the quiet spaces where even time forgot to watch. Their fulfilling love became a whispered promise between them, a secret carried on the wind. But their quiet solitude would come to an end. Tria was recalled to service, her temporary leave ending. As they left the Republic of Peace, she said her goodbyes to this tranquil place, hugging her little simian friend, Ozlo. Promising that she would return. His sad little face, making her almost reconsider leaving, but she had to, she had to return to her duties.

Tria knew her parents wouldn't understand her love for Amarax. At least not yet. To them, she was a daughter of the Republics, bound by duty, and the responsibility of their noble and respected legacies. It was a love that would seem like treason to most. Even with the Messengers visions. It didn't matter. The majority of people in the Republics held the visions that the Messengers bestowed as nothing more than fantasies. Most didn't believe in them. The public would destroy her if they ever found out, she was a Peacekeeper of the United Free Republics. Amarax, on the other hand was the polar opposite, a Grand Marshal of the Dominion, a servant of the Duality, a war criminal. Their worlds were at odds, their peoples were at war.

She had to keep her love a secret. But secrets as forsaken as this can never last. It began with glances from strangers that lingered too long, footsteps heard when no one should be there, the shaking of a branch or bush in the night, and the quiet knowledge that forbidden love, no matter how carefully hidden, has a way of betraying itself.

Chapter Forty-Six:
UNUM FALLS

I have stood beneath the dying light of Unum. Lost not to sword or flame, but to the fragile certainty that hope itself can fail. In that deepening shadow, I faced the cruel price of survival: the empty space left by sacrifice, and the weight of a tomorrow born from ashes.

Maxamas Rivenborne Hendrix,

Captain United Resistance Front, Personal Journals, circa 3,115 AD

Unum glowed with quiet life, suspended within the vast cavernous hollow of Earth's outer core. A hidden city veiled from the eyes of the galaxy. Its spires shimmered with bio-luminescent crystal, its structures sculpted from living alloys and radiant stone. Above, the artificial sky curved in pale amber hues, light refracted through layers of crystal strata built into the ceiling of the hollow earth.

Tria and Amarax stood side by side on a floating garden near the edge of the capital overlooking the vista. The pinnacle of the central spire shined in the distance. The air shimmered with warmth and peace. They had found sanctuary and a joy in their secret marriage. However temporary it might be. In one another's arms they had found a new kind of solace and hope. The scent of blooming oxygen-fruits and glowing nightblossoms filled the air. Beneath them, Unum sprawled like a dream.

The sky of Unum was a vaulted sea of crystal and light, suspended miles above within the hollow Earth's outer core. The secret capital of the Republics, a miracle of engineering and hope, shimmered beneath its false setting sun. Floating towers and suspended gardens wove between magnetic bridges, alive with the tranquil hum of their advanced civilization. The city bloomed like a flower of chrome and tranquility.

Tria and Amarax stood together in one of the highest sanctuaries. Their own private floating arboretum suspended above the Capitol like a star. The garden was quiet, the air sweet with drifting spores and glowing blossoms. Here, they had recently shared laughter, fears, secrets... love. They had chosen each other against the tides of war, bound by a forbidden marriage neither of their governments would honor. They held each other beneath the bio-sculpted canopy, lost in a rare, fleeting moment of peace.

Boom, their silent serenity was shattered. The entire garden shook. A deep, violent concussion echoed from above. Their heads snapped upward as another explosion thundered through the hollow sky. Then another. The vibrations became a violent tremor. The glowing dome far above began to fracture, fine lines of light spider-webbing across the simulated firmament. And then. It broke.

A section of the crystal ceiling miles wide collapsed, sending down shards the size of starships. A swirling dark void gaped above them. A short silence lingered as they gazed at the black void. Then they came. The Legions of the Duality.

Specialized, state of the art Dominion gunships, dark and sleek, poured through the wound in the sky like a divine punishment. Thousands upon thousands of them. No warning. No transmission. No hesitation.

Dropships followed, casting long shadows across the utopia. Troop carriers vomited endless lines of armored Legionaries and hulking monsters of war. Hovering artillery platforms rained down hellfire and destrcution. Civilians screamed as their world of peace turned into a torrent of ruin. Peacekeeper sirens howled across the city, trying to organize a resistance against the disorder.

Another rupture tore open in the ceiling of the grand cavern. Even wider this time, its edges glowing with an unnatural, searing light. A colossal slab of stone like material wrenched free and plummeted with unforgiving force, striking Unity Tower, the beating heart of the Republics. The very emblem of their way of life. The impact shattered the spire in a thunderous burst of fire and debris, its hovering platforms faltered, then gave way entirely, tumbling into the emerald canopy of the great ancient forests below.

From the fresh wound in the sky, more Dominion forces descended. Without any hesitation, no words or proclamations. Only the cold finality of divine judgment made manifest. A continual stream of more sleek, black gunships, perfect machines of war, poured through by the thousands and then tens of thousands, their formations blotted out the artificial sun. More dropships followed, dragging shadows like claws across the once pristine metropolis, troop carriers spewed endless ranks of armored Legionaries and towering beasts of metal and flesh, the personal Raddak'Khazmar of the Duality led the charge against the heretics. As the artillery platforms continued to hang in the void above, unleashing an relentless storm of molten fire into the structures below.

The air was filled with the screams of the innocent and the wail of the Peacekeeper sirens, the sounds crashed together into a chaotic symphony of despair.

Tria's breath caught, her eyes fixed on the ruin devouring her home. "No... no, this can't be happening! How did they find us?" she cried, her voice breaking into fury and disbelief. She ran, sprinting for the hovercar they had used to come to the gardens. Amarax was already at her heels. They dove in together, the craft's engines screaming as it tore into the airways, weaving between collapsing structures and the falling dead. Surging through the airways with a desperate plea to survive.

The skyline of Unum, once a beautiful testament of a people who had remained free against all odds, now burned, a punishment for their heretical assaults against the Dominion. Peacekeeper fighters and patrol craft engaged enemy formations in desperate dogfights, but the Dominion's attack was quick, coordinated, and unrelenting. There had been no time to prepare. The Peacekeepers of the Republics had been blindsided by their own assurance of secrecy and the arrogance of their technological superiority.

Tria's destination: Peacekeeper Base Alpha, the primary and largest Peacekeeper base within the capital cavern. A sprawling multi-leveled network of the finest Peacekeeper tech at the edge of Unum. The central command center stretched across a domed canyon and down steep cliffs, housing multiple launch hangars, energy artillery towers, a vertical barracks column, and a central AI war-core. It was supposed to be Unum's shield. The rally point for the Peacekeepers. But now, even that shield trembled.

As they approached, the base was already under siege. Heavy landers crashed into the canyon's ledges, deploying waves of Legionaries. Anti-air turrets blazed. Robotic drones screamed through the skies. The base's outer platforms were engulfed in a torrential storm of war-fire.

Tria barely had time to land the hovercar before enemy rounds struck the landing pad. The two leapt from the vehicle, dark matter bolts slicing past. Tria dove for a supply crate and grabbed a rifle and battle arm module from it. She instantly activated battle mode and Peacekeeper armor formed around her in a rippling nanite surge, like a wave of water over the shore.

Six Dominion Legionaries rushed at her, their armor burning with holy sigils of devotion to the Duality, songs of praise and loyalty to their Gods. They charged with an inhuman fervor.

Amarax moved faster. With a roar, he slammed into the first, breaking the Legionary's spine with his bare hands. The second fired, but Tria rolled and dropped him with two bursts to the chest. The third lunged with a Singublade. Amarax caught their arm mid-swing and tore their weapon from the attacker's grip, then drove it into his heart. He was a Grand Marshal, but he wouldn't let any Legionary kill his wife. He slashed and bludgeoned the other Legionaries without mercy.

"More incoming! Watch out!" Tria yelled.

Dozens more surged from the smoke and flames. Peacekeeper troops began pouring from the inner base to reinforce and protect Tria. Automated defense cannons activated and set to max power, turning the canyon into a molten kill-zone. The Peacekeepers didn't have time for high ideals, not now, not when the fate of everything hung in the balance. Mechs from both sides rolled forward and engaged, and battle drones darkened the skies. Amarax and Tria moved in sync, back-to-back, leading the Peacekeepers nearby, driving the enemy into a retreat. The Dominion forces began to falter under the ferocious defense that the Peacekeepers were putting up. Then the air above twisted and glitched.

Circular energy rifts opened in the canyon air everywhere, shimmering and howling portals. Hundreds of them. From each stepped out Tribunals. The children of the Gods. Armored in the finest and purest shining black obsidian, carrying weapons said to be forged in the stars themselves. They struck like an uncontrollable storm that was destined to destroy everything in its wake.

The Peacekeepers fought with everything they had: heavy war mechs which had been repaired after the battle of Antica, they teleported in from other bases. Missile platforms with the most powerful warheads available, pulse auto cannons. But no matter how hard they fought the tide was turning against them. It was as if every

Tribunal throughout the galaxy was descending upon them, wave after wave after wave.

Tria and the Peacekeepers around her were nearly overrun within a couple minutes. Amarax never left her side, using Dominion weapons against his own people. He still hated the heretics, but he wouldn't let his wife be killed. He loved Tria above anything else, even more than his duty.

Then a black flame of intense rippling energy ignited above them. Two beings descended from the largest portal. Massive, winged, and terrifying: The Holy Duality, the God Emperor and God Empress in their divine forms of wrathful judgement. The Gods of Terra leading their Legions together against the heretics of Terra. Their presence twisted gravity and cracked the earth around them. Fissures of lava began to erupt and the entire base rattled and shook, it began to collapse and break under the power of the divine pair as Peacekeepers began vanishing into clouds of nothingness.

Amarax saw Tria wounded, pinned beneath debris. He roared and charged recklessly at the twins. Alone. He fought like no man ever had. Striking as hard as he could as he bleed out, refusing to fall. But the Gods were merciless. A scream tore from Tria as she watched the God Empress smash him with her massive war-hammer. He was catapulted against the breaking ruins of the base. And then the God Emperor's holy blade pierced his body, ripping him in two.

Tria could do nothing, she was trapped and helpless, she could do nothing to stop his death. And then time froze. The world around her became a still image. Then, the battle was gone as quickly as it had began. Tria and Amarax found themselves in the crystal forest of the Messengers as it shimmered around them.

She gasped, stumbling back, finding herself not amid the chaos of conflict, but under the gentle glow of her crystal friends. Amarax stood beside her, whole, but confused, just as stunned. Before them stood the jagged crystal form of Tel'Mor'El, the Prime Messenger, bathed in flowing light.

"It was only one thread," the crystal being said in their minds. "One vision of what may come. But all things may yet be rewritten."

Tria gripped Amarax's hand, her breath trembling as she tried to recollect herself. Could they change the future? Or was destiny already set in stone and unfolding against them?

Thank You

I truly appreciate you reading the continuing story of the TAZM Saga and digging deeper into the STARVINITY universe. It means a lot. This is only the beginning. There are so many more adventures and tales to be told and discovered.

It would be wonderful if you could review on Amazon or other book review sites. I would love to know your thoughts. Please stop by and leave your thoughts on this book and the STARVINITY universe as a whole.

Thank you again for joining the journey that is STARVINITY, a journey that is beyond our known universe, a journey of infinite possibilities. Hoping that you always stay inspired.

Most Sincerely,

Grant-Grey Guda

Check out STARVINITY on Fandom and ask any questions you may have or add to the community. Go to our site to stay updated on the newest and latest additions to the universe.

www.starvinity.com

Starvinity can also be found on Youtube STARVINITY @Starvinity, Bluesky @Starvinity, TikTok @Starvinity, Twitter/X @Starvinity, Facebook @Starvinity, Instagram @Starvinity, Reddit @Starvinity

www.ingramcontent.com/pod-product-compliance
Lightning Source LLC
Chambersburg PA
CBHW020342180626
46812CB00001B/307